How to Fake a Southern Gentleman

How to Fake a Southern Gentleman

MAYRA CUEVAS
and
MARIE MARQUARDT

PRIMERO
SUEÑO PRESS

ATRIA

New York Amsterdam/Antwerp London
Toronto Sydney/Melbourne New Delhi

PRIMERO
SUEÑO PRESS

ATRIA
An Imprint of Simon & Schuster, LLC
1230 Avenue of the Americas
New York, NY 10020

This Primero Sueño Press/Atria Paperback edition April 2026

PRIMERO SUEÑO PRESS / ATRIA PAPERBACK and colophon are registered trademarks of Simon & Schuster, LLC

Interior design by Davina Mock-Maniscalco

Manufactured in the United States of America

1 3 5 7 9 10 8 6 4 2

The Library of Congress Cataloging-in-Publication Data has been applied for.

ISBN 978-1-6680-9895-0 (pbk)
ISBN 978-1-6680-9896-7 (ebook)

For Chris, my very own (Midwestern) gentleman.

Mayra

For Mayra, my favorite co-conspirator and partner in crime.

Marie

"The difference between a lady and a flower girl
is not how she behaves, but how she is treated."

—Eliza Doolittle, *My Fair Lady*

The story you're about to read is a work of fiction. And yeah, okay, maybe it's inspired by real places and real events. Truth, after all, is stranger than fiction.

CHAPTER 1

Luisa

Unfortunately, newspaper deadlines don't come with a twenty-four-hour birthday curse extension. I should've known my birthday would be the worst possible day of the year to turn in a story I've been working myself to the bone to write for months.

Abuela called me at the crack of dawn this morning, bursting into a sweet but abysmally off-key rendition of "Las Mañanitas," after which she delivered the "auspicious news" that she'd had a vision of San Juan Bautista, which meant all my shitty birthday luck was about to be over. "*This* is the year you will finally shake off the mal de ojo," she exclaimed in Spanish. "Your birthday falls on the spring equinox, mija! It's a sign."

Now it's midmorning and my thighs burn as I double my stride, praying Abuelita's right and this birthday will be different, calamity-free. I'm trying in vain to keep up with Nina, my managing editor. She's a five-foot-one force of nature with two speeds: sprinting and catch-me-if-you-can. Which is how I find myself panting as we climb three flights of stairs from the bowels of *The Georgia Times*, where the printing press is located, to the newsroom on the second floor. Apparently, Nina doesn't believe in elevators.

"Nina," I plead for the hundredth time, "this is ready for publication." In my hand, I'm brandishing a draft of my latest article as if it were a sword. The two of us have been going at it over this story for weeks: me pushing forward, Nina pushing back—and for no good reason. "I spoke with experts. I have multiple sources. What's this email about standing down? This is a solid story. Did Chip even read it?"

Chip is our publisher. Harold "Chip" F. Marshall IV, to be

precise. He's the kind of guy who loves to cry out "Show me the money!" at staff meetings, repeatedly rubbing his thumb and forefinger like some hapless, middle-aged Tom Cruise wannabe.

"Oh, Chip read it all right," she says, speed walking ahead of me, parting the newsroom in her electric-blue sheath dress, stylish short Afro, and diamond studs. This woman has mastered the busy boss lady look—laptop in the crook of her arm, eyes on her phone, thumb scrolling down the screen. No one dares interrupt her, except me.

"This family is about to lose their home, their farm—their livelihood!—over a deed that magically materialized in the clerk's office." My hands gesticulate wildly in front of me, trying and failing to catch up with my words. I know I'm getting worked up, but I don't care. I refuse to "tone it down" so other people can feel more comfortable with my loud (and proud) Puerto Ricanness. If there's one thing I've learned in the three years I've worked at *The Georgia Times*, it's that my Latinidad gives me access to the kind of stories most of my colleagues can't get on their own. Stories like this one.

Two months ago, I was working late when the crew boss for the night-cleaning service tapped me on the shoulder, scaring the bejesus out of me. In Spanish, she introduced me to her cousin, Gloria Castillo, the owner of a family-run, sustainable farm in Westlake, about forty miles east of Atlanta. Gloria explained that she and her husband were set to inherit their farm from her father-in-law, Don Luis, after he passed away from an aggressive form of cancer. But days after the funeral, the Castillos received notice of an unknown security deed placed on the property.

According to the deed documents, Don Luis had taken a six-figure loan against the property from a lender called Peachtree Holdings, LLC. Yet there was no paper trail confirming Don Luis had signed away his farm or that he'd received a transfer of funds to any of his bank accounts. And even though the deed was recorded with the clerk's office, Peachtree Holdings turned out to be a ghost company with no working phone number or email. The address on file belongs to an empty lot owned by the city of Westlake.

The Castillos called the police, but without solid evidence of fraud, there was nothing they could do. If they wanted their property back, they'd have to repay the loan. Money they don't have.

"What exactly is not clear about my email? Or the three others I sent previously?" Nina says, still speed walking and focused on her phone. "We're shutting the story down. Time to move on, Luisa."

I follow her into her office, pulling documents out of my research binder: photos of the Castillos, development plans, interviews with local officials, a copy of the security deed. I'm ready for a fight. As one of the paper's dying breed of investigative journalists, I must be equal parts detective, historian, forensic pathologist, psychologist, and entertainer, if I'm to have any chance in hell at (a) uncovering the truth, and (b) presenting the truth in a way that will make reel-obsessed audiences actually give a fuck.

"Look," I say, pointing to the photograph I've just placed on her desk. "This is the family: Gloria and Pablo, Little Mishel and Abelardo. They will be homeless soon." I leave unsaid that Pablo's kind eyes remind me of my late father—killed by a drunk driver during my freshman year in high school. I don't tell her that the kids burrowed their way into my heart, just like each of my three nieces did the second they were born. And I absolutely don't mention that after spending countless hours sharing meals over their kitchen table, there is nothing I won't do to keep them from losing their home. *Nothing*.

Losing your childhood home breaks you in ways you never knew possible. Sure, you can move. Even start over. But you'll never be the same. A part of you tears off and stays behind.

And yeah, maybe I'm breaching some objectivity rules, but my counterargument is this: anyone who works to screw over a family of dedicated, kind-hearted immigrants to build yet another golf course for rich white folks is objectively an asshole who must be taken down.

In the days and weeks that followed my first meeting with Gloria, I looked into her family's story. "Rage" is an appropriate word to describe how I felt when I came across plans for a future multimillion-dollar housing and golf course development called

The Preserve at Lake Chiaha. That's when everything clicked into place.

I roll open the plans for the Preserve, guiding Nina's attention with my finger. "The developer already scooped up all the land around the lake—future golf courses and clubhouses." I trace the familiar plans until I reach the community's main entrance. "The only way in and out is over the Castillos' property."

I go silent for a beat, expecting her to share in my moral outrage, but her expression remains impassive. "Nina, a bunch of rich white developers are ripping off a hard-working family—in a less-than-legal way—just to get even richer." I throw both hands in the air in disgust. "The city council approved the development outright. No bidding war. No competition. Apparently, this GCJ Construction promised they would include low-income housing, which is total bullshit. Since when do '*world-class*' private communities have housing for the poor?"

Nina settles into her Italian leather office chair and releases a sigh. I stand uncomfortably in front of her. There are no other chairs in Nina's office, which I've been told is by design.

"Maybe they're building living quarters for the help," she deadpans.

"They're set to break ground in the fall, just as the security deed expires." My stomach sinks at the reminder of that deadline. "The developer is some guy called Griggs Johnson, out of Atlanta."

"Some guy?" Nina scoffs, finally making eye contact. "Please tell me you know who Griggs Caldecott Johnson III is."

"I've already done a deep dive into his company and assets, if that's what you're asking. This man's dealings raise more red flags than a circus tent. He's using an offshore bank in Panama for his business, which only makes sense if you're trying to hide something."

I drop an organizational chart on the desk. "One of the main investors in the Lake Chiaha development, Jim Wade, sits on the state's Board of Natural Resources. And lo and behold, he also happens to hold the foundation's purse strings." I jab a finger over the man's simpering face. "There's zero oversight, Nina."

She doesn't react, so I press on, offering a series of spreadsheets and tax filings, everything I could find in public records. "I'm convinced this family foundation is a front. Money's probably getting diverted straight to the development." I leaf to the end of the company brochure, where I find a marked page containing photos of various happy families Griggs's foundation has allegedly helped with affordable housing. "But that's just a theory. I'll need more time to dig on that end."

"Oh, honey, that, right there, is your problem." Nina points one red, manicured fingernail in my direction. "That guy called Griggs," she says, tersely, "is a big fucking deal in this town."

"And he's the person who stands to win big if the Castillos lose their land," I counter. "Given the only road access to the development is through their parcel."

Nina shakes her head. "Chip thinks your story is one big hunk of Swiss cheese."

"Swiss cheese?" I ask, stumped and suddenly angry at the utter lack of chairs in this office.

"The man is a sap for worn-out metaphors." Nina waves a hand dismissively. "Look, you have no evidence of wrongdoing. For all we know, the old man signed this deed and forgot to tell his family. There's nothing illegal here. Sad? Yes. Unfair? Yes. Criminal? You've got nothing."

"So that's it?" I ask, unable to accept what I'm hearing. "I can't just call these people and tell them . . ." I trail off, suddenly overcome by the image of Little Mishel and Abelardo playing in the yard, laughing carelessly into the afternoon sun. I clear my throat, blinking away the surprising sting of tears. And, as a general rule, I don't cry in front of people. This news business, after all, is not for wimps. "Tell them what? That we don't care about their lives? I can't do that."

I think back to the first time Gloria and I met in the dead of night in the newsroom, when I asked her what she wanted me to do with the information she'd given me. *Investigate*, she said. *Isn't that what journalists do? Be a voice for people like us*.

"Nina, just tell me what I need to do to make someone like Chip care about this family. Hell, you know I love a challenge."

Nina exhales audibly. "I can't keep protecting you, Luisa. I've been trying to get you to drop this story for weeks now and you've paid no heed. I'm sorry, but—" She pauses, her lips tightening into a thin line as she fixes her dark brown eyes on a point in the newsroom, past the glass walls of her office. "Chip wants you out. He says your work is not up to the newspaper's standards. The newsroom's attorney agreed."

I follow her gaze, and that's when I see him—*Chip*—leaning all too casually against the newsroom's assignment desk. Watching us. Watching *me*.

A clammy sense of dread claws its way up my back. "And is this what you think, too? That my work isn't up to snuff?"

Nina doesn't say a word.

"Well, tell Chip to explain all the awards hanging above my desk, then. Or the insane number of stories I've broken for this paper!" I lean forward on her desk, my sweaty palms resting on the glass surface.

Silence.

"Nina?" I plead. "What's going on?"

"Luisa, you're fired."

CHAPTER 2

Holly

I wind through this posh playground for Atlanta's multigenerational families of wealth and status. The bridge ladies convene on the flower-strewn veranda that overlooks the pool deck, shuffling cards amid the clinking of tea glasses. A lifeguard blows his whistle, signaling the start of toddler swim lessons. Society moms in tennis dresses chat amiably and head toward the courts, passing by the distinguished gentlemen who gather in carts near our world-renowned golf course, puffing on cigars while they prepare to tee off.

But it's not just another Friday morning. It's the morning of Anna-Byrd Johnson's annual Baubles Brunch, where her go-to jewelry designer shares the latest shimmering trends with a select group of "girls in the know." And so here I am—on my precious day off.

During my eighteen years working at this club, including five years managing events, I've successfully served countless cocktails to Coca-Cola's founding families and organized elaborate weddings for hundreds of discerning guests. I've planned and executed dinners to honor governors and mayors, the sort of people who will, in fact, be here tonight, for the city's annual Philanthropy Banquet. But still: Anna-Byrd Johnson's Baubles Brunch for twelve sends my heart into palpitations. She is the absolute worst of this place's prim and judgy society ladies, all bright smiles and effervescent *how aaaaahhhhre you*s with the other ladies at the club—until they turn their backs. Then it's a litany of razor-sharp judgments, covering everything from their tennis skirts to where their toddlers go to preschool. No one is safe, not even her (purported) best friends. She and her lecher husband,

Griggs Caldecott Johnson III, are a perfect match—made in hell. They are Atlanta's Golden Couple, the city's country club royalty, and crossing either one of them has extreme consequences that I'm not willing or able to endure. I have a kid to feed.

Every single detail of this brunch must go precisely as Anna-Byrd planned, or that woman will have my head. Which is why I'm storming through the double doors into the kitchen.

"Ohmygod how could I not remember this?" I desperately call out to whoever might be within earshot. "And where the hell are my notes? Do the Davis sisters drink Bollinger or Taittinger?"

"Not your fault," Irma replies, slipping on red oven mitts. "Neptune's swimming through your tenth house of career, making details a little murky. You'll come through it." For Irma, the club's sous chef and amateur astrologer, everything's written in our stars.

"Before or after Anna-Byrd Johnson chops her head off?" Justine replies from the walk-in. She's not wrong. The Davis sisters are Anna-Byrd's closest friends and partners in crime, and perennial guests at the Baubles Brunch. Their every wish must be my command.

"I'm just sayin'." Justine shrugs, coming out of the fridge with four gallons of sweet tea balanced in her arms. "You'd better fucking get it right." Justine—the Dogwood Hills Country Club's head waitress and chief surliness officer—acts as sweet as tupelo honey when she's out serving club members, but back here, she's a drill sergeant. And I adore her.

"Taittinger," Byron announces from the other side of the room as he casually slides on his white bartender jacket. "Loula Davis Babb hates Bollinger. She thinks it's too bubbly."

"Too bubbly?" Irma replies with mock horror, pulling a tray of the club's signature crackers from the oven.

Can champagne be too bubbly? I shove the question from my mind, focusing on the task at hand. If the Davis sisters want mildly bubbly champagne, that's exactly what they'll get.

"And, by the way," Byron adds, gesturing toward the prep table, "I believe your beloved tablet is hiding under that tray of canapés."

"Bless you," I exclaim, rushing over to retrieve it. It's absolutely fitting that Byron has swooped in to rescue me. He is, without a doubt, the most consistent and reliable man in my life.

I tug my tablet out from under the canapés, open it, and scroll through my event notes.

Lavender hyacinths? *Check.*

Champagne flutes smooth, NOT cut glass? *Check.*

Taittinger, NOT Bollinger? *Check.*

"Now wish me luck," I say, grabbing two bottles from the fridge. "I'm heading into the fray to check on the boozy ladies."

Perfectly chilled Taittinger in hand, I make my way toward the Ivy Room, one of several small formal dining rooms that fan around the grand rotunda. These spaces, intended for such intimate gatherings as small birthday fetes, sweet sixteen luncheons, or special family dinners, have been decorated with the feminine feel of a ladies' parlor in a well-appointed Southern home, circa 1936.

I push open the door and step inside, noticing immediately how gorgeous the hyacinths are looking in that silver vase at the center of the table. I make a mental note to call my go-to florist and shower her with praise. And the white linens, crisp and perfectly draped, are a real testament to the entire team over in housekeeping.

The women are huddled, discussing in hushed tones the latest Posted Notice: Dogwood Hills's most arcane form of public humiliation. The husband of one of their—now spurned—friends just had his name taped to bulletin boards around the club. An announcement carefully printed on expensive ecru card stock reports the precise balance on his delinquent account.

"Holly!" Loula, the younger of the Davis sisters, says, her voice slurring just the slightest bit. "Come join us!"

I set Loula's not-too-bubbly champagne on ice and watch from an appropriate distance. Chatter about the Posted Notice abruptly stops, and Anna-Byrd extends her dainty hand, showing off the enormous emerald tennis bracelet dangling from her slim wrist.

Seeing that bracelet reminds me of the almost identical one

currently residing in a safe under my desk. The only difference? That one is sapphire, presumably to match the piercing blue eyes of Kasey Ketchum, the young third wife of banking magnate Miles Ketchum, and Griggs's erstwhile lover. According to Janey, the club's receptionist and resident gossip, Kasey lost the bracelet during a passionate after-hours encounter with Griggs on the squash court (gross) after which he unceremoniously dumped her. She'll probably never retrieve the bracelet since it was a gift from Griggs, and Mr. Ketchum appears to provide her with a shiny new object every week. In the meantime, a bauble worth several thousand dollars is gathering dust in my office.

"Come sit," Loula calls out to me, patting an empty seat beside her. "You *must* see this *absolutely to-die-for* ring."

Loula knows, of course, that there can be no "joining them," and I won't be cozying up beside her, since I am staff and they're club members. Nevertheless, she persistently invites me.

"That's a lovely piece, Mrs. Babb," I say, lying. I'm not really a fancy jewelry person.

"For the hundredth time," Loula says, gesturing for me to come closer, "please call me Loula! Mrs. Babb is my mother-in-law."

"And for the hundredth time," I reply, my voice gently teasing, "please don't make me call you by your first name. I could lose my job for it. And I happen to really like my job."

All the women around the table laugh uncomfortably. All but one, that is.

"Well, well, well. Isn't someone feeling cheeky this morning," Anna-Byrd Johnson says, through an utterly disingenuous smile. She shakes her head slowly, sending the bright blue tassels on her earrings bobbing about. The woman is obsessed with fringe earrings. Every time I see her she's wearing a different pair, to match whatever brightly patterned dress she's got on.

An uncomfortable silence ensues, during which I attempt to stare thoughtfully into the distance, or, in this case, at the strange array of eighteenth-century pastoral scenes gracing the walls of the Ivy Room.

Over many years, I've come to realize that the design of this antiquated, slightly shabby club is meant to convey something important about the people that fill it: They are *old money*, not new. Theirs is multigenerational wealth. Any unseemly displays of their status are, at best, tacky and, at worst, meriting quiet expulsion from their tightly monitored social world.

I happen to know a good deal about their world. Growing up, I lived on the other side of the member-staff divide. Not here, but at a club a whole lot like this one, in Mississippi. My father basically ignored me, electing instead to play endless rounds of golf and drink bottomless scotch. My mom spent most of her time preening and gossiping with the ladies. She only cared about what I did to the extent that it reflected on her. For my mother, discretion and propriety were the most important virtues, and so discreetly raising proper children was the ultimate goal of parenting.

By the time I hit puberty, I was through pretending to have a real family. Instead, I worked my little ass off to ensure that every single action I took made my mother look like an utter and complete failure. Desperate to escape my gilded cage, I threw myself repeatedly against the bars. My teen pregnancy was, for her, both the pinnacle of my indiscretion and the final proof of my reckless irresponsibility. There was one fleeting moment, though, after I got pregnant with my son, Aidan, when I thought I might stay a part of that world—maybe even build a little family with his father, play by the rules, and make a place for us there.

Aidan's father wasn't like me. I rebelled; he simply belonged. He lived comfortably with his good name, his lovely family, his sterling reputation.

As it turns out, in my Mississippi town, teenage boys who want to maintain sterling reputations don't become dads. They properly and discreetly pay to take care of the "problem."

So I left. I escaped the gilded cage, secretly carrying away the shame both our families said the pregnancy would bring, and I boarded a bus for the big city.

Here's the great irony: When I was utterly adrift, desperately seeking a job in Atlanta, this country club was the only place that would take me in. I landed a job here, with no family or community, and the staff made a home for us. Almost immediately, they became, for Aidan and me, the family I never had.

Marg, the older Davis sister, breaks into my memories. "Holly, be a dear and run down to the driving range. Let Chase know we'll be a tad late to pick the boys up from their golf lesson."

"Of course," I say, then leave the ladies to their jewelry chatter, to deliver the news that Chase will be babysitting the Davis sisters' little hellions for a while longer.

The heavy oak door hasn't even had a chance to thud shut behind me when Janey enthusiastically scurries toward me, sensible black pumps shuffling across the maroon carpet. Janey's face brightens as she calls out to me. "Holly! I didn't expect to see you here."

At least one of us is thrilled I'm at the club on my day off.

"You won't believe it," she says, somehow managing to simultaneously express deep distress and utter glee at having procured new information. "It's Reginald."

"Reginald, the new head of security?" He's been at the club for almost two years, but that makes him a real spring chicken, relative to old-timers like us.

"Fired!" she cries out.

"No!" My jaw goes slack with disbelief. Reginald is a great guy—honest to a fault, but also compassionate. Last summer, he did me a huge favor, and I'll forever be grateful to him. If it weren't for him, I'd probably be unemployed, and my son definitely wouldn't be out there living his best life in college.

"I overheard Lynn talking to Dennis, who'd just gotten off the phone with Buck Dorsey . . ."

I'm waiting patiently for Janey's story to unspool, wondering what the club's board chair has to do with any of this.

"Mr. Marshall said Mr. Johnson accused Reginald of some funny business. He insisted Reginald be fired—wouldn't take no for an answer."

"Griggs Johnson?" I ask, knowing the answer but still needing to hear it.

"Yes. You know, he just got elected to the board—youngest

member ever," she says, apropos of nothing. "He must have dug up some terrible scandal involving Reginald, because—*poof!*—Reginald's gone. Just like that."

Just like that, Reginald is gone. I sure hope he's taken my secret with him. But the sick feeling in my gut suggests otherwise.

CHAPTER 3

Luisa

By one in the afternoon, I'm hiding at the Road Queen Grill, sharing my misery with Ginny and Rhonda, the women who own and run this place. It's a legit biker bar on a back road between Atlanta and Athens. Over the last two months, I've turned the barstool I'm currently occupying into my Westlake headquarters.

"Fuck 'em," Ginny spits, pouring me a sympathy shot, because according to her biker bar gospel, *There's nothing that tequila can't fix*. I cradle the amber liquid between my fingers, my chest tight with self-pity and indignation, wishing I had one ounce of Ginny's bravado.

After quietly packing my cubicle, I sat in *The Georgia Times* parking lot, trying to process Nina's sucker punch and my bruising unemployment. A quick search confirmed what I already knew: Jobs for investigative reporters are virtually nonexistent. And even if I managed an interview somewhere, how would I explain getting fired to a prospective new employer? And what if they called Nina or Chip for a recommendation?

One glance at my banking app revealed that I can no longer afford my spacious apartment, or my season tickets to the Atlanta Opera—my one and only self-indulgent, bourgeois splurge. I will need my meager savings to pay—among other things—for the fancy SUV I just *had* to have because it was supposed to be my "grown-up" car. Well, there's nothing "grown-up" about having to ask Mami for a loan or, even worse, move back into my old room.

Clearly, my birthday curse has not been lifted. Though, this birthday isn't the worst I've ever had. The *Worst Birthday of My Life* designation belongs to my fifteenth. Days after my big Quinceañera celebration, our family gathered again for my father's wake. There, we learned Papi had another family on the opposite side of the Island, and I had a half sister almost exactly my age. I cried a lifetime's supply of tears that year, but whether I was crying out of grief, the discovery of a sister I didn't know existed, or realizing I didn't know my father at all, I'm not sure. All I know is that the man we most trusted to keep us safe, ended up wrecking our lives.

"You told the Castillos yet?" Rhonda asks, resting a heavy cardboard box against one of the coolers. Her mildly offensive T-shirt reads: *You, my friend*—one finger pointed at the reader—*should've been swallowed.* I'd laugh if I didn't feel so wretched.

"I left work and drove straight to Westlake," I tell them. "Chickened out and came here instead." I shrug, angry at my own spinelessness. "What am I supposed to say? 'Sucks to be you'?" I scoff, then down the shot of tequila. "Fuck, that burns."

Rhonda lets out a low whistle, moving beer bottles from the box to the inside of the cooler. "The devil's errand. Don't envy you one bit."

"Sometimes life is shit." Ginny taps one finger on the bar's wood surface. "I see it every fucking day." She opens one arm, gesturing past the row of neon beer signs, where a Willie Nelson look-alike drinks alone. His leather jacket is stitched with patches that read: *In memory of Chomper* and *Cheating Death* over the image of a reaper. Her voice takes on a hard edge as she says, "Even if life gives you a shitty hand, there's no backing out, you still gotta hedge your bet."

"Preach," Rhonda pipes in, beer bottles clinking in her hands.

"And then you figure out how to win with a shitty hand." Ginny winks one kohl-rimmed eye, then cuts her gaze over my shoulder toward whoever just walked in.

"Or you learn to bluff." Rhonda nods toward the stranger crossing the room.

Ginny moves down to chat with the new guy, a breezy familiarity between them. I know better than to stare at people in a place like this, but I can't help myself. He's about my age, tall and toned, with broad shoulders, a trim waist, and arm muscles that bulge slightly under his black T-shirt. An unkempt lumberjack beard and shoulder-length chestnut-brown hair cover most of his neck and face, barely revealing a pair of striking gray eyes that flicker with wolfish intensity. *This man could devour me*, I think hazily.

I'm so disconcerted by the bizarre thought that I forget to avert my gaze. When Lumberjack Guy's head turns, he finds me studying him with the concentration of someone about to take the bar exam. I should break away, but I'm transfixed by the soft lines around his eyes. They lay bare a kinder side—in stark contrast to his rugged facade. But there's also weariness in those lines. This man is tired, so very tired. Not tired as in "I worked all day at my lumberjack job," but tired as in, "Why is life so fucking hard?"

"Hey," he says in the low gruff voice of a country singer. I look straight ahead, my cheeks blushing in spite of every effort at self-control. I blame the alcohol. My skin feels warm and prickly. This is why drinking on an empty stomach is always a bad idea. The last thing I need today is some hairy, backwoods redneck chatting me up.

Ginny uncaps a beer bottle and passes it to Lumberjack Guy. He shows her something on his phone and her face softens, in the way people do when they're looking at a puppy or a baby, or a puppy cuddling with a baby.

"Hey, Rhonda," Ginny calls out. "Two burger orders to go. Extra onions and cheese for Pearl." Rhonda signals she's on it, then turns her attention to the open grill behind the bar, giving me a view of the raised middle finger on the back of her T-shirt. Classic Rhonda.

Ginny heads to the back room, and then it's just Lumberjack Guy and me on this side of the bar. Suddenly, I'm an awkward mess, self-conscious of his gaze on me.

"Haven't seen you around here before," he observes as if we'd been carrying on a conversation. He peers down at my black suede heeled booties. "You're a ways away from Atlanta."

My hackles stand on edge. I've gone out of my way to disappear into the background—one of the many reasons I've excelled at my job. There's nothing about my all-black outfit that attracts attention.

"This is a far cry from those snooty bars in Buckhead," he presses, casually taking another sip of his beer.

"I like it here just fine," I respond, cutting my eyes to his, boldly holding his gaze. His lips curl into a provoking, closed-lip, impish grin that transforms his expression and lifts some of the heaviness behind his eyes. The effect is striking, and because I can't seem to stop making bad choices today, I start wondering things like: *Why is he hiding that smile under all that facial hair?* and *What kind of face is attached to that chiseled body?* and *Why am I even thinking about this?* Because I'm stressed, and distraction is a potent survival mechanism. And also, well, I haven't had sex in a really long time on account of investigating country club criminals.

"Pretty sure this bar ain't on the map," he says, leaning casually in my direction. "So I'm curious, what brought a girl like you here? You lost or somethin'? Need a tour guide?"

"I don't get lost," I say pointedly. "And, call me crazy, but why should I go anywhere with a guy who's at a bar on a weekday, in the middle of the day?" I tip my beer bottle in his direction. "In my experience, there's a fifty-fifty chance you're either unemployed, an alcoholic, or on parole." I tilt my head as if drawing a new conclusion. "Or just an unemployed alcoholic on parole." This makes him laugh.

"Call *me* crazy," he says, arching an eyebrow, "but you're here, too." He mimics my stance, angling his bottle in my direction. "So maybe I'm the one taking a chance on *you*."

Before I can think of a pithy comeback, Rhonda breaks in to hand Lumberjack Guy his food order. He slides off the stool, grabs the bag, then drops a few dollars in the tip jar. He finishes what's left of his beer in one drink, then sets the bottle down.

"Don't stay too late," he says, ready to leave. "You'll get stuck in that nasty Atlanta traffic."

I check the time and begrudgingly realize that he is, in fact, correct. If I don't leave now, I'll be late to my own birthday party.

"All right, I'll bite." I testily face him, further aggrieved by his amused expression and that feral streak behind his eyes. I'm reminded that wolves are known to hold their prey's gaze as an intimidation tactic. I flaunt my own menacing glare in response. "What gave me away?"

He points toward the parking lot. "The brand-new, hoity-toity SUV," he says as if the answer should be obvious. "Fulton County plates." He walks out, leaving me slack-jawed and deeply annoyed. Who the hell is this guy, and where did he come from?

CHAPTER 4

Holly

And so, once again, my day off slowly dwindles away, as I battle with a sound system likely purchased around the time I shotgunned my first beer in a sand trap at the Jackson Golf Club—which is to say, a really freaking long time ago.

Good Lord, this club could use some updates. It's chockablock full of heavy gold-tassel curtains, dark mahogany furniture that looks like it was lifted out of the estate sale of a rich old lady, and audiovisual equipment from somewhere in the mid-twentieth century. Sure, part of the charm of Dogwood Hills is the time-warped nature of the space. Cell phone use is prohibited here, which, in this day and age, feels almost radical. I'm a fan of the "no cell phones" policy, but I simply don't understand why the club can't spring for a decent microphone or two.

At least I'm tangled so deep in audio cables that, mercifully, I don't have the mental bandwidth to dwell on poor Reginald and the scandal I hope he quietly took with him.

"Untangle one mess at a time, Holly," I whisper to myself, staring forlornly at the nest of black cords in my hand.

Most events at the club—rehearsal dinners, wedding receptions, retirement parties, debutante balls—don't require much in the way of technology, but this is not a club event. It's an event *at* the club—the annual Philanthropy Banquet, to which all of Atlanta's political and economic elite flock to pat themselves on the back for being so very charitable.

I've planned every detail of this event with absolute precision, from the arrangement of high-top tables to the fresh mint sprigs in each glass of iced tea. The event staff has been here since before dawn, steaming tablecloths, polishing forks, assembling the small stage from which awards will be distributed. I refuse to let their enormous effort be overshadowed by a staticky microphone or a buzzing amp.

Fiddling with the knobs on an ancient amplifier, I finally manage to produce clean sound. This is perhaps the one life skill I learned from Aidan's father. He was a musician—or, more precisely, the swoon-worthy frontman in his church's praise-and-worship band.

Aidan's father was a *nice boy.*

We grew up in the same neighborhood, but we didn't exactly run in the same circles. In high school, while I was sneaking onto the golf course to smoke weed and shotgun beers with the weirdos and skaters from our neighborhood public school, he was strumming a guitar and singing to the glory of God. Some girls at my prep school went to that church for the sole purpose of watching him play. But I had no interest in him, and I'm quite certain he felt the same way about me, if he felt any way about me at all.

We both ended up at Ole Miss—I had barely slid in, with the minimum GPA and SAT scores; he probably could have gone to any school he chose, with his excellent grades and extensive extracurriculars. But—like mine—his was the sort of family that went back for generations at the school, and there was never any question we'd both go there.

Classes hadn't even begun the first time we stumbled into each other at a frat party and ended up having sex in my dorm room. Over the next couple of months, this happened more times than I could count. Maybe he was clinging (literally) to the familiar, in an overwhelming world of new faces and different rules. After all, we had at least vaguely known each other since we were in diapers. Or maybe he considered our hookups a form of rebellion—doing what many kids from conservative families do when they show up at college.

At colleges like Ole Miss, though, nice Christian boys also got wasted on Saturday nights. Then they woke up on Sunday morning, took a hot shower, chugged a Liquid IV, put on their khakis and button-downs, and played in the praise-and-worship band.

I went to see him a few times, feeling very out of place as I watched him croon for Jesus while strumming on an acoustic guitar. Honestly, we had very little in common. I don't know why he kept finding me at parties. The real question is why I kept letting myself be found.

Looking back, I think the appeal of Aidan's father was this: If this *nice boy* always came to find me at the end of the night and let me help him pack up amps after Sunday morning worship, what sort of girl did that make me?

A pregnant girl, as it turned out. Pregnant and alone.

I hear a few people gathering early—the ones giving and receiving the awards—to review the run-of-show. Before I even look up from the tangle of wires, I know that Griggs Johnson has entered the Azalea Ballroom. The room shifts with a gravity that pulls the whole world into his orbit. When the man walks into a room, people can't help but stare. And when he opens his mouth to speak, everyone listens. He is, after all, Atlanta's Golden Boy.

Griggs pauses after entering the ballroom, perfect smile under piercing green eyes and a thick head of dark brown hair. He's wearing a slim-cut suit that fits him like a glove, but that appears effortlessly thrown on, with a sky-blue tie and brown loafers that suggest this award is important to him, but not really *that* important.

I watch as he and his golf buddies, Jim Wade and Billy Thacker, take their leave of a fourth man I've never seen before. Thanks to Janey's "Daily Dirt Dump," I know he grew up right here at the club, and he's solidly a part of their old boy network, but he's now working for a bank in Panama, of all places. He must be a big deal, if this threesome has deigned to spend time in his presence. Janey reports that he'll be joining them this weekend for their Sunday morning round of golf—after which, they'll all head to the Men's Grill for lunch and bourbon. Yes, the Dogwood Hills Country Club, two decades into the twenty-first century, still manages to have an enormously popular all-male bar and grill on the grounds. There, I presume, they sit around toasting their world domination. I wouldn't know. I've never stepped inside the Men's Grill. As the name suggests, I'm not allowed.

I turn away from the gathered men and rush toward the equipment closet, crossing my fingers that there's a microphone in there that actually works.

"Holly," Griggs Johnson's voice comes from behind me. "I've been looking for you."

"Oh, hello, Mr. Johnson," I say, turning to face him, my voice stiff. "Do you need to discuss something with me?"

"You might say that," he replies, stepping into the narrow service hall so that he's inches from me. "But I don't want to talk here." He pauses, as if considering something important. "Why don't you meet me for a drink at the Four Seasons tonight after the banquet?"

I flinch, stepping backward. Did he just openly proposition me?

"Relax. It's only business," he says. But nothing in his response, or his knowing smirk, makes me feel reassured. He steps toward me again, so close that I can smell the chemicals in his hair gel mixed with his expensive cologne. Gross.

"I don't do business at hotel bars, Mr. Johnson," I reply, mustering all my strength to stay calm. I'm twisting my necklace so tightly that I worry it might break, sending fake pearls flying.

A sudden anger flashes across Griggs's face, but he quickly rearranges his features into a controlled poise. "How's your son doin'? Aidan, right? He's up at University of Georgia?"

"Yes," I say curtly. As a general rule, I occasionally engage in idle chitchat about my personal life with club members, but that rule doesn't apply to Griggs Johnson. "He's fine."

"Janey told me he's earned himself a full-ride scholarship. That's quite a feat."

Not for the first time, I'm wishing Janey could keep her damn mouth shut. I nod, pasting a smile across my face.

"Maybe you should think about that son of yours before turning me down." He lets his eyes rove over my chest and up to my face. "Haven't done a whole lot of research into it, but I'm guessing a felony conviction might get that scholarship yanked right out from under him." Feeling myself begin to shake with a strange combination of fear and rage, I pray that he doesn't notice. "Wouldn't that be a shame?" he asks casually.

But we both know there's nothing casual about his words. Griggs Johnson just threatened my son because I refused to have a "business" drink with him at a hotel.

"What exactly are you saying, Mr. Johnson?" I reply, my voice shuddering.

"I'm saying people can lie—but video footage doesn't."

And with those simple words, my worst fears are realized. Reginald clearly did not take my secrets with him when Griggs had him fired. And I don't know exactly what Griggs was looking for when he searched through Reginald's office, but he found the only thing in the world that I need to hide.

He watches me, grinning, seeming to relish the game he's playing with my life. "Think about it," he says. But I won't think about it, not for a moment. I've committed my entire life to protecting my son. And I have no intention of stopping now.

He inspects my face, clearly hoping to find weakness, fear, all the things I'm desperate not to reveal. Then, maybe because he's not finding the evidence he seeks, Griggs leans in so close that I smell the bourbon on his breath, and then he slowly reaches around to cup my ass.

"After all," he whispers into my ear, "it's just a drink."

Before I can form a word, before I can respond to the audacity of this horrible man threatening my child and then causally groping me in my place of employment, Griggs Johnson brushes past me. He nonchalantly saunters into the Azalea Room, leaving a red-hot sting where his hand touched my body and a simmering fury in my soul.

CHAPTER 5

Luisa

The moment I step foot into Mami's house, all the glitter, streamers, and balloons I've managed to avoid in the office find their way into my day.

It's my twenty-ninth birthday, a fact that I—fortuitously—kept from everyone in the newsroom. The last thing I wanted was some well-meaning co-worker littering my cube with garish decorations, singing "Happy Birthday" in garbled Spanish, and forcing everyone to eat that too-sweet supermarket buttercream-frosting cake. Mercifully, I didn't have to contend with said decorations as I emptied out my desk.

On the stove sits Mami's mouthwatering paella, and beside it a bowl of sliced green plantains ready to be recast into fried tostones. The Spanish sounds of chisme and laughter glide through the patio door like the soothing notes of a favorite song. I take a deep breath and amble through the screen door and down the daffodil-lined path that connects the house with the converted barn where our family-owned beauty salon is.

This salon is the only piece of home we managed to rebuild after our first one was ripped out from under us. Like the daffodils, which come back every year, Abuela says our salon is a reminder that "la vida continúa," and even after a tragedy, good things can happen. For Mami, this salon was a way back to her confident self.

After my dad died, the other woman—or *La Otra Mujer*, as we still call her—and my mom almost came to blows at the velorio over the swift claim she made on Papi's estate. La Otra Mujer and her daughter wanted half of everything. Following the funeral, Mami decided the Island was too small for Federico Aurelio Martín's two families, so she sold her hair salon and relinquished two decades of loyal clients. Then, she was forced to sell my childhood home, a stunning colonial in the hills of San Germán—ironically called Casa Consuelo, as in, there was no consolation to be had. Three months after Papi's death, we collected half of his life insurance benefits and followed one of Mami's friends to Atlanta.

It took us a long minute to find our place in this sprawling city, with its dozens of distinct neighborhoods and noodle-like highways. Eventually, we came to appreciate its rich civil rights history and progressive art scene. We ate our way up the Buford Highway corridor, bursting with international flavors from every corner of the world, and in the process discovered a little suburban enclave called Norcross. On that fateful day, we were bound for an antique store in the town's historic center—treasure hunting being our family's team sport. Instead, we ended up following the train tracks past a road lined with magnolia trees and white cottages. At the end of the street, we found a dilapidated Victorian home for sale, like something out of a Southern Gothic novel, sitting on a one-acre lot with its own massive red barn in the back. Mami remodeled thc barn and reopened her salon, christening it The Barn Salón de Belleza. Abuela and our Spanish-speaking clients took to calling it La Barna.

This house was an unexpected gift—the ultimate antiquing project, and a much-needed distraction from our collective grief. This house brought us back from the dead. I'm just hoping the miracle will repeat. And since it looks like I'll be forced to move back in, I'm hoping that, once again, inhabiting this house will bring me back from the bardo state I've landed myself in.

"La bendición," I call out, the door to La Barna slamming shut behind me. The acrid smell of hair chemicals replaces the delicious food aroma from only a moment ago.

"Mija," Abuela exclaims from her perch in a La-Z-Boy chair, "you're gonna break the hinge one of these days." She's reading one of those trashy novels she likes. This one is called *Pirata del Deseo*, and it features a risqué, half-naked pirate on the cover.

I lean down and plant a kiss on her cheek.

"Que la Virgencita y San Antonio te bendigan," she says, peering at the upside-down statue of Saint Anthony behind the register. I roll my eyes. Abuela offers him a candle daily in the hopes that he'll find me a husband, as if saints have nothing better to do these days than play matchmakers. I wonder which saint finds new jobs for the recently unemployed. I'll light that candle myself.

"Happy birthday, hermanita," Carola sings from behind her styling chair. With one practiced move, she unfastens the salon cape from her last client of the day, then turns to sweep me into a hug. I hug her back, inhaling the familiar scent of hair dye and essential oils lingering on the fabric of her dress. Carola followed in Mami's footsteps: wife, mother, purveyor of all things beautifying. Which means I'm usually the third wheel in our relationship.

"There's the birthday girl!" As if on cue, Mami steps out of the laundry room, looking ever like the Puerto Rican version of Sophia Loren in a waist-hugging dress and bright red lipstick. She kisses me on both cheeks, then drops an armful of freshly laundered towels in my hands. "Fold these, nena. Neatly, please—into squares, not rectangles. I don't want to find them all bunched up every time I open the drawer."

I swallow a protest and start folding, aware that my squares are nowhere near as neat as she wants them to be. The moment I step out, my loving but controlling mother will refold them herself. Today, I have no patience for her neurotic demands. "Can we talk for a minute?" I ask. "In the back room?"

"Augusto and the kids will be here in a minute," Carola calls out from the register, where she is checking out a client. "Augusto is doing an overnight shift, so we're eating early."

"I'll go get the tostones started," Abuela says, leaving her perch on the La-Z-Boy and heading toward the house.

Mami's fastidious gaze falls on my face, and before I can pull away, her hands are on my skin, assessing. "You need a facial." Her fingers crawl over my cheeks. "You have to moisturize if you want any chance of getting a husband, Luisa."

"Maybe I should go help Abuela in the kitchen," I say, but then Carola shoves a broom in my hands, expecting me to use it. "It's my birthday," I cry out in mock indignation, which only makes her laugh.

"Vidalina was here this morning," Mami prattles on as I sweep the floors. "Says her son, Juan Pablo, just broke up with his floozy of a girlfriend." I ignore her, because who refers to women as floozies anymore, and the thought of getting set up with my very embarrassing teenage crush—who incidentally doesn't know I exist—feels like entering the seventh circle of hell. "Maybe I should have them over for dinner."

"Please don't—" I bark.

Mercifully, we're joined by my brother-in-law, Augusto, who decided from day one that his role in the family was "human buffer"—and we all love him for it. Augusto won over the family with his breezy Afro-Cuban manner, sharp wit, and shrewd intellect. His job as an Atlanta police detective earned him a special place in my heart as a fellow fact-finding geek.

"Happy birthday, hermanita," he coos, balancing my baby niece, Sarita, in one arm.

He plants a kiss on my temple and in turn I shower my niece with little pecks. She giggles into her daddy's chest.

"What about a makeover for your birthday weekend?" my sister squeals, eyes going wide with excitement. "Facial, blowout, nails."

"Keratin treatment," Mami offers. "Make that frizzy pelo malo smooth and shiny."

"You shouldn't say 'pelo malo,' Mami," I snap, collecting hair clippings from the floor with a dustpan, then dropping them in the garbage. "It's racist."

"Bah." Mami waves one hand in the air dismissively. "Everything is racist these days."

I know I should let this go. I am too stressed and too tired for this conversation. Plus, my mother, like most people on the Island, still identifies as white every time she ticks a race checkbox on an official form. She's brown, not permanently tanned as she likes to believe.

We finish closing the salon, then head back to the house, where Abuela busies herself beside the stove, smashing plantains on a tostonera and tossing them in hot oil. My nieces Rosita and Daniela storm past me, chasing after (i.e., terrorizing) Abuela's cat, Chapulín. I love these girls more than life itself, but at three and five years old, they are truly little demons.

Augusto, still holding Sarita, pours me a glass of chardonnay, filling it almost to the brim. I mouth a silent thanks, and we exchange a knowing smile. We do this a lot, talk without words. Augusto is the brother I never had and never thought I needed, until he stepped into our lives.

"Augusto is Black," Mami says abruptly, returning to our conversation in La Barna. Her eyebrows shoot up and her tone goes defensive toward me, and yet she lovingly offers a spoonful of paella to Augusto, which he eagerly accepts.

"I am?" Augusto responds with cartoonish surprise. "Oh. My. God," he exclaims, chewing. "Another kitchen miracle."

"See?" Mami turns to me. "How can I be racist when this man is one of the great loves of my life?" She pinches his cheek, then drops a piece of chorizo into his mouth.

"One does not beget the other, Mami. You only call it pelo malo because it's Black hair," I try to explain, exhaustion clawing back into my body. "Do you tell your blond, straight-haired clients that they have pelo malo? No. You don't."

"You think too much about these things, Luisa." She grabs a serrated knife, then slices into a crusty baguette. "Give it a rest. That mind of yours is always thinking. Always working. Can't you just unwind?"

Rosita and Daniela trap Chapulín in a corner and pull at his fluffy tail. He hisses at them, then releases a high-pitched yowl. "Leave that poor cat alone," Mami shrieks.

Temporary or not, one thing is certain: Moving back home will *feel* like forever. I make a mental note to run to the botanica and buy one of those San Judas Tadeo veladora candles for the lost and desperate. Maybe Abuela is onto something.

We gather around the table, eager to dive in. And after Abuela offers a blessing, we pass the dishes around.

"Luisa, amor, what did you want to talk about?" Mami asks, loud enough for everyone to hear. "Is everything okay, mija?"

"Later," I say, stuffing my mouth with a forkful of paella.

"Why?" she insists, arms open in a collective embrace. "It's just your familia here."

The rice and seafood go down like gravel. I set down my fork and take a long swig of wine, aware that all eyes—including the freaking cat's—are on me.

"I was thinking," I say hesitantly, "that maybe I should move back here with you and Abuela. Save up for a down payment. To buy my own place, you know?" The table goes quiet, so I'm forced to fill in the silence. "I'd like to put down twenty percent. Have a comfortable mortgage."

"You're so full of shit," Carola blurts out, sending her fork clattering against her plate.

"Carola," Abuela chastises. "Language. The girls." But it's too late. The little sponges are giggling uncontrollably, chanting in unison, "Titi Luisa's full of shit. Titi Luisa's full of shit."

I'd be pissed, if they weren't so freaking cute.

"She's doing that thing with her upper lip." Carola points one finger at my face. "It curls when she's lying."

"What thing?" I spit back.

"That lip thing," she says, mirroring my face by pinching and twisting her upper lip with her fingers. "Augusto, back me up."

"I'm staying out of it," he groans. My sister glares at him, then punches him in the left arm. I punch him in the right for not defending me. "Owww!" He rubs at his biceps, then glances at my lips, stifling a laugh.

"You suck," I hiss.

"What's going on, Luisa?" Mami glowers at me across the table.

"I . . ." I clear my throat, trying to find a way to spin my unemployment situation into something that doesn't make me sound like a total failure. My sister beats me to the punch. She gasps, bringing her hands over her mouth, eyes wide with horror.

"You got fired," she cries out, like some bruja mind reader. "Oh no, Luisa." She winces.

"Are you fucking kidding me?" I protest, slamming both hands hard against the table.

"Language," Abuela scolds. "Really, mija? And on your birthday?" she adds, her voice softening with pity, because apparently all the women in my family are mind readers—except me, that is.

"Is this true?" Mami demands. "Did you get fired?" The answer must be written on my upper lip as Carola keenly observed. But it's Mami's next question that sends me flying straight over the edge: "What did you do?"

Because of course, to my mother, this is somehow my fault.

"I don't know." I huff, pushing back my chair. The legs scrape against the hardwood floors. "Apparently, I'm a hunk of Swiss cheese. I have to pee."

My feet stumble to the bathroom, where I lock the door behind me. I pull down my jeans and sit on the toilet to pee—and think.

Why was I fired? That's the million-dollar question.

I take out my phone and search "Griggs Caldecott Johnson III." His company's website comes up first. There's an announcement for a banquet—which starts in an hour—celebrating National Philanthropy Day at Dogwood Hills Country Club. Griggs Caldecott Johnson III is receiving a Young Philanthropist award from the mayor.

I click on various links, featuring the GCJ Foundation's work with about two dozen affordable housing and urban development organizations. Some of them I've heard of: Glendale Community Gardens, Homewood Village, and the new housing development near the stadium. Others aren't familiar at all, but the list makes one thing clear: this man is everywhere.

Suddenly, I'm feeling very sorry for myself and wondering if Nina was right. Maybe I allowed my affection for the Castillos to cloud my judgment and I missed the obvious: The old man sold the farm and spent the cash. He was probably too embarrassed to tell his son. Heck, look at my own dad and how much he managed to hide from us in plain sight. Guilt and shame can make good people do terrible things—even destroy their family's lives in the process.

"Luisa," Carola whispers through the locked bathroom door. "What are you doing?"

"What do you think I'm doing?" I sigh, exasperated, browsing through the Dogwood Hills Facebook page, which hasn't been updated in years. Why do they even bother keeping the thing active? Still, I select the Photos section.

"Let me in!" Carola jiggles the door handle. "Pleeeease."

Ugh. I lean forward, unlock the door, and open it a crack. Carola squeezes inside.

"Are you done?" she asks, ignoring my question. "I need to pee."

"Why don't you use the bathroom upstairs?" I pull up my underwear and jeans, then move to the sink to wash my hands.

"This one's closer." She laughs at herself, a little tipsy, then sits on the toilet. "Why didn't you tell us you got fired? I would've done your hair real nice. A little pick-me-up."

I dry my hands, then reach for my phone to scroll through old photos of the club, mostly weddings and golf tournaments, until I find my answer.

"What the fuck?" I hear myself cry out. "What the fucking fuck? That fucker!"

"Who?" Carola demands. "Who's a fucker?"

"My publisher," I exclaim.

Chip, my asshole publisher, and Griggs Caldecott Johnson III are golfing buddies. Of course they are. A tournament photo shows them standing by a golf cart with their wives, chummy, toothpaste-ad smiles plastered to their faces.

Chip didn't just pass on my story; he outright killed it. The whole damn thing stinks of rich white boy networks and underhanded cover-ups.

Fuck Chip and fuck *The Georgia Times*.

I pull up driving directions to the Dogwood Hills Country Club.

CHAPTER 6

Holly

"Vodka soda, hold the soda," I tell Byron.

He smiles at me, concern gathering in his dark eyes and at the corners of his mouth.

"You off the clock?" he asks, glancing around the empty Magnolia Bar—a new, "modern" addition, which, at Dogwood Hills, is a relative term. Instead of flocked wallpaper, this room has white wainscoting and walls painted hydrangea blue. Instead of heavy oak or mahogany antique tables, it's filled with overstuffed leather sofas and armchairs, with marble cocktail tables dispersed throughout.

I nod, slumping onto a leather barstool.

"All right, then," Byron tells me, tucking a crisp white dish towel under the string of his equally white apron. "I suppose you can sit up here and keep me company while I prep to open."

I rushed straight here to hide, as soon as the official program began, still reeling from my encounters with Griggs. The first one—beside the equipment closet—shook me to my core. The second one, from which I've just run away? I think what concerned me the most about it was how unremarkable it probably appeared to everyone else in the room. Griggs had simply approached me to ask where the mayor was sitting, or more precisely to insist that I seat her next to him, at the head table. But he stood too close, watching me with roving eyes. I could almost see his mind calculating, strategizing his next move—deciding how long it would take to break me.

Is this how it will be now? Every day, when I arrive for work, will I worry that Griggs Johnson is lying in wait for me, ready to pounce?

I needed to stop spiraling, to gather myself somewhere safe before trying to walk through the crowded foyer and away from this place. And I knew that, with the Philanthropy Banquet in full swing, I'd find Byron alone here.

I watch, taking comfort as he falls into his expert rhythm, one that I've seen more times than I can begin to count.

When Byron tells the story of our first meeting, he says that he came around from behind the bar to introduce himself, and I confidently thrust out my little hand for a firm shake, all the while looking him directly in the eye, steady and resolved.

Needless to say, our recollections of that day differ. All I remember is that, terrified during my entire shift that I was leaking breast milk through my uniform, I compulsively stole glances at my tits. But we all need people in our lives who resolutely believe that we're stronger than we really are. And for me, Byron is one of those people.

He pulls a crystal tumbler from the shelf behind him and fills it with ice.

"Looks like you could use a Belvedere," he says.

I nod and drop my head into my hands.

He grabs the expensive vodka from the top shelf and pours me a double. "Wanna talk about it?"

"Nope," I say as he slides the vodka toward me, two limes expertly balanced on the rim.

"Well, you know I'm here when you do." He meets my gaze, his expression so kind that it physically hurts to look at him. I can't drag Byron into this mess.

I squeeze both limes into my drink and then lift the glass and take a long swig. The Belvedere burns on its way down, and the burn feels good. But even this can't keep my mind from obsessing over that secret—the one Reginald was keeping before he got fired. The one Griggs aims to use as a weapon of blackmail and harassment against me.

It was a few days after Aidan's eighteenth birthday. We had a dozen events lined up at the club that weekend, and on Friday afternoon, the new parking valet failed to show up—no notice, no excuse. Desperate, I called Aidan and begged him to come park cars for a rehearsal dinner.

Aidan rushed over, changed into a uniform, and dutifully began to park cars while I launched myself into the ballroom and started putting out a shit-ton of little fires. It was one of those events where everything that can go wrong does go wrong, from botched seating charts to pasta for the vegetarian bride—who not only avoided carbs like the plague but also happened to be gluten-intolerant. Irma blamed it all on Mercury's retrograde. I blamed it all on myself.

Just as the (mostly collapsed) chocolate soufflés were being served, Reginald arrived at my side, tapped my shoulder, and discreetly gestured for me to follow him.

"We have a situation," he said as soon as he had me alone.

The cause of the situation unfolded in a long conversation between Aidan, Reginald, and me—interspersed with a vast array of creative expletives from me.

The facts: Griggs and Anna-Byrd Johnson pulled up in Griggs's brand-new C-class Mercedes convertible. Aidan politely opened the door for Anna-Byrd, and she exited the vehicle. Aidan then walked around to the driver's side, and Griggs moved to the passenger seat, insisting that he ride along to park the car since Aidan was a new employee.

As Aidan drove into the garage, Griggs asked who'd hired him. Aidan said, "Holly, the events manager," but he left out that I was his mom, worried that it might appear I was doling out special favors. Griggs replied that I was "hot," and all the valets must want to "fuck" me. Aidan said nothing in reply. Then, as Griggs was leaving the car, he casually added that he planned to "find a way into" my "hot little pants." Aidan still said nothing. Instead, my eighteen-year-old son, in his infinite wisdom, made the decision that only an "adult" man with a not-fully-formed frontal lobe can make: He used the valet key to scrawl "prick" onto the driver's-side door of Griggs's brand-new hundred-thousand-dollar cabriolet. And—of course—he did this directly in a security camera's line of sight.

In a gesture of mercy—and after patiently listening as I berated Aidan for a full five minutes about his back-ass, misguided chivalry—Reginald offered to get rid of the security footage and say a grifter must have wandered in from Piedmont Park. We'd need to come up with the money to cover repairs, but he'd tell Griggs the club's insurance would pay.

At first I was appalled by Reginald's offer. "My son should take responsibility for his actions!" I proclaimed. Reginald then gently interjected that keying a car of that value was unequivocally a felony, which shut both Aidan and me up fast.

Felons don't receive full-ride scholarships from the state of Georgia, as Griggs so helpfully just reminded me.

I made a split-second decision. Aidan would work all summer in the most grueling job I could find. He'd earn enough to cover the cost of repairs, and we'd accept Reginald's offer with gratitude. Then, in August, Aidan would head to the University of Georgia on full scholarship, as planned. We'd try to forget the whole thing happened.

That's what we did, for better or worse. Griggs never found out who defaced his car, and Aidan spent a long, hot summer replacing roofs under the relentless sun. He paid for every penny of those repairs.

Now, I watch Byron work behind the bar, wondering if I made the right choice. I guess this is what it means to be a mother: I struggle to protect my son at all costs and then worry that I may have protected him too much. I make the impossible decisions and then accept the inevitable consequences.

Here's the thing I've learned about Griggs in my many years of observing his behavior with women: For him, sex isn't sex. It's power. He quietly has affairs with the wives of prominent men at the club as a way to prove his own dominance—not to other men, but to himself. And women who refuse to sleep with him—especially women of a lower social status—threaten to diminish his feeling of power, which is really all he cares about. As far as I've been able to observe, Griggs will do just about anything to prove to those who dare to refuse him that he's still the one on top.

Which means, in short, that I'm totally screwed (metaphorically speaking).

Byron arranges stirrers, chops limes, and fills the fridge with bottles of white wine, while I sit in silence nursing both my extreme self-pity and my second double.

How can I go after Griggs—reveal him for the grimy sexual predator that he is—if it means destroying my precious son's future?

"How about some water, Holly?" Byron asks after a while, gently pressing a glass into my hand. "Maybe some peanuts, too?"

I look down, my vision blurring. I thought I'd be fine having two doubles, but Byron's "country club" pours are heavy, and I'm not much of a drinker these days.

I clutch my gut, feeling my forehead sink to meet the cool steel bar top. Then I feel a warm hand on my shoulder.

"Let me get Justine to bring you over a burger from the grill," Byron says, clearly worried that he's overserved me. "Rare, with bacon and extra pickles, just the way you like it?"

"I think I might be sick." I lift my spinning head to exclaim to Byron. Then I jump to my feet and rush out past the Azalea Ballroom, making a beeline for the bathroom, just in time to hear the announcer exclaim through a crisp, perfectly calibrated sound system, "Griggs Caldecott Johnson III, this year's Young Philanthropist."

CHAPTER 7

Luisa

I'm chewing on my fourth melt-in-your-mouth cracker when Griggs Johnson is called to the podium to accept his award.

What do they put in these crackers, anyway? Some kind of secret butter from the gods? They're even served warm, as if they were baked exclusively for each guest. Of course rich people have access to more delicious saltines than the rest of us.

A server deposits a tall glass of tea with a fresh mint sprig on the high-top I'm occupying, then sets a small dish of lemon wedges wrapped in yellow mesh beside it. "Can I get more of these, please?" I gesture to the silver cracker dish, now empty. He nods and leaves. I squeeze a meshed lemon over my tea and swirl the straw, trailing Griggs with my eyes as he shakes hands with a few men on his way to the podium, while also scanning the room for the too-young, pearl-clutching Country Club Betty in the blue dress, now conspicuously absent. Where did she go?

Much to my family's dismay, I sped through the remainder of my birthday dinner, blew out my candles, opened my gifts, then hauled ass to Midtown in rush hour. I used my now-defunct *Georgia Times* press badge to check in at the media table when I first arrived. That's when I first saw Griggs Johnson in the flesh, wearing the same predatory smile I'd seen him parade online. He was muttering to the Betty in the pencil skirt, standing inappropriately close. Could she be his mistress? Maybe. She certainly isn't his wife. The wife was across the room glad-handing local politicians and berating a server because her sweet tea was "too sweet."

Griggs practically had the *Maybe Mistress* and her pearls pinned to the wall like some taxidermy butterfly. And either everyone's attention was too absorbed by the freely flowing alcohol and delicious canapés to notice, or these people just don't give a damn.

But I saw. I'd never laid eyes on him before today, but I already knew his type. Griggs is the kind of man who excels at hiding his despicable behavior in plain sight.

He is charming, I'll give him that. Charismatic in a way that seems almost genuine. He's also absurdly photogenic, as evidenced by a booklet about his family's charitable foundation, brimming with photo after photo of his well-boned face.

A fresh tray of buttery crackers arrives just as Griggs steps up to the podium. The wall of windows that forms one half of the circular ballroom only serves to highlight his tall frame and athletic build. He vigorously shakes the mayor's hand, then accepts a blown glass award sculpture.

"Thanks, Gail," he says into the microphone. "This will look just perfect next to my Peachtree Invitational trophy." Everyone around me laughs at his asinine inside joke. A clandestine search on my phone—I was sternly told it's a club rule to keep it turned off—reveals that the Peachtree Invitational is an amateur golf tournament at this very country club. The way he says it is almost dismissive, as if the award doesn't matter much. I'm annoyed that he's even comparing the two. Apparently, it's all one big fucking joke to him.

"No, really, folks. I'm getting a little choked up thinking about how proud my father would be if he were still with us today." He looks down, lips pursed, and pauses for a beat. I read somewhere that his dad was a big-time architect, built all of Atlanta's iconic skyscrapers. Tough to live in the shadow of that, I guess.

"This foundation and the good work it does—they meant the world to him," he continues. "And this recognition means the world to me." His slight Southern accent is warm and pleasant. His manner, easy and open. His smile, beguiling. I'm reminded that the devil was once an angel.

If only these people knew that—much like the country club itself—Griggs Caldecott Johnson III starts falling apart on closer inspection. Earlier, as I walked in, I couldn't help but scoff at the musty smell of the carpets, the dings and scratches on the furniture, the faded fabric of the sitting room sofa. There's even a landscape painting hanging on a wall with a hole in it the size of my thumb. A fucking hole. In a painting.

I've read that to join this place, people have to cough up a hundred-thousand-dollar-plus entry fee, as well as absurd monthly dues. I don't get it. Atlanta's most exclusive country club is an old, stuffy building that serves saltines (though admittedly delicious) as its specialty.

As Griggs finishes his speech, he looks back to his table, thanking his "lovely bride and partner in crime, Anna-Byrd," then winks at her from the podium. I observe her from across the room, eager for any inkling that this woman could become a trusted source. She waves a hand at the adoring crowd around them, like a small-town princess sitting atop a parade float. It's a studied move. This woman clearly knows what kind of douchebag she's married to, what the trade-off was when she married him, and is happy to look the other way from more unsavory matters. Like the extramarital affair her husband seems to be shamelessly flaunting with the (*Dear God, please let it be so!*) pearl-clutching Country Club Betty.

I search the room, but she's still nowhere to be found. Which, judging by Griggs's effusive and very public praise of his wife, can only mean one thing: The other woman must be pissed. Really pissed. And no one—no one—makes a better source than a woman scorned.

Griggs wraps up with the equivalent of a beauty pageant's "world peace" platitude, and the room erupts into applause. You'd think he just announced a universal cure for cancer. Then, he swaggers over to his wife, cups her head in his hands, and whispers something in her ear that makes her blush.

I need a source, someone to attest to Griggs's underhanded business dealings. And the wife ain't gonna cut it. Where did the *Maybe Mistress* go?

I spend the next fifteen minutes wandering around the maze that is the Dogwood Hills Country Club, searching for Griggs's hopefully jilted lover, while gently being redirected by the staff back to the Azalea Ballroom at every turn. In the process, I can't help but notice that I have yet to encounter a white staff person, other than the folks at the front desk. It's as if being Black or Latine is a requirement for any of the club's backroom service jobs.

A bulletin board notice grabs my attention, a public announcement of a member's past due account and the amount owed highlighted in bold. Jesus, what a sadistic form of public humiliation. I wonder if they will feel the same public obligation when they find out what Griggs is doing to the Castillos.

Needing a quiet moment to regroup, I step into the nearest bathroom, which incidentally is the biggest bathroom I've ever set eyes on—maybe this is what that obscene membership fee buys you? I'm greeted by a comfortable sitting area, upholstered in more faded fabric and an elaborate white rose flower bouquet arranged on a pedestal table. That's where I find *Maybe Mistress* slouched on a rattan settee, clutching her pearls with one hand and a glass of water in the other. Her skirt is rumpled and the waves in her strawberry blond hair have fallen, hanging limp around her shoulders.

I get ready to swoop in on my much-needed source, but her droopy eyelids and disheveled appearance stop me in mid-flight. *Is she drunk?* Annoyance claws at my chest. Is this woman too impaired to provide any useful information?

"Are you okay?" I ask, looking down at her.

"Yup," she says, sitting up a little straighter. Then, in a slow Southern drawl, she mutters, "Finer than frog hair split four ways." She shrugs absently, trying to appear less tipsy than she is.

Great. Not only is she drunk, she's also nonsensical.

She tilts her head to look up at me and I notice her eyes are wet, and her mascara is smudged, adding to the pitiful sight. Pain radiates off her.

"What's your name?" I ask, forcing a gentle tone.

"Holly," she says with a tired sigh. "And you are?"

"Luisa." I sit beside her on the settee. "Maybe we should get you some coffee?"

She nods once, but then her face crumples, overcome with fresh tears. I reach for a box of tissues, pull out a handful, and hand them to her. At the same time, the door to the bathroom opens and a distinguished-looking elderly woman in a powder-blue suit and flashy cat eyeglasses steps into the entryway.

Holly peers from behind the mountain of tissues in her hands. "Oh no," she whisper-shouts, ducking behind me on the sofa, "Birdie Beauregard. Oh Lord, please don't let her see me like this. I'll lose my job."

"Job? What job?" I ask.

Holly buries her face in the cushions, too overcome to explain, leaving me with no choice but to shoot up from the sofa and stop the old woman at the door.

"Excuse me, ma'am," I call out, feigning a thick Southern accent, cringing at the sound of my voice. I hold the door before she can shut it behind her. "This bathroom is closed for repairs." She complains, mouth agape, as I briskly usher her out. "Nasty sewage backup situation. There's another, clean bathroom down that way." I gesture down the hallway, then pay no heed to her huffing and puffing as I close the door in her face.

"Thank you," Holly manages, dabbing her eyes. "I'm so sorry. I'm really not usually like this, but . . . did you see that man up on the stage?" *Hiccup.* "He's trying to ruin my life."

I nod but all I can think is: This *is my infallible source? A drunk Country Club Betty having a total meltdown?*

She digs into her purse, nervously pulls out a package of crackers, then rips the foil open, sending crumbs flying everywhere. "What am I gonna do?" she blurts out, nibbling on broken pieces of cracker that have landed on her chest. "I can't start all over again from nothing. Once should be enough. Shouldn't it?" Her cheeks go pale as her hand suddenly drops to clutch her stomach. She sucks in a gulp of air before announcing, "I think I'm gonna be sick again."

She rushes past me, hitting the round table on the way and almost knocking down the giant flower arrangement. I catch it in the nick of time, then follow her into a well-stocked vanity room, like something from the Regency era. Her knees hit the tile floor of one of the floor-to-ceiling stalls, as her arms wrap around the toilet seat and her head sinks inside the bowl to retch. I move to hold her hair, stroking circles around her back, like Carola did with me so many times during my college years.

"You'll feel better after you get it all out," I say gently. When she's finished, I let go of her hair and flush the toilet. She leans against the stall, eyes closed, breathing hard, legs splayed on the cold tiles. I step back, giving her some space, debating what to do next.

"Are you a new member?" She opens her eyes to take me in. "You've been so nice. I'm so, so sorry," she blubbers, pulling way too hard on a too-long thread of toilet paper that she uses to wipe her face. "Please don't tell anyone you found me this way. I promise it's never happened in the eighteen years I've worked here."

"Wait, you work here?" I ask, reaching down with one hand to help her stand. She staggers toward a vanity and plops on top of a stool, which incidentally is also upholstered in faded fabric. *What's with this place?*

I sit beside her, rummaging through the free toiletry basket in search of makeup remover. The woman looks like a rabid raccoon. I fish around an absurd selection of hand lotion, toothbrushes, tampons, breath mints, and chocolates wrapped in royal-blue foil stamped with the Dogwood Hills coat of arms. I unwrap one and put it in my mouth. *Dammit to hell*, it's a little morsel of heaven. Fucking rich people always hoard all the best things for themselves—first the saltines and now the chocolates. Where does it end?

"I'm the events manager," Holly says. "It's supposed to be my day off."

God, this is worse than I imagined. This affair could bring her career to a dead end. And maybe even her livelihood. The women always pay the price of the affair. The men wear it like a badge of honor.

Against my better judgment, I feel a protective, sisterly instinct kick in as I hand her a brush and some makeup remover, then pull a scrunchie out of the backpack I use on assignments—used to use, anyway.

"He's got this hold over me," she says quietly, unwilling to lift her head enough to glance at her reflection in the mirror. "He will ruin my son's life. I know he will."

I manage to press my lips shut before the next logical question can burst out of me: *Does she have a child with that man?*

"I just don't know how we will ever extricate ourselves from that man," she whispers.

That makes two of us, I want to say.

A loud bang rips through the silence we've fallen into. It's followed by a violent rattling of the door handle. "Please open this door," a man's booming voice orders from the hallway.

"I can't even drive myself home," Holly says, her voice exhausted.

I decide to ignore the *Open this door right now!* command and try my luck with a door at the far end of the room.

"That's the service door," Holly remarks, dejected. She rests one elbow on the counter, then squeezes her temples between her thumb and index finger. "I'm so screwed. Everyone will know."

I peer out the door, which seems to shoot into a hallway near the kitchen. "Can you get us to the parking lot?" I ask, collecting our bags, then pulling Holly up to stand. She nods.

We make our way through the kitchen, dodging cooks and waiters. I only slow down at the sight of those buttery crackers, wishing I had time to ask for the recipe. Within seconds, we burst out of the service exit and into the pollen-covered parking lot, a by-product of the neighboring park's hundreds of April-blooming dogwoods.

"Thank God," Holly exclaims, swallowing a gulp of fresh air.

"Come on—" I force her to keep moving, away from this place. "I'll drive you home."

In the car, Holly pulls up her home address and gives me her phone. It takes precisely two minutes after we leave the Dogwood Hills Country Club for her to pass out.

I wind through the tree-lined streets of the Midtown Garden District, driving by a few 1970s-style brick apartment complexes, left over from Atlanta's brief period of white flight to the suburbs, and pull up to her address. The house is one of those slightly run-down Penn Avenue craftsman bungalows, split into four apartments. The property is surrounded by fully renovated American foursquares—tasteful, bespoke, ungodly expensive. Old Money meets Garden District meets Gay District in all its cultured, sophisticated, fabulous glory.

I pull over, then save my contact information in her phone, and nudge her awake.

"I saved my number in your contacts," I say, handing her the phone. "Griggs Johnson has a few other secrets I think you should know."

"Other secrets?" she mutters, still half-asleep.

I sigh. "Aside from—" *You*, I want to say. "He has some . . . business secrets," I tell her instead. "I may be able to help you and your son. Let's talk when you're—you know, not drunk."

Holly nods, her cheeks burning red.

"Call me when you're ready."

CHAPTER 8

Holly

My phone dings with the sound I've reserved just for Aidan's texts. Against my body's will, I roll over in bed and fumble to pick it up.

Hippopotamus?

I smile, scrolling down to see the photo Aidan's attached. It's of the foam on his morning latte, which I know he made in his dorm room with the fancy espresso machine my co-workers pitched in to buy him as a high school graduation gift.

Me

Hmmm. I'm feeling rhino. Note the pointy horn. Or maybe, actually, jackhammer on second glance?

Aidan

I see it! Def jackhammer.

Ugh. Like my pounding head.

Me

Glad we agree on the essential things.

I manage to reply, despite my blurred vision. Is this a hangover? Oh God. I think it is.

The last time I had a hangover was seven years ago—after way too many mojitos at Irma's wedding.

I'm not feeling quite as rough as I did that morning, but still, my mouth is parched and sticky, and I need a Tylenol—or four.

I haul myself to the edge of my bed, sit up, chug some water, then text Aidan.

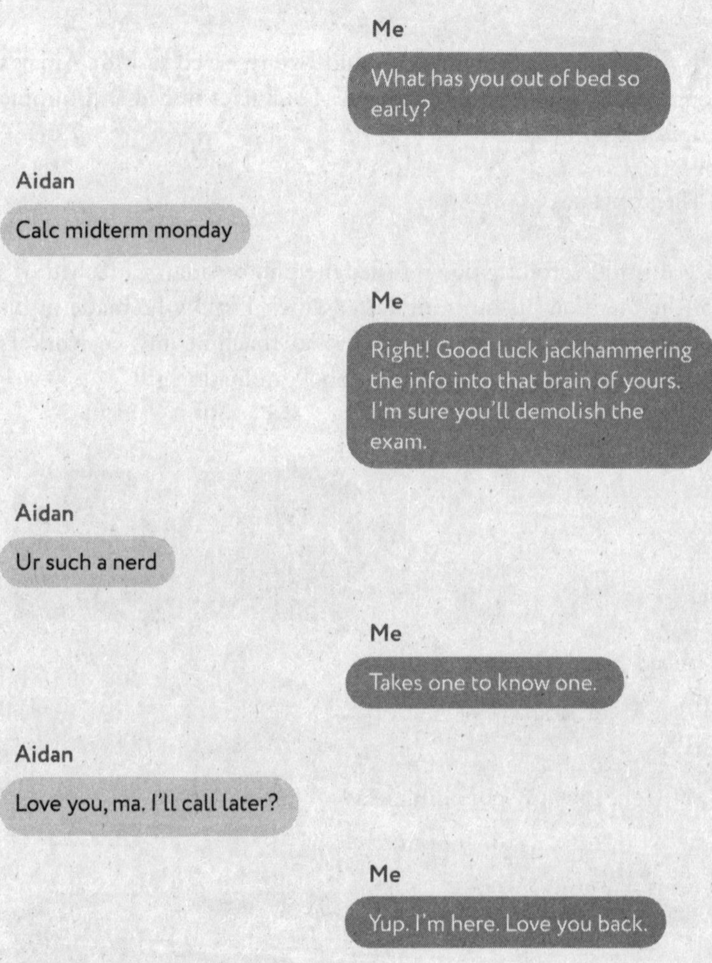

I drop my phone onto my bedside table, feeling quite smug that I've raised the sort of son who wakes up early on weekends to study—and can make his own fancy coffee.

I taught him the summer before his sophomore year of high school. My lessons came with an extensive economics calculation, comparing his hourly wage at the ice cream shop to the cost of a latte from the fancy coffeehouse around the corner. He's a fast learner, and even more of a penny-pincher than me (which is saying something). He quickly mastered the skill and took over our morning coffee routine. Somehow, when he makes my coffee, it always tastes better. Plus, he's quite the foam artist.

Even though I miss him desperately, I also love imagining Aidan waking up in his dorm and then making his morning cappuccino just the way he likes it. What if it all goes away? What if Griggs Johnson follows through with his threat?

I desperately need a distraction—and some good, strong coffee. I know just where to go.

After throwing on sweatpants and a ratty old cardigan, brushing my teeth, and downing a couple of Tylenol, I head downstairs and out the back door, then cut across my yard and through the gate onto Joel and Peter's impeccably manicured lawn. They're my next-door neighbors, and also my landlords. But none of these descriptors captures what they—and Peter's mom, whom I affectionately call Aunt Edna—mean to me. The three of them are perhaps the most generous people I have ever encountered. Their actions remind me every day that it's possible to both be immensely privileged and have a good heart. Also, they are all real pieces of work.

Through the casement windows I see Joel and Peter in their usual morning routine. Joel lounges on the sofa in his favorite batik robe, his thick white hair already perfectly combed, reading the Arts section of *The New York Times*. Peter sits in the wing chair beside him wearing L.L.Bean slippers, a white polo shirt, and pressed khakis. He's fiddling with his tablet.

I tug open the sliding glass door.

"Morning, sleepyhead," he says in his signature Kentucky accent. "And close the door behind you. No need to heat the great outdoors."

"Is there coffee made?" I grunt. "I'm out."

"Good Lord, Holly," Joel says, lifting his reading glasses to rest on top of his head. "What happened to you last night?"

"Rumor has it, you had a few too many at *the club*?" Peter says, feigning a scandalized tone. "Janey's very concerned."

Peter and Joel have been members of the Dogwood Hills Country Club for years, which conveniently allows all the old Atlanta families to pat themselves on the back for being "open-minded." They are the only club members that I've let myself become real friends with—an exception to my general rule. They're also besties with Janey, which means, of course, that they're in on *all* the gossip.

"I was off the clock," I say, shrugging. "Tough day." I put my head down and head resolutely toward the scent of freshly brewed coffee.

"And?" Joel stretches out the word, waiting for me to explain my unprecedented behavior. I'm not exactly one to drink on—or at—the job.

Aunt Edna wanders in, blessedly distracting us from the question that still hangs in the air. Her bejeweled cane sparkles in the sunlight, and a diamond bracelet dangles from her fingertip.

"Come on over here and give your aunt Edna a hand." She settles on the piano bench and motions for me to sit beside her.

I plop down next to her, and she stares hard at me, studying my face. "What you need, my darling, is a good strong Bloody Mary." She turns toward Peter, who is back to punching at his tablet as if it's a touch-tone phone from the 1980s. "Son, go on into that kitchen and make our sweet girl a drink. And while you're at it, make your mama one, too."

Peter places his tablet on the side table and dutifully heads to the bar.

"A little hair of the dog will fix you right up," she says. "Now, help me put this darn thing on. I think the clasp is broken and I'm about to go play bridge with the girls."

I take Aunt Edna's bracelet and wrap it around her pudgy wrist as Peter comes back with two Bloody Marys, complete with celery and three olives on a spear.

I accept one from him, admiring its peppery smell, then lift it to my lips. Aunt Edna was right. This is precisely what I need. I quietly nurse my Bloody Mary while she and Peter debate whether it's really "necessary" that she wear a diamond tennis bracelet to play cards.

"If you must know," Aunt Edna announces, standing up, "every week that Judy Swanson struts into bridge club with another gorgeous brooch or cocktail ring." She starts stabbing her cane into the air, which always signifies she means business. "I won't go having her think I'm some sort of country bumpkin, just because her daddy was a Kentucky coal baron and mine was a lowly horse trainer."

"No one thinks you're a country bumpkin," Joel replies, his voice, as always, even.

My heart aches with affection, watching their banter. I am eternally grateful that the universe placed me and Aidan in the house next door to these three.

It was the day after Thanksgiving, my freshman year of college, when I realized that I would be leaving Mississippi, probably forever. I was eighteen, almost three months pregnant, and terrified. Aidan's father and I had agreed that we would tell our parents after the club's annual post-Thanksgiving brunch. I saw him there, but we studiously avoided each other.

After we got home, I broke the news. My father said nothing to me. He stood up from our formal dining table, pushed his chair back, and announced to my mother, "You'll deal with her messes." By contrast, my mother said many things, most of them relating to her absolute incredulity that Aidan's father, that *nice boy* from such a *nice family*, would have managed to get me, of all people, pregnant.

She finally stood up from the table and began putting away the etched silver serving pieces that we only used on holidays. She was holding a chafing dish when she said it: "We'll take care of this quickly and discreetly. No need to drag his family into it."

"Too late," I replied. "He's telling them right now."

"Oh my Lord," she sighed. "What have you done?"

My mind reeled. Was she planning to take me for an abortion?

Was she worried they wouldn't let me do it? My parents went to church, of course. Everyone in our world went to church. They weren't particularly religious, though. By contrast to my parents, his parents were super religious, and vocally conservative. They definitely would not be down for an abortion. That's what I thought, at least.

My mom was putting the chafing dish in the sideboard when I saw him through the dining room window, walking toward our house. He was still wearing the khakis he'd had on at the club, and a checkered blue button-down. His hands were shoved into his pockets, and he was looking at his feet. His auburn hair had fallen into his eyes, and he appeared so sweet and innocent that I had a moment of hope. Maybe this would all work out. Maybe he would fling open the door and announce to my father that he loved me and wanted to marry me, and we'd have a lovely, intimate wedding beside a lake somewhere, and I'd wear blush pink. We'd find a cute little condo in Oxford that our parents would pay for, and even though it would be hard, we would both manage to finish school, and then I'd work while he went to medical school and I'd be a doctor's wife, maybe even become a nurse someday.

My father must have seen him coming, too, because he walked downstairs and greeted Aidan's father at the door with a shake of hands.

"I'm sorry for what I did, sir," he said, before even crossing the threshold.

My father gave a brief nod in reply, then stepped into the hallway.

"I talked with my parents, and they think I'm too young. I need to finish school."

I stared hard at him from across the room, but he couldn't look at me, or he wouldn't.

"So we think it probably will be best if she, uh, you know . . ." He fell silent.

I couldn't figure out how this was happening.

"If I what?" I said, my question reverberating through the cavernous room. "Say it."

"Holly," my mom scolded. "No need to raise your voice." This was her worry in such a moment: propriety. This was always her worry.

"You can't say it, can you?" I demanded, ignoring my mother.

"We think she should, um . . ."

"Look at *me*," I called out. "Talk to *me*."

But he didn't. Instead, he looked directly at my father and said, "We think she should end the pregnancy." And then he had the audacity to dig into his pocket, pull out a thick wad of cash, and hand it to my father. "It's my money," he said. "My parents thought it was important that I pay with money I earned." He failed to mention that he'd made that money playing in his conservative church's praise-and-worship band.

"I don't want an abortion," I heard myself announce, my voice even and strong, as my father pocketed the cash.

That may have been the truest moment of clarity I had ever had. I knew that even though not a single person in my life wanted it, this pregnancy was meant for me. Also, in this particular case, my choice wasn't just another ploy to piss off my parents. It was a clearheaded decision to become a mom—a good mom, maybe even an excellent mom—to my own beautiful child.

"Stop talking nonsense," my mother spat. "You heard the young man. We absolutely will not go running his family name through the mud with your bad decisions."

"I don't need him or his family," I mumbled. "I don't need any of you."

"Oh, isn't that just so rich," my mom said, a biting tease in her tone. "You, Holly Simmons, are most certainly not capable of raising a child on your own." She paused to let out a loud huff. "For heaven's sake, you can't even keep a job at the pool snack bar."

She was right. The only job I'd ever had was at the country club snack bar the summer after my sophomore year of high school. It lasted a week. I overslept once after a brutal night of period cramps, rushed in a half hour late, and my asshole boss called me an "irresponsible brat" and fired me on the spot. I told myself I didn't want the job anyway, and I spent the next two months stealing my mother's vodka, loitering by the pool where I should have been working, and day drinking from a plastic water bottle.

"Okay, I'll do it," I said, approaching my father. "I'll . . . take care of it." I made sure to glare right at the *nice boy* standing, ashamed, in my hallway. "But I want to do it alone." I held out my hand and waited for my father to give me the cash.

When he did, I turned my back on all of them, went up to my bedroom, and packed. Before dawn the next morning, I was on a bus to Atlanta, carrying three suitcases filled with the expensive clothes and jewelry that I would sell off in the ensuing months, five hundred dollars of praise-and-worship money, and the fetus that would become my Aidan.

This was way back when Midtown was still "transitional," and I felt so proud to have found a charmingly shabby-chic attic apartment in a chopped-up, sagging old bungalow. And then there was the blessing of Mrs. Babangida. She was a stern and capable Nigerian grandmother who lived in the corner apartment on the first floor, missed her own grandchildren desperately, and generously offered to babysit Aidan after I landed my first job at Dogwood Hills. She lovingly cared for my baby in exchange for occasional assistance navigating the bureaucracy of the U.S. citizenship process and free leftovers from the club. That woman loved a loaded baked potato, God rest her soul.

Unfortunately, Kyle, my smarmy landlord, was anything but a blessing. When rich couples like Joel and Peter moved in and started pouring hundreds of thousands of dollars into restoring neighboring homes, he smelled big profit. Shortly after Aidan's third birthday, Kyle threatened to evict us all so that the old dump could be torn down to build townhouses. But then, Joel and Peter, my knights in shining armor, jumped in to save the day and bought the place out from under him. Joel insisted that the act was far from charitable. He simply couldn't abide the thought of living adjacent to *townhomes*. And so, for fifteen years they've served as not only my dear friends but also my landlords. They haven't raised the rent even once.

"I don't mean to pry," Peter says, turning his attention to me, "but what in God's name drove you to drown your sorrows at *the club*, of all places?"

"Oh, the usual work nonsense," I tell him, trying not to sound evasive.

"I heard the head of security was let go," Joel says. "I've lost his name—"

"Reginald," I say, my voice faltering.

"Another one bites the dust," Peter adds, matter-of-factly.

Peter, Joel, and Aunt Edna wait for me to say more, but my lips press tight and my head resumes its pounding, as I force myself to remember the last two exemplary Dogwood Hills employees to "bite the dust." Both women. And, if Janey's intel can be trusted, also both victims of Griggs Johnson.

I could ask Joel to help me find a lawyer and sue Griggs for harassment—a fool's errand, since he'll almost certainly have the judge in his pocket. I could quit and never have to see Griggs's face again. But over the years, I've worked my way up to a level that I could never reach at another club or hotel, not without a diploma—*and* a fabulous recommendation from the board of directors. Even if another club wanted to hire me despite my lack of a hospitality degree, Griggs knows all the club presidents. He'd have me blackballed, for sure.

My skin crawls as I recall his eyes roving my form hungrily, his hand red-hot on my body. One thing is clear: I will never, ever give him what he wants.

How will I explain to Aidan that his bright future is going dark, fast?

As if my thoughts have summoned him, I hear my phone vibrating and look down to see the face of my sweet boy, his shaggy auburn hair shining in the sun. I step out onto the patio to take his call, but I just can't seem to pick up. I stare at his image, my knees weak and wobbly. Tears spring to my eyes and a wave of hopelessness washes over me.

But then I look back at Aidan's precious face, and I recall the desperate moments—the nights holding him as he wailed, burning hot with fever, the mornings I wasn't sure I could pull together a few dollars for his school field trips, the long afternoons sitting beside him at the kitchen table and trying to figure out how the hell to solve a linear algebra equation. I did it, though. I did it because I had no other alternative, and because I love this boy more than life itself.

I've gotten us both through the worst of situations, on my own. And I'll be damned if I don't get us through this one, too.

I dash off a quick text to Aidan, saying I'll call him back in ten. Then I find the new contact that has been added to my phone: Luisa Martín Moreno. Before I can lose my nerve, I press call.

CHAPTER 9

Luisa

"Must've been a helluva day, sweetheart," Ginny says, uncapping a beer bottle and handing it to the guy sitting two seats down.

"You have no idea," I sigh, slipping onto my barstool. "Can I get my usual?"

"One Luisa special, coming right up," Rhonda hollers from the grill. "Double patty, fries, *and* onion rings, just like you like 'em." Today's offensive T-shirt features a praying mantis gripping her mate's decapitated body, a red heart between them, the words *Thanks for a Good Time* arched across the top.

Ginny deposits a beer in front of me. "I'll be praying for a miracle," she offers.

I've spent the last three hours in Gloria's kitchen, poring over legal documents while the kids are in school. We found nothing new. In a few months, they'll lose their livelihood and their kids will be thrown out of the only home they've ever known. *And then what? What will become of them?* I stuff down my own wretched teenage memories. I, too, know how it feels to be displaced against your will. All because of my father's unforgivable choices.

And now, I've been displaced again, all because Griggs Caldecott Johnson is a crook, aided and abetted by my former boss. This time, though, I'm not a helpless teenager—even if I'm back living with my mom.

A cacophony of whoops and hollers breaks out at the pool tables, disrupting my private pity party. Someone has just walked through the main door of the bar, and their presence is causing a stir.

"Oh, honey, the church is about a half mile down the road," Ginny says to the newcomer, who is apparently standing behind me.

It's Holly, looking just like a church lady at a biker bar.

"What in God's name are you wearing?" I ask, forgetting to hide my contempt for her very flowery spring dress. I need this meeting to go well. But who wears a church dress to a dingy bar? Ginny's official dress code is shades of black. Or at least biker-gang denim.

"I came straight from work, a Junior League luncheon," Holly says defensively. Her eyes dart around, taking in every detail of Ginny's grungy establishment—the sticky tables that match the sticky floors, TVs broadcasting March Madness, and the *regulars*: about a dozen members of a local biker gang and their ole ladies. I wonder what she'll think of the *Silence of the Lambs* Buffalo Bill poster that is taped to the ceiling directly over the women's toilet. While you pee, a blond, psychotic man cradling a small fluffy dog stares directly at you through a stone tunnel.

"Also, it wouldn't have been crazy for me to think that Road Queen Grill was a cutesy Southern place. You know, the kind that serves tuna salad on croissants and has fried chicken . . . but only on Tuesdays. How was I supposed to know we were meeting at a bona fide *biker bar*?"

I open my mouth, at the ready with a snarky comment, but decide to swallow it. I remind myself that Holly is my *only* lead. If she turns around and walks away, I'm fresh out of ideas for how to get access to Griggs's business dealings. It was a miracle that she called me in the first place. Saint Jude came through for me after all.

With my beer bottle, I gesture to the empty stool beside me.

"Hope the food is good," she says, dropping her giant purse on the bar. "I'm starving."

"There won't be any cutesy Junior League cucumber sandwiches on the menu," I sizzle back, unable to help myself.

"For your information, I'm allergic to cucumbers."

Ginny interrupts our banter, sliding my food in front of me. She gives Holly a quizzical once-over, as if she's considering banning her from her bar, but then seems to decide against it, tossing her a flimsy paper menu instead. Holly doesn't bother to read it. "I'll have a double cheeseburger," she says without hesitation.

Ginny looks as surprised as I feel. I thought for sure Griggs's prim *Maybe Mistress* would shudder at the prospect of greasy meat (and greasier fries) and ask for a Caesar salad—*hold the anchovies, dressing, cheese, and croutons, please.*

"Anything else?" Ginny asks pointedly. "We serve beer and hard liquor only. No wine, no top-shelf shit, and definitely no spritzers. Spritzers are the devil."

"Couldn't agree more," Holly says. "An ice-cold PBR will do."

Interesting. Ginny and I exchange an arched brow, as she promptly uncaps a beer for Holly and a bonus one for me. She sets them in front of us with a dramatic thump. Holly tips the bottle in Ginny's direction—a silent *Cheers*—then takes a deep swig.

"So, why did you agree to meet me all the way out here?" I ask. I'm trying to square the pearl-clutching, Country Club Betty image I have of Holly in my head with the surprising reality of the woman in front of me, who seems more self-possessed and down-to-earth than I anticipated.

"I didn't want to run into anyone from the club. None of those people come out here."

"Well, I'd like to keep it that way," I say with more vinegar in my voice than is prudent.

I dig into my cheeseburger, trying to defuse the tension. Reddish meat juice drips down my fingers like blood, and all I can see in my mind's eye are visions of the destruction to come—of bulldozers clearing away land for Griggs's *world-class* development.

"A double cheeseburger for our Southern belle here," Ginny says, returning with Holly's food order.

Holly doesn't miss a beat. She matches Ginny's snarky tone, calling back in a full-on *Gone with the Wind* accent, "Oh, why thank you, daaahlin', so veeeehry kind of you."

The comeback seems to earn Ginny's respect. She laughs, shaking her head with amusement before going about her business.

I guess she'll allow this Country Club Betty to stay and eat at her bar after all.

"What did you mean the other day, about Griggs keeping business secrets?" Holly asks, finally getting to the point of this meeting. She takes a few bites of her burger, then sets it down to meet my gaze.

I clean my fingers with a napkin. I can no longer hold it in: the question that has been burning inside me since this woman and I crossed paths. "Why are you messing around with that man? He's awful."

Holly's face and neck flush red. "What? He's the one messing around with *me*," she exclaims, indignant.

"Sweetheart, it takes two to tango," Ginny chimes in. That woman has one ear perpetually pressed to the bar.

"Let's get something straight," Holly whisper-yells at me through gritted teeth. "I am *not* having an affair with Griggs Johnson. I'm not having an affair with anyone. That horrible man has been harassing me for years. I've never given him what he wants, which drives a power-hungry person like him crazy. And now he's found a way to blackmail me with my son's future."

I raise my eyebrows, trying to take it all in. "So, to be clear," I say tentatively, "you're not his mistress?" Are all my hopes for an inside source about to be dashed?

Holly doesn't answer. Instead, she eats in angry silence, practically fuming. "No," she says finally. "I'm not his mistress. And, frankly, I've had enough slut-shaming for one lifetime, thank you very much. Not that I owe you my life story or anything—but I got pregnant when I was eighteen, and I got slut-shamed for years. Skank, hussy, floozie, trollop—I've been called all the names. I'm done with it. I'm through with being punished." She shoots me a barbed glare. "I love my son, and I wouldn't change a damn thing about how he came into this world." She's breathing hard now, hands holding a bottle of ketchup a little too tightly.

"Shit." I take a swig of my beer, needing to buy myself a few seconds. I've totally misjudged this woman. Inadvertently slut-shamed her. *And* hit a big-ass nerve in the process. All because I prayed to God she was Griggs's mistress? *Fuck.*

"I'm sorry that happened to you," I add, remorseful.

Holly narrows her gaze on the ketchup bottle in her hands, seemingly trying to gather her emotions.

After a few beats, I ask, "How in God's name did you end up trashed inside that bathroom on Friday?"

She scoffs. "How far back do you want me to go?"

"All the way."

Over the next half hour, I learn all about Holly's upbringing in Jackson.

"Ironically, I wound up right back in the world I was trying to flee," Holly says, finishing the last of her onion rings. "But, honestly, I love my job. And I love the people I work with."

"Did you ever think of calling your family?" I ask, finding it hard to imagine life without my own. "Asking for help? It must've been hard for you, going it alone."

Holly shakes her head, eyes set on the empty basket in front of her. "They wanted me to give my son away." She takes a deep breath, then releases the air slowly. "I won't subject you to the cruel things my mother said." Her gaze turns to meet mine, and I can see the pain resurface with the memories. "Besides, I've made my own family."

"And now Griggs is threatening to take everything away from you?" I ask, already knowing the answer. Holly sighs, nodding in response. "How long has he been harassing you?" I add.

"I'm not sure when exactly it started," she tells me. "But about a year ago, he seemed to start testing how far he could go, like pushing the boundaries?" She shrugs, a shadow falling over her expression. "And then suddenly he got way more brazen. Like he knows he's untouchable." Then she tells me about Aidan keying Griggs's car, the video evidence, the club's security employee who was fired after Griggs joined the club's board.

"So let me get this straight," I say, enunciating the words slowly. "A grown-ass, misogynistic prick is going after a kid raised by a single mom so he can get in her pants?"

"That about sums it up." Holly taps the bottom of her beer bottle against the bar. "But just to be clear, this isn't about Griggs Johnson wanting *me*. He's just one of those guys who gets off on power."

Griggs, I recognize, is borrowing from the same harassment playbook so many other douchebags have used before him: coerce, threaten, discredit. He has positioned himself as a charming bastion of social good, an icon in a world of wealth, influence, and power. Without indisputable evidence of wrongdoing, it would be Holly's word against his. In which case, Griggs would spare no expense destroying her reputation. Also, Griggs joining the club's board meant he is now technically Holly's boss. He'll waste no time pegging Holly as difficult to work with, incompetent even. He'll dig up the names of every person she's dated or slept with, then frame her as a shameless flirt or even a gold-digging slut. Holly's life and career would be irreparably ruined.

My lungs collapse under the weight of a long, hopeless sigh. Holly is not the inside source I had prayed for. *Dammit, Saint Jude! How many more candles do you want?* Holly is a victim—no different from the Castillos, or even me. And like us, Holly and her son also stand to lose everything because of one greedy shitbag.

I search for Ginny among the steady stream of customers, collecting their drink and food orders, hoping she might be feeling generous with those sympathy tequila shots. I find her at the far end of the bar, listening to none other than Lumberjack Guy, who is whispering something in her ear. Naturally, my curiosity is piqued. Ginny's face sours, taking on a troubled expression. She nods and quickly gets to work, pouring about a half dozen vodka shots and setting them on a tray.

His heather-gray T-shirt hugs his arms and torso in all the right places, and a pair of very worn Wranglers highlight the curves of a well-toned ass. I'm ogling now.

Lumberjack Guy cuts his eyes to me, quirking an eyebrow, as if he can read my thoughts. *How does he do that?* I don't look away, though. Remembering our last encounter, I sit up taller, taking up space at the bar, brashly telegraphing that I belong here as much as he does. To my surprise, he breaks into a smile, waves his fingers at me cheekily before turning his attention back to Ginny.

"You know that guy?" Holly asks.

"He's a regular," I tell her.

"I think he likes you," Holly observes, poking at my shoulder. I cut a side-eye her way.

Ginny adds one last shot glass to the tray—tap water, positioned over a folded napkin. Lumberjack Guy sloppily carries the tray back to the pool table, stumbling along the way. I'm not fooled, though. I can tell by the clarity of those wolfish eyes—and the water spilling from his shot glass—that he's not drunk.

He hands out vodka shots to a bunch of white college bros wearing KA insignia polos—Kappa Alpha. A few years ago, I had the *pleasure* of writing about their Old South Ball, an antebellum-themed spring formal in which young women dress as Southern belles, and the young men pretend to be slave owners. Apparently, they still hail Robert E. Lee as Kappa Alpha's "spiritual founder." The scene immediately raises my hackles.

"I'm guessing those kids wandered down here from Athens, bored with the bar scene on West Broad," Holly says. "My son's at UGA. Says those guys are total asses."

We both watch as a KA sneering jackass puts one patronizing arm around Lumberjack Guy's shoulders. Lumberjack Guy then clinks his glass with the group and shoots it, stumbling backward and hitting a chair on his way to the floor. No one but me seems to notice the practiced way he breaks his fall with one hand. One of the KA bros helps him stand and pats him on the shoulder before dropping a stack of cash on the pool table. I'm frankly a little shocked when Lumberjack Guy pulls a large wad of cash from his own pocket and matches the bet.

And then I get it.

"What's happening?" Holly asks, turning to watch the first solid pool ball glide into a corner pocket.

I gesture toward Lumberjack Guy. "He's about to clean house."

Holly gives me a skeptical look. "He can barely stand."

"It's a scam. He's stone-cold sober." I'm impressed. He's good, this guy. He takes his time, giving the frat guy a few wins, but steadily striking solids into pockets.

I laugh out loud. Why didn't I see it before? Lumberjack Guy is a pool hustler.

I raise a hand to get Ginny's attention, my thoughts consumed with Griggs and the pack of entitled frat boys acting like they own the place. I realize there's not much difference between these KA assholes, Griggs, and his golf buddies—just another boys' club for privileged white men. I hope Lumberjack Guy takes them for all they're worth.

Ginny must sense the rage bubbling up inside me, because she strides over carrying a bottle of mezcal that she reserves for celebrations or desperate cases—which in my book only adds to her saintliness. *No candles required!* Saint Ginny pours one for me and Holly without saying one word.

I shoot back the smooth, smoky spirits, adding up the stakes in my head—the Castillos, Holly, Aidan, my future. How can one man be responsible for ruining the lives of so many people? And how do we turn the tables on him?

"I'm so sick and tired of these greedy, selfish, rich assholes taking and taking without consequence. Turning everything to shit for the rest of us." I set down the shot glass as Holly gulps hers down. I anxiously tap two fingers on the bar, a wordless *hit me* for two more shots, like a blackjack player whose entire luck rests on the next card. My gut reminds me: *The house always wins.*

CHAPTER 10

Holly

I might've been a little uneasy when I first walked into this dive bar, but as I settle in and chat with Luisa, I'm finding it kind of . . . cozy. And chatting openly with Luisa is refreshing. None of my co-workers actually like Griggs Johnson, but we can't exactly go around talking shit about club members. You never know who might be listening.

"So, why exactly do you care about Griggs Johnson?" I ask, setting my empty shot of mezcal on the bar.

"Are you familiar with the Preserve at Lake Chiaha?" Luisa asks me.

"The Westlake development?" I clean the corner of my mouth with the back of my hand. "He's been obsessed with it for at least three years. Is it finally getting off the ground?"

"On the backs of hard-working people whose land he stole," Luisa mutters.

My eyebrows shoot up. "Are you sure?" I ask, placing our now-empty food baskets one over the other, then cleaning the bar with my napkin. Force of habit. "Griggs may be a scumbag with an overinflated ego, but he doesn't need to steal. Trust me, that man is closing deals left and right. I know because almost all of them happen at the club."

"Unless he has no other option," Luisa says. She pulls out her notebook and starts telling me about the Castillos—a hard-working immigrant family who were set to inherit acres of land on what is now the Preserve at Lake Chiaha. She explains how the land was taken out from under them, something about a fake company and a fake deed.

"Without their plot, there's no way to access the land around the lake," she explains. "But they refused to sell. Griggs wouldn't take no for an answer."

I nod, not all that surprised. "Not many people say no to Griggs," I say with a defeated sigh. "What options do the Castillos have?"

"That's where I was hoping you'd come in." Luisa sighs. "When I still thought you were Griggs's mistress and could get close enough to him to secure proof of his underhanded dealings." Luisa hands me a heavy binder.

I riffle through the paper trail—legal documents, land surveys, financial spreadsheets.

"Griggs didn't just steal the Castillos' land"—Luisa points to a development plan—"he's bribing local officials, getting environmental regulations tossed, and I'm pretty sure there's something shady going on with his family's foundation."

"His family's foundation? The one he just accepted an award for, from the mayor?" I ask. That's low, even for Griggs.

"Same one," Luisa says, lifting another mezcal to her lips. "Problem is, I can't follow the money trail unless I have someone on the inside. Proof. Solid evidence a prosecutor will consider." She takes a long sip, then taps at her binder for emphasis. "And—*dammit all to hell*—I thought you were in bed with him, and the perfect person to get it."

"Sorry to disappoint." I grimace. "But I don't think you understand. Griggs is untouchable. He operates with absolute impunity. Also, he'd never share his secrets with a woman—not even one he's in bed with."

"So we've hit a dead end," Luisa says, dropping her head into her hands.

"Yup," I reply. "Tomorrow, you and I and the Castillos will wake up wondering when it's all gonna fall apart. Not Griggs, though. He'll be headed out to his standing tee time with Judge Thacker and Jim Wade—just another day on the course. Then he'll sip Macallan at the Men's Grill before a steak dinner with Anna-Byrd on the terrace."

Luisa lifts her head, eyes wide. "Wait, who's Griggs playing with?" she asks, grabbing the binder and then leafing through the handwritten pages of her notebook.

"Billy Thacker and Jim Wade—you know them?"

"Hell no, I don't know Griggs's golf buddies," she says, searching frantically for something in her notes. "But I know those names. Here, take a look."

Judge Billy Thacker: Shady judge overseeing Castillo's case. Why didn't he subpoena the deed holding company?

Jim Wade:

- *Griggs's family foundation money man*
- *Chair of State's Board of Natural Resources. Pushed through Lake Chiaha 100-year lease for nearly nothing. Why did the board go along with this?*

Offshore Bank in Panama: Who in the world is Dudley Magruder? Is he laundering money for Griggs?

Recognition dawns on me as I read through the notes. "A Panamanian banker was golfing with Griggs a few days ago," I exclaim. "I mean, he lives in Panama now, but his family's Old Atlanta, and he grew up here."

"Fuckers! All of 'em," Luisa grumbles. "These assholes are all in on the scheme, I'm sure of it. They're gonna cash in big when this development happens."

"But Jim Wade? Really?" I say. "I mean, Judge Thacker is a corrupt boozehound. I wouldn't rely on him to dispense justice on my behalf, that's for sure." I shudder at the thought. "But Jim's such a mild-mannered old guy." I read through Luisa's notes, tapping at the page with one finger. "I'm pretty sure he dedicated his retirement to protecting wildlife habitats. How can he be in on this scam?"

"The guy is a crooked SOB," Luisa assures me. "They all are. If only we could get solid evidence of criminal activity—bribes, fraud, money laundering, embezzlement, racketeering. If we could just catch them in the act. But how? And where?"

"The *where* is easy," I offer. "The Men's Grill, in the locker room at the club—that's where all the big deals go down."

Luisa lets out a hollow laugh. "Okay, first, don't even get

me started on why there's a grill in a locker room. Second, what would we do exactly? Turn ourselves into naked, sweaty white dudes in robes? That's one makeover I'd like to avoid."

A loud noise erupts from around the pool table. Distracted, we both look toward the hubbub just in time to see the bearded guy sweep a clump of dejected KAs' money off the table.

"He's good," I say, awed. "You were right."

"He's also a criminal," she responds matter-of-factly.

"When it comes down to it," I tell her, gesturing toward the pool hustler with my beer bottle, "that man is no different from Griggs. Look at him. He's cunning, smooth-talking, and charming as hell." Luisa quirks an eyebrow at me skeptically. "The only difference between him and the Golden Boy of the Dogwood Hills Country Club is a clean shave, a pressed oxford, and a crisp pair of selvage denim jeans."

"Can't say I have a lot of experience with country club criminals," Luisa says, still watching him closely. "But it would take a hell of a lot more than a makeover to turn that man into somebody like Griggs."

We watch the pool hustler saunter casually away from the frat boys, grinning as he slides the wad of cash into his pocket. And, just like that, a flash of intuition moves through me. I absolutely could turn that guy into a country club boy with cash to burn, a cocky kid who's desperate to prove himself a man.

"Wanna bet?" I ask, leaning back and folding my arms across my chest, as my utter dejection turns into hope.

"Bet on what?" Luisa says, turning to me.

"That we can make that pool hustler into a country club boy," I say, feeling bolder by the second.

Luisa looks at me like I have three heads. "You've lost your mind, Holly."

"He'll be in and out so fast," I argue. "It will work. I know the place. I know the people. I know the rules. I know them all—even better than Griggs does. I know the front *and* back of the house," I insist, undeterred. "Plus, with your investigative skills and my know-how, we can easily make him into a trust fund baby. We'll slide him into that golf foursome as a potential angel investor. In and out, with the proof we need." I snap my fingers beside my face for effect.

Ginny leans in to top off Luisa's mezcal. She nods appreciatively and takes a long sip. I'll say this about Luisa: The woman sure can handle her liquor.

"A pool-hustler makeover?" she scoffs, putting the glass down. "That's your brilliant idea? Why would they let a stranger in on their secrets?"

"This wouldn't be just any stranger," I say. "It would be a gullible young guy with tons of money to dump into their project. You have to understand—for Griggs, enough is *never* enough. I'll bet anything, if there's a big pile of cash sitting in front of him, under an impressionable young angel investor, he won't be able to resist."

"It's not a terrible plan." Luisa shrugs. "To find someone we can send inside for intel, but why not someone from their world? Someone already connected to them?"

"Have *you* lost your mind?" I exclaim. "No one—and I mean *no one*—from that world would risk double-crossing Griggs Johnson." I shake my head. "You have to believe me. We need a complete outsider."

I watch as Luisa thinks. I can see the wheels turning in her brain.

"Okay, let's just suspend disbelief for a moment and pretend we can find some outsider to say he wants to invest. And I don't mean Lumberjack Guy over there." She gestures toward the pool table. "There's no actual cash. Just a guy made over to seem like he has money. How exactly are we supposed to finance this grand scheme?"

It comes to me instantly, thanks to Janey embarking on a long and painfully irrelevant spill-the-tea session about Kasey and Miles Ketchum this morning before the Junior League luncheon. Apparently, they have suddenly quit the club and relocated to Scottsdale, Arizona. Clearly, Kasey Ketchum won't be coming for that gleaming bracelet sitting in the safe in my office at the club, and I'm sure as hell not returning it to Griggs.

I tell Luisa about the abandoned bracelet, and watch as the

corners of her lips turn down. "We can pawn it," I say. "And don't you worry. We'll get a good price. As it happens, I've got tons of experience."

"With pawnshops?" she asks, visibly surprised.

"How do you think I financed the first year of Aidan's life?" I lean forward in my chair, eager to prove my chops. "I sold off the designer deb gown I never got a chance to wear, along with the family pearls." I'm ticking items off with my fingers. "I got a great price for the huge diamond cross pendant my darling mother gave me when I turned sixteen. The trick is to never let them take gemstones to the back room. They'll try to—"

"But that was your stuff," she cuts me off, exasperated. "You're proposing that we steal a sapphire bracelet," she says through a grimace. "Or, more precisely, commit larceny."

"Okay, Miss Goody Two-Shoes," I shoot back. "If you saw a twenty-dollar bill on the street, would you lean down and pick it up?"

"I wouldn't get jail time for picking up twenty bucks out of the gutter," she scoffs.

"Here's the thing," I launch in, desperate to make her see that, while this plan may not exactly be legal, it's also not necessarily immoral. "Griggs bought this bracelet for a woman he slept with a few times and then discarded like an old pair of sneakers, and now she's long gone, starting fresh." Luisa tries to break in and say something, but I hold up my hand to stop her. "I know what you're thinking, but believe me, she does not need the money. So, the way I see it, this is just good old-fashioned karma, which can be—as we all know—a real bitch."

"I'm not so sure that argument will hold up in court," she says, gazing for a long while into her almost empty glass. "But it's not like we have another option. And, frankly, part of me loves the idea of using Griggs's dirty deeds against him."

"Then it's settled," I say, trying to sound resolute. I grab my beer and take a long gulp. Suddenly, I'm a rebellious teenager again. I'll be damned if I'm gonna fulfill my mother's prophecy and let her win. I'm a good mother and I'm keeping my job. "But hey," I offer. "If you have a better plan for getting justice for the

Castillos, getting your career back on track, and taking down Griggs, I'm all ears."

"I'm fucking gonna regret this," she groans. "Where do we find an angel investor?"

I smile slowly. "He's our angel. I can feel it in my gut." Luisa raises a brow as if to say, *Lumberjack Guy?* I nod vigorously as she narrows her gaze in his direction, possibly considering our options, or lack thereof. "I'll bet you anything."

This makes her laugh. "I don't do open-ended bets."

I glance over Luisa's shoulder, where a bright orange poster announces Karaoke Night every Thursday. "Loser comes back to the Road Queen to sing karaoke," I say. "Winner chooses the song."

A full-bellied laugh bursts out of her. "Screw it," she says. "You're on."

CHAPTER 11

Luisa

Two days later, Holly and I are inside my SUV, following the blue GPS line on my navigation screen down a Westlake back road, in pursuit of our only viable lead: a harebrained, half-baked scheme for a makeover and a phony angel investor.

We learned the pool shark's name is Eli—as in Elijah, a biblical name that means "man of God." And as I turn off the highway by a roadside marquee advertising *Live Bait & Tackle* and *HOT Boiled Peanuts*, I'm praying this man has God's luck on his side, because I can't believe we're trusting a country grifter to get us into a country club. I really need to rethink my life choices.

After Ginny proffered the pool shark's name, I ran a thorough search on Elijah Denvil Sweet Jr., age twenty-seven, of Westlake, Georgia. I was glad that my degree in investigative reporting was still useful, given the student loan repayments that would keep coming every month into perpetuity.

Granted—if I'm being honest with myself—my extraordinary sleuthing skills might also be the reason I've never gotten past a third date. Because at some point, an investigative journalist ends up researching *everyone*. This is how I found out that Lying Liam was still married—not divorced, as he insisted even after I confronted him. Delinquent Daniel had an outstanding arrest warrant for public urination. And Mama's Boy Marcus, age thirty-five and gainfully employed, still lived in his parents' basement for no good reason other than that his mother did his laundry.

Elijah Denvil Sweet Jr., though? Nothing. Beyond his home address and current place of employment, there was not much else available. Which could only mean one of two things: He'd gone through the trouble of expunging his online history, or he had intentionally avoided having a traceable history in the first place. Either scenario begged the question why. A red flag in and of itself. A flag I'm choosing to temporarily ignore, because short of a heavenly intervention, there's no other feasible plan.

I shift my SUV into park in front of Happy Hooker, Inc., then turn to Holly, one eyebrow raised.

"What?" she says. "It's charming."

Strands of multicolored Christmas lights hang across the porch, and a U.S. flag waves over a sign that reads *You might be a Redneck Fisherman if . . .* Number one on the list: *You made a homemade hot tub with a trolling motor.*

"What the hell is a trolling motor?" I ask.

"It's for fishing boats," Holly says, clearly feeling proud to know this. "I used to fish Crystal Lake with my neighbors. Good old-fashioned rod-and-reel. Bream mostly, but sometimes we'd catch a nice-size bass or a crappie—"

"I have no idea what you're talking about," I break in. "Let's go in before I realize what a huge mistake this all is."

We get out of the car and make our way toward the shack. Most of the porch is taken up by an ice machine and a giant wooden sign listing the types of bait for sale—a truly disgusting array including live crickets, leeches, and nightcrawlers. Holly flings open the screen door, and we step inside. It must be our lucky day, because our angel is sitting behind a very crowded counter, grasping several live worms in his left hand.

Our eyes meet and we stare at each other for a beat, his brow furrowed in confusion. "Didn't I see you in Ginny's bar a couple of times?" he asks in that deep, husky, brooding voice that reminds me of a woeful country song. His eyes cut behind me, past the window to the parking lot, then he snaps his fingers beside his face. "Hoity-toity SUV girl," he exclaims in recognition. In one slow gaze, he surveys the *country-girl fishing* outfit I painstakingly put together for our little outing. My stomach inexplicably flutters as his eyes travel down my body. Once again, he seems to recognize my efforts to blend in. I'm reminded that chameleons, even when deeply camouflaged, can recognize each other.

"Nice getup. Very authentic," he sneers. "You lost or somethin'?"

"Hi there," Holly exclaims brightly, no doubt trying to save me from his jabs. "We were looking for you."

"We have a proposition for you, Elijah," I say curtly, getting right to business.

He narrows his eyes, then dumps the worms into a plastic container. "It's Eli," he says, brushing dirt from his hands. There's a slight trace of grease under his clipped fingernails, which are framed by ragged cuticles. This man works with his hands, I realize. "Elijah's my deadbeat dad." Then, breaking into an utterly charming smile, he adds, "Whatever you have in mind, it's not my thing." He throws both hands in the air in mock surrender. "No judgment."

I roll my eyes. Holly's cheeks have turned tomato red. Did he think we were making *that* sort of proposition?

"It's not like that," I say, glancing at the laptop and various accounting reports laid out on the counter beside him. "I'm a journalist." I pass him my business card. "I'm working with a family a few miles from here. They're about to lose their home, and we need your help."

Eli's phone dings. He reads the screen and scowls. "Sorry, I'm not your guy. Now, if you'll excuse me, these ain't gonna count themselves." He gestures toward a few dozen containers in the fridge behind him.

Holly shoots me a panicked look, then marches past me, disappearing behind an extensive display of fishing rods, hooks, weights, and sinkers. *Where the hell is she going?*

"We'll make it worth your while," I say, briefly distracted by a list of *Carp Juice Flavors* set next to an extra-large jar of hard-boiled pickled eggs and another of pickled pig's feet. "Think of it as contract work," I add, moving closer to the counter, forcing him to meet my gaze.

He studies me intensely, turning my attempt at assertiveness into a moment of surprising intimacy. Oddly, a pang of panic settles in the pit of my stomach. It can only be yet one more sign that this plan is insane, but given our nonexistent options, I push on.

"We'll pay you to pose as an investor in a development right here on Westlake," I tell him, my tone pragmatic, professional. "All you have to do is record the deal."

"Y'all are barking up the wrong tree," he blurts out, his accent dropping into a thick backwoods drawl.

An enormous tabby cat jumps from his lap, momentarily pausing our conversation, and heads across the room, along rows of coolers and bins, all presumably crawling with live bait, above which hang about a dozen cricket cages. The cat yowls as he brushes past Holly, who is ambling back with a Happy Hooker trucker hat over her head and a heavy-looking golf bag behind her. In the same breath, she asks, "How much for the hat?" and "Are these your golf clubs?" She waves a driver in the air. "Would you happen to play golf?" She raises both eyebrows at me with a silent *Told you he's our guy!*

Eli grabs a pencil from inside a mason jar. "Twenty-five for the hat. And we don't take Amex." Then he scribbles something on an inventory sheet. "There's a few public golf courses round here. I caddy sometimes. Tips are good. Hustles are better."

"What do you mean, 'hustles'?" Holly asks.

"What's it to you?" he says, cutting an impatient glare to a wall clock hanging above a sign that reads *It's Fish O'Clock Somewhere*.

Holly slips the driver back in the bag. "Looks like you could use some new clubs."

"Those suit me just fine," he replies, nonchalant.

Eli types something on the laptop, then sets one of the blue containers from the fridge on the counter beside him. The lid has about three dozen tiny holes punctured through it, and a round sticker that reads *Not Your Ordinary Happy Hooker.*

"What the hell is that?" I ask.

"What? You ain't never been to a bait 'n' tackle before?" Once again, he leans into his backcountry lilt, the one he seems to turn on and off at will.

"I haven't had the pleasure," I say snarkily, watching him intently as he removes the container's lid with a flourish and drops the contents into what looks like . . . a roasting pan?

"Up in here, ma'am, we got some grade-A, top-of-the-line,

big catch, fishing worms." Thick, pinkish worms crawl out from under a handful of dirt. "And if worms ain't your thing, we got minnows, leeches, shrimp, shiners, goldfish, baby catfish, bream. We go through damn near twenty-four-hundred crickets a week in summertime." I ignore the sneering tone behind his facetious country-boy sales pitch, grateful when the store's phone rings and he turns to answer.

We've already wasted enough time. We need to get to the point of this little visit. I adjust the bill of my trucker hat, then mirror Eli's stance. If there's one thing I've learned in years of field reporting, it's that quickly earning a source's trust requires making eye contact, matching their inflection, and adjusting my posture to set them at ease. Coincidentally, these are also the same qualities that make for a great con artist. Eli, with his pool hustles, his secrets, and his untraceable history reminds me of every other trickster on the face of the planet—including my own father.

A growing list of indisputable facts makes it clear that Eli cannot be trusted, which, paradoxically, also makes him perfect for our scheme. But it doesn't mean I have to like it, or him. It does mean, however, I'll have to keep him at arm's length at all times—or risk losing my objectivity. If things get icky, we bail. I refuse to repeat my mother's mistakes and fall prey to a scammer.

"Thanks for showing us around," I say, "but we haven't got all day. Are you interested or not?"

"So let me see if I understand this—what did you call it?" he asks with a smirk. "Contract work?" He sits back on the stool, hands resting on top of his thighs. "You want me to pretend to be somebody else—"

"From a family with generational wealth," Holly says, not waiting for an answer. "Grandfather was a cotton magnate, and you just got your first trust fund payout."

The tabby cat jumps back into his lap, and he casually begins to stroke his fur. "You want me to pretend to be some Atlanta country club asshole—"

"Mississippi," Holly clarifies. "Mississippi country club asshole."

"Whatever," Eli says, adjusting the visor of his hat. "They're all the same."

"An angel investor type," I press on. "Do you know what that means?"

Holly elbows me in the ribs. Okay, fine, maybe that sounded a bit condescending.

"Well, I'll be damned," he exclaims, matching my contempt and leaning hard into his twang, "I'm just a good ol' country boy. Don't know nothin' 'bout—"

"Of course he knows." Holly steps between us, a big smile on her face, working overtime to smooth things over. "So, anyway, you just got your first trust fund payout," she explains to Eli. "You're desperate to show your daddy you can make it on your own, so you're looking for a rock-solid investment. We get you into the country club. Then you casually run into Griggs—"

"Griggs Johnson. He's the developer who's stealing land from innocent families up here," I interject. "The guy's a total snake, but he's also greedy as fuck."

"All you have to do is score an invite to be the fourth in his standing Sunday golf game," Holly adds. "At the nineteenth hole . . ." She pauses, looking up at him. "You know what that is, right?"

Eli rolls his eyes and keeps petting that cat but says nothing.

"Of course you know," she continues. "Because you were made to do this job!" She turns to me, beaming. "See?" she erupts, triumphantly. "I had a feeling about this one."

I, too, want to roll my eyes at *her*, but it's almost cute how excited she is by this plan. And I have to admit, she's good at stroking egos. Must be all the practice at the club.

"This one?" Eli asks, skeptical. "How many people have turned you down?"

"None," I reply. "And neither will you, because the plan is simple. You'll make Griggs think you're deep in his old boy network, but also young and naive enough not to get that he and his golfing buddies are criminals. Eventually, you'll make an offer to invest in his new development and ask him how he's getting access to the land. Or, really, anything—details on bribes, banking connections, money laundering, shell companies." I pause, lifting one finger in the air. "Anything to prove he's a scumbag. Record one simple detail of his many crimes and we're done."

"We'll give you a free makeover," Holly adds. "New haircut, new clothes . . ." Holly's voice trails off as she, like me, takes inventory of Eli's tragic ensemble. Greasy, muddy work boots; saggy, ill-fitting jeans; and a baggy T-shirt under an open flannel long-sleeve shirt that, frankly, should've been turned into cleaning rags long ago. Eli follows our gaze, staring down at himself.

"What?" he asks, oblivious.

"Maybe even new golf clubs," Holly swerves. "And I'll coach you on what to do and say—every step of the way."

"Oh," he exclaims sarcastically, marking something off with a pencil, "like a circus monkey."

"No," Holly apologizes. "That's not what I meant. I just—"

"Don't those people check bank records, financial history?" Eli cuts in, gently pushing the cat from his lap and then moving to tidy up a shelf of fishing weights and line reels. "I mean, don't take my word for it. I'm just some country boy running hustles for a living."

"Actually," Holly says, her voice rising, "that's the great thing about these old-money families. They barely have any public presence at all. You only know they're filthy rich if you're a part of their world. So we wouldn't need to create any physical record of your false identity. And I've already tracked down the perfect real-life person for you to pose as."

He sighs, takes off his hat, then runs a hand through his unkempt hair. "Listen, ladies. I could pull something like this off, sure. I'm a professional. But it would cost you."

We've got him now, I know it. Hook, line, and sinker.

Before he can change his mind, I tell him how much we can pay. He scratches his beard, releasing a low, long whistle. "We'll pay half up front, half upon completion of the deal." Eli doesn't fight me on the payment terms. Seeing an opening, I press on. "And to be clear, you work for us. We set the rules, and you follow. No arguing. No going rogue. Understood?" My hands instinctively go to my hips, and my eyebrows arch in an expression my sister, Carola, has dubbed my don't-fuck-with-me face. Which even my cop brother-in-law says is mildly terrifying.

Eli folds his arms tightly over his broad chest and nods in agreement. *Message received.*

"Well, all right, then, ladies," he says, slipping into a charming-as-hell smile and an honest-to-God, authentic Mississippi drawl that's so smooth it's actually almost sexy. "When do we start?"

CHAPTER 12

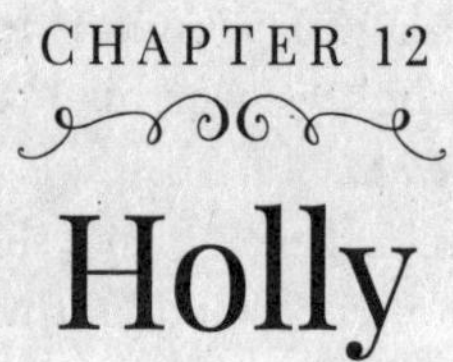

Holly

"Sand or toasted almond? Which works better with his complexion?" I turn to Luisa for her opinion, but she's distracted by her phone.

"I don't wanna sound like an idiot," Eli announces, looking perplexed as I hold out two pairs of flat-front performance trousers, "but why did we have to come all the way here, when the place we just left had perfectly good pants?"

Dressing him was supposed to be the easy part, the second step in our four-phase plan to turn our pool hustler into a guileless young angel investor.

> **Phase One:** Operation *Miss Congeniality*, the identity tutorial.
> **Phase Two:** Operation *Pretty Woman*, the shopping spree.
> **Phase Three:** Operation *Maid in Manhattan*, the full-body makeover.
> **Phase Four:** Operation *My Fair Lady*, the etiquette lesson (of course!).

Eli was a little less excited about my mnemonic device, but he's proving to be quite a good sport about the whole thing. And Luisa? She can't get enough of calling that poor boy Miss Congeniality.

The three of us have spent the past few mornings deep in Phase One, hovered over coffee and bagels at my kitchen table, working our way through the detailed lists of information Eli will need to memorize as he assumes his false identity.

Eli is sharp as a tack, and a real quick study, so we moved efficiently through most of Operation *Miss Congeniality*. This allowed me to review some more general principles, like the three key dispositions of our angel investor:

1. **Bubba:** He is handsome, well-heeled, mildly bigoted, and assertively masculine. He hunts and fishes and is naturally, though not excessively, athletic.
2. **Gentleman:** He has impeccable manners in mixed company and is especially polite to his elders. He makes his way through life without trying too hard.
3. **Misogynist Prick:** When alone with the guys, he at least occasionally acts as a blustering lecher, and he routinely degrades women.

These were a bit more difficult for Eli to process, so I had to offer several concrete examples. For instance, I explained to the enormous surprise of both Eli and Luisa, that "making his way through life without trying too hard" will be evidenced by a specific choice of clothing and accessories. Both of them assumed that since our angel investor is supposed to be filthy rich, he'd wear expensive watches, clothes with designer labels, etcetera.

"Absolutely not," I exclaimed. "Nothing garish, and certainly nothing prominently displaying a brand name!" Even polo-style shirts, I made clear, may bear the logo of a country club or event (preferably, of course, the Masters), but rarely the brand. That one really took the two of them by surprise. It is, I'll admit, a fine line to walk. Men like our angel investor are, in fact, very careful and thoughtful about their appearance, but they need to make it seem like they're not—which is why we came here to execute Operation *Pretty Woman*.

I actually took a vacation day for the first time in three years. I'm having so much fun with all this that it sort of feels like a vacation. Which is pathetic, I know. We've just left the outlet mall, for Chrissake. If I'm being honest, it's a relief to have a couple of days away from the club, or, more specifically, from the worry that Griggs could corner me in an empty hallway at any moment. I've become hypervigilant of his comings and goings, doing my best to avoid the driving range on Tuesday and Thursday mornings, the Terrace Restaurant on Sunday evenings—anyplace he seems to have a pattern of going. A tall order, given the man seems to spend most of his waking hours at that place.

Which is why we need to execute our plan, fast.

"As I already made clear in this morning's tutorial," I remind Eli, "Brooks Brothers is perfectly acceptable for a handful of basics." I return the sand trousers to the rack, since toasted almond brings out the highlights in Eli's hair. "But if you show up for your tee time wearing Brooks Brothers straight-fit chinos or—heaven forbid!—pleated khakis, everyone will assume you've raided your granddaddy's closet."

"Oh, right. The cotton king," he says, leaning hard on the sarcasm.

"Magnate," I correct. "And what's his name?" I urge, quizzing him on this morning's lesson, during which I carefully detailed the false identity he'll assume.

"Theodore Reynolds Bedford, God rest his soul," he replies dutifully. "T.R., for short. But his buddies all called him 'The Colonel.'" He crosses his arms, holding his chin with one hand thoughtfully. "Wait," he says, "don't these country club types all know each other? Won't they recognize the family name?"

"That's exactly the point," I tell him, my voice rising. "People in Atlanta will know *of* the Mississippi Bedfords, but no one will actually know them personally. They're one state removed and they're a reclusive bunch." I turn my attention to a display of belts and begin to sort through them. "Not even the Jackson Country Club crowd I grew up with really *knew* the Bedfords. That's why they're so perfect."

"And please at least *try* the Mississippi accent you've been practicing with Holly." Luisa sighs. "I heard you use it at the bait and tackle. Where the hell did it go?" Judging from the scowl on her face, she's having a little less fun. She's got a point, though. We both assumed, based on how effortlessly Eli switches between country and city accents, that he'd easily pick up how to talk like someone from Mississippi. I fear that we may have overestimated his abilities.

Eli studiously avoids Luisa's question, twists his face into a grimace, and continues, "Gentleman farmer from the Mississippi Delta, town of Greenwood. Lived his entire life at Bedford Hall, the family estate, except, of course, for his glory days at Ole Miss and the years he bravely fought for our country overseas. Upon his return, T.R. made a discreet but enormous fortune investing in the manufacture of weapons, while continuing to expand his cotton holdings." His details are perfect, but his accent is abysmal. "The Colonel is survived by his only son, T.R. Junior, and me, his beloved grandson, T.R. the third, known to all as Tripp."

Eli pauses, looks up at me with puppy-dog eyes. "C'mon. Does it have to be Tripp?"

"For the thousandth time, yes," I reply, frustrated. "Stop fighting it. And don't forget to elongate those vowels." I'm starting to really worry about Eli's ability to pull off the smooth Mississippi drawl. Maybe I should have gone with Tennessee. In addition to the frequent casual misogyny that spews from Griggs and company's mouths, I've overheard them say plenty of classist crap about accents. They'll suss out a fake in no time.

It's amazing how quickly my own accent returned, once I started trying to teach Eli, even though my childhood in Jackson feels like it was three or four lifetimes ago. I've almost completely lost the Mississippi cadence, which is fine by me. Luckily, though, I still have lots of useless cultural knowledge stored in this old brain, like what shoes a frat boy from Mississippi would wear—Rainbow flip-flops—when kicking back with a beer. It's really come in handy over the past couple of days.

I worked long and hard to find the right identity for Eli. I even reached out to "Aunt Peg," the house mother at Phi Delt, and told her I was working on a scrapbook for my second cousin Jack, who is five years younger than me and went to Ole Miss. I failed to mention that I haven't spoken with him, or anyone in my family, for eighteen and a half years. That detail didn't seem particularly relevant. Aunt Peg sent me photos of all the member boards from his years there, and I scoured the "not pictured" lists until I came across Theodore (Tripp) Reynolds Bedford III, blessedly absent from social media, and very fortuitously a descendant of The Colonel.

It's nearly impossible to garner praise from Luisa, but my strategy for finding Tripp earned me a nod of approval. It's a little pathetic how ecstatic I felt, to have impressed her. I even checked to be sure that none of the men Tripp will be hanging out with at the club—Griggs, the judge, and Jim Wade in particular—are Phi Delts, since those fraternities have all sorts of insider information I'll never be able to get my hands on.

Luisa also used her investigative skills to confirm Tripp's lack of digital footprint and run a thorough background check for details that could be helpful. I gotta say, we make quite the team.

"And Tripp's mother?" I ask Eli, resuming his quiz while I select a belt.

"Charlotte Walker Porter Bedford, of the esteemed Porter soybean dynasty. Tragic small plane crash back in 2007, when I was a child."

"When *aaaahhh* was a child," Luisa interrupts. "Christ, Eli. It's the easiest part of that accent to master. 'I' becomes *aaahhhh*."

"When aaaahhhh was a child," Eli says, his jaw stiffening into an angry scowl.

"Ooooh, the pear belt is nice!" I say, observing the way Eli recoils at her criticism, and trying to divert our attention back to the task at hand. "But maybe a bit too much?" I ask, weighing the boldness of the red against the Tripp we're creating. It's quite a delicate balance, perfecting this not-trying look.

"That there belt is *pink*," Eli interjects.

"It's more of a Nantucket red," I reply. "And please, for the love of God, remove the phrase 'that there' from your vocabulary immediately." I shake my head.

"'That there' makes you sound like a backwoods redneck," Luisa adds derisively.

I raise an eyebrow; Luisa's been cold to Eli ever since we first brought him into our scheme. This morning, as we were wrapping up Operation *Miss Congeniality*, she judged his cinnamon-raisin-with-berry-cream-cheese order so hard that I thought she might reach across the table, swipe his bagel, and toss it in the garbage. Instead, she glowered. I wonder what it is about him that gets under her skin. Besides, hasn't she ever heard that a spoonful of sugar helps the medicine go down?

"Well, ain't that there somethin'," Eli exclaims, slapping his knee as his voice dips deeper into the country drawl he intentionally uses to make her angry. "Pro'ly 'cuz I *am* one."

"I guess that decides it," Luisa says gruffly. "Red belt for our redneck."

I hand her the red belt, a marina-blue striped polo, and the performance trousers in a thirty-four waist. "Take him back to try these on for size," I say, "while I see if I can find some five-pocket trousers in highland green."

"Yes, ma'am," he replies.

"Also, please don't address me with 'ma'am,'" I remind him. "I'm not your mother's age."

I guess this has been another sticking point. For days I've been trying to explain to Eli the subtle differences between the country use of "ma'am" and the genteel use of "ma'am" in the South. "Tripp Bedford would only say 'ma'am' to women in his own social circle who are a generation or more older than him. When you say it to random strangers or women my age," I add, "it makes you sound like a hillbilly."

"Plus, it suggests that you might actually respect Holly," Luisa adds matter-of-factly. "Don't forget the *key dispositions*."

"Your key dispositions are confusing as hell," Eli says to me, and then he turns toward the dressing room, red belt in hand, Luisa stomping along in his wake.

I don't know what she's so worked up about. I'm making excellent progress on the four looks Eli will need to perfect to successfully undertake his mission. I glance down at my tablet and note with pride that we've already mastered Look One: Event Formal, which, contrary to popular belief, is the easiest. Any ol' properly fitting tux will do, even a rented one.

Look Two: Casual Business is a bit more of a challenge. Take the blazer, for example—perhaps the only clothing item that our Tripp might care a lick about. We'll need to go semi-custom, selecting patterns that are unique but not too unique, bold but not too bold, interesting though subtle.

The most surprisingly difficult look is Look Three: Getting Away from It All. This is what Tripp would pack in his Patagonia duffel for a weekend in Cashiers, where he'd tool around on a pontoon boat at Lake Glenville or chill with a beer after pickleball at the High Hampton Golf Club. We're hoping to get in and out so quickly that none of this will be necessary, but we also need to be prepared for a surprise invitation—expect the unexpected—which is why it's essential to get the look right.

Worn-out khaki shorts, leather flip-flops, and worn-in (but clean) T-shirt or golf shirt, from somewhere only people in the know would go. A bit of fraying around the edges is crucial. I've instructed Eli to wash his new shorts at least a dozen times in hot water before wearing them, and I've already gone to work finding the appropriate Ole Miss fraternity attire, as well as embroidered logo polos from the Jackson Country Club and River Hills. These, too, will need to be vigorously washed.

This brings us to Look Four: Golf. Since Peter Millar is essential, we're at the flagship store in a wealthy Atlanta suburb known to be *new money.* Which means that no one I work for at the club lives out here. Or so I'm confidently thinking when I spot Betty Preston MacArthur behind a sweater rack, looking right at me.

"Holly, dear!" she calls, hanging back the sweater in her hand. "What a surprise."

Mrs. MacArthur makes her way around a display table, while I launch into fight-or-flight mode. Did she spot me with Eli and his wild, furry beard? Is it too late to pretend I didn't see her and hightail it out of this store? She catches my gaze and, staring into those watery blue eyes, I know it's too late.

Shit. According to Janey, Betty Preston MacArthur is the queen of all gossipmongers in the older ladies' golf crowd.

"I had no idea . . . well, you know," she continues, "I wasn't aware that you play golf." She leans in for a kiss on the cheek. "Where have you been hiding this little secret?"

"Oh, you know," I tell her, just as I spot Luisa coming toward me with a camo golf shirt. In a panic, still holding Mrs. MacArthur close, I send a pleading look at Luisa. She gives me a thumbs-up and steps toward the women's skorts.

"Will I see you on the course anytime soon?" she asks. As soon as the words slip out, she steps back and brings a hand to her mouth. "I've gone and done it now, haven't I?" She sighs dramatically. "Of course you can't play at the club," she says. "Since you're an *employee*."

I give a wan smile.

"It's a crying shame," she continues. "You're absolutely essential to the place, after all. And you've been there how many years?" she asks.

"Eighteen," I reply, trying hard to hold my smile.

"We really should find a way to offer more benefits to the help," she muses. "Maybe set aside undesirable tee times or let you out on the course after hours. Wouldn't that be nice?"

"No need, Mrs. MacArthur," I tell her, standing straight and tall. "Atlanta has some great municipal courses." I'm frankly assuming this is the case, since I've never once teed off. The only thing I've done on a golf course is drink beer, smoke weed, and hook up with boys, back when I was a teenage hellion in Jackson.

"Why yes, I imagine it does," she proclaims, nodding vigorously and then glancing down at her watch. "Oh goodness. I must head on back into town. Beat this horrible suburban traffic."

I say my goodbyes, then watch in blessed silence as she checks out and leaves.

"Who the fuck was that Country Club Betty?" Luisa exclaims as soon as Mrs. MacArthur disappears from sight.

"Her name is in fact Betty," I say, trying to sidestep the tirade I know is coming.

"More benefits to the *help*?" she repeats, mimicking Mrs. MacArthur's elaborate Southern cadence. "Undesirable tee times?" She throws up her hands in exasperation. "What a grade-A bitch! Why do you let her treat you that way, Holly?"

"It's my job," I reply, suddenly dejected.

"Well, then maybe it's time for you to look for another job," Luisa shoots back. "Stop waiting on nosy old hags and find a workplace where you get the respect you've earned." She gestures angrily with that god-awful camo shirt still dangling from her wrist.

"But I like my job," I say, knowing full well that I sound unconvinced.

Is that a totally pathetic thing to admit, that I enjoy working for rich people, some of whom can be outrageously patronizing, but many of whom are perfectly nice and respectful? Honestly, I can't imagine not working at the club—not spending every day with Byron and Justine, not getting regular astrological checkups from Irma. And how would I survive without Janey's daily dirt dumps? Who would I even be without all of them?

"Christ Almighty, Luisa," Eli says, coming up behind her, "How 'bout a little sympathy?"

We both turn to look at him, and for the first time today, I feel encouraged. If it weren't for the scruffy beard hiding half his face and the long hair that sticks out from underneath his baseball cap, he'd be a perfect Tripp Bedford.

"Ain't no way I'm wearin' this here thang," he says, thrusting a salmon-striped golf shirt in my direction. "But that one there's all right, I reckon." He points to the terrible camo shirt.

Well, I guess it will have to do. After all, the shirt accentuates his Bubba disposition.

Operation *Pretty Woman* complete, I take the shirt from Luisa and head to the cash register, reminding myself that sometimes we have to make small compromises along the way to achieve our greater goals. Calling to mind my conversation with Ms. MacArthur, though, I'm starting to wonder whether I've let myself make way too many of them.

CHAPTER 13

Luisa

Late at night, after spending the day on our sapphire bracelet–funded shopping spree, I slink out of the house and take the garden path toward La Barna, behaving like the criminal I now am.

I've been a jittery mess since we drove to Cheshire Bridge Road this morning, to find a pawnshop with no security cameras and no paper trail. The place was a total dump—tucked between a strip club and a fried chicken 'n' catfish shack. Holly stressed that under no circumstances should we let them take the jewels to the back room, or risk losing a few diamonds. Apparently, she's something of a pawnshop expert. Blessedly, they paid cash and didn't ask any questions.

Our cat, Chapulín, slips out of the house beside me, reminding me that Mami and Abuela are asleep upstairs and there will be hell to pay if they catch me sneaking around with a stranger in the dark.

Operation *Maid in Manhattan* is set for a midnight launch. I should be excited that our plan is in motion, that I'm closer than ever to getting justice for the Castillos, and with any luck, resuscitating my career. So why do I feel so lousy?

Maybe it has to do with the infuriating way that Eli gets under my skin. I hate that he sees past my usual disguises, rendering useless my attempts at becoming invisible. I hate how much effort it takes to keep him on the other side of every boundary line I've created for myself. And I especially hate his unnerving habit of locking that wolfish gaze on mine every time he walks into a room—just like the first time we saw each other at Ginny's bar.

He's nothing like the brutish, narrow-minded swindler I

expected him to be. And yet I can't figure it out: What's his story? Who is he? Where does he come from? Why does nothing about him add up? Eli has proven to be clever and sharp, handsome and insouciant, but can we really trust him to help us? I'm still not sure. I hope Holly's faith in him isn't misplaced—that I won't come to regret all of this.

I enter La Barna and find Eli standing, as instructed, by the hair dye station. He's washed in moonlight, studying color swatches under the light of his phone. Behind him, San Antonio rests upside down on Abuela's altar, in hopes he will find me a man. I'm pretty sure this is not what Abuela had in mind. She might, however, approve of the bespoke Japanese denim jeans Holly picked out and which accentuate his toned thighs and ass, and the smoked cashmere quarter zip that brings out the gray in his eyes. I push away any thoughts of his thighs, eyes—or ass, for that matter—or risk losing both my mind and my objectivity.

"Deep Purple Dream?" he asks, holding up a sample of violet-tinted hair. "Sounds like a Prince song."

"Middle-aged white ladies love it," I tell him, taking the sample from his fingers and placing it back inside the color book. "I think it makes them feel rebellious."

He chuckles. "Against what?"

"Their privileged yet tedious suburban existence?"

He flashes me a lopsided grin that transforms his face into that of someone softer, almost boyish. I'm momentarily disarmed by the sincere glint in his eyes. A confusing mix of irritation and yearning churns in my gut, forcing me to take a step back.

To my disbelief, Chapulín ambles toward his feet, then circles his leg, shamelessly soliciting pets. This cat hates everyone. Is he really that deprived of attention?

"When do we start?" he asks, crouching down to stroke the cat's fur.

I scan the salon. Everything we need is here. After considering our options, La Barna After Dark seemed like the safest place to transform Eli into something resembling the heir to a wealthy Mississippi cotton empire. And given my family's proclivity to meddle, interfere, and ask too many questions, I judged it best to schedule a midnight makeover session.

"Now—" I say, trying to sound more confident than I feel. "Holly's on her way."

But then I hear the loud echo of my full name, bouncing off the walls. "Luisa María Martín Moreno," Mami exclaims as the bright lights come on. Chapulín darts outside with a howl, and I yelp in alarm, regressing a whole fifteen years to the night I was caught making out with a boy in my mother's old salon in San Germán. "What's going on here? Is this what you do when I go to sleep? *Who* is this man?" She's standing impossibly tall, arms crossed tight over her very large breasts, her own don't-fuck-with-me expression contorting her face.

Shit.

"Jesus Christ, Mami," I exclaim. "Are you trying to kill me? My heart almost came out of my mouth."

"Count yourself dead, señorita, if you don't start explaining," she says, tapping her chancleta against the linoleum, her face twisted into a scowl.

I'm a grown-ass woman, for Chrissake. I shouldn't be afraid of my own mother.

And yet.

Maybe it's a Puerto Rican mother thing.

"It's for work," I say, my hands in the air, gesticulating God knows what.

Eli raises an eyebrow in surprise.

"Work?" Mami asks, unconvinced. "It's past midnight!"

"I'm not exactly in the position to turn down jobs, am I?" I say defiantly.

"What work?" she presses. Then switching to Spanish, she adds, "What is this, some homeless makeover?" She glares at Eli, wrinkling her nose as if she's smelling sour milk.

"Oh my God, Mami," I cry out in Spanish. "Do you even hear yourself? That's so offensive." My face burns with embarrassment. I cut Eli an apologetic look, praying he can't understand. And maybe he doesn't, because he seems quite entertained by this whole shit show.

She rolls her eyes. "Miss high-and-mighty. You could've been a lawyer. You could be married already! Instead, you're wasting your time and talent. Getting fired—why? You won't say. And now this? Who *is* this gringo you're sneaking around with?"

I dig my fingers into my scalp, pulling at my hair by the roots. Implied in "this gringo" is the staunch Islander belief that all mainland white men are colonialist pricks whose only aspiration is to pillage and plunder—they take and take and take until there's nothing left. *This gringo*—she's really saying—cannot be trusted.

I mean, sure, in this case, she's probably right. But I'm not about to give her an inch.

"This *man*"—I motion to Eli, switching back into English, arms hovering up and down his body as if showing off a prize in a game show—"is Eli. He's a . . ." My brain sputters, struggling to come up with an airtight story. This is exactly why I don't do unprepared.

"An actor," Eli asserts without missing a beat.

"That's right," I say, following his lead. "A friend of mine hired me to be his publicist. She works with one of those film companies always shooting around town."

"A friend?" Mami asks pointedly. "What friend? You've never mentioned any friends?"

"Holly," Eli offers. "She's on her way. Excellent film producer."

I stare at him, searching his face for any indications of a lie, but I find none. I'm both impressed and alarmed at his seemingly innate ability to deceive on the spot.

I should be thrilled, I tell myself. After all, that's exactly why we hired him.

"He's got a big audition in the morning," I continue. "Playing a young, rich investor."

"It's a thespian emergency," Eli deadpans.

I snort, then pretend to sneeze to cover it up. *Thespian emergency?*

"God bless you," he says with a wink.

Mami stares dubiously between us, then evaluates Eli with

the fastidiousness of someone about to buy a used car. I can almost hear her mind ticking off a makeover checklist inside her head. Shave. Haircut. Nails. Eyebrows. Skin.

"Fine," Mami says, as if answering a request that was never verbalized. "I'll have to change into my work clothes." And with that, she swivels and marches back into the house.

I watch her leave, then close my eyes in a strained attempt to find some calm.

"Taking a standing nap, are we?" Eli asks. I open my eyes to find him staring down at me, his expression bemused.

"More like contemplating matricide," I mutter. "Do you have any experience digging graves?" I narrow my eyes, then rethink my question. "Actually, don't answer that." I put up a hand between us. "I don't want to know."

I text Holly, filling her in on the rickety details of our story. Ten minutes later, Mami's back, Holly in tow. She arrives in a University of Georgia sweatshirt, carrying a tablet in one arm and a tray of coffees and a box of pastries in the other, as if she's here for a college study session.

"A midnight makeover," she exclaims, passing around hot coffee cups. "This is so fun." Then she proffers the tablet, showing off a collection of photos that can only be described as *Country Club Hotties*. "Let's get to work!"

Mami's hands are already clutching a pair of scissors. Eli sits on her salon chair before I cover him in a black styling cape. "Sit up straight," Mami demands, her tone uncompromising.

"Yes, ma'am." He quickly obliges.

I bring a hand to cover my mouth, trying not to laugh. This man was a shark when it came to hustling those frat guys at the bar, but now, under Mami's scrutiny, there's a childlike alarm in his eyes.

Mami takes off his trucker hat and tosses it aside. She runs her fingers through his hair and beard, *tsk*ing and shaking her head. "This all has to go."

Eli winces. "All of it?" Then, turning to Holly's tablet, he adds, "One of those guys must have long hair. Look again."

"Let's start with the hair and beard," Mami says mercilessly.

Eli's right hand catches his beard, wretchedly stroking the hair about to come off. "Then we'll tackle his skin, eyebrows, and those nails." Mami's face twists into a grimace.

"I'll look like a toddler." Eli grunts.

"Baby face," Holly chirps, nodding encouragingly. "The younger you look, the better."

Eli's eyes find mine in the full-length mirror on the wall. "You didn't say anything about shaving off my beard," he says to me.

I shrug. Once you're in Mami's chair, resistance is futile.

"Luisa," Mami calls out to me, "get him washed."

"Why me?" I exclaim.

"Because I'm getting the clippers ready and this is your job, after all." She grabs me by the wrist and drops a clean towel onto my open palm. "Make yourself useful, mija."

Eli dutifully moves to the hair washing station, leans back, and closes his eyes. I sit behind him, checking the water temperature as it runs through his long mane of hair. I pump shampoo into my hand, then add Mami's signature essential oils blend into the mix and plunge my fingers into Eli's scalp. He relaxes at the touch, exhaling slowly, sinking deeper into the chair. I rub circles around his hairline and massage his temples with my fingertips like I've been trained to do. The soothing scent of jasmine and vanilla fills the air between us. The muscles along my neck and down my back slacken, unwinding a little with the repetitive movement of my hands, giving in to the pleasant sensation of water, soap, and warm skin between my fingers.

"This feels nice," he says in a low, husky voice.

I rinse his head, half distracted by the copper highlights of his brown hair, the long eyelashes framing his eyelids, and the smattering of freckles on the bridge of his nose.

Stop it, Luisa. Just no.

I open the faucet to full pressure and finish the job, wrapping his head in a warm towel.

"Do we get to do this shampoo thing again?" he asks through hazy lids.

I can't tell if he's joking. It doesn't sound like a joke. I don't answer.

He returns to Mami's styling chair, his shoulders going taut with apprehension. Mami unceremoniously bunches up all his hair in one hand, brings her scissors to the back of his head, and cuts. Eli flinches under her grasp. It's cute, really, the way he's holding on to the armrests like his plane is about to go down.

Holly hovers, peppering Mami with suggestions, while simultaneously pulling up photos of the "look" she's put together.

"Tousled," Holly explains. "Fairly tight around the back and over the ears, but not too short on top. Shaggy under a cap, you know? He can't look like he's trying too hard. Needs to seem like he doesn't care all that much."

"You mean like before?" Eli asks sarcastically. "Because I didn't care before, either."

Holly sighs dramatically. "No, not like before." She taps at an example on her screen, growing impatient. "You do care, but you want to *look* like you don't care. That's the look."

"That makes no sense," I add unhelpfully. "You get that, right?"

Holly shrugs. "I know. But that is the first rule of the world where this, um, film is set," she says, glancing over at Mami. "You never flaunt your prosperity. That's *gauche*."

"Gauche?" Mami asks. "Like, it's tacky to show you're a rich man?"

"It's absurd," Holly concedes. "Trust me, I know."

"Fine," Mami says, reaching for her feathering scissors. "Lazy chic it is."

Mami finishes Eli's haircut, but we won't see the full effect until later. She's caked on a hair mask and wrapped his head with a thermal foil cap.

Meanwhile, I take the shears to his sideburns, but when I try to press the buzzing contraption to his face, he twitches back.

"You're gonna have to sit still," I tell him, cupping his jaw with one hand in an effort to angle his face. He reaches for my hand on his jaw, covering it with his warm palm, his gray eyes searching for mine. My breath inadvertently catches in my lungs the moment our gazes meet, filling my chest with an ache I haven't felt in a really long time. There's a vulnerability behind those eyes that I recognize.

"I . . . I just . . ." He stutters in a low voice. "I *need* my beard."

The unguarded tone in his voice stabs at my heart. I stare into his eyes for way longer than I should.

Against all good judgment, I run my thumb over the edge of his beard, appraising. "It'll grow back," I quietly assure him, then push down any inkling of emotion and break away from all eye contact. Eli clears his throat, averting his gaze to the reflection in the mirror.

I steady his face with one hand, working the shears over his beard with the other. Inside my head, the left and right parts of my brain go at it. My operating system defaults to analyzing, assessing, and searching for answers—no feelings required, regardless of how strong those feelings may be.

My life and career have taught me that emotions only serve to impair judgment. Under the influence of emotion, humans become irrational beings, incapable of thinking objectively and making decisions based on facts. Just look at my own mother. Either my dad was extraordinarily adept at lying or my mother ignored a trail of evidence fifteen years long, given that my half sister and I were the same age when the truth finally came out.

When I'm done with the beard trim, I push Eli back in the chair, then lather his face in shaving cream for a wet shave. I stretch the skin, slowly angling the blade around his cheeks, jawline, and neck. Behind me, Mami holds up a pair of tweezers over his forehead, preparing for the next stage—the plucking of the brow. At the sight of the tweezers poised over his head, Eli recoils under me.

"You realize you have a Japanese steel blade to your throat, right?" I say, holding up the straight razor in my hand in warning.

"Christ Almighty," he exclaims, as the blade makes contact with his chin, and I swipe upward, finishing the shave.

I'm barely done wrapping his face in a hot towel, when Mami savagely attacks his left brow. I know her well enough to see the sadistic pleasure she's getting from inflicting pain on this poor man.

"Why would anyone actually choose to do this?" Eli mutters.

"Who's the tough guy now?" Holly teases.

"You want to look the part, don't you?" Mami asks, pulling yet another hair.

"Right." Eli grimaces. "For my audition."

By the time Mami's done plucking his brows, Eli's clean-shaven face is caked in a charcoal mask. He moves to the mani-pedi station, where Mami scrubs and cuts his nails.

"Buffed finish," Holly tells her. "Not too shiny. He can't look like he got a manicure."

"Well, how 'bout we just don't buff the nails, then?" Eli deadpans.

"They have to be clean and well-maintained," Holly says as if all of this should be evident. "But if they're too shiny, you'll look like you're trying. And—"

Eli cuts her off. "Lemme guess—I can't look like I'm trying."

It takes another two hours, and as many rounds of coffee, for Mami to finish his nails, then blow-dry and style Eli into the perfect "Lazy Frat Bro" look.

Holly and I sit back, awaiting the big reveal like the audience of a runway show. Mami pulls back a curtain to introduce a completely transformed Eli, proudly twirling him in a slow circle. His clean-shaven cheeks blush crimson at the echo of Holly's loud claps and whistles.

I swallow hard at the vision of the man standing before me—clean face, soft skin, rumpled hair that begs you to sink your hands into it and pull—hard. My stomach flutters against my own better judgment. Blotches of red crawl from my chest to my neck as the siren equivalent of a five-alarm fire goes off in the back of my mind.

"Dolores, you are an absolute miracle worker." Holly pats my mother on the shoulder.

"I look like a frat boy," Eli sighs, checking himself out in the mirror.

"Precisely," Holly says. "A very handsome, guileless Phi Delt. Nice, clean-cut, laid-back, but still knows how to have a good time." Then she turns to me and grins from ear to ear. "See?" she exclaims. "I told you he'd be perfect."

I meet Eli's eyes, not saying a word, just wondering why in God's name he's been hiding all this. Every feature of his face is magnified—the long muscles of his neck, the high cheekbones, the hard lines of his jaw, the vivid gray of his eyes. But he also looks strangely vulnerable. Like all that facial hair was guarding him from the world. A protective, territorial instinct—the one I usually only reserve for my own family—settles in my gut. It's absurd, really. I don't know this man, or so I keep telling myself.

"He looks good." I clear my throat, then turn to my phone. "Great job, Mami."

Eli steps in front of the full-length mirror and grumbles in that godforsaken redneck accent, "I've become a *got'dam* pretty boy."

"That word!" I cringe. "Your Georgia backwoods twang has got to go."

"Don't they have people for that?" Mami offers, straightening her pile of trashy gossip magazines. "Like voice coaches or accent teachers? My telenovela actors use them all the time."

I scoff. "Short of finding a world-renowned linguistics expert, we're gonna need a fucking rhetorical miracle."

Eli gives me a once-over. "Honey, who licked the red off your candy?" And once more, I'm reminded we're not even close to being ready.

CHAPTER 14

Holly

I'm wandering the labyrinthine campus of Emory University in search of the Modern Languages Building—the place where I, Holly Simmons, college dropout, will be meeting with Professor Hugh Pridmore, a sociolinguist and world-renowned scholar of dialectology (I had to look up what that last word even means). He's come all the way from Cambridge University to serve as Emory's Distinguished Visiting Professor of Linguistics. And, miraculously, he agreed to meet with little ol' me.

Days after our late-night session at La Barna, I was driving to work and stressing that, despite Eli's fabulous makeover and the great success of Operation *Maid in Manhattan*, his terrible Mississippi accent was going to do us in. To distract myself from our impending failure, I turned on *Lunchtime Luminaries*, just in time to hear the Atlanta radio icon Doris Lorenz, in her charmingly wobbly voice, introduce the esteemed Professor Hugh Pridmore. Listening to their interview, I thought: *If he's doing this sort of research, would he consider helping us? Could we arrange some sort of barter?* I've become a master of the barter, given my years of negotiating with stingy vendors on behalf of the club. So I've shown up here to make a deal.

I finally locate the building, tucked behind the campus's leafy quad, and rush to his second-floor office. The door is open, revealing a sparse room with nothing but a crammed-full bookshelf and a laptop, open and abandoned on an otherwise bare desk. I lean against the doorway, waiting, watching the wall clock. Fifteen long minutes pass. Did he forget about our appointment? Maybe it was all too good to be true. Maybe Professor Hugh Pridmore isn't the rhetorical miracle we need.

I had been so hopeful when he replied immediately to the message I fired off through Professor Pridmore's Emory Contact page. I used the same story we cooked up for Luisa's mom: We're working with a promising actor from the north Georgia mountains, and he is having a hard time nailing the Mississippi Delta accent. Might Professor Pridmore be of assistance? He replied immediately, asking me to meet him in his office. Now pushing twenty minutes ago.

Defeat begins to creep over me. We only have one more phase of the plan to get through: Operation *My Fair Lady*. Of course, neither of us expected that Eli's accent would pose such a big problem, and there's no way we can move on with the etiquette lessons until we have this little setback squared away. But I feel it in my gut. This Pridmore guy just might be our very own Henry Higgins, the key to our success. First, though, I need to track him down.

Hearing muffled sounds from the adjacent language laboratory, I decide to walk over to investigate. I peer through a transom window to see two men inside a large booth with thick gray foam undulating along the walls. One appears to be a college student, wearing a backward baseball cap over an impressive low drop fade, speaking into a large tabletop microphone. The man sitting across from him seems a little older, but it's hard to tell, since his back is to me. He's lean, with broad shoulders and a full head of thick dark hair, wearing a crisp white linen button-down and jeans. He's sitting at the very edge of his seat, grasping a handheld recording device. Maybe he manages the research lab?

I tap on the glass. The student seems amused. The other guy scowls, visibly annoyed.

"May I help you?" the researcher asks in a posh British accent, his almost boyish face twisted into a grimace. Did Professor Pridmore bring this guy with him from Cambridge? Is he such a big deal that he travels with an entourage?

"I'm sorry to interrupt your . . ." I pause, unsure exactly what I've walked into.

"Acoustic-phonetic research," he says matter-of-factly. His face is smooth and tanned, his eyes deep brown. He has incredibly thick eyebrows and dark stubble. The only indication that he may be as old as me is the subtle crow's-feet around his eyes.

"Do you know where I can find Professor Hugh Pridmore? I have an appointment."

"Oh, bloody hell," he exclaims, pressing his palm to his forehead. "I've gone and lost track of time again, haven't I?"

I stare at him, confused. Could this linen-and-denim-wearing thirtysomething be the distinguished visiting professor of linguistics? *No way.*

"Hugh Pridmore, at your service," he says, grasping my hand to shake it. "So sorry about that." His hand is cool and smooth in mine, and while his grasp is firm, it's not the sort of handshake that's designed to project dominance or bravado. I stare at our intertwined palms for a beat too long and, when he pulls his hand away, I glance quickly toward the glass booth, hoping that my cheeks haven't gone pink or, if they have, that the distinguished professor hasn't noticed.

I hear Professor Pridmore clear his throat softly as he steps back to put more space between us. "Raymond," he says, gesturing toward the student in the glass booth, "is from Louvale—are you familiar with the town?" I shake my head. "Southwest Georgia," he clarifies. "And when I heard him calling across the quad to a friend this morning, it was simply imperative that I get him into the lab for elicitation. He has the most fascinating patterns of morphology."

Patterns of morphology? Elicitation? I have no idea what this man is talking about. He's clearly one of those high-and-mighty academic types. When I come up with absolutely nothing in reply, he grins awkwardly, and I'm sure he must already have decided: meeting with me is a waste of his precious time.

As if on cue, Raymond of the "fascinating morphology" comes out of the booth. The professor gives him a broad, white-toothed smile that disproves the British bad-teeth stereotype. "Well, Raymond. I'm sorry we were interrupted, but I'm afraid I'm already late for a meeting with Ms. Simmons," he says, glancing toward me in acknowledgment, "who has an appointment. I'd like to have you back next week. Does that work?"

Raymond smiles sheepishly. "Just to talk into a microphone some more?" he asks. "Yeah, okay, cool," he says as the professor escorts us both out of the lab.

"I'm afraid we'll need to walk and talk," the professor tells me, glancing at his watch. "I've squeezed you in during my lunch hour, between engagements."

"No worries," I mumble, suddenly feeling annoyed by Mr. Oh-So-Important and his packed schedule. Personally, I take great pride in my punctuality. It's essential to my job. But not the professor, who seems perfectly comfortable making me sit around and wait.

We head outside, walking at a rapid clip, neither one of us saying a thing.

"I'm sorry if you missed lunch on my account," I launch in, nervously filling the silence as we make our way along a redbrick path. "I've probably got some Nabs somewhere in my purse, to hold you over." I fish around in my enormous bag, then lift the pack triumphantly. "Found 'em!" I add.

He glances at the crumpled package of cheese crackers in my hand with what can only be described as mild disgust. Admittedly, they've seen better days, and Professor Pridmore doesn't strike me as the type to tip up a baggie and down the crumbs, as I've been known to do in a blood-sugar emergency.

"That's enormously kind of you," he says, his voice dripping with condescension. "But I'll have time for a proper meal after my class."

A proper meal. I can almost see it now: The esteemed Professor Hugh Pridmore perched at a gleaming mahogany table, set with a linen place mat and silver candelabra, nibbling on canapés served on a dainty china plate. Well, he's definitely snooty enough to be our Henry Higgins.

Professor Pridmore pauses, looks over at me. "You're Mississippi-born," he says, lifting a finger to his lower lip. "Jackson, I presume? Lovely cadence. But masked." He studies my face, which makes me mildly uncomfortable. Or maybe it's the way his fingertip strokes that plump lip, grazing the top of his five-o'clock shadow. "I'd gather you've spent your entire adulthood in Atlanta."

"You're freaking me out a little," I say, feeling a blush rise to my cheeks. "How did you know that?"

"Nabs," he says. "A simple matter of word choice."

His eyes gleam as he smiles, clearly pleased with his sleuthing. I'd never thought about it, but no one around here calls those little cracker packets "Nabs." I guess I did pick that up in Jackson.

I don't smile back. Instead, I shove them back into my purse, focus my attention straight ahead, and keep walking.

"It's a shibboleth, a linguistic giveaway. But I digress," he says, stopping and gesturing for me to sit on a bench in the shade of an elm tree. I plop down, trying to recall whether I've ever heard anyone use "digress" in conversation.

"Now, back to your request. The predicament facing your actor friend is in my field of inquiry." He takes a seat beside me. "My research interests have long centered on the relationship between social class and dialect," he says, then crosses his legs on the bench, "beginning with my graduate studies, when I examined variations in my mother's first language of Punjabi. It's always fascinated me that a person's accent can open or close doors to their social mobility."

"I guess I never thought about it that way," I reply, thinking about my own social standing. Because in a way, it's the very reason I'm here: a rich and powerful man has me completely trapped.

"Well," he says, "I grew up with an Oxbridge father and a mother for whom English was a second language. She was entirely fluent, of course. But that didn't seem relevant." His hands fold on his knee, as his top leg slowly taps out a silent rhythm. "As a child, I noticed how differently people in London perceived her—and by extension, me—particularly when my father wasn't with us."

"I get that," I say, even though I have no idea what an Oxbridge father is. I'm assuming from context it's someone very fancy. "My neighbor is from Eastern Kentucky," I add. "And her accent's a bit twangy. She thinks people treat her like a country bumpkin."

"And is your neighbor, as you say, a 'country bumpkin'?" he asks.

I shrug but don't answer. Professor Pridmore here is a piece of work. I can just feel the judgment rolling off him in waves—me, living next door to a country bumpkin, using such charming turns of phrase as "freaking out," while he's over there piling on the SAT words. It's as if a snobbish old British dude got trapped in the (frankly not unattractive) body of a worldly thirtysomething.

"If I can find the time, we might perchance arrange to bring your actor friend into the lab," he says, his expression suddenly thoughtful. I watch as he lifts his hand to the nape of his neck, then runs his fingers through his thick, dark hair. "I occasionally take on outside consulting."

Consulting? That sounds expensive. I'm studying him too closely, trying to tear my eyes away, wondering how much this is going to cost us and where in the world we'll manage to come up with the money. I'm fresh out of sapphire tennis bracelets. I absolutely must convince him to do this for free.

"You know," I say, "our young actor friend also has . . . what did you call it?" I pause for effect. "Ah yes. Fascinating patterns of morphology." I bring my hand to my chin and squint my eyes a little, in a feeble attempt to look smart and thoughtful. "Among the most fascinating I've ever heard in the South, and, believe me, I've been around."

As soon as I say it, I feel that pink flush return to my cheeks. *I've been around?* Sounds like I'm sharing the details of my sex life, which I'm obviously not. (Since it's basically nonexistent.)

"Wonderful," he states, his voice rising with enthusiasm. "I'd love to investigate his southern Appalachian speech patterns." Clearly, he hasn't picked up on my unintended double meaning, which emboldens me to try closing the deal.

"So." I paste on my most guileless expression. "It's an even swap? In exchange for his time in the lab, you can help him learn—"

"I like it," he breaks in, nodding vigorously. "He'll record in the lab for me, and I'll teach him that . . ." He pauses, leans in toward me. "What did you term it? Ah yes, that Mississippi drawl."

"You've got yourself a deal," I respond, thrusting out my right hand for a shake.

"Fabulous," he says, clasping my hand with his and smiling, but—this time—also gently squeezing, as if the two of us are entering into some sort of secret pact. I can't help but smile back. After all, I've nabbed a world-renowned dialectologist to help us—and for free. Sure, he's a little snooty, but he knows what he's talking about, and the price is right. Luisa will be so proud.

CHAPTER 15

Luisa

Living at home is getting so old, so fast. I know she cares, but Mami's constant stream of unsolicited advice is driving me up a wall. Juan Pablo's mother, Vidalina, came by yesterday for her weekly blowout, which meant I had to endure my own weekly nag session. Nothing is outside the purview of my mother's expertise, whether it be my hair, career, or marriage prospects.

To add to my growing anxiety, I rarely wake up without thinking of the Castillos and how little time they have left in their home. This week, I threw myself into a forensic financial analysis of every nonprofit Griggs's family's foundation has supported in the last five years, like a newshound picking up a scent. It'll take me weeks to cross-reference donation records and tax filings, but there's nothing like a spreadsheet to make sense of chaos.

I was actually relieved when Holly called with the news she'd landed a speech expert—a perfect excuse to get out of the house. She somehow managed to pull off the rhetorical miracle, considering our foray into Emory's linguistics lab isn't costing us a dime. The heavens must be smiling down on us today, because the only thing missing as we glide down the campus hallway is San Pedro holding the pearly lab doors open, ushering us into the bright lights.

"I was thinking more like a voice coach," I remark, a little awestruck by the brand-new, state-of-the-art facility, "not a whole research lab at one of the top colleges in the country."

"You said to get a professional . . ." Holly trails off, nervously smoothing the split ends around her face, then thinking better of it and tucking the too-long strands behind her ears. "He's got some grant to get people to talk into a mic," she explains.

"Wait—" Eli cuts in. "I could be getting paid extra for this?"

Holly and I both roll our eyes.

"Tell me ya didn't turn money down?" Eli groans. Neither one of us bothers to dignify the question with an answer.

Before us, the lab's high walls are covered from floor to ceiling in acoustic slat panels. A row of computers, each with its own set of noise-canceling headphones and recording-grade microphones, display some sort of sound spectrum and wavelength analysis. All other available space is occupied by sound meters, mixers, and equalizers.

"He's coming," Holly adds in a whisper, brushing down her hair again. I wonder if she knows how badly she needs a haircut, and maybe some layers, too. But, I remind myself, we're not here to make Holly over; we're here to make Eli into someone Griggs Caldecott Johnson III will trust, and quickly.

I glance behind Holly, expecting an old white guy in a tweed blazer and elbow pads, horn-rimmed glasses framing his face. But seeing him, my head tilts sideways in confusion. *Is this the world-renowned Professor Pridmore?* He looks like a graduate student doing a semester abroad.

"Welcome, friends," he says, shaking our hands. "We won't have time for everything today, but we can dive right into phonetics. And if we're lucky, we might have time to get started with morphology and a little bit of syntax?"

I gotta hand it to Holly, this Pridmore guy is kinda cute—until he opens his mouth and sounds like some sort of genteel British nerd.

Holly steps forward. "Absolutely," she chirps.

Eli and I nod, then make a concerted effort to smile politely.

We discuss Eli's burgeoning acting career as Pridmore directs us to a small conference table by one of the large windows. Holly takes the chair closest to him, engrossed with every scholarly word that comes out of his mouth. Once again, I'm impressed by her questions and depth of understanding. She told me last night that she had been relying on Google University to do some linguistics research because she didn't want to seem dumb. Holly, I've realized, is really fucking smart. I don't get why she doesn't wear her brain on her sleeve more often.

Eli, meanwhile, seems as stiff as the acoustic boards behind him. The muscles around his jaw are rigid, and even though he's casually resting his elbows on the armrest, his shoulder blades seem uncomfortably taut.

"Tell me about yourself," Pridmore says, turning to face Eli directly.

"Not much to tell." Eli shrugs, his voice plunging hard into a default North Georgia twang, which wasn't there a minute ago.

"Tell me about your family, your upbringing," Pridmore prods, leaning forward. From what I learned about linguistics, dialects, and elocution (because I've also done my research at Google University), I gather he's listening for cues in Eli's speech, watching the movements of his mouth.

Eli rubs his palms hard over his thighs. He shrugs again, eyes quickly cutting to me, then back to Pridmore. "Family's from Westlake. Just me and my lil' sister left. Moved around a lot when we were kids." He licks his lower lip, then pauses, and takes a breath. "Like I said, not much to tell."

"What about your parents? What are their backgrounds?" Pridmore asks, as I begin to wonder if the linguistics doctor—like so many intellectuals—is oblivious to nonverbal cues.

"Why do y'all need to get up in my business?" Eli says, turning to me as if I'm the one interrogating him. "How's this gonna help?"

Pridmore offers a gracious smile, relaxing back into his chair. Something tells me he's heard all this before. "I'm trying to gauge your levels of exposure to other accents and dialects," he explains patiently. "Childhood exposure to a language shapes the brain's ability to recognize its sounds, structures, and patterns, making it easier to understand or even gain fluency later in life."

Eli nods, loosening a little, seemingly satisfied with the academic spiel.

"Can you tell me about some of the places you lived as a child?" Pridmore asks, his voice more cautious this time.

Eli winces slightly as he says, "We lived in every state below the Mason-Dixon Line. Like I said, we moved around a bit."

"Did that include Mississippi? The Delta, possibly?" Pridmore asks.

Eli nods, his cheeks coloring a little. "I was a kid, though," Eli repeats. "Don't remember much."

Pridmore claps his hands excitedly. "Fantastic," he exclaims.

"How exactly is this fantastic?" I ask impatiently, and to my surprise, also slightly defensive. Because it doesn't take a genius to interpret what Eli is saying: He grew up in a transient family. And given his apprehension, he probably went through some heavy shit. Did he go to bed hungry? Or spend nights at a shelter? Or, even worse, did someone abuse him? My chest tightens at the thought of a child-aged Eli surviving under those conditions. "He said he doesn't remember," I add. "Maybe we need to move on."

But the professor remains undeterred by my sharp tongue or resting bitch face. "Part of the reason Eli can reproduce Atlanta dialect so well is his exposure to it," he explains breezily. "Somewhere in the back of his brain, there's a bank of memories layered with a rural Mississippi dialect. We just need to tap into it." He raps one finger on the table for emphasis, then gestures to Eli with open palms. "And to our great advantage, Eli is a proficient code-switcher."

I grip the armrest on my chair as an icy tingle spreads down my spine. I think I've known on a subconscious level that Eli—like me—is a master code-switcher. But acknowledging it would mean that he and I actually have something in common. And not just *any* something, but a whole language born out of necessity and oppression. That all-too-familiar feeling of panic squeezes my lungs. I have to quietly remind myself to take measured breaths, to keep a clear and rational head on my shoulders.

Pridmore manages to elicit a few more childhood memories from Eli's brain, but I'm barely listening to the content. Instead, I'm narrowly tuning in to the nuances of his pronunciation, the cadence of his voice, the shifts in his inflection. It dawns on me that he leans on his North Georgia twang when he's nervous, tired, or irritated, turning it on and off at will. Not much different from me and my Puerto Rican Spanish accent.

I wonder if, like me, he had to teach himself to code-switch just to avoid the bullshit of people in power, or to fit in with his own people. Or—as I've been guilty of numerous times—to get people to trust him simply because he sounds like them. Deceitful? Yes. Necessary? Probably.

It never occurred to me that a guy like Eli—Southern, straight, white—would have to employ similar tactics to survive. *Wait, he is straight, isn't he?*

I'm so deep in my own musings that I've lost track of the conversation. Holly is now talking about her own childhood in Jackson, which apparently Pridmore was able to identify within fifteen minutes of meeting her. "Can you tell where Luisa is from?" Holly asks, like a kid asking a birthday magician to pull a rabbit from a top hat.

"We're here for Eli, not for me," I say curtly. "Plus, the professor's academic research is not a party trick." There's a guarded edge to my voice, despite my every effort to keep it composed.

"Interesting," Pridmore says thoughtfully.

"What is?" Holly asks, inching toward him.

"Luisa's accent is exceptionally hard to pinpoint," he observes in that highly erudite, clinical tone that grinds at my insides. "It's almost as if—" He pauses, once more unable (or unwilling) to read the room. I'm about to call for a bathroom break, but then he blurts out, "Almost as if you've gone out of the way to erase any markers from your speech pattern."

All eyes are on me. My face grows blistering hot.

What exactly do they think they see? I've lost count of how many times I've been told "But you don't have an accent?!" in a tone that reeks of disappointment, as if my speech is part of a little puzzle they must solve. *Who is this Luisa woman? And where does she come from? Because she certainly doesn't belong here.*

Suddenly, I'm thrown back into the small bedroom of our first Atlanta apartment the summer we moved to the States. I'm on my bed, sitting with my laptop open, headphones on, listening to movies in English for hours, saying the words aloud until my voice, raspy from exertion, sounds exactly like the voices of the Americanas on the screen.

From the moment we landed in Georgia, I witnessed the way people demeaned and condescended to my mother as soon as they heard her thick Puerto Rican Spanish accent. They made assumptions about her intelligence, education, competence, and even her trustworthiness. I'd be damned if that would be me, come the first day in a new school. It took me eight weeks to chameleon my speech into what linguists like Professor Pridmore call "prestige dialect"—also known as the language of white, privileged, wealthy folks—the language of power. All through high school I kept pushing myself, excelling in English Lit and Composition until my proficiency surpassed that of my native-speaking peers.

"She's from Puerto Rico," Eli offers on my behalf when I don't say anything. "She's fluent in Spanish, too—spoken *and* written."

I stare at him, partly furious, partly dumbfounded. Why and how does he know all this? It's almost as if he's quoting something he's read about me somewhere.

He must see the question on my face, because he says, "I read your bio on *The Georgia Times* website." My cheeks burn even hotter.

"Puerto Rican Spanish is such a complex, multifaceted language. It embodies elements of Taíno, African, Spanish, and English vernacular," Pridmore observes. "I hope I can visit there sometime. It's a short flight from Atlanta, I understand."

"Only three and a half hours," Holly adds, suddenly the helpful travel agent.

"Can we please refocus," I break in abruptly, any semblance of my nonexistent patience gone. We've already wasted half the morning in this little therapy session. "Can you help Eli learn the Mississippi accent? That's why we're here."

"What Luisa is trying to say is"—Holly cuts me a side-eye—"do you have any techniques that would be helpful?"

"I have a language crossing plan," Pridmore replies. "Been developing it since we first spoke." He stands, motioning for us to follow him inside a sound booth at the far end of the room.

We cram inside, ogling various articulation devices—an airflow mask, a sonogram, and a torturous-looking metal octopus. Eli takes a deep, long breath, inflating his lungs as if he's about to go underwater. Pridmore sits by the audio console, then directs Eli to the chair beside him. Holly and I stand behind them, trying to stay out of the way.

"I've created a list of words that are representative of the dialect." Pridmore points to a series of black-and-white wavelengths on the screen. "The computer will enunciate the word, then Eli will repeat it." He adjusts the tentacles of a black metal contraption protruding from the desk, then directs Eli to press his forehead and chin against the felt resting pads on the device. A small microphone sits directly in front of Eli's mouth. "If the intonation matches the wavelength, we move on to the next word. If not, you must repeat the word until the system hears a match."

"You mean, until I get it right," Eli clarifies, then clears his throat, fidgeting in his chair.

"There's a physicality to the language," Pridmore says, lifting his hands under Eli's face. "May I?" he asks. Eli nods. Pridmore nudges Eli's jaw with his fingers, positioning the muscles around his cheeks. "The jaw is slightly elevated, so if you sigh through that oral posture you have *ahh*."

Eli repeats, "Ahhh."

"The Mississippi accent is a very lengthened, slow drawl," Pridmore remarks. "So slow that you create diphthongs."

"Deep thongs? What the hell is a deep thong?" Eli asks, his backwoods twang so thick it sounds as if his mouth's been sewn shut.

An unexplainable burst of anger bubbles to the surface, and before I can contain the words, I'm snarling at Eli. "Jesus, a diphthong—two vowels in one syllable. What are they teaching kids in Westlake these days?"

Eli's head slowly turns, searching for me. When his narrowed eyes find mine, I'm certain I've gone too far. His gray irises are clouded with ire, but also hurt.

I'm about to apologize, but before I can say anything, he cries out, "Well, that there is one highfalutin word!" He digs deeper into his twang, and I narrow my eyes right back at him, feeling like I'm about to self-combust. "Guess I must've been catfish noodling or maybe muddin' the day they taught that there big word in school."

Holly bursts into laughter, clearly entertained by the way Eli provokes me.

"I must know. What in the world is mudding?" Pridmore asks, still smiling, genuinely curious.

"Driving in the mud," I snap. "Please don't encourage him."

"What? Don't tell me you ain't never hit a mudhole!?" Eli blurts out.

Holly tugs hard at my sleeve. "Let's take a potty break, shall we?"

I trail Holly as she grabs my hand and leads me around the corner into a hallway, then opens the door to a nearby all-gender restroom and beckons me inside.

"Luisa," Holly says, shutting the door firmly behind us. "Are you aware that you're being just plain ugly to Eli?"

"Ugly?" I point at myself, dismayed. "I'm being ugly?"

"Mean," she clarifies, arms crossed over her chest.

In my mind's eye, I see Eli adjusting his headphones, deep in concentration. A thousand feeble excuses cross my mind—mostly some ludicrous, childish version of *He started it*, I begrudgingly realize.

"Be careful not to confuse kindness with weakness, Luisa," Holly says, her tone low and soft. She gives me a long, pitying gaze before turning on her heel and exiting the bathroom.

I scoff to myself, growing agitated by the lack of space in the small bathroom. I push my way into the hallway, but I come to a standstill before rounding the corner into the lab. I have a clear view of Eli sitting behind a thick pane of glass, moving his mouth, presumably repeating Pridmore's list of words. When his gaze finds mine, there's no mistaking what I see: scars, deep and tender. Behind those gray eyes, I recognize the trauma of language. Accents, dialects, phonetics—weaponized, manipulated, controlled.

All of it, reflected like a mirror straight back at me. Am I frustrated with Eli because I had to do this on my own? And now here we are, in an academic research facility, working with an expert, and he still can't grasp the most basic concepts? Or is it about much more than that?

A voice deep in my gut whispers what I can't admit—even to myself. The certainty that ever since my own father betrayed us with his double life, with his blatant lies, I expect every man I meet to do the same.

CHAPTER 16

Holly

It's an hour past my bedtime, and I'm crammed into the Amsterdam, clutching my soda with lime, trying to score a table near the front. The venue is intimate, and the crowd is huge—all waiting for the Wednesday Jazz Jam to begin.

Luisa called me just as I was pulling into the parking lot. She flew into a frenzy about how far we had to go with Eli's accent, and she assured me that we'd never get there.

I patiently tried to talk her off a ledge, but she has a point. Operation *My Fair Lady* is our final phase of training, but will Eli be ready? Luisa and I both agreed that before we throw our Tripp Bedford into the pool of sharks, we need some sort of final exam—a low-stakes trial run among the Southern elite, to be sure he's got what it takes to hang with Griggs and his golfing buddies. We need to take him to an event outside of Atlanta, but where? Highlands? Cashiers, maybe? Too risky? I'm not sure.

I toss my phone to the bottom of my purse, urging myself to set all this scheming aside for one night and be fully present for my son.

Aidan came down from Athens for the jam, since he misses playing with all his bandmates from the Atlanta Youth Jazz Orchestra. Ever since he was eight years old and first held a pair of sticks, watching my son play drums has been an experience of seeing him at his most true and authentic self, confident and relaxed, fully present.

A seat opens at a table near the front of the room, and I rush to snag it. Aware of someone moving rapidly through the dark from the direction of the bar, I pick up speed and slide in to score the empty chair, just as none other than Professor Hugh Pridmore arrives at my side, holding a glass of red wine.

"Fancy meeting you here," I say, wondering how in God's name the highfalutin Professor Pridmore ended up in a Midtown dive bar, at a jazz jam for locals. He must be lost.

"Indeed," he replies, bowing slightly. "And you're fortunate that I'm too much of a gentleman to note that you've just stolen my chair."

"Finders keepers," I say, flashing what I hope is my most confident smile.

From the stage, the band director calls out for the audience's attention, mercifully distracting Professor Pridmore and me from our awkward predicament. He takes the mic and announces, "There's extraordinary talent assembled here tonight, and I'll do my best to give all the musicians a chance to play." He then gestures toward our table. "Jeremiah Goldwin, come on up to the stage and bring your tenor sax."

Jeremiah is the adorable early twentysomething sitting next to me in a black beanie and very stylish kicks. He gets up and motions for the professor to take his seat. "All yours, Prof," he says, an offer Pridmore very politely accepts.

"Jeremiah is one of my students," the professor explains as he sits down to watch Jeremiah take the stage. "We bonded over our shared love of American jazz music the other day after class, and he invited me to the jam," he tells me. "Not a chance I'd pass it up."

I nod, although I wouldn't have thought he'd be a jazz fan.

"And what brings you here?" he asks, his tone cordial if a bit stiff.

I spot Aidan coming through the door with a couple of his friends. "That kid—the one with the shaggy hair, dressed like he shops at thrift stores." I elect not to mention that he dresses like he shops at thrift stores because he, in fact, does shop at thrift stores. I thank God every day that Aidan and his friends prefer thrifting over buying new, name-brand clothes. Needless to say, my service-industry pay doesn't quite support a label-conscious lifestyle.

"A friend?" he asks.

"My son," I reply.

To his credit, Professor Pridmore doesn't show the shock that I'm certain he must feel, to learn that a full-fledged adult is my child. Before he can say anything, Aidan and his friends spot me and begin heading through the crowd toward us. I stand to greet them, and Aidan enfolds me in a huge hug, lifting me off my feet. He's lanky, like his father, a foot taller than me.

"Hey, Ma," he says into my ear. "I've missed you."

I've missed him, too, so much that I squeeze him tight and don't let go, my chest lightening in his presence. But then I remember the secret I'm keeping from him, and a heaviness descends. I don't want to be overprotective or coddling. But I also can't bear the thought of him stressing about the house of cards we're both living in, when there's not a damn thing he can do to keep it from collapsing. That's all on me.

He puts me down and, pushing my worry aside, I give equally warm hugs to his buddies Jay and Nikki, whom I've known since they were pimply middle schoolers starting out in jazz.

"You gonna introduce us to your friend?" Jay asks, smiling in a way that I know he thinks is real cute, but that makes me want to grab his ear and turn it.

"Oh, well, n-not exactly my friend," I stutter. "This is Dr. Hugh Pridmore, a professor at Emory."

I see my son's eyebrows shoot up. Pridmore's not exactly my type, historically speaking. But I don't see a good way to correct him, since Pridmore and I are very much *not* on a date. Plus, can I even have a type, when I can count on one hand the dates I've had since Aidan was born? I know my priorities, and dating simply hasn't been among them. Now that Aidan's in college, I sometimes wonder if I should try to get back in the game, so to speak. But it all seems so exhausting and time-consuming, and I question whether dating is really worth the effort.

"I recently had the chance to work with your mother in a professional capacity," the professor says, falling deep into his Pridmore self. "I was so pleased to run into her tonight."

Aidan looks over to me, puzzled. Just as I'm trying to figure out how to explain what on earth I'm doing working with a linguistics professor, Pridmore, clearly sensing that I need to divert the conversation, jumps in to tell Aidan he's here to see Jeremiah. He gestures toward the stage just as the band launches into Charlie Parker's "Ornithology."

We all fall into a trance, watching Jeremiah play. I find that I'm involuntarily letting my shoulders sway along with the snappy tune. Beside me, I can feel Professor Pridmore watching me, and I sense that he, too, is swaying to the rhythm. With my focus trained intensely on that sax, I'm suddenly reluctant to look at the professor, feeling a little disoriented by this new jazz-loving, toe-tapping version of Hugh Pridmore.

Jeremiah leaves the stage to thunderous applause, then comes to join us. Of course, he knows Aidan and his friends already. Much like the country club world, the world of young jazz musicians in Atlanta is small. Their chitchat is easy, relaxed, and to my great surprise, Pridmore is right in there with them, asking all the right questions and listening intently. Hugh Pridmore knows a thing or two about American jazz music, much more than I can claim to know, but he doesn't, as the esteemed Professor Pridmore would himself say, "pontificate." Rather, he expresses real interest in what the kids have to teach him. It's strange, but not in a bad way, to hear Aidan and the professor chatting comfortably with each other.

"I'm spotting not one but three of our talented young musicians that have gone away for school," the band director calls out when the next song ends. He's pointing toward our table. "Come on up here, Aidan, Jay, and Nikki. It's great to have you back in the ATL."

Jay grabs his guitar case, Aidan clutches his sticks, and the three of them head up to the stage, confident and relaxed. They greet each member of the house band with hugs and fist bumps, chatting as they set up.

"'Blue Skies,'" Nikki announces, heading toward the mic.

"Tempo?" Aidan asks, already settled on his throne, as drummers call their stools.

"Let's go medium up," Nikki says, and then my heart soars as Aidan launches smoothly and comfortably into an opening fill and the pianist drops in with the melody. They're off and running and I'm awed, once again.

"Damn, they're talented," Pridmore asserts from beside me.

"Don't I know it," I say, looking over at the professor. Tears have filled my eyes, as they always do when I watch Aidan play. Pridmore notices, but he just smiles. He's wearing a buttery leather jacket, and I feel an intense urge to reach out and stroke it. *Could it be as soft as it looks?* I judiciously focus my attention on Aidan instead. I can tell he's now fully in what he calls "the pocket": eyes down, mouth hanging slightly open, hands and feet moving each to their own beat, in ways that appear so effortless, but also somehow impossible.

When the song ends and the applause is over, the band huddles to discuss their next piece, and conversation swells around us.

"I'm guessing you're a musician, too," Pridmore says, gesturing at Aidan up onstage. "That kind of talent runs in the family."

"Oh no, not me," I say, turning back to smile at the professor. "I'm not quite tone-deaf, but I can barely carry a tune." I laugh. "And my hand-eye coordination is for shit."

He laughs, deep and throaty, throwing back his head. "That makes two of us," he says. "But we appreciate the gift that natural musicians have, while they often assume that, with effort, anyone could achieve their skill level."

"It came naturally to Aidan's father, too." As soon as the words slip from my mouth, I wish I could take them back. I have no business chatting with this man about my personal life.

"Not in the picture anymore?" Pridmore asks, in a way that feels casual, not probing.

"Not since before Aidan was born. He was a front man—just as talented as Aidan," I say, figuring it's probably too late to turn back now. "Big star in a very small world. Always surrounded by adoring fans. You know the type."

"Does that worry you?" he asks. "That your son might chase the same thing?"

"Not at all," I tell him, and I mean it. "Aidan's father needed the spotlight. It fed him. He loved to be onstage—any stage—

because he loved to be adored." I pause, take a sip of my soda, and look back to Pridmore, who seems to urge me on with his silent attentiveness. "Aidan doesn't need any of that. He just wants to make great music with great musicians. That's what feeds him."

Nikki steps off the stage and heads toward the water jug at the bar. The saxophonist for the house band, Billy June, returns to the stage, and Aidan and the keyboardist launch right into an up-tempo piece I don't immediately recognize.

"Ah, 'L's Bop,'" Professor Pridmore says, closing his eyes. "One of my all-time favorites."

We listen for a while, enraptured by the wailing sax and smooth stand-up bass. Aidan is where he loves most to be, in the background, working his subtle magic to let the soloists shine.

"It's lovely"—Professor Pridmore leans in, unnervingly close to me, to be heard over the music—"the look on your face when you watch him play."

"I can't help it," I say, feeling a flush rise to my cheeks. "Even when the lead singer in his emo band is yelling at the top of her lungs and Aidan's beating at the drums so fast I can barely see his arms and legs, I'm totally mesmerized."

"I'd like to see that sometime," he says, pulling back enough to look me in the eye, but still close enough that I can smell the leather and clove wafting off him. Does he notice the unexpected effect of his proximity?

"Screamo?" I say too loudly, right into the silence between the song's last note and the thundering applause. "I can't imagine you'd enjoy it," I whisper, embarrassed. "I don't think wailing, angsty teens and squealing guitars are your cup of tea."

"You might be surprised," he whispers back, as a trumpet player takes the stage. We watch Aidan count in, and the band eases into the sort of slow, sexy tune that Chet Baker probably played at romantic hole-in-the-wall clubs across Europe. "You should have seen me back when I was your son's age," Pridmore continues, smiling in a way that's almost mischievous.

"What are you trying to tell me, Professor Pridmore?" I ask, feigning a scandalized tone. "Were you *perchance* a wild child like me?"

"It's Hugh," he says, then pauses to take a sip of his wine. "And oh, how I longed to be. My Mohawk days weren't my best look," he says, grinning. "But I don't regret a moment of it. Frankly, the punk community saved me from myself." He leans back in his chair, and we both watch the bassist pluck gently on the strings of her instrument while grasping tightly to the neck, her eyes closed. "Oddly enough," he continues, turning to look at me, "it was a bunch of middle-aged punk rockers—not my scholarly parents or my erudite teachers—who set me on the path I've followed."

The bassist ends her solo to gentle applause, just as the trumpet eases into a lovely melody. I want to ask Hugh what he means, but I wait, listening to the music, hoping he'll say more.

"I suppose it might be anachronistic," he eventually continues, "but those old-school anarchists made me start asking questions about what it means to belong." He pauses, seeming to sink into memories. "Hanging out with them also got me arrested a couple of times."

"Noooo," I exclaim, trying to imagine a Mohawked Pridmore in handcuffs. The mental image forms more easily than I would have expected.

"Indeed," he says, his brown eyes twinkling. "Stealing Noam Chomsky from Borders."

"You stole books?" I ask, holding back a laugh.

"Evil corporation and all that," he replies, which makes us both laugh. Hugh whispers conspiratorially, "But those blokes, and the books I stole with them"—he nudges my arm gently with his own, sending a lovely and unexpected sensation right down to the pit of my stomach—"they gave me purpose, gave my life meaning."

"It's funny how our supposed mistakes can set us on exactly the right path, you know?" I suggest. He looks at me, searching, and an intense energy fills the air between us. Over the next few tunes, I tell him more about my life—as much as I can that's true, without having to restate the movie producer lie—about how getting pregnant with Aidan shifted my course; about how hard it's been at times, raising Aidan on my own, without the support of family; about how despite all that, if given the chance, I'd do it exactly the same way again. Wondering if I've overshared, I struggle to find a way to lighten things up. "If you think I'm a hot mess now, you should have seen me before that kid came along," I say, nodding toward Aidan.

"I don't think you're a hot mess, Holly," he says, his voice low.

Smiling through the blush I feel rising to my cheeks, I reply, "Well, thank you, Professor Pridmore."

"Hugh," he urges. "Please call me Hugh."

"Hugh," I reply, and it feels good to finally say his name aloud.

We sit in silence, close enough that with any subtle movement we'd be touching. But neither of us moves. Instead, we listen together to the trumpet and piano, as their notes intimately intertwine, bringing the song to a gentle close.

When the applause begins, I look over to see Aidan, easing back on his throne, clapping slowly for his bandmates, but gazing directly at me, his expression searching. Aidan and Jay leave the stage to make room for other musicians, and when they arrive beside us, Hugh gushes with genuine warmth about the quality of their playing.

"Have you been to the Monday night jam at the Switchyards Lounge yet?" Aidan asks Hugh. "You'd love it." He turns to me, his expression eager. "Right, Ma?"

"I can confirm," I say. "It's a great jam."

"You should take him," Aidan says to me, grinning. Then he looks at Hugh and adds, "Monday's her night off."

I feel my palms begin to sweat—both at the implication of Aidan's words and the fact that Hugh thinks I'm a movie producer, and as far as I know, movie producers don't have nights off.

"Sadly, I've got to travel to London next weekend, and I'll be there for a couple of weeks. But if you're available when I return, It's a date!" Hugh says cheerfully.

It's a date? Dear sweet Jesus. I think my son just set me up on my first real date in years.

CHAPTER 17

Luisa

Holly had to work at the club today, so it's just Eli and me. And after three excruciating hours in another one of Pridmore's "language crossing" sessions, I'm not feeling very optimistic. Today, the professor strapped Eli into a mask to measure the nasal airflow in his vowels. If I never again hear the phrase *Pee-can whai-ne tastes deh-vai-ne*, it will be too soon.

Beside me, Eli holds on for dear life, making some kind of strangled cat noise as I hurl my SUV into the inches of space available between a monster truck and some hapless old lady in a Prius. In my defense, there's only one way to merge onto the connector at the height of Atlanta rush hour: aggressively.

I grip the steering wheel a little harder, annoyed by the infuriatingly slow-moving traffic and unsettled by this stifling silence between us. Unable to do anything about the traffic, I reach for my phone, scanning my playlists—*Greatest Opera Arias*, *Rock en Español Radio*, the *Tropical Boleros* mix I keep on tap for Abuela. I hit play on *This Is Billie Holiday*, and the nostalgic notes of "I'll Be Seeing You" pour into the cabin. At the sound, my shoulders sink lower into my leather seat. I'm exhausted, yet my heart makes room for memories of Holiday's voice pouring out of Papi's office on a sunny Sunday afternoon, mixing with the mouthwatering aroma of Mami's sofrito as she prepared a big family dinner—back when we were all happy. Or at least I thought we were.

The beeping noise of the tire pressure gauge brings me back to the present. A dashboard warning illuminates, but it's not until Eli asks me to pull over that I register it's a flat tire.

I veer onto the shoulder and stop. Eli props his elbow over the center console to inspect the dashboard. "How many lights do you have on?" he asks, leaning so far into my seat that his shoulder brushes my arm. The hard sensation of his forearm muscle lingering over my skin sends a ripple of warmth flowing through my whole body—I'm too tired to fight it or push it away. "When was the last time you got an oil change?"

"I've been busy," I say, my tone prickly. "Our little project is a bit of a time suck, in case you haven't noticed."

He shakes his head and mutters something under his breath. "Pop the trunk," he says, opening his door and stepping outside.

"What are you doing?" I ask.

"Changing your tire and then taking you to get an oil change." He shuts the door and walks to the back of my SUV. A wall of toxic fumes and burnt rubber punches me in the face the moment I step out of the car. I follow Eli, unnerved by the asphalt hellhole that is the connector.

Eli opens the trunk and removes the cover for the underside compartment. He takes out the spare tire, a black box marked by a bright red triangle, and other metal tools I didn't know lived there.

"You don't have to do this," I say, searching on my phone for my car's roadside assistance app. "I'll call for help."

"It'll take those guys an hour to get here. Maybe more with this traffic."

I glance back at the highway, where thousands of vehicles are crammed bumper-to-bumper, all because some engineer, in their infinite wisdom, decided the solution to this city's traffic nightmare was merging two highways into a twelve-lane sprawl.

Eli takes off his new sweater and shirt, stripping down to a white undershirt. His undershirt rises slightly, offering me a glimpse of the very toned torso underneath. *San Antonio, what are you doing to me?* Is this who I've become? A single, almost thirty, unemployed disaster, leering at an unpredictable (albeit smoking hot) man on the side of the highway?

I step back as he effortlessly rolls the spare to the flat side of the car. "It'll take me ten minutes."

"Wait," I say with so much urgency that he stops cold. "It's my car." I take off my brand-new jacket and my watch, then pull my hair up. "I should be able to do this."

Eli watches me with that sardonic amusement he seems to save only for me. I can't tell whether he finds me silly or just plain insufferable—maybe both. I'm going for badass feminist, as in, got-it-together gal who can change a tire in heels and doesn't need a man's help. And yeah, maybe I need to prove to myself that I don't need his help.

I got this.

"Okay," he says, passing me the black box, which admittedly weighs a ton. "Have at it."

He leans the spare against the side of the SUV and steps back. I squat next to the flat, assessing the situation and trying my hardest to remember Papi's tire-changing lesson on the day I got my learner's permit fourteen years ago. In theory, I know I have to use a jack to lift the car, unfasten the nut bolts, swap the tire, replace the nuts, then bring the car down again.

I open the black box and study its contents—a jack and something that looks like a drill? I pull out my phone and search "how to change a flat tire" on YouTube. I add "on the side of the highway" for good measure. The options seem endless. Dozens of men explain the exact same thing in as many different ways.

I sense Eli standing quietly behind me, watching over my shoulder.

"You've got a fancy electric jack," he says after I've hit stop and play for the fourth or fifth time. "The ones in the videos are all manual."

"Thanks," I mutter, opening the electric jack's instructions to page one.

Behind me, Eli exhales—hard. I peer over my shoulder and find him staring down at me, one arm crossed over his abs, the other pulling at his face, wrapped tightly around his jaw.

"You can go wait inside the car if you want," I say coolly. "I'm not in a hurry."

"God, you're stubborn," he says, shaking his head.

"Not the first time I've heard that one," I grumble, then more loudly, "I prefer strong-willed." I leaf through the manual, trying in vain to speed-read the contents, refusing to call it quits on a matter of principle. "Maybe even endearingly so."

This makes him snort. "Well, I hope you're willing to die out here," he observes. "'Cause any minute now, we may get crushed against that concrete wall." He nods toward the cement barricades lining the emergency lane. "Not to mention, you're about to be doing this in the dark."

I ignore the commentary, because no, I don't have a death wish, or a flashlight for that matter—other than the one on the phone I'm currently using to translate the lingo in this manual. And yes, I'll admit that maybe it is dangerous to be out here in the dark.

Eli crouches down next to me so that we're at eye level. "Luisa," he says, but I'm only half listening.

"Uh-huh," I respond, my attention completely absorbed by this stupid manual, which I'm convinced was written by a German aeronautical engineer. Apparently, I need to block the tires in the front before lifting, but with what?

Eli places his warm hand on my arm. "Luisa," he repeats. The touch startles me. I gaze up to meet his eyes, staring back at me. "Let me do this for you." The kindness in his voice momentarily disarms me. "You've spent weeks washing my hair, buying me new clothes—"

"That was part of the agreement," I interject, my tone businesslike, transactional, eager to put some distance between us. "We made a deal. Let's just agree we're both in this for our own purposes." I pull away and, instantly, a burning sensation pricks at my skin in the spot where his hand touched my arm. "I don't need you to pretend to care about me or my problems. Okay?"

"Jesus Christ, Luisa," he cries out in frustration, jumping to his feet. "We're standing on the side of the damn connector in rush hour. Let me help you." Then, more softly, "I want to help you."

He leans down, then slowly extends his hand for the manual I'm grasping. The whizzing and whooshing of the highway grow faint as his gaze holds mine. He doesn't take the booklet away. He waits instead for me to offer it. A beat of stillness passes between us, in which I remind myself that not everyone is my dad.

Not everyone fails to keep their promises.

Finally, I sigh and pass the manual to him. "Okay," I say, standing to face him, then stepping back. "Thanks."

"Anytime." He nods but doesn't smile. It's his earnest expression, the one he uses on the rare occasion that he's not deflecting or being sarcastic. It's the same sincere expression that makes me want to trust him, in spite of what I know to be true. "Let me—" he says, taking my hand in his. The fight drains off me as I let him hold me, watching as he carefully cleans the grease off my fingers.

He slowly rubs into my palm with his thumb, standing so close that I can smell the sweet musk of his cologne, the tea tree oil essence in his shampoo. My legs weaken beneath me at the warmth of his scent, the gentleness of his touch, at the proximity of his solid form, the firm contour of his body. For a fleeting moment, I allow myself to imagine what it would feel like to sink into his chest, to close my eyes and rest against his bare skin, to—for just this once—let myself go.

After all the grease is wiped clean, he slowly releases my hand. We stand still for a few seconds, neither of us certain of what to say or do next, both aware that we can't stay like this for long.

Eli clears his throat and passes me the rag he's been holding. "I'll get us on the road in no time," he says, bending to position the jack under the SUV, then presses a button. Within seconds, the tire is hovering a few inches from the ground.

"I'm sorry if I've been . . ." I shrug, struggling to find the right thing to say. "If I've been unkind to you." Holly's admonishment from a few days ago echoes in my mind. "I know it's not an excuse, but I have a lot riding on this mad scheme." I shake my head. I can't seem to stop myself as I confess, "I lost my job because of the Castillos' story—because of Griggs. I had to move back home with my mom, which is utterly humiliating on so many levels. And it may be all for nothing." I stare down the infernal highway, letting out the breath I've been holding. "The Castillos may lose everything in the end." Eli stops what he's doing, turning his head to study my expression. I step closer, meeting his eyes. "And if I'm being totally honest," I continue, "it scares the shit out of me to put our collective fate in the hands of someone who runs hustles for a living." My voice goes quiet as I admit, "I'm not good at trusting people." So quiet that I wonder if he even heard me.

He appraises me thoughtfully, a crease forming between his thick eyebrows. After a beat, he nods. "No need to apologize," he says, turning back to the tire, huffing through the words as he forces the nuts loose. "Most people do terrible things with your trust."

I watch him, wondering: How did he come about this hard-earned wisdom? Who let him down?

It takes him exactly ten minutes to change the tire, after which he insists on taking me to a quick lube shop where a friend owes him a favor.

I press the gas and ease back onto the highway. Then I hit play on the blues music station, where a Nina Simone track pops up. I ease back into the seat, anticipating the mellow effect of her husky voice, the soothing power of her melodies, but as the first notes of "Mississippi Goddam" stream into the SUV's cabin, I can't help but burst out laughing. Next to me, Eli chuckles to himself, his face breaking into the widest of grins.

He turns up the volume, our hands tapping, heads bobbing to the buoyant piano vamp and the incongruous cabaret beat framing the lyrics of these incendiary blues. This legendary song is Simone's soulful cry against acts of violence and the oppression of Black communities in the segregated South. And as I think of the Castillos and every injustice still brutalizing our communities, my own "Mississippi Goddam" erupts from somewhere deep inside me. Eli joins the revelry until we're practically screaming "Do it slow!" at the top of our lungs. I'm bent over the steering wheel, roaring hard. Eli nails a final "Mississippi Goddam" in that flowery Mississippi accent he's been practicing all day.

"Goddam, that was good," I bellow, punching him teasingly on the arm.

He laughs—a genuine laugh. When the song ends, the space between us feels lighter. My shoulders unwind against the snug backrest and my breathing calms.

"That was good," he agrees, still chuckling as he lowers the volume. "We sound good together."

For some godforsaken reason my mind attaches itself to the pronoun "we," followed by the adverb "together." The unexpected combination of the two sends my face into an all-out blush, mainly because he's right. We do sound good together.

And maybe, even more than that, we make a good team. Over the time we've spent together, I've confirmed what I already knew on some level: Eli is bright and resourceful. He's internalized our insane scheme and built on our ideas. And along the way, he's also asserted himself, pushing back when he thinks something's not right. It's certainly been annoying at times, but if I'm honest, the man is slowly earning my respect.

If I weren't so worried about staying fair-minded, I might admit that I like him.

I clear my throat, scrambling to find a dark mental closet where I can shove my thoughts, reminding myself how little I know about this man and the reasons he chose to take this job.

I tap on the screen of my phone until I find a different song—something that doesn't feel so intimate. In the end, I just turn the radio off, and we fade into a more comfortable silence than before.

"So, what's your deal?" I ask a few minutes later.

"What do you mean, what's my deal?" He chuckles to himself, amused by the question.

"I don't know." I shrug. "We've been spending all this time preparing for this thing, but we know nothing about you."

"Trust me," he says, "you know plenty."

"Why did you move so much as a kid?" I ask instead. The question has been nagging me all week, poking at the raw corners of my mind.

Eli stares out the window, his expression quickly shifting from carefree to brooding. I keep my eyes focused on the road, both hands on the steering wheel, giving him space.

"You can only run so many hustles in one place before you have to skip town," he finally says.

Not exactly what I was expecting to hear. Was Eli running hustles as a kid? And if so, where the hell were his parents?

"What do you mean?" I ask, slowing down slightly, not quite ready to arrive at our destination.

He sighs, drumming the tips of his fingers against the side panel of the door. "You're right not to trust people," he says, turning to face me. "The world is full of selfish men, capable of fleecing even their own kids." His voice sours.

I know there's a story there, but I also know that I'd be crossing an invisible line if I tried to fish for details. I can sense the anger underlying his words, the resentment in his tone. I'm reminded of yet another reason that I was good at my job—trust must be earned, not demanded.

After a long, silent stretch, we finally exit the highway, then take a rural road in the direction of the lube shop.

"I'm not keen to dredge up any childhood memories of Mississippi," Eli suddenly says, his voice low and serious, "but I'll try. I'll do my best to pull this off." The shop comes into view ahead of us. "For all of us."

I turn into the parking lot, then slide the SUV into park. "Eli," I say, shifting to face him. "Why are you doing this, really?"

He pauses, glances back at me with that oh-so-fake smile, and says, "Can't you tell? I'm a hustler with a heart of gold."

And, when he says this, his Mississippi accent is so spot-on that I can't help but smile back.

CHAPTER 18

Holly

I enter the Ivy Room to find Eli, alone, perusing the display menu. With just one glance at our "Tripp," my spirits rise. We've come so far in such a short time. Eli has memorized every detail of Tripp's backstory, he's nailed the clean-cut frat boy haircut and shave, and he looks fabulous in the business-casual clothes I ordered last week: crisp slacks and a blue-gray sport coat with subtle overplaid and a butterfly finish.

After squeezing in three more arduous sessions in the language lab, Eli suddenly broke through the accent. My hunch is that Eli and Luisa's incident on the side of the highway fixed more than a flat tire. She blushed furiously when I suggested that her moment of kindness did the trick, then quickly redirected the conversation to my upcoming date with Professor Hugh Pridmore.

At the end of the night, as Hugh and I exchanged numbers, I did manage to sneak a quick two-fingered touch, and that jacket was just as soft as I'd imagined. Since then, I've been checking my phone constantly, hoping for texts from Hugh and daydreaming about being close to him again.

Thankfully, I didn't have to wait long for the first text. Hugh followed up first thing the next day:

> Woke up to blue skies
> this morning and thought
> of our surprise encounter.

Reading his text brought me right back to that strange sensation I had, my entire body on high alert, sitting so close to Hugh while Nikki belted out "Blue Skies."

ME

Really fun to see you there and yeah its really a beautiful day

HUGH

Is springtime in atlanta always this lovely?

ME

As long as you can see through the pollen

HUGH

I quite like the pollen. Gives everything it lands on a lovely chartreuse tint.

ME

You may be the only person in the world who finds pollen lovely

HUGH

Me and the bees! Dreading my return to dreary london.

I was deep in concentration, trying to come up with some pithy response about the weather in England, when his next text came through, saving me from feeble attempts to appear clever.

HUGH

At least i have our Monday date to look forward to when I'm back. Dinner first?

ME

Perfect

So we're going on a real date—dinner and the Switchyards jam—when he gets back in a couple of weeks. Exactly fourteen days from today, but who's counting? I can't get all swoony now, there's work to do: three phases down, one to go. It's time to commence with Operation *My Fair Lady*—the etiquette lesson.

Luisa and I decided to bring Eli to a private dining room at the club for the fourth, and hopefully final, stage of our preparations. We thought that conducting the etiquette lesson here would give him a chance to become familiar with the club and seem at ease in this type of environment, where he's supposedly spent a lot of time.

"Didn't you tell me that my most important run-in with these guys was gonna be over wings and beer in a locker room?" Eli asks, a puzzled look on his face.

"Not exactly a locker room," I say. "The Men's Grill, adjacent to the locker room," I explain, gesturing down the maroon-carpeted hall. "It's at the other end of the building."

"Well, as far as I can tell, there's nothing locker-room-adjacent about this place," Eli replies, "or the weird menu."

"Which is why we're here," I reply cheerfully. "So you can learn the ins and outs of table setting and dining etiquette, while also practicing that lovely new Mississippi accent."

Justine breezes through the room, takes a hard look at me, and then pastes a disingenuous smile across her face. As I expected, she bit her tongue when I asked her to come in today. I explained Eli/Tripp would be spending time at the club as the guest of a member, and since he's a fellow Mississippian, I offered to help him feel less nervous about the whole thing. She knows I'm full of shit, but she also knows not to ask questions, *God bless her.*

The club is closed on Mondays, so no one's here except for Byron and Justine, whom I convinced to serve as our sommelier and waitress, respectively, and Irma, who never turns down an opportunity to play in the kitchen.

I point to the framed page. "Just think of the prix fixe menu as a cheat sheet," I tell Eli. "You pick one item from each category, which helps you understand the structure of rich-people dining, in case Griggs invites you out for dinner to seal the deal."

"Well, alll riiight," he says, still inspecting the menu while also beautifully capturing the slow and lilting musicality of his new accent. "But there doooon't appeeear to be any priiices," he says.

"It's a set price," I reply, pointing to the small print. "That's what 'prix fixe' means."

"One hundred and twenty-five dollars a person?" Eli blurts out, the lilting accent gone.

"Not including cocktails and wine," I add. "Absurd, I know."

"That's *got'dam* highway robbery," he exclaims, sliding back into his country twang.

Anxiety rises in my chest as I take in his last lingering slip—the North Georgia expression Eli can't seem to drop: *got'dam*. I just hope the new accent will stick around long enough for us to get our information on Griggs and get out.

As if on cue, Justine returns. "May I bring you a cocktail while you wait?"

This, of course, is precisely the trick question that I told Justine to start with. I've already instructed Tripp that under no circumstances will he order a cocktail. He will order bourbon, neat. This does not mean a shot of Wild Turkey, as he initially assumed. It means he will make his way down a priority-ordered list of Kentucky bourbons, beginning with Blanton's—which feels very *Tripp Bedford* to me, but can be hard to find. If he wants to mix it up, he can order Widow Jane from a hipster distillery in Brooklyn, but he'll need to joke that it doesn't really count as bourbon, since it's from above the Mason-Dixon Line. Excellent opportunity to demonstrate that he's a Bubba at heart.

Eli sails through his first test smoothly, and when Justine returns with our drinks, he even remembers to sip on (not shoot!) his Blanton's, as we peruse the menu together. Luisa arrives, late and stressed, as tends to be the case for her, but looking fabulous in a fire-engine-red dress with matching lipstick.

"God, I could use a drink," Luisa mutters over an anxious breath. "Finally made some progress on my forensic audit side project." Her voice drops as she adds, "A third of the nonprofits Griggs's family foundation gives money to, don't actually exist."

"Are you sure?" I ask, disbelieving. "How is he getting away with that?"

"Easy—" she scoffs. "You move the money enough times, it becomes untraceable. And Jim Wade is probably making sure nothing is audited." She pulls up a very complex-looking spreadsheet on her phone. "I scoured their tax records. The money trail leads straight to that offshore bank in Panama."

"Is that enough to take Griggs down?" I ask, hopeful. Luisa shakes her head.

"I'll get you what you need," Eli assures her, resting his hand on her shoulder and giving her a gentle squeeze.

To my surprise, Luisa doesn't recoil from the touch. *Interesting.*

"My source at the DA's office says we'll need the bank statements," she adds, leaning into Eli's hand. "Or a way to track the money back to Griggs's development."

Justine interrupts, then discreetly ushers us to our table. We take our seats, and she heads back to the kitchen. Luisa and Eli bicker over whether he should have pulled out her chair (which he did), or stood until the women were seated (which Luisa insists he should have done).

"I have news!" I clap my hands together, vying for their attention. "I found the perfect place for our trial run." They stop their banter to look at me, their expressions expectant. "This morning, as I was dragging my recycling bin to the corner—"

"Jesus. What's the headline, Holly?" Luisa cuts in.

"My neighbor Aunt Edna rushed over," I continue, ignoring her, "calling out that she was *just desperate* for someone to drive her to Madison next weekend for the bridge ladies' event of the season." I pause for effect, thrilled that the universe must find our cause just, because it had dropped the perfect invitation into our laps. "Judy Swanson's Annual Kentucky Derby Party," I exclaim.

"Won't there be Atlanta people there?" Luisa asks, unconvinced.

"The Swansons are members of the club," I explain, "but they split time between Atlanta and Madison. They don't run in the same circles as Griggs."

"Do I need to wear one of those hats?" Eli asks derisively.

"We all will," I respond effusively, much to Luisa's dismay. "It's going to be perfect!"

Luisa and Eli launch into a debate, and I excuse myself to head into the kitchen. I want to make sure Irma has found all the ingredients I ordered and then hid in the back of the walk-in.

"I hope you know what you're doing," Justine fires off as I come into the kitchen. "'Cuz that *got'dam* boy ain't from Mississippi."

Leave it to Justine to nail our one lingering weakness.

"I don't know where he's from," Irma says, her voice swoony, "but I know he's gooooorgeous." She turns to me. "When was he born? I bet he's a Libra rising."

"I have no idea, Irma." I laugh. "I don't have a habit of asking people exactly what time of day they were born."

"You'd need to know the location, too," she says in a tone that suggests I'd seriously consider grilling a recent acquaintance on these minuscule details. "But you don't even need to ask your friend Luisa. I'm sure she's triple Aries." She waves her hand as if to stoke a flame. "That one's pure fire sign."

"And totally hot for the not-from-Mississippi kid," Justine adds.

"Wait, what?" I ask, suddenly anxious. Eli and Luisa? That would complicate things.

"Don't give her a hard time, ladies," Byron coos, sidling up beside me and wrapping an arm around my shoulder. "Our little Holly Berry can be a bit naive when it comes to—"

"Blatant sexual attraction," Justine snorts.

"I am not naive!" I retort. "Plus, you're wrong. Luisa's not, like, into him. It's a professional relationship." Justine raises her eyebrows but doesn't push back.

Anxious to avoid this conversation, I grab Irma by the elbow and drag her into the walk-in, pointing out the stash of extra ingredients. Then I make my way back to the Ivy Room, studiously avoiding Byron and Justine.

I return to my seat, just in time to hear Luisa asking Eli, "All right, *My Fair Guy*, are you a squeamish eater?"

"I'm not a squeamish *anything*," Eli responds, judiciously avoiding the nickname she's assigned him for Phase Four. "Why?" he asks.

"I'd say your best bet is to just dive in and order," she replies. "That's the only surefire way to avoid asking a very dumb question."

"Like, what the fuck is preserved yuzu?" Eli asks, pointing at an item on the menu. "And aren't truffles those little round chocolate balls? Seems weird to serve with tuna fish."

"Which is why you'll not ask any questions," Luisa says, laughing despite herself. "Confidently order your starter and main course, avoid words you can't pronounce, and be sure to let any women at the table order first."

"And speaking of women," I jump in, "try not to order anything too feminine."

"Feminine," Eli repeats slowly, staring down at the menu. "And how might a gentleman know if a food is, uh, *feminine*?"

"A good rule of thumb," I instruct, "is to stay away from anything that seems healthy, like something you might eat on a diet."

"So, meat and potatoes," he says in a lovely slow cadence. "Well, thaaat I caaan do." He winks at Luisa.

Seeing no sign of Justine or Byron, I start to worry that some disaster may be unfolding back there. *Where is everyone?*

"Can we get some of those crackers?" Luisa asks, looking toward the kitchen longingly.

"You mean the saltines?" I ask, incredulous. "Do people really like those?"

"They're, like, the only reason I came." Luisa smirks.

I sigh and excuse myself from the table again, to rustle up some saltines. Heading through the door, I hear her call out, "Make sure they're warm, please."

At least she asked nicely.

"What's going on back here?" I ask, bursting into the kitchen to find the three of them huddled close. "We need some warm crackers out there. Luisa's getting hangry."

"Sorry, sweetheart," Irma says. "We got distracted by juicy gossip."

"Did you hear Dennis is retiring?" Byron asks.

Dennis is the club's general manager—the sixth since I arrived at Dogwood Hills, and among the best of them. He's not the brightest bulb on the circuit, if I'm being honest, but he's reliable, and a good enough boss to know when to step aside and let those of us who've been around for longer make and execute the plans—as long as they don't include such earth-shattering propositions as replacing mimeographed locker lease forms with online documents. That sort of thing simply wouldn't fly.

I shudder, recalling a particularly foreboding moment last spring when, entering my shoebox office, I found Griggs already standing inside the doorway, demanding to lease a second locker in the men's locker room. Though I've never been in there, Byron tells me the lockers are enormous—nearly the size of my office. I was so busy wondering how many pairs of golf shoes that man must have that I didn't notice until it was too late: He had positioned himself so that I'd be forced to brush against him to approach my desk, where I keep the stack of mimeographed lease forms. Seriously, the forms are in triplicate—the kind you have to press hard on with a ballpoint pen. And then I file them in an actual folder, in an old-school metal file cabinet. Another part of the club's timeless charm, I suppose. But also a pain in the ass for staff. I had to make the split-second decision as to whether I'd let my tits or my thigh brush against his body. I went with thigh. Looking back, I should have known where all this was going.

"Dennis is headed out to pasture," Justine says, "which means he's about to move to Carrolton and join a bowling league, or maybe take a bus tour of America's national parks, or something equally dull—"

"Don't be cruel, Justine," Irma interjects.

"Well, you're the one who called him mediocre the other day," Justine retorts.

"I said trustworthy and reliable," Irma replies, her voice rising. "He's a classic Taurus."

I know these two all too well, and their play-fighting banter could go on for days. Before we know it, Irma will be explaining the planets in Dennis's first house or his moon or something equally incomprehensible, and Justine will be calling bullshit on her astrological insights.

"You should apply for the GM position." Justine turns to me with sudden clarity, all hint of banter gone. I look to Irma and then at Byron, and they both nod vigorously in unison.

Have these people lost their minds? There's no way I'm qualified to be the general manager of this club. I wonder for a moment how Luisa would respond if she were in my situation. If her three closest friends were to tell her she had the chops to be their boss, she'd say, *Hell yeah, I do. Thanks for finally noticing.*

But I'm not Luisa. (And, come to think of it, I'm not sure Luisa actually has three friends.) So instead, I shake my head and do what I do best: get back to the task at hand.

"Focus, people," I announce. "We have a meal to serve." They all stand at attention, and Byron even gives a little salute.

It doesn't matter what I want, anyway. Before I can even consider seeking a promotion, I have one enormous obstacle to deal with: Griggs Caldecott Johnson III. That man stands firmly between me, my son, and our future, and we're way past the days when I could awkwardly slip by him. Our Tripp is the only person with any chance of knocking him down.

CHAPTER 19

Luisa

On the first Saturday in May, Tripp makes his debut into old-money, genteel Southern society.

The day began early, when Eli and I met Holly and Aunt Edna at the old dame's swanky Midtown address. The instant Aunt Edna's Fleetwood came into view, Eli turned into a starry-eyed schoolboy with a crush. Aunt Edna tossed him the keys, then gingerly slid into the passenger seat, where she spent the hour-long drive chattering and flirting, Holly and I practically forgotten in the back seat. Needless to say, Aunt Edna is smitten with our Tripp.

Now, Eli veers the Cadillac off Madison's main street, then glides into the driveway of a stunning Greek Revival that covers an entire city block. We learn from Aunt Edna that her bridge partner, Judy Swanson, married one of Georgia's Cotton Kings, who then bought her a "house on a quiet little street" in Madison, a town south of Atlanta that was spared by General Sherman's troops. Two Southern red oaks, aptly nicknamed "The Generals," welcome us to the estate. I guess this is what some would call Antebellum "charm."

Eli parks the Fleetwood, and we pour into a magnificent azalea garden in full bloom. Aunt Edna's friends quickly whisk her away, several dozen diamonds sparkling in her wake. I'm convinced the oversize floral brooch pinned to her hat is worth the equivalent of a developing country's GDP.

"Okay, this is it," Holly whispers, her voice shaky with nerves. "We can do this." She's wearing a peach nightmare of a ruffled dress, and half her face is shaded by a giant hat, with bird feathers in various shapes and lengths shooting into the sky like the plumage of a cockatoo. She's really leaning into her Southern rich girl heritage today.

"Don't talk unless you have to." Holly brushes away a microscopic speck of lint from Eli's shoulder. "And if you do, stick to the weather or sports. Safe topics. Got it?"

Eli nods, opening and closing his mouth, barely swallowing a "Yes, ma'am" that would've likely launched Holly into another lecture about the expression's proper use. I've gotten so used to native Southerners *sir*ing and *ma'am*ing, that it never occurred to me there was a whole rule book to follow.

Eli nods, sliding an index finger inside his collar, then tugging at the shirt. "This bow tie is strangling me," he protests. To be fair, it's unseasonably hot for May—even in the South. I'm quickly regretting my choice to wear a tulle "statement skirt." Equally regretful is the stupid fascinator that keeps digging into my scalp.

"I look ridiculous"—Eli yanks at the carnivalesque fabric of his shorts and takes off his boater hat—"like a circus act." He turns to me for support, and I stifle a laugh.

"Don't look at me," I say. "I'm practically wearing a tutu."

"You look perfect," he says, his tone straightforward. "You have great legs."

I struggle to think of something funny to deflect his compliment, but I'm too agitated by the unpredictable heart sputter that comes when his eyes trail up from my legs, hungrily roaming over my body. My mind goes blank. I pat at the pleats of my skirt, trying to contain the warmth spreading over my cheeks, deeply annoyed by the effect that penetrating gaze has on every one of my limbs.

"I, on the other hand," Eli continues, "should not be showing this much skin. These shorts are too damn short."

Our Tripp is dressed in what Holly described as "derby chic"—blue blazer, button-down oxford, madras bow tie, loafers, and a matching brown belt. Holly completed the look with a pair of red-and-white striped shorts—currently the bane of Eli's existence. They would be full-on hilarious if it weren't for the very masculine, very athletic legs they're barely concealing. Like the long beard that was hiding his chiseled face, Eli's ill-fitting jeans were concealing a pair of well-defined thighs over rock-hard calves. And yeah, I may have ogled a little when he arrived this morning.

"You look festive," I say cheerfully.

"Festive?" he asks, giving me a death stare from under his new Ray-Bans.

"Festive," Holly repeats. "And if you're going to complain, please do it with that charming Mississippi accent."

"Pee-can whai-ne tastes deh-vai-ne," he practices earnestly.

"Pee-can whai-ne tastes like pee-can pah-ie," Holly joins in, making us all laugh.

Eli pushes his sunglasses up the bridge of his nose and impishly grins, fully transforming into Tripp before our eyes.

"After you, Miss Simmons," he says, gesturing for Holly to lead the way. He then turns to me and crooks his elbow. "May I?" he asks, and I loop my arm in his.

Tripp Bedford has arrived.

We follow the lively sounds of a zydeco band into the back garden, where dozens of people are decked in full derby regalia. They eat and drink, mill around in small groups, crowd around the Churchill Downs live stream, and play croquet on the lawn.

Every inch of this space has been transformed into an equestrian-themed bacchanalia. Red roses are gathered into wreaths, garlands and vases intersperse with vintage horseshoe and jockey decor.

About a dozen round tables have been arranged on the stone patio that's spread under an ancient oak. An extravagant buffet sparkles with silver—ornate trays, serving spoons, forks, and delicate tongs. The menu is written in tight script on a betting chalkboard: hot browns, fried chicken, pickled shrimp, burgoo, deviled eggs, hush puppies, and for the more health conscious, a smattering of salads. The equally impressive dessert table boasts a towering chocolate fountain surrounded by tiers of derby pie, hummingbird cake, bourbon balls, and banana pudding. The whole thing is wildly over-the-top.

A server comes around with a tray of the party's signature mint juleps, poured into what Holly explains are traditional "pewter"—not silver!—cups. Each is individually monogrammed with Judy Swanson's initials—because, why not? I take my first sip, praying a little bourbon will help me relax. Just as Holly told us to expect, there are tons of Southern country club types, but only a few are from Atlanta. And just as I suspected, it's a mostly white crowd, except for a few outliers—myself included—and the waitstaff, which is mostly Black and Latine.

Tripp downs his mint julep like he's gulping water. "Want another?" he asks me, searching for the bar, which seems to be tucked inside a remodeled carriage house. The triple garage doors are open to show off the custom mahogany bar and large TV screen.

"Easy there, tiger," I say, elbowing him slightly. "We just got here."

"May I remind you, you are not here to get wasted," Holly whisper-yells.

"It's hot," Tripp grumbles. Then, taking in Holly's sour expression, he goes all-out Mississippi: "Good Lord, it's hotter than a two-dollar pistol!" And with that, he leaves to get himself another drink.

Holly exhales in one long, hard breath. She nods at a few passing guests, smiling through clenched teeth. Tripp orders a drink, then laughs about something with the bartender and a tall blond wearing a stylish, body-hugging tube dress and wide-brim hat embellished with a giant magnolia. She paws at the breast of his blazer, laughing as she leans into him.

My hand grips my cup a little tighter. Next to me, I sense Holly cringing. "Oh Lord," she mutters. "That's Virginia Thacker. Judge Thacker's granddaughter. Why is she here? And why in God's name is he flirting with her?"

"Looks like Virginia is flirting with *him*," I mutter.

We watch as she laughs, head tossed back, at whatever idiotic thing Tripp is saying.

"What the . . ." Holly trails off as Virginia slips her arm through Tripp's, just where mine was minutes ago.

"Well, you told him to charm everyone," I say, throwing back my drink until the cup is empty. "Technically, he's following *your* instructions." Inexplicably, I'm rattled by the whole scene.

I'm a feminist, for fuck's sake. What do I care if some hot, legs-for-days blond is flirting with the con man we've hired to deceive an entire club on our behalf? It's not like Tripp, or Eli, or whatever his name is, owes me anything. It's not like we set boundaries around his interactions with other women. But, as absurd and naive as it sounds, it didn't occur to me—until right now—that Tripp would draw the attention of this world's very young, very rich, very attractive women.

I need another drink. And these dainty pewter cups ain't gonna cut it.

"Holly, darling!" Aunt Edna calls out, beckoning us from the plush sofa on the back porch, where the Southern Grande Dames appear to have gathered. She introduces us to our hostess, Judy Swanson, dressed in a flowery puff-sleeved muumuu and wearing so many glinting stones that she could partner with Aunt Edna to open a jewelry store. I know Holly keeps saying people in this world don't show off their wealth, but let's be honest—these ladies love their baubles.

Holly and I sit, sharing a wicker settee. Tripp joins us, Virginia dangling from his arm like a wet towel. My spine stiffens and the low-level throbbing in my head intensifies. The headband of my fascinator is actively digging holes into the sides of my scalp.

"And this . . ." Holly stutters, blinking a few times, "this is . . ."

Tripp and I watch in disbelief as Holly stammers. Did she just forget his name?

"Tripp Bedford," Tripp smoothly interjects, reaching out his hand. "How do you do?"

"Of the Mississippi Bedfords?" Judy Swanson asks as a server (finally) refills our cups.

"Why, yes, ma'am. Theodore Reynolds Bedford III, at your service."

"Well, how do you do, young man?" Judy shakes Tripp's hand, her cheeks gleaming. Something tells me that she, too, has been enchanted by our creation. Beside me, Holly exhales in visible relief.

"He just moved to Atlanta," Aunt Edna offers. "I may have to take him under my wing for a bit." She winks at Tripp, and he responds with that irresistible smile.

I shift in my seat, uncomfortable. The last thing I want is to unwittingly bring a gullible old lady into our scheme.

"And I see you've met our Virginia," Judy says, gesturing for them to join us. They sit side by side on the sofa, way too close for comfort in this muggy heat. I set my feminist values aside for a moment, just long enough to imagine myself tearing that stupid magnolia hat right off her head.

"We're already old friends!" Virginia smiles, resting one hand on his bicep. Tripp plays along, laughing at her inanity. "Even our derby looks are color-coordinated."

They look made for each other—white, Southern, genteel. I can easily see them gracing the cover of a *Southern Living* magazine. Despite knowing better, I can't help but feel like a smudge in an otherwise perfect photograph.

"I saw him in those fabulous shorts standing by the bar," she recounts. "I said, 'I must know where you got those!'"

Tripp gestures dismissively. "These old things? Well, they *are* festive." He glances over at me from under his Ray-Bans. I offer him a tight, closed-lip smile.

"Carnivalesque," I exclaim abruptly, narrowing my gaze at him. "They remind me of that old Turkish proverb," I add, pointedly. "When a clown moves into a palace, he doesn't become a king. The palace becomes a circus."

Tripp smiles, quirking an eyebrow, seeming to grasp my full meaning. Holly elbows me in the side.

"Never heard the saying," Virginia says, drawing out the vocals so that "never" sounds like "nevahh." "But I like it." I guess she missed the backhanded insult I was throwing her way. "Anyway—" she says, turning to address Judy and Aunt Edna. "Tripp's a Rebel, just like my cousin Shuggs."

"Hotty Toddy, Gosh almighty," Tripp chants, much to Virginia's delight.

I glance anxiously at Holly, worried that Virginia is about to blow our cover. In a school with twenty thousand students, what are the odds that we've run into someone who knows the real Tripp?

"I can't wait for y'all to meet sometime," she gushes, squeezing Tripp's arm. "He's a senior, so smart. Can't believe my little Shuggy will be going off to med school in the fall."

Holly sighs, pressing into my forearm with her hand. The look in her eyes seems to say, *Little Shuggy is too young to know the real Tripp*. I shoot her back a mental response that clearly telegraphs, *You better make fucking sure Little Shuggy is not gonna turn up at the club.*

Holly nods in understanding before exclaiming in her best fake, cheerful voice, "Oh, that's so exciting! What are his plans for the big summer of freedom before the med-school grind?"

"Oh, you know," Virginia says dismissively. "Big Eurail tour with his Sigma Nu brothers, right up to the day he starts."

Thank goodness for European frat bro adventures. I should let out the breath I'm holding, but I'm too worked up to relax. One single person, in the wrong place at the wrong time, could undo all our hard work and derail our plans.

Blessedly, Virginia moves on. "Tripp joins us all the way from the *other* Madison, in Mississippi." She laughs at her own insipid joke. "Family's all from Greenwood, in the Delta."

"Greenwood?" Judy asks wistfully. "Oh, how I enjoy the Grand Boulevard. It's one of the crowning conservation efforts in the South, if you ask me." She stares at Tripp expectantly. For the briefest of moments, his smile falters, his eyebrow twitches. We covered the Grand Boulevard in a prep session, and the hundreds of oaks that form a cathedral over it.

"Those oaks are spectacular," I proffer, trying to jog his memory. But there's no need. Tripp skillfully spins away from Greenwood and the oaks.

"Unfortunately, I didn't get to enjoy it as much as I would've liked." His tone goes solemn, and the gathered women tilt forward, curious. "Our family suffered a tragic small plane crash back in oh-seven. My momma—God rest her soul—died in the accident."

Virginia may just cry. "You poor thing," she coos, moving her hand to cover the top of his bare thigh. Tripp's muscles tense under the touch, but he doesn't pull away. I'm so torn inside, I can barely sit still. Tripp's feigned vulnerability is so seductive that I honestly can't blame Virginia or anyone else for being charmed by it—part of me can't help but be proud of him. This is all confusing as hell.

"Daddy remarried and we moved to Madison. Those were lonely years, but what can you do? Eventually, trouble finds you." Virginia shakes her head in understanding. Holly silently nods, doing a much better job than me at keeping a straight face. "After Momma's death, I went a little off the rails, to be honest. But I'm back on the straight and narrow now." He offers his most beguiling grin, an expression assiduously crafted for maximum intrigue and allure. With one calculated smile, he's able to arouse equal parts hope and desire. It's a little too tempting, that grin of his.

"Oh, Trippy," Virginia cries out. *Trippy?* "You poor, poor thing." She presses herself to his side in a shameless side-boob rub. And that's when I remove my fascinator. Between the heat and the bourbon in the mint juleps, my head is pounding.

"But here I am, among new friends." He smiles again. "On this beautiful day for a horse race," Tripp says, then pauses to sip on his mint julep.

"We may have sun and fun today, but it rained all day yesterday," Aunt Edna observes, one hand wrapped around the top of her bejeweled cane. "That track will be one and a quarter miles of pure slop. Our champion must rise from the mud."

"Aunt Edna's father was a horse trainer," Holly explains. "She's something of a derby expert." I, too, have become "something of a derby expert" during the past week, combing the Kentucky Derby and Churchill Downs websites, watching documentaries and YouTube videos. My chest swelled with pride when I learned the world's best jockey school is in Puerto Rico.

"Are you a betting man, Tripp?" Aunt Edna asks, eyeing him curiously.

"Ma'am"—his left hand covers his heart and his body inches forward, shaking off Virginia's hand—"I'm not a man of many vices. But I thoroughly enjoy a friendly wager."

Tripp removes his sunglasses to reveal a foreboding glint in his eyes. A chill runs down my spine. I'm reminded of the pool shark we met at the Westlake biker bar, the one who fleeced a room full of frat guys.

"You want a little betting advice?" Aunt Edna asks, moving toward the edge of her seat. "Clean out everyone's pockets?"

"Go on," Tripp says, placing both feet on the floor, creeping closer to Aunt Edna.

I poke at Holly's side, urging her to jump in. To release Eli's predator instincts among these unsuspecting rich people would be a very bad idea.

"Tripp probably doesn't want to take money from all these folks he just met," Holly says, forcing a smile. "That wouldn't make the best first impression."

"Bah," Aunt Edna exclaims, waving her cane in the air. "Everyone's here to clean up."

"That's right," Judy chimes in, eagerly rubbing her hands together, making me question the real nature of their old ladies' bridge club. "Errol Dean is taking bets in the garage. Odds are on the chalkboard." She points to a list next to the TV, broadcasting the horse races. Twenty horse names appear in order of their program numbers. Next to each is their starting gate position, winning odds, and potential payout. "Just fill out your slip and pay up."

"My money is on the Queen's Curse," Aunt Edna loud-whispers to Tripp. "Are you with me?"

"Hogwash," Judy cries out. "The Queen's Curse is dead last. Odds are fifty to one. Seventeenth post position, the kiss of death."

"It's the most unlucky position at the starting gate," Holly adds. "That position has never produced a winner. Some people say it's cursed." Then, glaring at Tripp, she adds, "Which is why it's such a terrible idea to place a bet."

"Maybe it takes one curse to break another," Tripp replies breezily. "But fifty to one? Those are some mighty high odds."

Aunt Edna directs the top of her staff at Tripp, piercing him with her blue eyes as she declares, "She's a mudder. A mudlark, you understand?"

Tripp nods, watching her with rapt intensity. These two seem to be having a one-on-one conversation that none of us are invited into—not even poor Virginia.

"The Queen's Curse knows how to spin mud into gold," Aunt Edna says, her eyes going a little wild. "Mark my words, young man, she will conquer the slop."

And then to our extreme dismay, Tripp cries out, "I'm in!"

Two hours later—mostly thanks to Virginia's extraordinary gossip prowess—news of Tripp, his mother's tragic death, Bedford Hall, and The Colonel has swept through the hearts of every last one of the partygoers like a wildfire consuming grassland. Incidentally, several of the women have been plying him with drinks, in spite of our best efforts to take control.

Seen from a pragmatic point of view, I should be delighted that Tripp's foray into this world has been so unexpectedly effortless. Today, after all, has brought us a step closer to completing our mission. But as we head inside the coach house for the main derby event, betting slips in hand, I'm only growing more tense and restless.

Virginia takes Tripp by the arm, pulling him to the front, where they catch up with Aunt Edna to huddle in a mass in front of the giant TV screen. I grab Holly's arm and force our way to the front beside them. Tripp went all in with Aunt Edna on the Queen's Curse, blatantly ignoring our repeated warnings.

The crowd holds a collective breath as the horses are loaded into position and a camera pulls back to pan over the starting line. More people squeeze into the garage, pushing us even closer together, until I'm standing in front of Tripp, my back pressed flat against him, so close that I can sense his almost feverish body heat through the thin fabric of his shirt. It's like a sauna in here. A bead of sweat travels down my neck and disappears into my bra. This race can't be over fast enough.

I peer up, ready to apologize for the tight space intrusion, but I find him staring down at me, a soft closed-mouth smile on his lips. In that instant, Tripp disappears. The crowd around us and all the chaos seem to fade. I'm staring back into Eli's gray eyes, so much older than his years, wondering what's crossing that clever mind of his. Why is he here, doing all this? Is it just about the money for him? Or does he actually care about our mission? About me?

I wish I could ask him—and get an honest answer.

Then the starting bell rings and we're back at the center of the raucous crowd. "And they're off!" the race announcer calls out, to cheers and applause.

Everyone, it seems, has a horse in this race. There's pointing and yelling, all-out screaming and hollering as the twenty horses gallop around the muddy track. "Well behind the rest of them is the Queen's Curse," the announcer says.

Tripp pulls at his hair, yelling out at the screen, "Come on, Queeny, move your damn ass! Move your ass!"

Oh no. No. No. No. He's slipped out of that Mississippi lilt and into his full-on North Georgia twang. This can't be good. To my left I hear Holly through the commotion, muttering an "Oh God."

Oh God, indeed. These are the most stressful two minutes of my life.

The announcer is spitting horse's names and positions so fast, it's impossible to keep up.

Tripp is doing his own jockeying behind me, shouting at the TV with one first raised. "Eat that mud! Eat that mud!" He sounds like a full-on redneck.

To my—and Holly's—absolute shock, Aunt Edna joins him, falling into a Kentucky hillbilly holler. My jaw drops, nearly scratching the floor.

"Dig in there, Queenie," she yelps, waving her betting slip in the air. "Shoo, shoo, shoo! Bring it on home, girl!"

"Make it rain," Tripp yowls in unison with Aunt Edna.

"The Queen's Curse is exploding through the rail!" the voice on the TV shouts as the horses round a corner. The announcer is now tripping over his words. The man can't seem to speak fast enough to keep up with the action. "She's taking the lead as she comes down to the finish. A spectacular, spectacular, monumental upset at fifty to one!"

"Well, hot damn! Hot *diggity* damn!" I hear Eli shout as the announcer declares, "The Queen's Curse has won the Kentucky Derby."

I don't have to look at Holly to know it. "Hot diggity damn" is not going to fly.

But none of it matters. Virginia throws her arms over Tripp's shoulders and plants a pink-stained kiss on his lips. Tripp pulls back in surprise, his smile stiffening in mild shock.

Without warning, my heart sinks to my feet. Instinctively, I walk back, arms folded over myself, eager to put distance between us, eager to get my head on straight. In the process, I almost trip into a waiter carrying a tray of Kentucky mules. Eli searches for me over the horde, his apologetic gaze landing on my bewildered expression. I turn away fast, trudging my way out of the commotion, desperate for fresh air.

Why do I feel so wrecked by that kiss?

CHAPTER 20

Holly

Setting aside the unfortunate "hot diggity damn" outburst, Eli proved himself at the derby party. And so, despite my extreme jitters, the time has come to put our plan in motion. Our Tripp will make his society debut this evening at the Altamaha Country Club, Atlanta's second-most-exclusive private club. With its rolling lawns, pristine gardens, and string of beautiful small lakes, it's an enticing venue for large outdoor gatherings. Many Dogwood Hills members elect to hold their wedding receptions here, after a tasteful, intimate rehearsal dinner at the Dogwood Hills Club. I'm often called in to help ensure a smooth thematic transition between the two signature wedding events.

This long-standing connection offered me the perfect in. When I called Diana, the events manager at the Altamaha Club, offering to be "on the ground" for this evening's reception, she enthusiastically accepted the extra help, thereby proffering the perfect opportunity. My only official responsibility here is to stroll through the reception all evening, making sure that guests are enjoying themselves and potential crises are averted. Fortuitously, the "on the ground" staff wear headsets—allowing for my smooth, undetected communication with Luisa and Eli. They'll be the "plus-twos" of dear Aunt Edna, who enthusiastically scored invites for both of her new besties.

In the right tux, I knew our Tripp would blend right in. But we didn't plan on the bride and groom bucking Southern tradition and going for a seated dinner, and now we're scrambling to improvise at the last minute. Guests are already trickling in from the ceremony, and I'm staring up at a champagne tower, trying very hard not to freak out.

"Why couldn't they just stick with place cards?" Luisa asks me, anxiously surveying the hundreds of champagne glasses before us, searching for Griggs's name. She looks fantastic in a glitzy designer gown, her hair pulled into a sleek updo. She also looks *pissed.*

The grand reception is about to get underway, but in lieu of a printed seating chart, the couple has opted for a "Sip & Seat" display. Guests' names and their table numbers are displayed on stirrers inside crystal champagne flutes, officially throwing a Dom Pérignon–labeled grenade into our carefully laid plans.

"Don't even get me started," I say, wiping clean the table numbers written in delicate calligraphy on the surface of two acrylic stirrers. We're hastily playing a game of musical chairs in which Aunt Edna and Tripp will end up seated beside Griggs, with Luisa at the table directly behind them. "The bride is from California, and she clearly doesn't care much for Southern wedding traditions. The whole seated dinner thing is very unconventional," I huff, moving down to a new shelf, speed-reading names while Luisa keeps watch.

"The cocktail hour is almost over," Luisa warns.

I peer back across the lawn at the country club's massive French doors, where guests are busy enjoying copious amounts of alcohol and, in my humble opinion, a somewhat over-the-top buffet, complete with an ice sculpture raw bar. *We're a long way from Malibu, honey.* That's what I'd have told the sweet bride, had I been the one to help her plan this event.

"Found it!" I call out triumphantly, brandishing a champagne flute just as the guests start to stroll down the lawn, among them Griggs and Anna-Byrd, drinking and laughing as if they don't have a care in the world. Because, really . . . do they?

I see Tripp make his way across the lawn with the other guests, Virginia beside him. She is carrying one of the wedding's signature pineapple mule cocktails and has pulled off looking both Southern-wedding-appropriate and sexy in a silky, powder-pink dress with a V-neck plunge. Meanwhile, Tripp is casually sipping a bourbon on the rocks and somehow standing out in the very best way, wearing a most inconspicuous tux. Luisa's mom really is a miracle worker.

"What is she doing here?" Luisa grumbles.

"That girl is our golden ticket," I admonish, passing Luisa one of the champagne flutes.

"Or our undoing," she mutters, as if speaking to herself.

"You're at lucky table seven, by the way," I add.

Luisa takes the bubbly without even a nod of thanks, and I can't help noticing the wistful look in her eyes as she watches Virginia cling to Tripp. I guess Justine was onto something after all.

For the first time in a long time, I can relate. Every time my phone screen lights up with Hugh's name, my stomach fills with butterflies, like I'm some lovesick teenager. Just this morning, he sent a photo of a London street under gray skies, crowded with grimacing people, heads down, in a sea of black umbrellas.

Good morning! Did I happen to mention how dreary it is here? And they say this is the best season to visit London.

I rushed outside in my PJs, to my pollen-drenched car, and I used my finger to write in loopy cursive through the chartreuse dust: *Atlanta misses you!* I even dared to make the dot below the exclamation point a silly little heart before texting him the photo.

To my surprise, he replied with another photo: this one of him looking into the camera with sad puppy-dog eyes, his dark hair slick with rain and the collar of a trench coat turned up around his neck.

I dashed over to Joel and Peter's riotously blooming pink dogwood and, before I could lose my nerve, took a PJ selfie, grinning madly with the flowering tree and sun-drenched sky behind me. His simple response made my heart stutter.

Sigh. So lovely

I can't possibly know whether he meant the dogwood tree or me, but I'm pretty sure he meant both, at the very least.

It's been fun to see Hugh at this angle—still the Esteemed Professor Pridmore, but also just a normal guy who's a little bit goofy and sweet. There's something so real and honest about him, beneath all the big words and fancy titles. I think he's revealing a part of himself that most people fail to notice, behind the big-shot-professor mask—the part that once got a regrettable Mohawk and stole nerdy books; the part that hates rain and longs for sunshine, that can be so gloriously optimistic that he actually enjoys pollen season. He even texted *LOL* the other day, when I randomly sent him a baby ducks meme. That was a real shocker.

I keep itching to pull my phone from its perch inside my bra and stare at that photo of Hugh standing on a street corner in the drizzle, managing to look both very sexy and utterly pathetic. But I shake off the urge. Like the Dogwood Hills Country Club, this place has a "no cell phones" policy. And even if I could use my phone, I can't exactly dig around in my bra while greeting guests. Plus, I need to focus.

"First off . . ." I say, returning to the task at hand, "I'm certain that, thanks to Virginia, news has already spread about the cute Phi Delt from Ole Miss planning to spend the summer in Atlanta."

"Fine," Luisa says begrudgingly. "I guess that helps our cause."

"And second . . ." I continue as we spot Virginia taking a sip of Tripp's cocktail, "having the judge's favorite granddaughter in our pocket is the quickest way into that golf quartet. Plus, Tripp doesn't seem to mind."

"You mean, he doesn't mind stringing her along?" Luisa replies. "Isn't that a little anti-feminist?"

"Maybe," I say with a shrug, "but also highly effective. And we're not asking him to do anything *physical* with her—"

"Other than the kiss at the derby party, you mean?" Luisa blurts out. "Not to mention today's spit swapping." She gestures toward the two of them, now passing the mule back and forth.

"In his defense," I jump in, "*she* kissed *him*."

Luisa opens her mouth to respond, but we are cut off by Diane's stressed-out voice blaring through my headset, reminding us that I'm on the clock. We put a mic on Tripp, too, so if I switch channels on my walkie-talkie, I can hear him. The whole thing feels very James Bond.

"On my way," I say into the microphone, wondering if I should have picked a code name. I'm feeling Honey Badger for me. Sweet and ferocious at the same time.

"Don't let Griggs see you," Luisa reminds me.

"Ten-four, Jade Jackal," I say.

"What the hell are you talking about?" Luisa demands.

"We need code names," I say. "I'm Honey Badger. Eli is Wolf Man, and with that fabulous green dress, you have to be Jade Jackal."

There's silence on the channel, and I'm thinking maybe she turned off her walkie-talkie?

"Okay fine," she admits hesitantly. "Jade Jackal sounds badass."

"Over and out," I say, pretty proud of myself. We're so cool.

Then I hurry toward the back of the tent where a small army of service workers are laboring behind the scenes to make every detail of the event flawless. I can't help thinking that none of these drunken revelers will pause for even a second to acknowledge the hard work of so many underpaid and overworked people, myself included. All they will see is a high tent strewn with floor-to-ceiling greenery, including a twenty-foot-wide botanical wreath floating above us like a halo. There's a stage for an eighteen-piece band, a custom-painted dance floor, and an artist set up in the corner, working on an oil painting of the bride and groom. Every table is covered in stunning floral centerpieces, candles, glassware, silverware, and monogrammed napkins. Each gorgeous detail has been seamlessly executed. I remind myself that, even if no one else notices, that's what counts.

I jump in to help the waiters wipe down the rims of plates, peeking out every so often to see how things are progressing. I spot Griggs, Anna-Byrd, Aunt Edna, and Tripp sliding into their seats. Luisa is at the table behind them. I click over to a different channel on my walkie-talkie, and Tripp's voice comes in loud and clear.

"Theodore Reynolds Bedford III," he says, introducing himself to the table. "But my friends call me Tripp." He pauses, and muffled sounds indicate that he's shaking Griggs's hand. Then Griggs introduces himself, and his "lovely bride, Anna-Byrd."

As if in a classic movie montage, my mind races through all the work that brought us to this moment. I feel a swell of pride, observing the Tripp that we created, followed by a rush of anxiety that he may not be ready. What if he forgets the Bedford family tree? What if he botches the diphthongs? What if—God forbid!—he calls Anna-Byrd "ma'am"?

"Our young Tripp here's visiting from Mississippi for the summer," Aunt Edna offers helpfully. Bless that woman. "We had quite the run at Judy Swanson's derby party. Emptied out everyone's pockets."

"So, you're a Mississippi Bedford?" Griggs asks, his interest immediately piqued. "I thought that might be the case."

As the salad course is served, Tripp lets Griggs take the lead in the conversation, but he carefully drops crumbs of his family history, his Ole Miss days, and his newfound love of Atlanta. Griggs puts on his charm offensive, aided by the freely flowing wine and easy conversation. The servers deliver the second course—a small lobster tail in a white lemon sauce. Tripp takes a few bites, and as far as I can tell from the audio feed, he manages to balance conversation with tiny-forked lobster-eating remarkably well. By the time the steak course arrives, I'm straining to hear over the spirited cacophony of laughter, music, and the constant clink of silverware, dishes, and glasses. But when I poke my head out of the tent and lock eyes with Luisa, she gives me a covert nod, confirming what my gut tells me: all is proceeding according to plan.

The noise dies down as the servers clear the dinner plates, and I hear Tripp divulge in that glorious Mississippi Delta accent, "I'm a country boy at heart. But there's so much damn investment opportunity here in Atlanta, I'd be a fool not to stay awhile."

Our happy hooker has dropped the bait.

But before Griggs has a chance to respond, Tripp abruptly excuses himself. "Enough business talk," he adds dismissively, "time for a bourbon intermission." He abandons his monogrammed napkin on the table, stands, and walks away.

Did he just say "a bourbon intermission"?

I switch the channel on my walkie-talkie, and blurt out, "Honey Badger to Jade Jackal: What's going on? Why is Wolf Man walking away?"

And then, before she can even reply, it hits me. *God, this man is good.* Men like Griggs and their primal caveman brains can smell desperation a mile away. They will pay no heed to someone who is trying too hard, but they'll kill themselves to get the attention of anyone who completely ignores them. They want what they can't have; they desperately need control. I should know, since Griggs's thirst for power is threatening to ruin my life—and our Tripp certainly knows it, too.

Sure enough, Griggs follows eagerly behind Tripp, both of them heading toward the bar.

Hot diggity damn.

We're in.

CHAPTER 21

Luisa

I make a beeline for the bar, then stand out of view, blending with the other guests. Tripp orders a Blanton's neat, just as Holly instructed. In an instant, Virginia appears by his side.

This woman is like a persistent rash. I wrap my fingers tighter around my wineglass, pulling myself a little taller. Why am I getting so worked up over this? I need to focus, stay rational, shrewd, and keep a lid on my emotions.

"Make that two," Griggs tells the bartender, joining them. He kisses Virginia on the cheek, then compliments her dress and orders her a spritzer.

"Reel him in, Tripp," I say. "You got this."

Instead, Tripp does what Tripp does best—takes his sweet time.

He laughs cheerfully as Virginia regales Griggs with tales and photos of the derby party, inserting enough anecdotes to quickly cement Tripp into this world. Then, for what feels like forever, they talk about the upcoming college football season. Tripp passionately defends "his" Ole Miss Rebels, while Griggs clamors after the Georgia Bulldogs. Virginia bursts out with a proud "Roll Tide!" that makes everyone guffaw.

Tripp is careful to steer the conversation to topics we practiced and for which Holly provided insight into Griggs's likes and dislikes: football was first on the list, then golf, skiing, tennis, hunting, fly-fishing, and deep-sea fishing.

Each one of these activities became part of Tripp's photo reel, a series of AI-altered images of Tripp living the one-percent life, any of which would drive home the point that he's got trust fund money to burn.

And because I'm an overachiever at heart, I even included a few photos of Tripp's around-the-world moments: island hopping in Bali, sunbathing on a sailboat in Croatia, hitting the bars in Ibiza, deep-sea fishing off the coast of Mexico.

Right now, he's casually thumbing over a few of these photos, in blatant disregard of the club's "no cell phones" policy. Griggs peers over his shoulder, proffering his own photos, as Tripp searches for the one where he's pulling the fin of a blue marlin off the side of a charter boat in Cozumel. I guess like every other entitled man under this tent, Tripp and Griggs assume the rules don't apply to them.

Virginia, blessedly, has taken a bathroom break.

"That bad boy was almost four feet," Tripp exclaims. "Took three of us to get him out of the water." He slides off the screen and tucks the phone into his jacket pocket. "I'm headed to Belize in the fall."

"Belize?" Griggs asks, seemingly impressed.

"Some of the best deep-sea fishing in the world," Tripp assures him. Then, lowering his voice, "And the women . . ." Tripp pauses, chuckles to himself. "Tanned, in love with their tiny bikinis, ready to party. Like shooting fish in a barrel." Tripp cocks and shoots off an imaginary shotgun.

I barf internally. But Griggs is eating it up. He laughs, because apparently, the sexual objectification of women is so very funny.

"But first, I need to get my shit together," Tripp says, leaning against the bar. "Prove to the old man that I can make something of myself, put that trust money to good use. You know?" Tripp takes a long swig of bourbon, and I pray that he's keeping tabs on his alcohol intake. There's no Ginny behind the bar pouring him shots of water, and the last thing we need is a repeat of the derby party.

"I get it," Griggs says, leaning in beside Tripp. "This whole family legacy thing can put a lot of pressure on a man. You're never just you," he says, eyes distant. "You're always part of something bigger, grander. Something impossible to live up to." Griggs finishes his bourbon, then immediately orders another round. I set down my wine and ask a server for a coffee.

"I miss the days when my biggest problem was remembering the names of every girl I'd fuck on Sorority Row." Griggs laughs at the revolting reminiscence.

"Tell me about it," Tripp says, leaning in conspiratorially. I catch an almost imperceptible wince in his eyes, a sign of Eli breaking through the disgusting display of misogyny.

Two other men join Griggs and Tripp at the bar. Griggs introduces them as Judge Billy Thacker and Jim Wade.

"I think we're in," I whisper to Holly, dropping a sugar cube into my coffee and swirling in a splash of creamer.

Virginia plants a kiss on Granddaddy Thacker's cheek, then saunters over to Tripp's side, presenting him like some prize she won at one of the club's many tournaments.

"I'll be showing him around the club this weekend," she squeals—or so it sounds to me. "Giving him a taste of the Peach City's Southern hospitality."

I walk away, searching for Holly, unable to handle another minute near this nonsense. I find her hiding behind a huge wisteria tree, pretending to organize glassware. I hover beside her, looking like any other guest, sipping on my delicious coffee and swaying to the beat of the band's instrumental jazz intermission.

"I hate that you're right about Virginia and her granddaddy," I reluctantly admit. "And who the hell calls Atlanta the Peach City? Is that a Junior League thing?"

"She can call it whatever she wants," Holly replies, discreetly passing me one of the earbuds on her headset so I can listen in. "Hate to say I told you so, but that woman is our golden ticket," she gloats. "The universe is definitely out to help us."

Holly taps her index finger against the screen of her tablet, keeping track of multiple schedules at once, and a guest list of six hundred.

"You're like a professional juggler," I observe, nodding toward her tablet.

She tilts her head sideways in confusion, eyebrows raised in a *What the heck is that supposed to mean?* expression.

"Relax," I exclaim. "It's a compliment. Maybe you should consider going on your own." I gesture at the reception unfolding before us. "Plan events, weddings and such. Work for yourself. Maybe even have your own team."

Holly stares back at me, a glint in her green eyes. "You really think I could do it?"

"Abso-fucking-lutely." I nod without hesitation. "You're in your element, Holly."

She pauses, considering. "Yeah, but starting a business takes money in the bank and great networks," she debates. "And that disgusting man"—she gestures toward Griggs—"will demolish both for me unless this plan works."

Virginia squeals through Tripp's mic, drawing back our attention.

"So let's focus on one grand scheme at a time," Holly says, surprising me once again with her sagacious practicality and intense focus.

"Granddaddy, I told Trippy about the club's famous course," we hear Virginia exclaim. "I'm sure he'd love to play a round with you three."

"Yeah? You up for a round?" Griggs asks Tripp. "Think you can drag your ass out of bed for a seven thirty tee time after all those bourbons?"

I silently thank our lucky stars, San Judas Tadeo, and every single saint that has interceded on our behalf. We. Are. So. In.

"Believe me, I can handle my liquor, but my clubs are back home." Tripp tosses around that beguiling smile of his, making himself just slightly unavailable. And also, we couldn't afford a fancy set of clubs. "Wasn't planning on staying in town this long."

Griggs puts one hand on his shoulder, and I can feel the tight squeeze as he says, "Tripp, my boy, don't you worry 'bout a thing. We've got you covered."

As the wedding winds down, I find Eli waiting for me at the driving range. Holly still has another hour left of her shift before we can debrief and go home. I walk toward him, holding a box of wedding cake. "Dessert?" I ask, lifting the box.

"I'm starving," Eli sighs, offering to carry the cake. "I was so worried that I barely ate. Shame, the food looked amazing."

"You didn't seem worried," I observe, working to sound cool and unconcerned. "You, Griggs, and Virginia looked like you were having a blast."

Eli scoffs. "That girl's like a bad tattoo." He stares past me in the direction of the tent. "She finally hit the dance floor with her girlfriends, and I managed to break free."

"You handled Griggs masterfully," I say, more sincerely. "You're really good at reading people."

Eli responds with a bashful shrug, his cheeks glowing at the compliment. "Griggs is the type of man who *wants* to be challenged," he says, slipping his hands into the pockets of his tux. "His whole life he's been handed everything on a silver platter, so the possibility of risk gets him off." The muscles around his shoulders go tense under the jacket. "I'll have to prove that I'm my own man, but also that I respect him."

"Kinda like the not-trying look," I tease.

"Exactly." He chuckles, relaxing a little.

"So what type of man are you, really?" I ask, shifting the mood of the conversation. It's an honest question, and implied in my thoughtful tone is the need for an honest answer.

Eli holds my gaze as if debating how to respond. *I just want the truth*, I plead with my eyes. *Be honest with me*, my heart implores.

"I've had to fight for everything I've got, Luisa," he tells me, pronouncing my name the way it was intended. "I'm no Griggs." He glances down at his tux, adding, "I'm no Tripp, either."

I have so many more questions, but then his eyes travel back to me, lingering on the bare skin of my exposed collarbone, trailing up my neck, pausing on my lips, stopping only when he's reached my eyes. He bites his lower lip, pinning me in place with a gaze that's deep and burning—it reverberates all the way from my chest to my knees. I'm both grateful and mildly terrified that we're all alone out here. I'm not sure I have it in me to resist this gorgeous man, in a tux, under the moonlight, with the sweet scent of summer in the air and the faint echo of an eighteen-piece orchestra in the background.

"It's nice to sneak away," he says, his voice thick and full of meaning. "Enjoy what's left of the night with you."

I nod, suddenly at a loss for words. My dress feels impossibly tight, as if my lungs have forgotten how to process oxygen. My hand travels to my hair, where the bobby pins are digging into my scalp. Unfortunately, Mami did too good a job fastening my unruly curls, so that try as I may, I can't reach the pins hidden in the back of my head. Watching me struggle, Eli steps closer.

"Let me," he says, reaching for my waist, slowly turning me around with both hands. I close my eyes, a drumline exploding in my chest. He reaches for my updo, carefully pulling pins out of my hair. The release is instant, causing a soft moan to spill out of me.

"That feels so good." I exhale as the tendrils come loose over my shoulders, and a strange combination of relief and yearning flushes through my body. His fingertips dig into my hair, sending my long curls cascading down my back.

"Much better," he whispers into my ear. His warm breath turns my skin to gooseflesh, melting what little resolve I have left. I can't help but dissolve into him, relaxing my back against his chest. His hands settle over my hips, holding me in place.

"Where to?" he asks, his face angling down so that his lips are brushing my temple. I tilt my head upward, pressing my nose against his neck. His scent is so deliciously warm and honeyed that I can almost feel it trickling under my dress, sticking to my skin like dew.

This is a terrible idea. I know it, but I can't seem to get out of my own way. At this exact moment, I should push hard on the brakes. I should shift to reverse and add a few feet of distance between us before these runaway feelings collide into one fiery crash.

This gorgeous man seems full of secrets he's not willing to share. And the few breadcrumbs he's scattered have only made me more ravenous. What exactly is he serving me here and now?

"Wherever," I say, biting my lower lip.

He gazes down at me, then moves one of my curls behind my ear, grazing my cheek in the process. With his free hand, he skims my fingers, tentatively taking me by the hand. I let him hold on, too overcome by the sensation of his touch, of his skin on mine.

"Let's get out of here," he says, leading me down a dimly lit path to the golf course. We amble toward a pond, deserted this late into the night, stumbling upon a magnificent maple tree that's set on a hill overlooking the party. Eli takes off his jacket and spreads it across the ground, gesturing for me to sit on it. I oblige, and he takes a seat beside me, then digs into the box of cake. We indulge in the silence for a while, gazing at the fireflies, breathing in the scent of gardenias in full bloom, passing the cake between us.

"The entire time we were down there"—he nods toward the lights of the tent in the distance—"I kept thinking of all the things I would do with that kind of money, you know?" The faint sounds of Frank Sinatra's "Fly Me to the Moon" reach us. Eli turns to me, his eyes bright and expectant. "Instead of blowing it all in one party, one night." He glances down at his feet. He's taken off his shoes and socks and is sinking his toes into the grass. I follow his lead. It feels good to toss aside my heels, press my soles into the ground.

"What would you do?" I ask, curious. I had the same thought at various points in the evening, and my answer to the question came easily: I would give the money to the Castillos, to save their home.

Eli sets the empty cake box on the ground beside him and wipes his fingers with a napkin. "Help a person out," he finally answers. "I know what it's like to be in a bind. I'd love—just once—to give somebody a chance that they couldn't afford otherwise." He turns to face me. "I reckon that would feel pretty darn good." He tosses me a sly, crooked grin.

I smile back, unsure what to make of this heartfelt revelation, of the genuine kindness in his voice. He sits back, hands resting on the grass, lost in his thoughts. I wonder if he's talking about himself. His life. His chances.

"My dad used to say, you have to make your own luck in the world," I tell him. "'Take what you want, Luisa,' he'd say. 'Don't wait for things to come your way, because you may be waiting forever.'" I can almost hear the echo of Papi's voice, the beautiful cadence of his Puerto Rican Spanish. I haven't spoken about him in a long time. Mami's expression would sour every time Carola and I mentioned his name, so at some point, we stopped. "Recently, I've begun to wonder if he was wrong." I hear myself continuing, "Maybe even the strongest people need someone to rely on. And maybe it's okay to ask for help."

"What does your father think about all this?" Eli asks, gesturing toward the tent. "Everything that's happened to you? The risks you're taking to help a family you barely know?"

"Couldn't tell you," I say truthfully. "He left us when I was fifteen. We shared the father-daughter dance at my quinceañera, and a week later a drunk driver pushed him off the road, wrapped his car around a tree. He died instantly." I leave out the rest of the story—about Papi's second family, how we discovered his betrayal at his funeral. Telling Eli about his death is enough for this moment.

Eli stares at me, mouth slightly parted. His expression is serious, warm even, instead of the pity that usually follows that pronouncement. He doesn't speak, doesn't try to ease the pain or smooth over the scars. I'm deeply grateful for his silence. Instead, he takes my hand in his and runs slow circles over my palm, sending soothing waves of energy up my arm, into my chest. I melt inside. My heart softens more with every circle, until I'm leaning into his shoulder, inhaling the scent of his skin through his cotton shirt, the woodsy notes of the cologne I picked out for him, weaved with a bouquet of freshly cut grass and a Georgia summer breeze.

I glance up to find those deep gray eyes staring at me—into me—like I've seen him do every time I walk into a room. There's no Tripp in these eyes, they are pure Eli—Eli searching for me; Eli finding me.

I know I shouldn't let him in. I know at this exact moment I should build a wall, protect myself, my heart. After all, we purposely sought him out because of his ability to deceive. Is he pretending to be caring and kind just to get what he wants out of me? Whatever that may be?

His open palm brushes my cheek, and I close my eyes, captive to the sensation of his soft touch on my face. And in an instant, reason loses out to all physical sensation.

Unable to hold back—or maybe unwilling to fight—I surrender.

His fingers gently slide down my jawline, then he tenderly cradles my neck. I rest my head into his hand, succumbing to his touch. My lips part, and I offer one hesitant kiss, then another, full and feverish. Eli wraps his free arm around my waist, tugging me toward him. I curl into him, letting my legs drape across his, aching for his hands to travel under the skirt of my dress. Aching for the raw sensation of our bare skin touching. His hand wraps around my hip and he pulls me closer, as I cling to his chest. I run my open palms past his shoulders, then grasp the back of his neck, sinking my fingers deep into his hair. I'm out of breath and so desperate for more. Now that I've had a taste of him, there is no satisfaction to be had.

Into the silence and the echo of another jazz song, a ringtone cuts through the darkness around us. Eli freezes in my arms. His shoulders sink and his head drops into my chest, as a heavy exhale escapes his lungs.

"I'm sorry," he mutters, gently guiding me back onto the solid ground next to him before he takes out his phone. "My sister is home alone. I should get this."

As he stands, I glimpse the screen of his phone—a photo of Virginia, blowing an air-kiss.

Maybe tonight was just another deception after all.

CHAPTER 22

Holly

Eli's official introduction to Griggs at the wedding couldn't have gone any better. This morning, our Tripp begins dismantling the evil machine that Griggs and his cronies built. And for the first time since this whole thing began, I'm feeling confident, optimistic, and, frankly, quite fabulous.

Maybe it's because I know we've done absolutely everything we can to prepare Eli, or maybe it's because tomorrow I'm going on my very first date with a sexy British professor. I can almost see Hugh sauntering into the Switchyards in that buttery leather jacket; I can practically feel the ice-cold martini in my hand and hear the jazz wafting around us as we speak in hushed whispers. But first, I have a golf foursome to stalk.

"Holly, my darling one, come over here," Peter says, standing up and gesturing for me to join him and Joel. My next-door neighbors have spent the past couple of hours bellied up to the Golf House Bar, as they tend to do on Sunday mornings. "We've got a proposition for you."

"I don't accept propositions from strange men at bars," I say, smiling. "Particularly not when I'm on the clock." And then, for good measure, I add, "But I'm not surprised by your come-on. I'm looking *damn* good this morning, if I do say so myself."

"Loving the blowout," Joel enthuses. "So sexy."

Luisa took me shopping for the wedding, and then we headed over to La Barna, where her mom gave me the best blowout of my entire life. I don't typically invest time or money in my look. But I thought, *Why not?* Well, actually, I thought, *It wouldn't hurt to show up at Monday night's jazz jam looking hot.*

While we were trying on dresses, I found myself chatting excitedly with Luisa about the date, but then worried that maybe I was crossing a line. We are, after all, business partners (so to speak), and I don't want to come across as unprofessional. Still, I feel like we're moving toward being friends—slowly—even if Luisa still hasn't spilled on what the hell is going on with her and Eli.

In the meantime, at least I've got Peter and Joel. They're quite skilled at dishing.

"Get your adorable little ass over here and listen to what we have to say," Joel commands in his most bossy-pants voice. "Or I'll evict you *and* that ragamuffin son of yours."

Byron stands behind the bar, smirking. Clearly, he's in on whatever they're cooking up.

"All right," I sigh, knowing it's useless to resist. "But make it fast. Because, unlike you two"—I point accusingly back and forth to Peter and Joel—"I don't get a Sunday Funday. This is my place of business, I'll remind you."

It's a perfect May weekend, crisp warm air, clear blue sky, and I've conveniently arranged to work setup for the club's Sunday brunch, which is held on the terrace, adjacent to the Men's Grill, and overlooking the eighteenth green. Eli is somewhere out there now, playing a round with Griggs, Jim Wade, and Judge Billy Thacker. His goal is simple: Slide right into the foursome and drop subtle hints about his deep pockets, lack of experience, and desire to invest. If he plays his cards right, he'll be invited back by the time they leave the green. Meanwhile, I'm making myself look busy here beside the nineteenth hole, hoping to get intel when he returns.

Joel and Peter both swivel on their stools to face me, and Byron leans across the bar and rests his chin in his hand. Byron's resting-chin pose is a surefire sign that he means business, so I'm starting to feel a little stressed about whatever it is they're going to tell me.

"You need to be the next general manager of this place, Holly," Joel says.

Oh, this again.

"You're far and away the most qualified person for the job," Peter adds.

"Exactly how many drinks have these two had?" I ask Byron, my voice teasing. "Because, as I told you, that's never gonna happen."

He shakes his head in response, and then, with his most authoritative deep voice, he says, "They're right, Holly. And you know it."

"Y'all are on drugs," I announce, shooing them away with my hand.

Except, this time, I find that I really am thinking about being the general manager. Maybe it was my experience at the Altamaha Country Club, realizing how much more of an expert I am than most event managers—how much I've learned over the years, and how my peers respect me. I guess this whole scheme with Luisa has also helped me see that I can set a big goal and stick to it. I can problem-solve my way out of unexpected predicaments (hello, Eli's perfect accent; hello, Hugh Pridmore). And I can keep my cool in a crisis. Aren't all these classic managerial skills? Maybe they're right about the GM job, maybe I should apply. I think back to what Luisa said last night, and I wonder if she could be onto something. Would it be possible to use these skills while also being my own boss?

It's all moot as long as the whole Griggs situation sucks up my free time and energy. So instead of replying, I fall back, as I tend to do, on a self-deprecating joke.

"Come clean, Byron. Have you been adding 'shrooms to your signature Bloody Mary mix?"

This elicits laughs all around—until Joel rearranges his face into that plastic fake smile he wears when someone he deplores is coming close. Peter and Byron stare in the same direction and their laughter fades away. I look over my shoulder, following their collective gaze, and see none other than Griggs Caldecott Johnson III. My eyes dart around the room, searching for Eli. How did I miss them leaving the course? And where in God's name is Eli?

Joel stands up stiffly, extending his hand. "Hello there, Griggs. It's good to see you." That's a lie and I know it.

Griggs shakes Joel's hand, smiling amiably. "How are you, buddy?" Then he steps in and places the same hand on my shoulder. I flinch at his touch, which I'm sure the entire bar notices.

"Hello, Peter," Griggs says, his voice booming. He tends to be especially warm and gregarious around the two of them, as if to demonstrate that he's a modern man, in line with the times, *perfectly okay with the gays.*

"Griggs," Peter says in response, his tone low and maybe even a little threatening.

I'm watching their exchange, a part of me seething with anger at Griggs's casual touch, feeling the terrible burn of it through my magnificent new dress.

"And what are you folks over here gossiping about?" Griggs asks, inspecting my freshly styled hair as he casually keeps his hand on my shoulder. Then he turns to look at Byron. "Am I imagining it, or is our Holly all gussied up for us today?"

"We're actually over here deciding that Holly should be the club's next GM," Joel says confidently, standing up to face Griggs. "She'll be submitting her application in no time."

"Well, good for you, Holly," Griggs exclaims, his voice too jovial. "I'm a voting member of the board, so you have the right connections," he says. "If you butter me up a bit, that is."

Disgusting man. We're all silent for a beat, until Griggs lets out a burst of too-loud laughter.

"Kidding, only kidding," he says, flashing a huge smile. "Anyway, I'm off to enjoy free drinks, courtesy of the young whippersnapper who just won the round."

My heart begins to stutter. Please, God, let that young whippersnapper not be our Tripp.

I made it abundantly clear to Eli that no matter how good a player he might be, he should not, under any circumstances, show these men up. Their egos are way too fragile. Judge Thacker *must* win. If he doesn't, there's absolute hell to pay. Janey told me that, a few years ago, he even found a way to land their fourth in jail after a particularly humiliating loss on the course. Called a few of his buddies at the sheriff's office and set the poor guy up for a

DUI after having paid the guy's bar tab himself. The story may be a classic Janey exaggeration, but knowing Judge Thacker, I'm inclined to believe it.

"Well, I'll be damned," Joel says, shaking his head. "Did you lose any money off him?"

"Hell yeah." Griggs snorts a laugh. "The old judge kept upping the stakes, sure he was gonna eventually turn the thing around."

"Stakes?" I ask, my face flushing hot with anger. "You mean, he won a bet?"

"Cleaned us all out." Griggs laughs, gesturing toward the adjacent Men's Grill patio, and I finally spot Tripp, joking along with the guys as if he doesn't have a care in the world. "Tripp Bedford's his name," Griggs continues. "Of the Mississippi Bedfords. That boy has a damn-near-perfect golf swing."

"And how's Judge Thacker handling it?" Joel asks, smirking.

My legs turn to jelly. I have to hold on to the back of Peter's chair.

"Well, you wouldn't know by looking at him, but the esteemed judge is mad as hell." Griggs couldn't be more amused. "Thinks the kid sandbagged us on his handicap. Doubt Tripp Bedford will be joining our standing threesome again." He sounds entertained, as if our plan's literal demise is oh-so-funny. "Crying shame—he's a solid young man and a fabulous golfer. At least we get a round or two of bourbon out of him."

My mouth goes so dry that I involuntarily reach for Peter's blood orange mimosa and take a long swallow. Why did he not follow my instructions? They couldn't have been clearer.

I think back to the derby party, and how quick Eli was to place a bet. Does he have a gambling problem? Is he just using me and Luisa to get in among the high rollers? Whatever the answer, I have to extract Eli from that situation before he's saddled with a huge bar tab or a DUI. Or, God forbid, both.

Griggs starts to walk away, then seems to think better of it. He pauses, turns back, and then speaks directly to me. "Oh, and, Holly, I thought you should know . . ." He smiles wickedly, and I know that whatever's coming next is not good. "The Undergraduate Dean over at UGA—he's my college buddy's uncle—he'll be comin' down to join me at the club in a few weeks, for a round of golf and brunch." My mouth falls open against my will, but I can't seem to utter a word. "I'll be sure to tell him all about your son, Aidan. I know he'll be intrigued." And then, the despicable man has the audacity to wink, as he calls out "Go Dawgs!" and then takes his leave of us.

As soon as Griggs walks away, I jump back, tipping over Joel's Bloody Mary and knocking the stool to the ground with a loud thud. Every single person at the Golf House turns to look at me, but there's just one person whose attention I need: Eli's.

"Oh, goodness," I cry, grabbing a napkin from the table and sopping up Joel's drink. "I am so clumsy today."

Just as I hoped, Judge Thacker and the rest of his foursome turn and look across the patio toward the commotion. I make eye contact with Eli and tilt my head subtly toward the restrooms.

"It's all right," Peter says, his voice kind. "Not even a drop landed on us."

"I'm going to go see if I can find a dishrag," I reply, stepping away from the table.

As I make my way inside, I'm followed by a dozen piercing stares. I can hear the talk already:

Poor Holly, she must be so exhausted. I can't even begin to imagine what it's like to be a single mom, working night and day for all these years.

Can you believe that Holly was so drunk at work, before noon, that she knocked a stool right over?

And to think she'd consider applying to be general manager. What a lark!

Soon they'll be gossiping about my felon son and how he got kicked out of college—or lost his scholarship and had to quit—after the Undergraduate Dean learned of crimes he committed *right here at the club*!

How are we ever going to stop Griggs now? A stomach-churning defeat threatens to overwhelm me, but I shove it down deep. When I get to the hallway, I duck into a broom closet, feigning an attempt to find dishrags. Our Tripp comes sauntering by, utterly cool and collected. I grab him by the arm and yank him into the closet, closing the door behind us.

"What the hell, Holly?" he whispers. "Have you lost your damn mind?"

"Yes, and it's entirely your fault," I spit. "What have you *done*?"

"Things are going great out there," he replies, gesturing toward the bar.

"No, Eli. Things are not going great. Are we not paying you enough?" I ask him, my voice accusing. "Because it seems that you just can't resist any opportunity to skim more cash off this deal."

"Hold on," he says, head going sideways. "Are you pissed about the illegal betting in *your* place of employment, or about the fact that I cleaned out those rich assholes' pockets?"

"I'm pissed, Eli, because our plan has just hit a big fat dead end." I gesture wildly with my hands. "Why, you ask. I'll tell you why," I loud-whisper. "Because you failed to follow my instructions and you beat out all three of those egotistical men." My cheeks are flushed, my arms still flailing. "You were supposed to play it safe," I whisper-shriek. "What happened?"

"That huge-ass bet happened," Eli says, shrugging. "Just before we teed up, Griggs said we needed to make this round interesting. I tried to turn them down, but the judge kept goading me on, heckling me." He shakes his head. "That guy's a real dickhead." Then he shrugs and says casually, "So I agreed to their bet, and I won a shit-ton of money off them."

And with those words, Eli confirms my worst suspicions: He's using us to get to the big payouts, and he doesn't give a damn whether it ruins our plans. I'm so furious that I want to scream. Or cry. But instead, I suck in a deep breath and then try to make him understand the huge mistake he's made.

"Oh, you'll pay. We *all* will pay!" I hiss. "You've ruined any chance of Judge Thacker agreeing to let you in on their business dealings." I let out a frustrated groan. "The man *hates* to lose." Eli shrugs in response, which only has the effect of making me angrier. "And Griggs has already made perfectly clear that you're not going to be invited back," I snap.

Eli bites his lower lip, his chest deflating. Our cocky Tripp has suddenly vanished.

"Okay, I get that you're angry," he says, his voice pleading. "And I'm sorry. But you have to understand—with guys like this, if I turned down a bet, I'd look weak. Like a total loser. They'd never respect me enough to do business with me. I did the right thing, Holly. I promise," he begs. "Please just let me follow through with this. Send me back out there and I can make it work."

"The thing is," I tell him, "I just don't know whether we can trust you. You've put our entire plan—and us—at risk."

I suddenly feel nauseous. Elijah Denvil Sweet Jr. is a con artist, and a good one. Now, instead of wasting his time on dollar bets at a pool table in Westlake, he's hit the big leagues, and it's all thanks to me.

Well, not anymore. My head begins to ache as I recall what I told Luisa back at that biker bar: When it comes down to it, Griggs and Eli are virtually identical. They're both cunning, smooth-talking, and charming as hell. They also both happen to be criminals, and I refuse to be taken advantage of by either of them for even one more moment.

It must stop here. All our work, all the time and energy we invested, all those risks we took to set this plan into motion, they're all for nothing. How could I have been so stupid and naive, relying on a small-town pool hustler to rescue me and my son?

With the thought of Aidan, my anger turns to sorrow.

"Just go back there and tell them you had a family emergency or something," I tell him, holding back tears. "And then please get the hell out of here before they think too hard and realize who you really are."

He stares at me, his mouth agape, as I walk away. I head straight to the powder room, lock myself in a stall, pull out my phone, and text Luisa.

Call me ASAP. It's over.

She will be furious when she learns of Eli's mistake. Meanwhile, I'm just plain *defeated*.

As I wait for her reply, my phone buzzes with a text from Hugh.

> I was so looking forward to tomorrow night, but unfortunately I'm still stuck across the pond. Sorry to miss.

My chest sinks in on itself, literally deflating as I take in the news. I guess I hadn't realized how much hope I'd pinned on tomorrow's date until it slipped away. My fingers hover over the keyboard while my mind struggles to compose a breezy, nonchalant response. Then another text comes in.

> By the way, I promise I'm not cyberstalking you, but must admit I did some googling and I can't find information on your production company anywhere... What am I missing?

Hugh found out I was lying. *Of course* he found out. And now, instead of rescheduling our date, he's backing out for good.

I squeeze my eyes together tightly, trying in vain to come up with any words at all that might explain what he's "missing."

I could tell him the truth, but he'd never want to talk to me again, not after he learns about the scheme he's been participating in without his knowledge or consent. I feel completely and utterly foolish. How could I have thought this ridiculous scheme with Luisa could actually work? How delusional am I?

My head sinks to my knees, and, once again, I'm falling apart in the powder room of the Dogwood Hills Club. At least this time I'm not puking.

CHAPTER 23

Luisa

I take another sip of Gloria Castillo's horchata, hoping its cool, creamy sweetness will soothe the ache in my chest. We sit beside each other in silence, lulled by the rhythmic creak of her rocking chairs, watching Little Mishel and Abelardo ride their bikes down a dirt driveway lined with Southern live oaks. Pablo has gone to the cemetery to visit Don Luis's grave.

"He's been going on longer and longer walks," Gloria says, her voice low and tired. The shadows under her eyes are more pronounced since I last saw her, but somehow she still manages to smile for the kids, pretend their world isn't about to be turned upside down.

"Have you told them anything?" I ask. It's been five days since the golf fiasco, and at this juncture, our plan to outmaneuver Griggs seems unsalvageable.

Gloria shakes her head. "I've been on my knees every night," she says, kissing the cross of the rosary around her neck. "Praying to La Virgencita for a miracle."

I stare at the milky horchata in my glass, absently stirring the long cinnamon stick protruding through the ice cubes. After we moved to Atlanta, I, too, prayed on my knees. I prayed to return home to Puerto Rico. Homesick and lonely, I missed my cousins and friends, missed our lazy weekends on sunny Buyé Beach, the tangy taste of an icy piragüa de tamarindo on my tongue, the wonder of surfing in Rincón at sunset, and the joy of living my life in Spanish. But pray as I might, Mami refused to reverse course. Puerto Rico was our past, she would tell us, angry and resentful. Atlanta was our future, and hell would freeze over before we moved back.

By the time I returned to the Island in my early twenties, my Puerto Rican Spanish accent and fluency were atrophied. My aunts and cousins teasingly called me *La Gringa*. I laughed at their jokes, taking them in stride, but inside, an essential part of my identity bifurcated, eroding any fanciful, childish beliefs that one day I could return to my life just as it used to be. On that homecoming trip, I realized that the woman I had grown into didn't fully belong on the Island, and didn't fully belong in the States. The day my father's lies became known, I lost my home and became irrevocably torn as a result. No amount of prayers could put me back together again.

In the distance, Abelardo's laugh rings out as the kids circle the trunk of a massive oak, heads thrown back with mirth, carefree and happy. I can't blame Gloria and Pablo for keeping the terrible news from them, for keeping them whole for as long as possible.

"You don't believe in miracles?" Gloria asks, pulling me back to the rocking chair beside her. I meet her curious gaze, unsure of how to respond. I usually keep any opinions on faith to myself, but Gloria seems to already know the answer.

I shrug, admitting for the first time, "I don't believe anyone's listening."

Gloria rests one hand on my forearm. "Our prayers brought you here," she says with conviction. "You listened."

Her words just about break me. I want to confess that in the beginning, the only reason I listened was my drive to ferret out a good story and land the top headline. I want to tell her that her faith in me is misplaced, that I can't save myself, much less her family.

If miracles existed, we'd still have a shot at taking Griggs down, saving her home, and getting my job back. Instead, our plan is dead on arrival, with no Tripp and no Eli. And yeah, maybe it's heedless of me, considering what's at stake for these kids, but I'd be lying if I said the thought of never seeing Eli again isn't crushing me from the inside.

Holly called me after the mess at the golf course to explain and commiserate. We haven't talked since. I've been busy chastising myself for feeling let down by Eli and his impulsive behavior. What did I expect? Frankly, I'm surprised it took this long for our absurd scheme to fall apart. We've known from day one that our angel investor is no angel. *So why did I think I could trust him?* And why can't I bring myself to confront him—choosing instead to ignore his relentless calls and texts?

"I don't know where we go from here, Gloria," I concede in a tone so defeated, it fills me with self-loathing. I've barely slept these past few days, trying in vain to identify a potential whistleblower at the offshore bank in Panama—a desperate long shot—while also reaching out to governmental regulators in that region, certain there's something I've overlooked.

Gloria taps my arm, then gives it a gentle squeeze. "It's okay to ask for help," she says, gazing up at the heavens. Voluminous, bright white clouds, the kind a child would draw, are scattered across a dazzling cornflower-blue sky. I've never seen a more oppressive sight in my life.

By the time I pull into Mami's driveway two hours later, my face is a red, puffy mess. I stress-cried all the way home, to the tune of a playlist titled *Break My Heart: Tragic Opera Arias*, because apparently misery has its own soundtrack. I slide out of the SUV and head inside, spent and so not in the mood for Friday family dinner.

"Luisa, is that you?" Mami calls out from the kitchen the instant I'm through the front door. "Where have you been?"

A stampede of tiny feet bursts from the living room to greet me in the foyer.

"Titi Luisa," Rosita and Daniela sing in unison, opening their arms to enfold me in a hug. Behind them, Carola rocks Sarita in the crook of one arm, dressed in a pretty summer dress that accentuates the curves of her post-baby body.

"You look nice," I observe. "Are you going out? I thought we were having pizza night."

"What happened to you?" Carola asks, taking my chin in her free hand, inspecting my face at close range. "Have you been crying?" Her voice drops to a whisper. "Is this about the hairy guy

Mami keeps talking about? The actor?" I wriggle myself loose, turning to my nieces, who are clamoring for more hugs and kisses. "Why didn't you tell me about the midnight makeover?" she asks, her tone tinged with hurt. "I could've helped you."

"You have enough on your plate, Carola." I lift Rosita, swing her onto my hip. "Besides, it was a last-minute thing." The injured look in her face only adds to the guilt I already feel.

"Titi hubband," Rosita exclaims puckishly. "Hubband su-pppprissssee." She presses her tiny hands over my cheeks, blows a raspberry, then dissolves into a fit of giggles. "It's a secret!"

"Is she saying 'husband surprise'?" I ask Carola.

"She's just being silly." Carola titters nervously, pulling Rosita off me with the swift acrobatic maneuver of an expert juggler. "Give Titi Luisa some time to freshen up her makeup."

"What's going on?" I ask, my tone suspicious. "It's pizza night—sweatpants and a Disney movie."

"I told Mami you wouldn't like it . . ." Carola trails off, striding back into the kitchen, shamelessly using her children as a shield.

"I won't like what?" I demand, just as Augusto and Abuela cross the kitchen door, arms heavy with bottles of wine, flowers, and a cake box from a newly opened Italian bakery.

"There it is," Mami squeals, taking the cake box. She removes an exquisite lemon meringue cake. I'd be excited at the sight of the candied lemons and torched meringue, if it weren't for the certainty that my own family is about to make a flambé out of me.

I count two extra place settings on the table. For a fleeting moment, I have the nonsensical thought that maybe Holly and Eli are coming over for dinner, and my spirits rally.

"Who's coming to dinner?" I ask, irrationally hopeful.

"Luisa, for the love of God," Mami cries out, striding past me with the cake platter. "Fix your hair. Put on some lipstick." She drops the cake on the sideboard before marching back to the kitchen. "Do I have to think of everything?"

"I'm eating in my room." I decide that I'm done playing whatever game this is. I reach for a plate, then storm toward the oven, where the mouthwatering aroma of Mami's decadent lasagna sends my knees buckling. I haven't eaten all day and I'm ravenous.

Mami angles herself beside me. "You're eating at the table, with your family," she snaps, shutting the oven door with her hip. "My roof, my rules." And with those four words—uttered with the same terrifying expression of my youth—I turn into a helpless teenager living under my mother's iron fist. I open my mouth to protest and stand up to her, like the adult woman I pretend to be, but then she's up in my face, scrutinizing me under the too-bright lights of the hood.

"Why are your eyes red?" She narrows her gaze in concern. "Mija, are you okay?" Her touch is so motherly, so tender, that for a second I consider dissolving into her chest with a loud and snotty sob.

"It's just allergies," I mutter instead, wiping at my nose. "Summer ragweed."

I'm saved by Daniela, who runs in, shouting, "They're here! They're here!"

Suddenly, Mami's most pressing worry is the state of my hair and washed-out makeup. A red lipstick materializes in front of my face.

"What are you doing?" I groan, unable to pull away from her death grip.

"You look like death, mija." She holds my jaw in place with one hand, pressing the lipstick to my lips with the other. "Blot," she orders, pushing a napkin between my lips. I mechanically obey, zapped of all remaining energy.

The doorbell rings. Mami ushers me out of the kitchen and into the foyer. She tosses aside her apron, glancing at her reflection on the console mirror. Then she takes one last full breath before throwing the front door open like some deranged game show host to reveal . . . a man. But not just any man—Juan Pablo Bustamante, the son of one of Mami's oldest friends and my first Atlanta crush. My jaw nearly scratches the hardwood floors.

I first met Juan Pablo over a decade ago. I was an awkward, nerdy, pimple-faced high school senior, swooning over a med-school student six years my senior. Even then, Juan Pablo had telenovela leading-man charm, and the kind of smarts that got him into one of the country's top med schools. Juan Pablo, with his shiny college life, his Ultimate Frisbee league, and his summer trips to new and exotic destinations, represented everything about our new Atlanta life Mami wanted us to embrace. But to me, he was always out of reach. The kind of poised young man who'd never bother with a girl still trying to figure out her place in the world.

And now, here we are. Juan Pablo and his mother, Vidalina, stride into our foyer. Mami shamelessly spreads kisses, looking ridiculously abashed when he passes her a bouquet of hydrangeas and a bottle of champagne. A dozen roses eventually make their way to me with more kisses and salutations as we move to take our seats around the dinner table.

I try pulling the seat between Carola and Augusto, but Mami makes a not-so-subtle gesture for me to seat myself next to Juan Pablo. My embarrassed cheeks probably match the red of her lipstick. Blessedly, Augusto pours me a generous glass of wine. Drunk may be the only way to survive this evening.

For most of the salad course, I only half listen. I'm so checked out that Augusto has to nudge me when Vidalina's questions turn to me and whatever lies Mami has told her about my career. But, unfortunately for my mother, I'm too tired to shine up my life and make things appear less grim than they are. So I tell her that, in fact, she's mistaken, and I didn't leave *The Georgia Times* for a career in film, but that I was fired because my boss is a snake. Mami glares at me as I pass my empty wineglass to Augusto, and he tops it off.

When it's time to serve the lasagna, I try to stand and help serve, but Mami pushes me back down, glowering at me behind Juan Pablo, mouthing for me to *TALK TO HIM!*

I'll give her this: Mami has brought home a doctor. A pediatric cardiologist who started his own charity, giving access to free life-changing surgery for families in need. He spends six weeks out of the year visiting rural clinics all over Latin America. On paper, Juan Pablo Bustamante is perfect. Sweet. Smart. Well-mannered. So why can't I muster the energy to care?

My heart whispers that I already know the answer. But my head tells me—too loud to ignore—that nothing good will come from analyzing my feelings for Eli too closely.

At some point, after my third slice of lasagna, I'm comatose on all the wine, noodles, and cheese. Juan Pablo and I run out of small talk, which gives Mami and Vidalina license to exchange a list of our interests. I learn that I'm a remarkable cook, *oh-so-talented* with a thread and needle, a terrific party host, and utterly devoted to my nieces—only the last one is true.

"I tell Juan Pablo he should have his own show," Vidalina exclaims proudly. "He's handsome enough to be one of those TV doctors."

"So handsome." Mami winks, ogling in his direction. *Jesus Christ.*

"He just needs a good wife by his side," Vidalina suggests, cutting her eyes to me. "Someone pretty and bright. And ready to give me some grandbabies."

Beside me, Juan Pablo fidgets with a low groan. I top off his wineglass, and he thanks me, his expression mortified. As the conversation officially descends into arranged marriage territory, I want to slide under the table, steal the cake, and eat alone while hiding in my room.

"Is it true you like the opera, or is that also made-up?" Juan Pablo whispers beside me. He tilts his head, angling his very high cheekbones until our eyes meet. Only a few inches away, I'm treated to a close encounter with his flawless facial structure—strong jawline, defined brow ridge, well-proportioned nose. Eighteen-year-old me has to resist the urge to giggle.

"That is true," I acknowledge. "And also true: I would lay down my own life for these three little monsters." I glance to the end of the table where Rosita and Daniela are absorbed playing a wood block game of tic-tac-toe.

"I have season tickets to the Atlanta Opera," Juan Pablo says, low enough so that only I can hear. I want to tell him that I, too, once had season tickets to the opera, but the admission that I can no longer afford said luxury is too embarrassing. "*La Bohème* is playing tomorrow night," he adds, tempting me. "We can grab dinner and get to know each other." He gazes at our overbearing mothers. "Just the two of us. Out in Midtown on a Saturday night."

I stare back into those dark telenovela eyes, thinking how easy it would be to be with someone like him, someone who fits perfectly into his own life. Someone who has adulthood all figured out. In spite of my mother's dubious machinations, I find myself considering his offer. It's true, I love everything about the opera—the drama, the costumes, the live orchestra. And it's Puccini, for Chrissake. If you are not sobbing in your velvet chair by the end of Act IV, you're surely dead inside.

I close my eyes and release the air I've been holding, letting my shoulders sag in defeat. Maybe Mami is right. Maybe I should just stop fighting, stop thinking so hard about, well, everything. Maybe, for once, I should just go to the opera, enjoy the flowers, the dinner, and the champagne, and (possibly) even break my sex dry spell with someone who can offer me a real future. *With a handsome pediatric cardiologist, Luisa!* I hear my mother's voice cry out.

Before I can give him an answer, a "Mississippi Goddam!" breaks out from the back pocket of my jeans, sending the girls into peals of laughter and cries of "Goddam!"

It's Eli's ringtone. The one I assigned him after that afternoon on the connector. It rings again, but I can't bring myself to answer or peer at the screen.

"Luisa, por Dios," Abuela chastises. "What is that noise? No phones at the table, mija."

I take out my phone and turn off the ringer, ignoring the string of texts and missed calls from Eli. He's been trying to reach me all week, surely to apologize. But the last things I want or need right now are his hollow regrets. Holly's words from our call have been replaying in my head on a loop: *He's just using us. We can't trust him. It's over.*

I turn off the screen and tuck the phone away.

"So, are we on for a date?" Juan Pablo asks beside me.

"Sure," I say, trying to smile like I mean it. "A night at the opera sounds like a dream."

CHAPTER 24

Holly

The morning that Kyle, my smarmy landlord, showed up at my front door to evict me, I was still in my pajamas, wrangling Aidan into his booster seat for breakfast. Kyle was wearing that stupid black puffer vest that he always wore—even in the dead-ass heat of summer—with his company's logo stitched on the chest: *KW Housing Solutions*. In pressed khakis and spit-polished loafers, Kyle always looked a little too smooth. And behind that clean-shaven facade and neatly stitched logo was a heart as cold as stone.

Aidan sat at the kitchen table, patiently awaiting his toad-in-a-hole burning on the stove, while Kyle, glancing repeatedly at my braless chest, calmly relayed that we would have two weeks to "vacate the property." Not exactly a Housing Solution.

I remember feeling proud, before Kyle arrived, to be the kind of mother who makes eggs and toast for her toddler, instead of sugary Pop-Tarts or Fruity Pebbles. But who was I kidding? I was the kind of mother who couldn't even figure out how to keep a roof over my son's head.

In the days and nights that followed, it became abundantly clear that I would never find an apartment that I could afford within walking distance of the club, and that owning a car and paying insurance were out of the question. My neighbor, Mrs. Babangida would be moving to the exurbs to live with her niece, taking with her my only affordable childcare option. The life I had so precariously—but also so lovingly—built with Aidan was falling apart.

And yet, in those stressed-out days and sleepless nights before Joel and Peter swooped in to buy the house, all I could do was obsess over a beanbag. I had impulsively ordered it for our living room the night before. It was on clearance and conjured images of Aidan and me snuggled up together, so close that the bright scent of his bubble bath lingered in the air around us, while I read his favorite book, *Skippyjon Jones*, again and again, and he giggled so hard that his body, still damp from the tub, shook against my side.

Would I be able to return the beanbag? Would I have to pay for shipping? And what in the hell was I thinking, going with the color *cheeky pink*? Aidan's grimy little fingers would stain it within moments of arrival. How had I failed to notice that the stupid thing had to be professionally dry-cleaned? As if I could afford that!

I knew I should be focusing on the real, actual issue facing me. But freaking out about the color of a beanbag felt like a safer way to move through the crisis.

Right now, my metaphorical beanbag appears to be the texts I'm not receiving from Professor Hugh Pridmore. I had one sort-of, kind-of moment with a man at a jazz club, followed by a handful of silly text exchanges, and now I'm acting as if some guy ignoring my messages is the most extreme crisis in my life. Not, say, that I may get fired from my job, or that my son is likely to lose his scholarship.

I can't stop staring at the string of unanswered texts I sent in response to his *What am I missing?* Over the course of a long and painful week, I've pressed send on every single one of these little gems:

So sorry yes absolutely I can explain next time I see you. Would really rather in person if that's okay?

Okay since you havent replied . . . Im not a producer. But Im really not a bad person I promise and I dont lie

Well okay I hardly ever lie unless I have a really good reason I don't like lie on my tax returns or anything

I guess since you havent responded you dont want me to explain which really is okay I totally understand

You are a great person and I hope you have a really nice life

Even when not staring at them, I'm obsessing over them. Last night, between two and four in the morning, I tossed in my bed while cycling through this oh-so-helpful jumble of thoughts: *The man is a college professor, for Chrissake. Use some freaking punctuation, Holly! Enough with the word "really"! Maybe I'll tell him the whole story in a text. But what if Griggs comes after me and the cops confiscate my phone and I get arrested because there's concrete evidence of my wrongdoing? What about a voicemail? Yes, a voicemail. That's safer. No!!! Not a voicemail. It's the middle of the night, you lunatic. But it's nine in the morning in the UK, where he is.*

Now, it's nine on a Monday morning where *I am*, and I'm exhausted from last night's mental acrobatics. In the end, I went ahead and explained the entire situation in a three-minute-and-twenty-seven-second voicemail word-vomit. I even rambled on about how I work at a country club and he should stop by sometime and we can go for a walk or get a drink or something. I mean, I think that's what I said. It's all a bit of a blur.

No response. No surprise there.

Seeking a distraction, I text Luisa:

Coming over with doughnuts. Get the coffee ready.

"Can I make a life proclamation?" Luisa asks, sitting cross-legged on the cozy bed swing that hangs from the ceiling of her mom's wraparound porch.

"Please," I urge.

"Onesies should be an acceptable form of office attire," she exclaims, brushing crumbs off her galaxy-cats-and-tacos onesie pajamas. She is stretched out across from me, a box of fancy doughnuts and a carafe of hot coffee between us.

"Agreed," I say, splitting a coconut creme concoction, then passing half to her.

We've only talked twice since the Sunday morning golf course debacle, which unfolded more than a week ago. The first time, for me to tell her the whole scheme was over; the second time, for her to tell me that things are so grim, she may be entering an arranged marriage. Well, not really. But apparently, she let her mom set her up on a date, which is a damn good indicator of our collective emotional state. Judging from the puffy dark circles under her normally bright eyes, I'd guess she's been sleeping about as well as me.

She rips a hunk of doughnut off and shoves it in her mouth. We both sit in silence, savoring the extreme sweetness.

"Did I tell you I went to see the Castillos?" she asks, leaning back against a pillow, gaze set on the coconut filling.

"Oh God, Luisa," I reply, sighing. "That must have been hard."

"It was fucking heartbreaking," she says quietly. "This is exactly why my first rule of journalism is never to get involved with my sources," she continues, licking a dollop of cream off her finger. "Once you start caring, it's all over."

I study Luisa's expression, steely and determined, wondering not for the first time where she finds all that drive. What makes this woman tick, so loud and so fast?

"But isn't caring what it's all about, when it comes down to it?" I ask, ready to probe just a little bit. "If you didn't care, you wouldn't work so hard to get your stories right."

"That sounds so idealistic." She shakes her head slowly. "When I was in J-school, I had this idea that I could make a difference, change the world." She raises one closed fist in the air. "I could use my investigative skills to uncover the truth, make the bad guys pay." She sits up, an intense expression crossing her face. "I learned pretty early on the power of a lie to ruin lives." She lets out a held breath as she adds, "But then you realize, it's all a business—a corporation. Instead of trying to present the facts, you're left cheapening stories and headlines for easy clicks. And, as I recently discovered, sometimes you're actually working for the bad guys."

I know she's right, about corporations and profit, and all the things that drive journalism. But I also sense that, for Luisa, that's not the whole story. What changed for her? What made her build that wall around her own heart, fill her life with work and deadlines?

"I don't even know why I'm doing any of this anymore." She balls a napkin in her fist and then drops it into the half-empty box. "And now my mom thinks I'll never get another job and is trying to marry me off."

I can't resist laughing out loud. "Oh, wait," I say, handing her half of a bright purple "galaxy" doughnut, which conveniently matches the theme of her PJs. "How was your opera date?"

"Something came up," she says, picking at the sprinkles on her doughnut. "It's on my to-do list."

"Wow," I respond, a sly grin spreading across my face. "Sounds romantic. What came up? Laundry day?" I eye her onesie knowingly. She shoves my thigh with her bootie. "Ouch!" I laugh, swiping purple icing from my mouth.

A part of me wishes she had gone on the date, and he was wonderful and sexy and kind, everything she wants in a man. I'd relish the chance to know Luisa vulnerable and connected—Luisa in love.

She takes a bite of her doughnut. "This one is surprisingly yummy," she announces.

"So, will you put him off forever?" I ask.

"Not likely," she says. "Mami has been harassing me nonstop."

She looks toward the front door of her house. "I love my family, but sometimes they can feel a little . . . smothering? Mami's so deep in my business." Luisa falls silent, and I decide not to respond. Something in her expression tells me she may be working up the courage to open up to me, just a little bit. "I guess one reason I loved my work," she says slowly, "was because, there, I could be completely independent, totally in control of the story."

Yes, control. That's clearly a key driver for Luisa, along with radical independence. I wonder what it would feel like to be entirely independent and in control of my life. I also wonder why Luisa can't see the gift that's right inside her house—the love and connection and support.

"I get what you're saying, but—as I think you know—I don't exactly have a family, apart from Aidan," I respond, deciding that honesty is the best approach. "So when I look at your family, and how big and boisterous and loving it seems to be, I honestly feel a little envious."

We so often want what we don't have.

"What happened to your family?" she asks, her voice gently breaking into my thoughts. "Why *are* you and Aidan all alone?"

"It was just me and my parents in Jackson," I say. "They kind of sucked as parents—all they ever cared about was appearances, looking like a good family, which, to them, meant a respectable family." An image of my mother comes to mind, for the first time in many years. She's in the kitchen, polishing a silver chafing dish, the same one she gripped so tightly the last day I saw her.

"So, you didn't want to live by their rules?" Luisa asks.

"It wasn't exactly that straightforward," I tell her. "When I got pregnant, they thought it was their decision what would happen next—the path that brought the least shame on them. We lived in a very conservative community."

"You mean they wanted you to quietly get rid of the pregnancy."

"Yeah," I say, smiling in spite of myself. They wanted me to do everything quietly. I was always too loud, too attention-grabbing. "And so did Aidan's father," I tell her.

"But you didn't want an abortion?" she asks. "Even though you knew you'd have to raise him alone?"

"I mean, I wasn't really thinking about it on a philosophical level. It's just that . . ." I pause, trying to form the words that might explain how I decided to leave everything and everyone I knew. "So, you know how people are always talking about 'my body, my choice'?" I ask her. "Well, I just watched as they all stood around determining what was best for me, as if I had no say. And I had this instinctive feeling—deep down in my gut—that I was meant to carry that pregnancy. It wasn't about *all* people and *all* pregnancies. It wasn't a rational decision or a moral choice. It was a sense, so profound, that I wanted to be Aidan's mom," I say. "And I decided that if I was going to be a mom, I would try to be a good mom, which is why I left my family behind."

Luisa looks at me, clearly puzzled.

"I felt like I couldn't even begin to do that with them in my life, reminding me that I'd never amount to anything, that I was bringing shame on them and on Aidan's father, just by existing. So I told them I'd 'take care of it,' and I left." I look up at her, desperate to avoid the hurt of it all, but still forcing myself to say the words. "Wanna know the last thing my mother told me before I walked out?" The image of her holding that damned chafing dish returns to my mind. "She said that I couldn't possibly raise a child. I'd be incapable of keeping a job and I'd fail as a mother." I shrug. "And now here we are. I guess she was right. It's a miracle that we've warded off disaster for this long."

My heart sinks into my gut, and I try to push away all the worry, the anxiety about what might be next for my little family.

"And that was the last time you saw them?" Luisa asks.

"Yeah." I nod. "I've only spoken to my parents once since I left Mississippi—to tell them I didn't have an abortion, and they have a grandson." I feel the ache swelling in my chest, recalling that conversation. "It was Aidan's first birthday. I had made him chocolate cake from a box. We were sitting together at the kitchen table, while he smeared icing all over his face." I smile, remembering those fat little cheeks. "Byron and Justine had just left—they came over with streamers and silly hats, and we had an impromptu birthday party." I recall the bright orange kitty-cat piano Justine gave him, which Aidan banged on incessantly—his first musical instrument. "I was so outrageously happy," I continue. "I had this amazing kid—this precious, healthy, thriving son—and together we had pulled through the hardest year of my life." I can still see Byron coming through the doorway of my apartment on that day, a gallon of ice cream in one hand and a carefully wrapped gift in the other, smiling like a proud uncle. And Justine, looking goofy in the very best way, wearing that pointy blue paper hat, while she taped bright streamers to my rickety old ceiling fan. "I realized that I didn't *need* my parents," I say, "but it seemed somehow cruel to keep Aidan a secret from them. So I called."

"What did they say?" Luisa asks softly.

"Basically that I made a huge mistake, and they would have nothing to do with me or my son or the embarrassment he brought on our family," I tell her, wanting to push away the sadness, but knowing that—even after all these years—it's impossible. "I told them I felt sorry for them, because they had no idea what they were missing." I recall ending the conversation, my sweet boy babbling in the background, still stuffing fistfuls of cake into his mouth, while I exchanged those final words with my parents. "And so," I tell Luisa, "that was that."

"You're amazing, Holly," Luisa says, her voice swelling with admiration. "You didn't let them define you. You did what I want so badly to do—struck out on your own, courageous and independent."

"I guess that's one way of looking at it," I reply.

What I wish I could explain is that the choice led me to exactly the opposite of independence. It sent me into an intense and profound connection to another person—the kind of bond that never, ever allows me to make a decision for myself without concern about how it might affect Aidan. And even though, every once in a while, this connectedness feels like an almost unbearable burden, most of the time it's the ground under my feet and the source of every true joy I have in my life.

Luisa, seeming lost in her own thoughts, doesn't reply. Instead, she sits silent for a while, and then blurts out: "I should have been more brave." Her tone is defiant. "I should have set my mind to it, put on my big-girl panties, and gotten the job done." She pauses to shove half a doughnut into her mouth. "And now it's over and—"

"You didn't even get the chance to take off your big-girl panties for Eli," I interject, trying to bring some levity into the situation.

She does laugh, but when she stops, she wipes her mouth with the back of her hand and growls. "That guy. Another huge mistake."

"Has he tried to reach out to you?" I ask.

"Like every five minutes," she says, shaking her head slowly. "I feel like such an idiot." She pulls her legs into her chest. "We should have never brought him into this."

"Lots of avoidance going on right now," I say. "The esteemed Professor Pridmore is ghosting me."

"Seriously?" she asks. "I thought you two were really going somewhere."

"Professor Pridmore would beg to differ," I tell her, feigning a British accent, which makes Luisa laugh.

"His loss," Luisa replies. "If he can't get over a tiny white lie"—she pinches her thumb and index finger together to demonstrate—"he's just another snooty Brit with a stick up his ass."

"Well, it wasn't exactly *tiny*—the lie we told him," I retort, swatting her hand away. "It's okay, though. At least now I know that I'm ready to get back out there. I mean, I haven't even tried to go on a date in ages." I peer into the pastry box, grab the last doughnut, split it, and hand half to Luisa. "I guess it was finally time to get out of my comfort zone, start taking risks. What is it that Irma's always saying? 'If there's no risk, there's no reward.'"

Seen from this perspective, I guess my decision to spew out our whole story in a voicemail to Hugh wasn't a terrible one after all. Maybe it was exactly what I needed to do—take a chance, even if the whole thing went nowhere.

"We need more coffee," Luisa announces, lifting herself from the swing. "Then we'll unpack what to do about the whole Pridmore situation. Be right back."

I'm cleaning up the remains of our doughnut binge, gathering a wad of sticky napkins, when a familiar truck approaches. And then none other than Elijah Denvil Sweet Jr. gets out and comes sauntering up the brick path—looking like he doesn't have a care in the world.

What the hell is he doing here? That's what I'm thinking when I hear the screen door slam shut. Then I turn to see Luisa, holding two steaming mugs in her hands.

"What the hell are you doing here?" she calls out.

Great minds *do* think alike. Or in this case, greatly distressed minds.

"Well, good mornin' to you, too," he says, in what I must admit to be a perfect Mississippi drawl. He reaches up to grasp the edge of his beat-up Happy Hooker baseball cap and tips his head, like a real Southern gentleman, then steps onto the porch and stands across from Luisa, who has set the mugs onto a side table and is shooting him a fierce glare.

He stares down at her pajamas and grins. "Are those cats and tacos?"

"Galaxy taco cats," she snaps back.

"Ohhhkay," he responds warily. "I tried to call you both. A bunch of times. Since you didn't pick up, I just came down here to share the big news."

We stare at him. Silent. I can feel the rage radiating from Luisa's body. Or is it desire? Sometimes the two are hard to distinguish.

"Well, since you asked . . ." He pauses for effect, then stretches his arms wide. "You ladies just might be looking at the next inductee into the Midnight Society."

"What are you talking about?" Luisa spits back at him, arms crossed over her chest.

Too dumbfounded to utter a single word, I plop down on the swing, my mouth agape.

"Holly," Luisa barks, then actually snaps her fingers, like she's trying to pull me out of hypnosis. "What's he talking about? Is this one of those creepy secret societies?"

"Not secret. More like exclusive—Atlanta's oldest and most

prestigious social club for men," I say, awed that Eli got an invite. "I'm pretty sure only bachelors can join, but then they stay in for life." I shake my head, still not believing our good fortune.

"Is this another one of those pat-yourself-on-the-back charity things?" Luisa asks.

I shake my head. "They just exist as an excuse to get together and have a good time," I explain. "Most of their parties are only for the male members, but they hold two events a year at the club—the only ones with spouses and dates: a New Year's Eve white-tie formal and an annual costume ball—"

"Costumes?" Luisa sneers. "What is this? Halloween in June?"

"We're not talking those polyester getups that you buy from the pharmacy in a plastic bag," I scoff, recalling the year Buck Dorsey, a Midnight Society old-timer and the current chair of the Dogwood Hills board of directors, paid thirty thousand dollars for a Robocop costume—at least, that's what Jancy reported. "People go all out," I tell Eli and Luisa. "It's a huge freaking deal."

"And yours truly scored an invite," Eli gloats, "from the esteemed judge himself." He leans back against the white porch railing and crosses one foot over the other. "They want me to meet one of their business partners," Eli says. "A banker flying in from Panama."

"Wait—" Luisa blurts out, holding up one hand, then searching for something on her phone with the other. "Is his name Dudley Magruder?"

"The very one," Eli confirms. "But the judge calls him 'Mags.' Judge says they've known each other since they were kids playin' hide-and-seek on Peachtree Battle, whatever that means. Apparently, Ol' Mags has a house down at Palmetto Bluff—really nice golf course out there, with undulating greens, lots of beautiful oaks. You have to be careful with the alligators, though," Eli offers unhelpfully. "I told you both, I knew what I was doing. You just chose not to believe me."

My mind races back through our fight after his big golf win. I was so mad that he refused to follow my instructions, I couldn't even process what he was trying to explain. But I guess he was right about earning their trust with that bet, because this introduction is exactly what we need, and Eli has managed to get it for us.

"Dudley Magruder is our guy," Luisa exclaims, jamming her index finger against her phone screen. "Griggs's family foundation money is getting diverted to his bank. Then laundered via shell companies, including Peachtree Holdings—the same company that holds the Castillos' fake deed." She's pacing the length of the porch. "I need to call my source at the Treasury Department, see what they have on Magruder. The man is a ghost online. I was starting to doubt he even existed in real life."

"Judge Thacker wants me to take Virginia," Eli says, apparently choosing to ignore Luisa's stressed-out pacing and musing. "She already texted. Says she's absolutely *thrilled* to introduce me to *everyone*."

"I'm sure she is," Luisa grumbles under her breath, just as I'm exclaiming, "That's amazing, Eli. You did it!"

"Does this mean we're back on?" he asks, a puppy-dog pleading expression in his eyes. "Because I've already got the perfect costume in mind."

Luisa and I glance at each other for just a beat, then nod in unison. Looks like our Tripp is going to the ball.

CHAPTER 25

Luisa

Eli asks me to meet him at Fort Yargo State Park, just down the road from the Happy Hooker, where he's making deliveries for bait 'n' tackle and fishing supplies. It gave me an excuse to drop in on the Castillos, deliver a home-cooked meal and bilingual picture books for the kids, and quickly update Pablo and Gloria on our progress.

I wind through the park's narrow roads, snaking my way under a lush canopy of green. I pass several families on bikes, and others readying for a hike on one of the many trails. A wrong turn lands me on a side road dotted with campers, RVs, cozy-looking cabins, and even a handful of yurts. It's a popular state park, I realize, taking in the multiple gatherings in picnic shelters and the conference pavilion.

I find Eli by the boat ramp, where he's teaching two freckled boys how to cast a fishing line. They look at him with a mixture of respect and admiration. Eli must say something funny, because the boys laugh, then follow his lead, pulling the rod tip back over their shoulders, then forward.

Eli sees me and smiles, beckoning me to the ramp where they're standing. I gather the collection of Jackson Country Club and Phi Delt golf polos, and the Ole Miss Rebels driver cover I came here to deliver, then jump out of my SUV. Holly ordered them after our shopping spree, and they've just arrived.

"Let's pick a nice juicy one," Eli is saying, proffering a container full of live worms.

"Please don't," I yelp. All three stare back at me like I've lost my mind. "I can't watch you impale a helpless worm. They feel pain."

The boys' expressions turn aghast.

"You said they couldn't feel anything," one of them reproaches.

Eli rolls his eyes, grunting in frustration. "Thanks," he says to me sarcastically, before covering the container and storing it back in a cooler.

"You're welcome," I respond, matching his sarcasm.

Worms safely tucked away, he gives the boys an artificial silverfish bait, instead. The boys throw their lines into the lake, smiling back at Eli with satisfaction, and I bite my tongue, so as not to share that the fish will *also* feel pain when hooked.

"You in a hurry?" he asks, gathering his fishing supplies.

"Depends," I say. "I have no intention of fishing, if that's why you're asking." I get a second eye roll in response.

It's sweltering hot and the air is sticky, so we leave the boys and return to Eli's truck. We grab some cold drinks from his cooler and store the new golf gear. Eli brings down the tailgate and I sit, watching him store his fishing supplies in the bed's metal toolbox. With his back to me—and his T-shirt drenched in sweat and practically painted on his lean body—I can appreciate the contours of his upper arms and broad shoulders, the athletic lines framing his spine.

I'm thrown back to that night on the golf course—the surprising softness of his lips, the way my body felt grounded by his solid form, and the mind-blowing sensation of his hands gripping my thighs under the skirt of my dress. What else can those capable hands do if left to their own devices? How much more can that gorgeous mouth accomplish, given the time?

I bite my lower lip, shuddering at the thought, reminding myself that I have no business thinking about Eli's mouth, or hands, or any other body part for that matter. Not when I don't know what Virginia expects from their upcoming date, or what Eli is willing to give.

I've tossed and turned all week obsessing about this thought, while also trying to do a deep dive into Dudley Magruder, even though I already knew he has virtually no digital footprint. Eli will be meeting him unprepared, and I may just get an ulcer counting all the ways their encounter can go wrong.

But without a paper trail, there's no way to prove the link between the bank, the development, and Griggs's family foundation. So we'll have to settle on Eli recording a conversation of the business deal, hopefully one exposing criminal activity.

"Holly ordered the Ricky Bobby NASCAR fire suit you asked for," I say, taking a cold Coke can from his hand, then opening it with a hiss. "*If you ain't first, you're last*? Really?"

He sits on the tailgate beside me, his voice suddenly dropping into a backwoods North Carolina drawl. "Here's the deal. I'm the best there is. Plain and simple. I wake up in the morning and I piss excellence." His Ricky Bobby impersonation is so on point, I can't help but laugh.

"You're gonna blow them away." I raise my soda can at him.

"I expect Griggs and his buddies won't waste any time making fun of a backwoods redneck," he says, one corner of his lips ticking upward, "but I'll enjoy knowing they're on the losing end of the joke." He stares at the can sweating in his palm. "I've wondered what they'd think of me, if they knew where I actually come from." There's an almost imperceptible layer of shame under his words, and I muse whether he's thinking back to his childhood. I want to know more, but I also don't want to push him to reveal the painful parts of his life before he's ready.

I need to be patient, I tell myself. But it's easier said than done.

"It's so damn hot," I say instead, pulling at my T-shirt, damp with sweat. "I may actually melt." I take a long swig of my Coke.

"You got a swimsuit in that fancy SUV of yours?" he asks, jumping off the tailgate, then tugging off his T-shirt.

"I didn't realize I'd be needing one," I counter, my voice dropping off at the sight of his bare torso. *Ave María, Madre de Dios.* I'm wonderstruck at the real-life six-pack before me, and the stunning watercolor tattoo of a mountain landscape on the left side of his chest. My fingers itch to touch the pine trees etched on his skin, the mountain ridges behind them, the full moon that perfectly complements his wolfish eyes, the two little birds inked over his heart.

"You're good like this." Eli gives my T-shirt and shorts, my bare arms and legs, a once-over. His Adam's apple bobs as he brings his hands to my waist, then pulls me to a stand before him. He then takes me by the hand, teasing me as he drags us along Fort Yargo's sandy beach, threatening to throw me over his shoulder when I complain that I can't go in the water fully dressed, and then insist that a lake beach is, in fact, not a real beach.

"It really doesn't get any more redneck than this," he exclaims as we plunge into the glorious cool water. Eli's self-deprecating laugh illuminates his entire face in a way I've never seen before. His eyes glint, mirroring the sun's bright reflection on the water. His cheeks radiate with an easy contentment that permeates even his speech. His words come out natural and relaxed, not artificial and defensive, as they tend to be when we're around other people.

This is the real Eli, I think. I laugh, too, diving into the sweet release from the oppressive heat. When I come back up for air, I tilt my head up, relishing the tingle of sunshine on my skin and the sand against my toes.

We wade in place for a while, watching the families spread out across the beach—parents grilling hot dogs, toddlers in little arm floaties, teenagers playing volleyball.

"I used to love those carbon-smoked hot dogs," he observes, smiling wistfully to himself. "My mamaw used to bring us here over the summer."

"Is she still around?" I ask.

"She died a few years ago." His gaze is intent on the shoreline, where some kids are building a sandcastle. "She left us her house, in Westlake. I'm not sure we could've managed otherwise."

In the weeks we've spent together, this is the first time he's offered a part of himself unprompted. I contemplate what it means, that he's finally trusting me with pieces of his real life. Could I do the same? Could I open myself up to him, too? Be vulnerable? Or as Holly said, step outside my comfort zone, take a risk.

I suck in a deep breath and ready myself to sink or swim.

"Eli?" I start, tentatively. "Is there anything going on? With you and Virginia, I mean?" I let go of his hand, slowly paddle my arms, pushing the water around me. "And trust me . . ." I add, self-aware, "I know how nuts that question sounds given that we've been pushing you to do whatever it takes to make this crazy scheme work." I look at him in earnest, my eyes fixed on his gray irises. "But if I'm being honest, I didn't know what we were asking. I didn't know you. And now . . ." He glides closer to me, holding my gaze. "It's different. We're different. And I just need to know. Okay?" I shrug dismissively, but my heart couldn't feel more defenseless and exposed.

"Luisa," he says, reaching for my arms under the water. "Nothing has happened between Virginia and me. And nothing *will* happen. I promise you." I study his expression, searching for any indication of a lie, but I find none. He can see my apprehension, and he releases an audible sigh, his head angled slightly. "I know you think I'm some kind of hustler or whatever," he says, sounding disgusted at the thought, "but I don't go around hooking up randomly. That's not my thing." His thumbs run over my biceps, lightly caressing my skin in a way that implores me to stay, to believe him. "I'm not exactly a no-strings-attached kinda guy."

"What does that even mean?" I ask. The current shifts and our legs brush against each other, moving us even closer. "You are, after all, a single guy."

"What I mean is that I don't really date, or hook up, or whatever." At the admission, a flush creeps over his cheeks. "I'm responsible for my younger sister, Pearl," he says, surveying my expression for a response. "I'm her legal guardian. So when I'm not working to keep us afloat, I'm essentially her parent, which doesn't leave much time for anything else—or anyone else."

He runs one hand over his wet hair. I glance down to his chest, over his heart, where two little birds are frozen mid-flight. I venture one fingertip over the ink. "Are these meant to be you and your sister?"

He nods, reaching for my hand over his chest, then interlacing my fingers with his. My heartbeat speeds up at the touch.

"How old is she now?" I ask, trying to absorb the details of his reality, process the weight of his responsibility.

"She's almost eighteen," he says, squeezing my hand under water. "She'll be heading to college in the fall." He smiles proudly, like a father would, and I see in the corners of his eyes that this has been a hard-earned accomplishment. I don't know the whole story yet, but I can sense how much he's had to struggle just to get by, to ensure a good future for his sister. My chest swells with affection and tenderness, and also curiosity. I want to be the person he trusts with his secrets, I realize. I want to earn that place in his life.

"So what are you saying exactly?" I ask, leaning into a more playful energy, finally relaxing into the sunlight and wild landscape around us. "I shouldn't expect you to take me out on a real date?"

Eli grins, his whole body slackening as he pulls me into him with both hands. My legs wrap tightly around his waist. I throw my arms around his bare shoulders, skin warm from the sun. "What are you doing tonight?" he asks.

Our first official date winds up at the White Windmill Bakery & Cafe. My sun-kissed skin glows from our time at the lake, and I'm giddy with sugar and pure joy. Eli asked his sister to help him plan the ideal "foodie night out," a tall order considering I once reviewed restaurants for *The Georgia Times*. They drew up a list of five Buford Highway "hidden gems" and dishes to taste at each stop, all part of a global culinary extravaganza that, so far, rates as the best date night of my entire life.

We savored Thai street food at Tum Pok Pok, revolving sushi and sake at E-Gyu, pork dumplings at Northern China Eatery, a taco tasting at La Guelaguetza, and now, dessert at what happens to be my all-time favorite French Korean bakery and cafe.

I'm glad I listened to Holly and took a risk. I guess she was right after all—this feels like such a sweet reward.

"I'm not gonna lie," I say, bubbling with laughter, "watching you attempt to order a taco de cabeza from that very confused abuelita at Plaza Fiesta was probably the highlight of my year." I gasp for air, remembering how she kept pushing a platter with a whole roasted pig's head in his direction, and the hysterical bewildered expression on his face.

"Thanks for the help," he says, laughing over the table. We're seated across from each other at one of the cafe's small tables for two. "I didn't want to be disrespectful, but there's no way I was having dead pig eyes staring at us on a first date. There's no coming back from that."

I clutch at my stomach. "Stop it," I cry out, unable to stop laughing. "I'm so full, it hurts." Still, I can't help but take another bite of the decadent berry Chantilly cake we're sharing. "The whole thing reminded me of the lechoneras in Puerto Rico. Entire pigs roasting on a spit."

"You go back often?" he asks, setting down his fork, then cleaning the sides of his mouth with a napkin.

"It's complicated." I fidget in my chair, leaning on my elbows, picking at the whipped cream with my fork. "When I'm there, I don't have to constantly explain myself. I have this sense of ease that I can't seem to access anywhere else." I sit up straight, abandoning my fork. "But other times people treat me like an outsider because I've lived in the States for so long." Beside us, a couple of kids set up a chess board, readying themselves to play. I take a sip of my honey tea. "At the same time, Atlanta also feels like home, even if people treat me like an outsider here, too." I fold both hands around the cup of hot tea, comforted by the warmth. "I'm one of those people who lives in the *in-between*, I guess."

"I get that," Eli says reassuringly. "Summers in Westlake with Mamaw were the only times it felt like we had a home, but they also meant missing my mom." His gaze cuts to the parking lot, busy even though it's past ten at night.

I'm so grateful he seems to have finally dropped his defenses. And maybe it's because I've dropped mine, too. Is this what it takes to fully trust someone?

"My mom was a wreck. But she kept our family together somehow." He stabs a piece of strawberry but doesn't eat it. "And then she got real sick. Died when I was twelve. And that's when the guardrails came off." I reach for him under the table, resting my hand on his knee.

He cups my fingers in his, before his gaze cuts behind me, his forehead crumpling into a frown. A warm hand slides over my shoulder and gives it a squeeze. Startled, I whip my head around to find Augusto, sharply dressed in his detective uniform—dark suit, light shirt, sensible tie, gun holster and badge.

"What are you doing here?" I stand to give him a hug. "I thought you were off today—" I mock glare at him. "Otherwise, I would've stayed far away from your favorite coffeehouse."

"Got the night shift all month." He gestures toward his partner, who is placing an order at the counter. "It's so much easier to solve a murder when you're properly caffeinated." Then, leaning into my ear, he asks, "Is this the hairy one?"

I punch his arm, and he pretends to whimper.

I'm debating how exactly to introduce Eli, when he saves me the trouble. Eli stands, one palm outstretched, inviting Augusto to shake his hand. There's a row of tiny beads of sweat over his brow that I swear wasn't there a few minutes ago.

"This is my brother-in-law, Augusto," I say. "He's a detective."

"Eli," he says, pumping Augusto's hand, offering a smile that doesn't reach his eyes. Something is off in Eli's demeanor, but I have no idea what. Tension has creeped over his shoulders, and I can sense he's making an effort to appear cheerful.

"You two on a date?" Augusto asks, aiming his shrewd cop eyes in Eli's direction. I put up a hand to stop Eli from answering.

"Don't say a word," I demand. "Because my dear Augusto can't keep anything from my sister, Carola. And my sister, Carola, can't keep anything from our mother." I jab at Augusto with one fingernail. "So you're not getting anything from us."

Augusto laughs, dropping a meaty hand on Eli's shoulder. Eli flinches in response.

"This woman can more than handle herself," Augusto remarks.

"So grateful to have a man to speak for me." I roll my eyes, crossing my arms over my chest.

"But if anyone ever dares fuck with her"—Augusto grins, increasing the pressure on Eli's shoulder—"they're fucking with me, too."

"You done?" I ask Augusto, jutting my hip at this absurd display of misplaced valor. "Can we please go back to our date now?"

"So, it *is* a date," Augusto exclaims, rubbing his hands impishly. I answer with a silent *Are you kidding me?* "It's always nice to be handed a voluntary confession." He winks, pulling me into a side hug and kissing the side of my forehead.

"You can go now," I say, sliding one arm around his waist and hugging him back.

He glances down at a cellophane bag of cookies on the table and cheekily says, "I'm confiscating these." He turns to leave, and just when I think we're finally rid of him, he points one finger at Eli, and says, "She's a keeper."

I groan, but then Eli's eyes land on mine, and his warm, husky voice murmurs, "That's what I'm hoping for." And that's when I melt into a puddle, right here at the White Windmill.

For what feels like an eternity, I'm at a loss for words. All I can do is hold Eli's gaze and bite my lower lip, trying to calm my racing heart. I'm also trying to make sense of Eli's odd reaction to Augusto.

"Did Augusto say something to upset you?" I ask gently.

"God, no," he's quick to respond. "I'm sorry if I was awkward." He shakes his head with a sigh, then takes a long drink of water, his Adam's apple bobbing hard with every gulp. "I have a . . . complicated relationship with cops."

"What happened, Eli?" I ask, resting my palm over his forearm.

He sets down the glass of water, releasing a low, painful exhale. "After my mom died, my dad just . . ." He shrugs, as if struggling to find the right words. "Drove us off a cliff, in a sense. He started running scams. Pretending my sister and I had cancer or needed an operation." I wince, already hating his father. What kind of man uses his kids like that? I move my palm to hold his hand, reminding him that I'm on his side. "Pearl has always been a good kid." He brings his free hand to his face, rubs at his chin with his fingers. "I didn't want her getting in trouble. So I volunteered to take the brunt of it."

"Fuck," I whisper, resisting the urge to pull him closer to me, fold him into a hug.

"High school was a shit show." His hand trails his neck, scratching at the back of his head. "We moved all over. We'd be at a big-box store—Walmart, Target, Kmart—and I'd pretend to slip on one of those waxy papers they put inside shoeboxes." He motions a sliding gesture over the table, landing with the butt of his palm. "Then he'd threaten the managers with a lawsuit. A few weeks later, we'd get a check in the mail from some insurance company."

"So after he scammed the stores in one area, you had to move on," I say in understanding, remembering his words from our day on the connector, his despondent expression as he said: *You can only run so many hustles in one place before you have to skip town.*

He nods in confirmation.

"I'm so sorry, Eli."

He leans back, clearly needing some space. His hair falls over his forehead in a way that gives me a glimpse of the teenage boy he used to be, scared and alone, but also resourceful and resilient. I feel a sudden visceral urge to protect us both from the world and all the shitty people in it, including our own parents.

"I got caught a few times," he admits. "The store manager would always call some cop, or detective, or a child services officer to come deal with me." He stares toward the door, where Augusto just walked out minutes ago. "My dad would always blame everything on me."

"And they always believed him?" I add, more a statement than a question.

"Of the two of us, he definitely is the more talented con man." Eli tries to give the words a sarcastic edge, but the truth behind them is too sad to be funny.

"Where is he now?" I ask, hoping his dad has disappeared for good.

"We hadn't seen him in years, but back in March," he says, the line of his jaw hardening, "he showed up, spewing some bullshit about making amends." His eyes cloud over, their expression turning angry and resentful. "I wasn't home, and Pearl let him in. He stole a checkbook, left straight for the bank. Cleaned out Pearl's college fund."

"What?" I ask in disbelief, leaning forward in my chair. "How could he do that?" Immediately, it dawns on me. "You have the same name." I think back to that first meeting at the Happy Hooker, how prickly he became when I called him by his father's name.

"I was about to lose my fucking mind." He shakes his head, pulling at his hair, one leg wrestling under the table. "Pearl had been working her ass off to get into art school in Savannah. We'd been saving for years. And in an instant, it was all gone. Every last penny."

We sit back in our chairs, Eli looking exhausted from all the awful memories.

"Is that why you were running hustles at Ginny's?" I ask, knowing the answer.

He nods, his eyes cutting away uncomfortably, shame coloring his cheeks. He avoided his father's fraudulent way of life for so long, and now his own father's actions made it his only option.

"I didn't know what else to do," he tells me earnestly. "We pieced together some scholarships, but they wouldn't cover everything. Student enrollment and housing fees were due." He looks away, past the window to the highway. "I was desperate."

"Did Pearl know?" I watch him sink into the chair, getting smaller under the weight of it all.

"No," he says tightly. "And I'd like to keep it that way." He meets my gaze expectantly. I nod. "You and Holly walking through the doors of the Happy Hooker"—he scoffs—"it was like a fucking miracle. I never thought it possible."

I think back to the sapphire bracelet and that awful trip to the pawnshop, how sick I felt selling that piece of jewelry to pay off someone I believed to be an unscrupulous scammer. How wrong I was. Little did I know that my crime just might fix one man's life, and save a young woman's future, in some crazy karmic justice payback that I never could have imagined.

And maybe, just maybe, meeting Eli was—for me—a lucky twist of karma, too.

CHAPTER 26

Holly

We're sitting around a conference table, forty-five minutes into an hour-long, end-of-day event staffing meeting, and Irma's in full-on astrology guru mode. She's already informed us, in excruciating detail, about Pluto's long transit through Sagittarius and next Thursday's Mercury cazimi. It's time for me to get this meeting back on track.

"Okay, folks," I announce. "Let's move on to the Midnight Society's Costume Ball."

A collective groan fills the small conference room, and Justine dramatically slouches onto the table, her forehead resting in her hands. "God, I hate this event," she says.

I pull up a checklist on my tablet and prepare to move us through the details of the Midnight Society Costume Ball, which will kick off the summer season.

The ball appears, on the page, to be more or less the same as an evening wedding reception, a debutante ball, or a black-tie charity fundraiser. But, in practice, there is something radically different about this event. Members and their dates see dressing in costume as a chance to cut loose, to "live a little." For staff, this "good time" brings out a side of these high-society types that we'd rather not witness, and it generally translates into a cluster of ugly messes, lawsuit-worthy slip-and-falls, broken stemware, and trashed powder rooms. In other words, our worst nightmare.

"I'm hiring an extra cater waiter, and I'll take floor duty," I announce, trying to sound nonchalant. If Luisa, Eli, and I want our plan to go off without a hitch, I'll need to be right in the middle of things. And we've decided the best way for Luisa to show up incognito is as a member of the waitstaff.

"Wait," Justine cuts in. "You're just gonna volunteer for the most hellish task on the most hellish night of the year? Without even putting up a fight?"

"You stayed on floor 'til the bitter end last year," I say, even though the real reason is that I want to be able to keep an eye on Eli and help out if I need to. "So it's probably my turn."

"And oh how bitter it was," she spits. "Eighty-pound grown-ass women should know better than to drink a gallon of Long Island iced tea."

After the party finally shut down, Justine had to call an ambulance for the out-of-town date of one of the Midnight Society's new inductees. Alcohol poisoning. The guy wandered off to a strip club with his new buddies and left her passed out on a bench in the courtyard—ironically, dressed as a naughty nurse. It was not pretty.

We don't typically talk trash about club events, or about club members. Most of us, with the notable exception of Janey, won't bother to waste our breath on members' silly indiscretions or social drama that has nothing to do with us. But I won't begrudge this crowd the opportunity to let off a little steam when it comes to the Midnight Society. They've earned it.

"Just so we can get ourselves emotionally prepared," Irma says, her voice suddenly serious, "what's the theme this year?"

"Y'allywood," I announce, consulting the details listed on my tablet, as if I need them. Of course, Eli had already filled Luisa and me in. The three of us have been talking daily since he showed up at Luisa's house to break the big news. Eli seems very concerned to prove to me that he's reliable and trustworthy. From what Luisa's shared with me, he has somewhat loftier goals when it comes to her. At first I was worried when she spilled the news that their relationship had taken a romantic turn. But I wasn't concerned for long, after hearing the thrill in her voice when she told me about their adorable first date on Buford Highway. I'm so happy for them both, but I also feel a little wistful, recalling what could have been with Hugh.

It's going on two weeks, and he still hasn't called or texted. Not a word.

"How's Y'allywood likely to rank us on the offensiveness scale?" Byron asks, bringing me back to the task at hand.

"Can't be as bad as 'Divas and Dudes,'" Irma scoffs.

"When Mr. Wilkerson showed up dressed as Diana Ross," Justine recalls, laughing in spite of herself. "Old white man wearing a two-foot-tall Afro and a tight sequined gown. That's messed up."

Honestly, I still can't look at Mr. Wilkerson the same way. I'm constantly pushing away the image of his veiny, gray-haired leg peeking out from behind the long slit of a silver gown.

Hearing a series of soft taps on the conference room door, we all turn to see Janey peeking through, her sensible brown loafer nudged into the doorway.

"So sorry to interrupt," Janey whispers, as if we're in a library and not a windowless room along the dingy service hallway. "But there's someone at the gatehouse," she says, turning her gaze toward me. "Who needs to speak with Holly."

I pick up my phone and glance through texts, wondering whether I've missed something from Luisa. She's meeting with a source at the FBI's economic crimes squad. And Eli scored an invite for a weekday fly-fishing trip with Griggs and Jim Wade. They're up at Brigadoon Lodge, on one of northwest Georgia's most exclusive private rivers. I made it clear that he absolutely, under no circumstances, will catch one of their renowned trophy-size rainbow trout. He laughed at that one, then assured me that he would "make no such promises."

Seeing no text from either of them, I look at Janey, puzzled.

"A British gentleman," she adds, her eyebrows arching oh-so-subtly. "He says he needs to speak with you."

I feel a fierce blush rise to my cheeks, as the attention of the entire room turns in my direction. "We're just about finished here," I say. "I'll take care of it."

I quickly adjourn the meeting and then rush out, trying to push aside the full knowledge that this absolutely will make it into tomorrow's episode of Janey's Daily Dirt Dump.

I arrive at the guard station to find Hugh leaning casually against an oak tree. He's looking up, studiously observing a branch waving in the breeze. His distraction gives me an opportunity to study the curve of his neck, the angle of his nose, the way his dark hair gleams in the dappled sunlight.

Hugh turns to look at me, and a broad smile spreads across his face. "I finally found you," he exclaims, making his way across the lawn toward me. He stops short of reaching out to grab my hand or hug me, which causes me to ache a little inside.

"How long have you been looking?" I ask, surprised that he seems to have been in search of me. I have a phone, after all, and he could have texted.

"Suffice it to say, I've had a lovely and informative tour of Atlanta's most exclusive country clubs. I'm awash in salmon-pink polos." My expression must betray my bafflement, because he continues without pause. "I hope I haven't made a mistake in coming here. You mentioned in your voicemail—"

"So you listened to the voicemail," I say sheepishly. "You read my texts, too?" I wince, embarrassed.

"I did, eventually," Hugh replies. Lionel, the security guard on duty, sends a Range Rover through and then steps out of the guardhouse to give us both a friendly wave. "I was away from my phone for several days," Hugh continues, waving back. "Trying and failing to finish drafting a monograph."

"Oh," I say, relief washing over me. I decide not to ask what a monograph is, or whether he noticed my extreme use of the word "really" in the string of texts. Watching another member pull in, I gesture for Hugh to follow me around the corner to the edge of the club's property. We stand together beside a stone wall, overlooking the rolling green hills of Piedmont Park.

"I felt—" He pauses and runs a hand through his thick hair. "I felt awful that you might have imagined I was ignoring you, and I wanted to explain in person. So I decided to accept your kind invitation. Shall we walk and talk?" he asks, looking back toward the park. "Or are you on the clock?"

"Not anymore," I say. "Free as a bird."

We head into Piedmont Park and follow a wide path toward the Beltline, under a broad canopy of trees. It's my favorite season in Atlanta, early summer, when the canopy fills out with a dozen shades of green, and fragrant flowers blossom in every direction—gardenia, wisteria, spray rose, and iris infuse my city with a gentle sweetness and the fresh feeling of possibility. Soon, the chartreuse leaves will deepen to green, bright scents will turn to heavy decay, and the delicate flowers will wilt in the extreme heat of summer. But somehow, every year—as spring fades to summer—knowing what's to come makes the moment all the more special.

We pass under an arch, twined with star jasmine, and Hugh asks me how I came to work at a members-only country club. I tell him about those early months in Atlanta, alone with Aidan, and my desperation. I explain that it may seem strange, but Dogwood Hills has been a gift to me, has given Aidan and me a family, and in so many ways has been a home. I tell him that working there, as an eighteen-year-old single mom, was the first time I ever held down a job, and it felt good to take responsibility, to build some structure and purpose into a life that had been, until then, adrift.

"I guess my fellow country club employees were kinda like your punk rock buddies," I say, recalling what he told me that night at the jazz club, about how he fell in with anarchists and stole his very first linguistics book. "They helped me pull my shit together."

We arrive at the Beltline and gaze into a sea of walkers, joggers, and cyclists. It feels strange to start cruising along this path in my wrap dress and sensible flats, but it's also lovely to be here with Hugh, skirting the edge of Midtown.

"Well, what I failed to share with you that night," he says, dodging a Great Dane whose owner is too busy talking on the phone to notice, "is that those punk rockers also landed me in jail."

"Seriously?" I say, my voice pitching high as I stop and turn to look at him. It's exercise rush hour out here, and I get a fierce glare from two power walkers in coordinating jumpsuits, as they swerve past us.

"Seriously," he responds, gesturing for me to keep walking. "In a charming little suburb on the outskirts of Paris."

Sensing my anxiety, Hugh looks back toward the small lake at the center of Piedmont Park, where an empty bench beckons. "Perhaps not the best time of day for a casual stroll," he says. "Let's sit instead."

We escape the flow of exercisers, and I feel my shoulders relax as we walk across a broad lawn toward the placid lake. We settle onto the bench and watch, in silence, as a pair of white swans glide away from us.

"I don't want to pry," I say, "so there's no need to answer, but what exactly happened in Paris?"

"Well, as it happens, I was in the wrong place at the wrong time. I had traveled with some friends to visit a small community of anarchists who were attempting to live off the grid." He's looking across the lake, his gaze fixed on a mallard taking flight. "What I didn't know," Hugh continues, "was that they also were sabotaging the grid—cutting power lines and the like. It seemed like a harmless thing to do, chopping through a skinny wire with garden shears. And so I gave it a try, just as the federal police were arriving to arrest them. Well, more accurately, to arrest *us*."

"And you went to prison?" I ask. I want to look at him, to see if something in his expression conveys the emotion he must have, talking about these events from his past. But I decide instead to watch the swans make their slow loops.

"I was seventeen years and eleven months old, thank God, or I might be in prison still," Hugh says. "I still recall how terrified I was when I called home, to tell my father what I had done. But my mother picked up instead."

"And she told your father for you?" I ask.

"No. She got on a train and traveled to Paris. My mother was a wise and intelligent woman, but she had a rather sheltered childhood and never dared travel alone. Not until then."

His words, so matter-of-fact, make my heart ache. I know what it's like to be that mother—one who does the unimaginable because there's no other option. He looks toward me, clearly sensing that I'll understand his words, and I turn to hold his gaze.

"She overcame her anxieties and even took public transportation for the first time, directly into Paris's sketchiest neighborhood." He smiles, and I can't help smiling back, as I watch those soft wrinkles form at the edges of his dark eyes. "I'll never forget watching her walk into that jail to arrange for my release," he says. "It was so extreme, the juxtaposition of my glamorous mother in her gold jhumka earrings, against the rusty yellow cell bars, that seeing her brought me to tears." He leans forward, resting his elbows on his knees. "I don't know where she found the courage to come alone, to bail her son out of a grimy jail in a Paris suburb. I walked out with her on that day, and we never said a word to my father."

"So you went back to London and left your anarchist phase behind?" I ask, probing.

"Something like that, I suppose. But after that experience, and living with this great act of love my mother undertook for me—" He leans back and looks up at the sky. "I determined not to squander what I had been given—a second chance."

"And so began your glamorous life as an academic?"

He laughs, deep and loud. "And so began my transient life," he corrects. "Let me assure you, there's nothing glamorous about the life of a professor."

"But you have to admit that you're one of those cosmopolitan types who never settles down in one place for more than a couple of years," I announce, shifting on the bench so that I'm also looking up.

"I don't know whether I'd identify as 'cosmopolitan.'" He laughs. "But I do travel unceasingly, and I find it exhilarating. I've built a research program that requires me to be in constant motion, and it's made for a lovely—if not glamorous—life. I haven't a single regret."

It makes me strangely wistful, knowing that this man's life is so very different from my own. I let myself wonder, for a moment, what it would be like to have such freedom, to have no strings tethering me firmly in place.

I sit upright, face him, and ask, "What's the awesomest place you've traveled?"

"Impossible to say," he replies, turning back toward me so

that we're face-to-face. I can tell he's ready to be grilled. "But I'd put Pamukkale, Turkey, and Punta del Este, Uruguay, high on the list."

"The ugliest?" I continue.

"No place is ugly, if one knows where to look." He shrugs.

"Well, aren't you the optimist," I tease. "The coldest?"

"Edmonton, Alberta, Canada, in January. Obscene."

"Sexiest?" I ask. *Holy crap. Where did that come from?*

He pauses to study my face, and I feel a flush rise to my cheeks. "You'll have to give me some time to come up with an answer to that one," he says, his voice suddenly low and thick.

He looks away, back across the pond, and we sit in silence. A breeze blows up and I watch as ripples form on the surface of the pond. It's remarkable, really, the stillness of this forested park, carved from the heart of Midtown. I feel grateful to be here, in a steady, calm place, beside Hugh. Though I wouldn't mind being in Turkey or Uruguay—okay, maybe not Alberta. I wouldn't mind having a life like Hugh's, but I also know that his life is not mine. I know that I belong right here.

"Is it ever lonely?" I dare to ask. "All the travel, I mean."

He ponders for a long minute, then turns to face me. "I hadn't thought so, until now."

I feel my heart stutter, and I'm not sure how to reply. Is he suggesting that something has changed? Could that "something" possibly be me?

"What I wanted to tell you," he says, breaking the silence, "is that when I heard your voicemail—"

"You mean my five-minute rant?" I ask, then let out a heavy sigh.

"It wasn't five minutes, and your words were so genuine, so deeply felt," he says. "I experienced this rush of recognition, and of gratitude for my own mother. I suppose what I'm trying to say is that I understand."

My heart wells with emotion, the sort that only comes from unsolicited kindness. I feel tears in the corners of my eyes, and I worry that one might spill over.

"And I still want to help, if there's any way that I can," he says, reaching into his jacket pocket to pull out a clean white handkerchief, perfectly pressed.

Who is this kind ex-punk sitting beside me on a park bench, handing me a fancy handkerchief to wipe my tears?

"Thank you for your offer to help," I say. "But now that I know you have a criminal record, you probably shouldn't risk getting thrown back in jail."

He laughs again, his head thrown back, and stretches his left arm across the bench.

"I'm not joking," I say.

His arm brushes my shoulder. He doesn't move it.

"Neither am I," he replies. "I'll do whatever you need."

"We might be in over our heads," I say. "But I think it will all be over soon. Just a couple more weeks." My fist flexes around the crisp linen of his handkerchief. "I'm trying not to stress too hard until then."

"Then might I at least offer a distraction?" he asks. "A night on the town?"

"Like, a date?" I reply.

"I was thinking an actual date, not *like* a date," he teases.

"Okay then, an actual date," I reply.

"Perfect," he says, his voice so lovely and smooth that I find myself wishing he were the kind of man who stayed in one place.

CHAPTER 27

Luisa

My stomach flutters irrationally, as I ready myself to knock on Eli's front door. *It's just an afternoon cookout, for Chrissake. Why am I so nervous?*

The exterior of the house is charming and inviting, with bright white siding, a vibrant yellow door, and a set of colorful, hanging flower baskets that have been artfully tended. Eli's truck is in the driveway, and the mere sight of it sends fresh frissons through my gut.

After our first date ended at the White Windmill—now a week ago—Eli drove me home, then walked me to the porch. We stood staring into each other's eyes for a long beat, the promise of a kiss lingering between us—that is until Mami abruptly turned on the porch lights and scowled at us through the sidelight window by the door. So much for privacy.

Holly burst out laughing when I told her what happened. Luckily, she won't have a nosy Puerto Rican mother lurking about for her date tonight with the professor.

Meanwhile, I'll be at Eli's—meeting his sister for the first time. When Eli texted me midweek to invite me over, I relished the idea of a break from the all-consuming money laundering and embezzlement investigation. I'm turning into quite the expert, if I say so myself. Maybe I should take Mami's advice and get that law degree after all.

But even though I was looking forward to a night off from sleuthing, I was so nervous about the prospect of meeting Eli's only family that I finally asked Carola to make good on her promise of a makeover.

Now here I am, sporting a fresh blowout, feeling restless. I run my newly manicured hands over the pleats of my dress, thinking for the hundredth time that I'm overdressed. I should've worn jeans. I should've worn that new pair of jeweled sandals. But just then, the door swings open and a young woman beams back at me. *Too late now.*

"You're Luisa," she exclaims, pulling at the screen door to lead me inside. "I'm Pearl. You like chocolate cake? Eli wasn't sure. Went ahead and made it anyway! Mamaw's Coca-Cola cake. It's Eli's favorite. I hope you'll like it." She says all of this in one breath, then lifts a cake platter. A lopsided three-tiered cake is festooned with cherries, marshmallows, and rainbow-colored sprinkles, like something out of the Mad Hatter's tea party.

I'm perplexed by the cake, and by Pearl. She's an explosion of color in a red scarf, wrapped over two long braids of wispy blond hair, and a pair of navy coveralls coated in vibrant paint spatter. The jumpsuit is unzipped at the top, hanging around her waist, a worn Pink Floyd *Dark Side of the Moon* T-shirt underneath. And I am so, so overdressed.

"So good to meet you, Pearl," I say warmly, stepping inside the house. "And yes, I love chocolate cake." I smile, my gaze roaming the room in search of Eli.

"He's on the back deck," she says. "On grill duty." She stands by the door, smiling and staring, her slanted cake propped between us. "You have a very pretty face," she observes matter-of-factly. "You remind me of an Amrita Sher-Gil portrait. Must be the red mouth."

"Thanks," I say, blushing under the scrutiny of Pearl's keen gaze.

My fingers instinctively reach for the Flamenco Red shade of lipstick covering my lips—a gift from my mother. Pretty sure she didn't intend for me to use it on a date with "the hairy one." After the hasty end to our Buford Highway date, I endured an hour-long nagging session on why I was wasting my time with an actor when I could be gearing toward an engagement with a doctor. I told her maybe she should date Juan Pablo herself, but that didn't go down well.

"I like your dress," Pearl remarks, peering at my emerald-green skirt. "Eli said you were very sophisticated."

My cheeks go hot, embarrassed at the compliment. "These are for you," I say, showing off the gift bag in my hand, an attempt to deflect attention away from myself. "Chocolates and macaroons. Each one is like a little piece of art."

"Thank you," she says giddily. "We're eating out back. Hope you're hungry."

"Can I help you with something?" I ask, following her down a long hallway, noting the boho decor—a tangerine couch set against white wood paneling, a magenta Persian rug covering the parquet floor, eye-catching throw pillows, art books, and plants dotted around the room. The house is cozy, tidy, and clean. There are gorgeous paintings hanging from almost every wall.

"Wow," I exclaim, awed. "Who made these?" Bold, figurative scenes stretch out on large canvases, painted in striking Southern colors—barn red, haint blue, creole pink, verdigris green. They are interspersed with mixed-media compositions, embroidered textiles, and photographs. The images feel intimate, chaotic, honest, and also painful.

"They're part of my art school portfolio," she says, her expression abashed and self-conscious as we pause to admire the haunting figure of a teenage boy underwater, pushing toward the surface, just on the verge of breaking through. "That's my brother," she says quietly. "Before we came to live here."

"Where were you living then?" I ask, appraising the fluid lines of the water, the fragile expression on the boy's face.

"Biloxi, I think," she says absently. Something murky and glum flashes across her eyes, but she doesn't allow it to linger. I wonder what she remembers of her transient childhood, being ten years younger than Eli. It was probably a blessing having her older brother to rely on.

Her manner shifts abruptly, leaning into the cheerfulness from moments ago. "The water is turbid there. Nothing like Puerto Rico." A smile returns to her lips as she leads me to the back deck.

Eli is standing by the grill wearing an apron that reads: *This is a manly apron, for a manly man, doing manly things, while cooking manly food.* I can't help but laugh out loud.

"See?" Pearl exclaims in Eli's direction. "I told you it was funny." She sets her cake down on the table, then turns to me, adding proudly, "It was my Father's Day gift."

Eli turns to me, his face breaking open with the most arresting smile.

"You made it okay?" he asks. I move to him as if in a trance, lulled by the pleasant summer breeze coming off the back garden, the dim light of the stringed bulbs above us and the opening guitar melody of Tracy Chapman and Luke Combs's "Fast Car" duet, playing in the background. When I reach him, his arm slides around my waist, and I fuse into his side, into the solid contours of his body.

"Hi," he whispers, staring into my eyes.

"Hi," I say, staring back at him, my heart beating furiously.

"I'm so glad you're here," he says, brushing my lips with a chaste, lingering kiss that leaves me breathless and wanting.

Behind us, Pearl clears her throat, reminding us that we're not alone. "Luisa, can I get you something to drink?" she asks politely. "Eli got some wine." She picks up the bottle from the table, reading the label. "Sancerre?"

"That's perfect," I say, giving Eli a meaningful look. I'll have to tell Holly her wine lessons have stuck, and that I'm personally reaping the benefits. I help Pearl with the corkscrew and pour a glass for myself. Eli sips from a beer bottle, and Pearl nurses a very festive Shirley Temple.

"These are almost done," Eli says. He opens the grill, then bastes butter over two steaks.

"It smells incredible," I say, moving aside the little flower vases on the table so that Pearl can fit a bowl of creamy mashed potatoes and a platter of roasted asparagus.

"He watched a million recipes online," Pearl whispers. "And he changed like ten times before you got here. I think he really wants to impress you."

"Don't believe a word she says," Eli exclaims, transferring the steaks onto a board. He cuts the flame, then joins us, carrying the steaks in one hand and a plate with grilled portobello caps in the other. "For the vegetarian," he says, placing the mushrooms in front of Pearl with a flourish.

"Vegetarians are the future," she says to me. "Meat consumption is unsustainable."

"Which is why," Eli retorts, slicing the meat, "we're enjoying this juicy steak while we still can." He slides a few pieces onto my plate. Pearl passes me a serving spoon for the mashed potatoes.

We load up our plates and dig in. The steak is perfectly cooked, the potatoes have a bliss-inducing amount of butter, and the asparagus is tender and fresh.

"So this is what manly food tastes like," I tease, dabbing at the sides of my mouth with a napkin. Pearl laughs.

"I told you: meat and potatoes, I can do," Eli says, grinning.

"I've learned not to underestimate you," I prod. "What other secret talents are you hiding?"

"The night is still young," he responds, his tone flirty, one eyebrow curved upward. "Plenty of time to find me out."

A sudden heat wave creeps up my skirt, leaving me desperate to shift away from the physical tension between us. "So, Pearl," I say, my voice coming out shrill, "how are you feeling about moving to Savannah?"

She looks to Eli before answering. "I'm a little nervous," she admits. "I've never been on my own before." She shrugs, sinking into her chair. "New place. New people. I'm excited, but also, a little terrified?"

Eli reaches for her, placing his hand on her back reassuringly.

"You're only a few hours away," he says. "You call and I'm there."

Pearl nods appreciatively, and it strikes me that she has no doubt that Eli will show up if she calls him, that she can count on him. I can barely contain the swell of emotion inside my chest.

I clear my throat before sharing, "When I moved here from Puerto Rico, I didn't know anyone, either." I set down my silverware, giving her my full attention. "Can I give you some unsolicited advice?"

"Yeah," she says, her loaded fork suspended over the plate. "I'll take all the advice."

"Find a place that you can claim for yourself," I say, resting the back of my forearms on the table. "A cafe table or a park bench. Somewhere you can go and dream."

"Is that what you did?" Eli asks, pouring more water into my glass.

"I'd walk to this used bookstore down the street," I recall. The store was part bookstore, part hoarding project. But the memory of the dusty shelves, cluttered aisles, and chaotic classifications only brings a smile to my face. "I'd spend hours in that place, sitting in front of the shelves, pulling down whatever called to me, reading the first page."

"Just the first page?" Pearl asks, her face open with curiosity.

"First pages are full of promise," I say, remembering the girl I used to be. "And my world felt pretty small back then."

Eli reaches for me under the table, gently pressing the top of my thigh with his thumb. His touch puts me at ease, connecting me to the present moment.

Over dinner and cake, I learn about their grandmother Mamaw Tillie, the strong Southern woman who practically raised them, and the house they inherited from her, and which they have turned into a refuge. Pearl delights in sharing Eli's most excruciating guardianship moments—that time he baked cookies for the PTA's Spring Fling and forgot to add sugar; or the meeting with a young teacher, who repeatedly hit on him. Through the laughter, and the memories, one thing is abundantly clear: Eli has stepped in to give Pearl the kind of stable home he didn't have growing up.

I'm angry at myself for not seeing him for the man he is, from the very beginning. For failing to recognize the good, devoted, loving man sitting beside me. I watch him tease Pearl, making her laugh, knowing that he's done everything in his power to secure her future. My feelings for him, for the man that he's proven to be, are more than my heart can contain. They fill me with warmth and longing.

And also fear.

What will happen if our plan goes south? If Eli gets caught

and—heaven forbid—thrown in jail? What will become of Pearl without her brother to take care of her? I add up the repercussions in my head, a mixture of guilt and regret churning in my stomach.

It won't come to that, I assure myself. We are three nimble, think-on-your-feet people—that's what it's taken for Holly, Eli, and me to survive. We know how to adapt. Eli will go to the ball, get the information, and get out. We will drive back to Westlake, and in a few weeks, he will drop off Pearl at her art school in Savannah. Maybe I can join them. Maybe we can spend a few days on Tybee Island. I smile at the idea, at the possibility of a fresh start for both of us.

After dinner, we crowd into the small kitchen, where Pearl and Eli work to put away leftovers and load the dishwasher. I'm wandering about, curiously exploring every nook and cranny, when I notice a series of intriguing photographs on the wall beside the cabinets. They're a ghostly, almost fantastical image of abandoned vintage cars in an old forest.

"Where were these taken?" I ask, gesturing toward the frames.

Pearl moves beside me, studying the images over my shoulder.

"That's Eli's favorite junkyard," she says. "Old Car City in White, Georgia."

I chuckle. "You have a favorite junkyard?" I ask, turning to Eli, who is scrubbing a pot in the sink.

"Don't you?" he asks, deadpan.

"That's where Mabel came from," Pearl exclaims.

"Mabel?" I ask, my expression drawing a blank. "Who's Mabel?"

The dirty dishes are abandoned as a very eager Pearl leads me to the garage and introduces me to Mabel—a 1966 Ford Bronco that Eli has been painstakingly restoring.

Mabel is jaw-droppingly beautiful. The pastel-mint body exudes retro beach vibes. The creamy leather interiors and shiny chrome details add a touch of classic elegance. She's a perfectly calibrated blend of charm and ruggedness.

"She was rusting under this big magnolia tree," Pearl explains, pointing to a series of Polaroids pinned to the wall of the garage. "Eli rescued her."

"I think she rescued me." Eli runs one hand over the hood, eyes glinting with pride. "I'm still tinkering with the engine. She needed a brand-new transmission, brakes, exhaust system, driveshaft. Everything had to be replaced." He pops open the hood, offering me a glimpse of his work.

"Is this what you do?" I ask, mesmerized, even though I have no idea how the inside of a car works and I'm finding it hard to reconcile the corroded scrap of metal in the wall photos with the gorgeous vintage car under my fingertips.

"I'm a mechanic," Eli says, his chin jutting with pride. "I like pulling things apart, putting them back together again. Giving a wreck a new life." He closes the hood, pushing it down until it locks in place. Then guides me to the open side door, gesturing for me to climb in. I do.

"What's next for her—after you're done?" I ask, sliding both hands over the soft leather steering wheel. Eli takes the passenger seat beside me.

"A potential buyer came through last week," he says, rubbing a speck of dust off the dashboard with the back of his palm.

"He offered three hundred thousand dollars," Pearl exclaims enthusiastically.

I shoot Eli a dubious look. "I think she added an extra zero," I say, unable to believe anyone would pay the price of a condo for this car. "Who has that kind of money?"

"Jackson Hole ranchers, apparently." He shrugs sheepishly in response. "The deal is far from done," he says, "but if it goes through, I'll be driving Mabel out to Wyoming before Labor Day. Wanna come?"

A few months ago, the mere suggestion of a road trip to Wyoming would seem ludicrous. For one, when would I find the time? Most of the vacation I accrued at *The Georgia Times* went unused. But standing here beside Eli and this dream of a car, it's easy to imagine myself in the passenger seat, a silk scarf over my long, windswept hair, the sun lapping at my bare shoulders, a vast cloudless sky over an expansive stretch of road—and the endless possibility of it all.

Pearl's phone pings, breaking into my thoughts. "My friends are here," she announces, texting something back. "It was so awesome to meet you, Luisa." In a sudden frenzy, she opens the driver's door and throws her arms around me, giving me a tight hug. I hug her back, unaware that she would be leaving.

"I'm staying at Paulina's," she says to Eli. "We're having a horror movie marathon. Can I take the leftover cake?"

"I thought you made that for me," Eli exclaims in mock indignation. "What are Luisa and I supposed to have for breakfast?" He cuts me a sly glance, and my cheeks go red at the suggestion that I'll be spending the night.

Pearl sets her gaze on me and smiles. "You kids make good choices," she sings on her way out.

CHAPTER 28

Holly

Ma, this is weird."

Aidan is propped on the phone screen in the corner of my bedroom, and I'm grilling him about which jeans I should wear for my date tonight. I've tried on two pairs, twice each.

"Is it any weirder than my son setting me up?" I ask, teasing.

Aidan's semester has ended, but he stayed in Athens to play a couple of paying gigs and apartment hunt for next fall. I wish he were here to offer in-person advice, but I can't exactly be mad that he's earning good money while also finding a place to live. I glance out my bedroom window toward Joel and Peter's darkened house, silently cursing them for choosing this particular stretch of time to take Aunt Edna on a Norwegian fjord cruise. Joel can always be depended on for brutally honest fashion judgments.

Aidan sighs, resigned. "Okay, go with the flared ones. But they both look great—you're beautiful, Ma." I watch as he pushes shaggy bangs from his eyes, wondering whether it's still my responsibility to arrange (and pay for?) my son's haircuts, now that he's technically an adult. "But it doesn't even matter," he says, "because that Pridmore guy is super into you—as he should be. You're awesome."

"See," I exclaim. "I knew there was a reason I kept you."

We joke about this sometimes. What else can we do?

Aidan was near the end of seventh grade the day he walked into the kitchen, opened the fridge to grab a bottle of chocolate milk, and asked me point-blank: "Did you ever think about having an abortion?"

I was glad that he knew what an abortion was, and also relieved that he had the courage to ask. His candor felt like a solid indication that he trusted me, that he could talk about difficult things with me, be vulnerable. Basically, all the things I never had with my own parents.

I had hoped the day would eventually come when I could explain my choice to bring him into the world. But still, I wasn't prepared.

"Honestly, yes," I told him, sinking into a chair at the kitchen table. *I considered it.*

"So, I was unplanned," he replied, taking the top off the milk and chugging. I wondered where he'd heard that term: "unplanned." Strange coming from a barely adolescent boy.

"Well, I wasn't much of a planner back then. I couldn't even find space in my life to do laundry," I explained, standing up to take a glass from the shelf, and then handing it to him. "So, technically, you were unplanned. But I think you're really asking whether you were a mistake."

"Were you using protection?" he asked me, pouring milk into the glass and not daring to look at me directly.

"You weren't a mistake, Aidan," I answered, deciding not to go into the details of sloppy, drunk teenage sex. That was a conversation for another time. I took hold of his arm, gave it a light squeeze, and then my mouth formed the most truthful words I have ever uttered: "You are precisely the opposite of a mistake, every single day."

He didn't reply, but he did look at me and nodded. And that was that. We never spoke of it seriously again. But Aidan did start to joke regularly about how cool it was that I decided to "keep" him, and so I started to joke about it, too.

"Don't lie to me," Aidan says now from my phone screen, "You didn't keep me for the unsolicited compliments. It was always my excellent coffee-making skills."

"I almost forgot about your coffee." I laugh, sitting at the edge of the bed to strap on my wedge heels. "It's been so long."

"I'll be home to make it for you soon," he tells me. "In the meantime, have fun on your date." We say our goodbyes and I reach across to hang up the phone, just as Aidan calls out, "And don't forget to use protection!"

Cheeky bastard, I think, smiling in spite of myself. *He can pay for his own haircuts.*

I do love Atlanta, I find myself musing, several hours later. I love this vibrant, young, diverse city that has become my adoptive home. I love the way the azaleas flame pink in March and the maples blaze red in October. I love the quirky little neighborhoods, where flower shops and bookstores crop up at random intersections, and where purple-haired women with a dozen piercings serve biscuits and grits in shabby diners. I even love the grimy blue seats in our radically inadequate metro system, and the twelve lanes of clogged highways that pulse through the center of downtown.

I love my city, almost all the time. Except at seven thirty on a Saturday night, when I'm on a first date, and we're trying to get a table for two at a trendy restaurant. Since it was my idea to just "pop in" to Deer and Dove for our date, I had no room to complain when we were politely informed of our two-hour wait.

I was getting hangry, and after we tried unsuccessfully to walk into three other nearby places, I was about to suggest that we give up and go to the Chili's at the mostly demolished North DeKalb Mall—site of filming for many postapocalyptic and dystopian films. That's when Hugh suggested that he could make something simple at his place, but we'd need to do a quick grocery run—which is how we ended up at Your DeKalb Farmers Market, where my first date with the esteemed Professor Hugh Pridmore isn't going exactly as planned.

My stomach is growling fiercely, and my fingertips are so frozen that they're tingling, which makes it impossible to determine the ripeness of mangoes. This is the one simple task that I took on when we walked into this freezing-cold place to execute plan B: pick out two mangoes from the mountains of fruits and vegetables surrounding me.

This place is an Atlanta treasure, where the unusual scent of seafood and bleach and pungent fruits somehow entices, where an entire wall of spices and seasonings rises above rows and rows of fresh produce from around the world, and where for some reason the temperature always hovers just barely above the freezing point. Even though I'm not much of a cook, I come here occasionally to pick up a bag of their house-made ravioli or a pint of fresh pesto. In a pinch, I've even rushed over to buy flowers for the club—they always have an excellent selection for dirt cheap.

My hands too numb to function, I abandon any attempt at testing ripeness and grab a couple of mangoes from the top of the pile. I'm clutching a huge, firm mango in each hand when Hugh shows up beside me, carrying a basket with basmati rice, cilantro, and a large squash or melon I don't recognize.

"It's a bit nippy in here," he says, taking the mangoes from my icy fingers to put in his basket. "Christ, your hands are cold," he exclaims. "You have actual goose bumps."

We both look at my bare arms below a whisper-thin silk tank. I was aiming for dressy casual: a bright summer patterned top with spaghetti straps, the jeans Aidan helped me choose, and wedge heels. Hugh looks damn near perfect in dark-wash denim and a white linen button-down. He also looks a tad warmer than me.

He places the basket on the floor, wraps his hands around mine, and begins rubbing vigorously. I watch, mesmerized, inspecting his oval nails and clean cuticles, feeling the pads of his fingers press against my palms.

"Is this helping at all?" he asks, smiling so wide that those adorable thin lines take shape around his eyes. I simply nod in response, because I'd be embarrassed to share how very much his touch is warming me, and in how many unexpected places. He releases my hands, then lets his own hand fall tentatively to the small of my back, gently urging me toward the exit.

We amble along a long row of produce, and even though I'm starving, I can't help moving slowly, with Hugh walking so close beside me that I can feel the heat radiating from him, warming my bare skin. Or maybe it's the peppers. They are a marvel: dried and fresh, Thai, habañero, scotch bonnet, chipotle. Piles of peppers squeeze between banana flowers and hunks of fresh ginger bigger than my hand.

"Have you ever tried granadilla?" he asks, touching my upper arm to guide me toward an adjacent aisle filled with fruits. I savor the feel of his touch on my skin.

Fingers still resting on my arm, he lifts a smooth orange fruit with small yellow spots from a precarious pile, and presses it into my hand.

"Will I sound painfully uncultured if I admit to you I've never even seen one?" I ask, studying the way our hands look against its bright flesh.

"Not at all," he replies, smiling. "You simply sound like someone who hasn't had the opportunity to travel to Bolivia."

"Yet," I say.

"Yet," he repeats, and then he takes the fruit from my hand and places it gingerly in the basket. "In the meantime," he says, "we'll break open the granadilla when we get to my place—prepare you for your journey."

I can't resist letting my mind wander as we head toward the cashier bays, envisioning all the places I could go with Hugh, if he were to invite me along. I know I'll never live abroad, but it's not impossible to conceive of traveling a bit, now that Aidan is mostly self-sufficient. After all, I have months and months of accrued vacation time. I envision myself in a flowy yellow sundress, wandering an outdoor market while Hugh gives a talk or teaches a class or whatever he does in all those places he goes. I'd fill my basket with fruits for us to try together, bring them back to our apartment or hotel, wait impatiently for his return.

Hugh presses his hand against my back again, this time less tentative, as he guides me through a sea of Atlanta residents from every corner of the world. They crowd around us, on the damp concrete floors, carts piled high with produce, fish, meat, cheeses, pastries, and dried goods, most of the jostling shoppers bundled up in jackets and gloves, even on a Saturday in June.

"Let's get out of here," he says. Then he pays for our groceries and leads me into the balmy evening, reminding me of another thing I love about Atlanta: the gentle summer nights that follow scorching-hot days.

It's a short drive to Hugh's place, a carriage house in the historic and affluent Druid Hills neighborhood, less than a block from

Emory's campus. Towering elms line the steep driveway leading to a lovely brick Tudor Revival home. Hugh parks and gestures for me to lead the way up a rickety exterior stairway beside the garage.

"Welcome to my glamorous home," he says, turning the key in the lock and then easing the door open.

The first thing I notice is a small kitchenette, with a Formica counter the size of a school desk, above which are open shelves painted white and neatly stacked with four plates and four bowls. The oven, against the edge of the counter, is a two-burner type that wouldn't even fit a casserole dish inside, and the squat refrigerator looks like it belongs in a dorm.

"Needless to say, I don't entertain much," he says as we step into the room.

He turns to close the door behind us, giving me a chance to do a quick scan of the room—the *only* room. It's a studio apartment, the key feature being a full-size bed, neatly made with a duvet covered in white cotton and two fluffed pillows. In some ways, it's a classic graduate student crash pad, but the very small number of items filling it are of much higher quality and are much more artfully arranged.

Hugh slips off his shoes and sets them on a wooden rack beside the door, where a row of leather loafers lines up neatly beside one pair of gently used running shoes.

"Force of habit," he says. "You don't need to—"

But I'm already leaning down to remove my heels, relishing the feel of cool tile under my bare feet.

"No sofa?" I ask, glancing up to see him set the grocery bags on the small counter.

"No room," he replies, then walks toward a worn leather armchair in the corner, between two full-to-bursting bookcases. The chair, which is the only one in the apartment, besides two small metal dining chairs, sits on an antique Persian rug. When he reaches over to turn on the reading lamp, the area fills with warm light. "Please, have a seat," he tells me, gesturing toward the plush cushion. "Let me pour you a glass of wine."

I sink in, savoring the commingled scents of leather, old books, and freshly washed sheets. It seems that Hugh wasn't exaggerating when he said his life is far from glamorous, but there's something so inviting about this small apartment that I can't help feeling at home.

Hugh walks across the room and pulls a wine bottle from the kitchen shelf. He opens it and fills two glasses, brings one to me. We silently clink our glasses together, and I take a sip—a rich, complex Bordeaux in a delicate crystal goblet.

Unable to resist tucking my legs under me, I curl deeper in and let myself watch him, his back turned to me while he unloads groceries, sets a speaker on the counter, and pulls a cutting board and knife from under the sink. John Coltrane's "Naima" quietly fills the small space.

"Music okay?" he asks.

I nod, remembering the first time I heard Coltrane, played barely adequately by a middle-school jazz band, and the many times and places I've heard him since. I never imagined I'd hear "Naima" in a garage apartment in Druid Hills, while watching a sexy British man cook for me.

Hugh fills an electric rice cooker and sets the timer. "Your meal will be served in approximately twenty-four minutes," he announces, taking a glass bowl from the shelf and pouring something from a jar. He walks toward me and sets the bowl beside me, handing me a cloth napkin. "Spicy pickled okra to hold you over," he says.

"Ohmygod, I love pickled okra so much," I exclaim, because it's true, and because I'm genuinely shocked that the esteemed professor is serving it.

"Well, then," he replies, heading back into the kitchen to run a bunch of cilantro under water, "that's something else we share in common."

I wonder what in the world else Hugh could believe we share in common. Maybe our ill-spent youth? I decide not to ask.

He pulls items from the fridge and arranges them on the small counter: onions, cucumber, tomatoes, carrot, radish, and a lemon. He places them beside a hunk of ginger, a head of garlic, and several spice jars, then removes a Tupperware container, sets a pot on the stove, and pours in the contents.

I'm feeling more relaxed, sipping fine wine in this cozy studio apartment, than I've felt in weeks, maybe months. I have the strange sensation, here, of having been transported to another time and place, where douchey men, shady business transactions, and blackmail simply don't belong.

Last night, we met up with Eli and prepared him to bait the hook for Griggs. Over "pregame" drinks at Griggs and Anna-Byrd's before the gala, Tripp will ask Griggs for advice on how to invest his trust fund. We're betting on the fact that Griggs won't be able to resist luring Tripp into the Lake Chiaha scheme. A pretty safe bet.

But the last person I want to think about right now is Griggs Johnson.

"Can I help?" I ask Hugh, pushing all thoughts of our scheme out of my mind for just one night.

"No need," Hugh says. "Just never tell my mother that you saw me do this." Then he takes an Instant Pot from the cabinet and sets it beside the rice cooker. "I love her recipes, but it seems I rarely have three days to set aside for preparing the meals I enjoyed as a child."

"Your secret's safe with me," I tell him.

He pours oil into the Instant Pot, then sprinkles in cumin seeds. While they sizzle and fill the air with their bright aroma, Hugh expertly dices an onion, then tosses it in. He continues to add ingredients, while I crunch my way through hot okra and wash it down with bold red wine.

I'm mesmerized, watching him chop and stir with a confidence that reveals he's done this many times before. On a whim, I snap a photo of him at work and send it to Luisa. After Eli left last night, I filled Luisa in on how Hugh arrived at the club to explain his long silence, and the sweet and supportive things he told me in the park.

She responds immediately:

Sexy British Professor cooks????
too good to be true?

I read her text and smile as a picture of Eli, standing beside a Weber grill in an apron, downloads.

Eli says "hi" and his meat is tastier than pridmore's

I laugh out loud at that one, causing Hugh to turn toward me, questioning.

"Luisa," I say, gesturing toward the phone, which seems to appease him. I shoot back a quick reply:

Eli wins. Pretty sure Hugh is vegetarian

Then I slide my phone into my purse and turn my full attention to the moment.

Hugh begins to set the small kitchen table with cloth napkins and water glasses. He opens the door and steps out to the landing, cuts three bright zinnias from a window box attached to the metal stair rail. He puts them in a bud vase and sets it at the center of the table, then returns to a stove to warm parathas on a griddle. I let myself observe the back of his neck, the place where his neatly trimmed, dark hairline meets freshly shaved skin. I find myself wondering what it would feel like to run my fingers across that skin, and whether he might want me to do that. I wonder if it would be smooth, or if I'd feel dark stubble under my fingertips.

"Dinner is served," he announces.

I climb out of the armchair, running my hand along the smooth leather as I walk away. By the time I reach the table, he has already set a low bowl, heaped with steaming rice, a dish that looks a bit like scrambled eggs, and a couple of other deliciously scented sides. He brushes a steaming paratha with ghee and then sets it on my plate.

"You're not one of those people who thinks cilantro tastes like soap, are you?" he asks. I shake my head, and he releases a handful of fresh herbs over my bowl. "My mum still calls it coriander," he muses, "even when it's fresh." He refills my wine and comes to sit across from me.

"Paneer bhurji and dal makhani," he tells me, "with a kachumber salad. The simple comfort food I carry with me wherever I go in this world. I hope you enjoy."

Following his lead, I tear an edge off the soft buttery paratha and dip it into the dal. I honestly can't remember the last time someone cooked for me, much less in their home kitchen. I feel overcome with gratitude for the delicate balance of this meal, and the simple pleasure of being in this place with Hugh.

"It's a miracle that you made all of this fabulous food in an Instant Pot, in less time than it would take for us to get a table at Deer and Dove," I exclaim.

"I actually made the paneer yesterday," he responds. "It's absurd, really, to make paneer when it's easily found at the corner shop. But somehow it relaxes me at the end of a long work week, to press the curd through cheesecloth. It's a bit like meditation."

"But yummier," I reply.

"I'm so glad you're enjoying it." His face shows genuine delight. "And the dal? Not too spicy?"

"Bring on the spice," I tell him. "I love it."

"Then next time, I absolutely will add more heat," he replies, smiling.

I feel a blush rise to my cheeks, imagining the next time he cooks for me, and all the ways we might find to add heat. He glances away, toward my almost empty water glass, his expression making clear that he's also considering the double meaning of his words. Then he jumps up to refill my water.

We both spoon generous second helpings onto our plates and somehow still manage to clean them, sopping up the last of the gravy with paneer. While we feast, he asks me questions, none of them probing, but instead curious—about my life with Aidan, my friends, what I love about my work and about living in this city.

"The general manager is leaving," I find myself telling him. "And some friends and co-workers have been telling me to apply."

"Would you enjoy the work?" he asks.

Such a simple question, but I struggle to devise a simple answer.

"I'd be really good at it," I respond, finishing my last sip of wine while Hugh stands to clear the table. "I know what it takes to run that club, and I have all the skills."

"Of course," he replies, setting the bowls in the sink and then opening the freezer. "But that doesn't necessarily mean it's the job for you."

"That's what I need to work out," I say, watching as he busies himself in the kitchen, his back turned away from me, then returns with two bowls, each filled with a scoop of vanilla ice cream, slices of mango, and a single sprig of mint.

"I'm certain of this," he says, sitting across from me again. "The club would be fortunate to have you in charge."

Sinking my spoon into dessert, then savoring the sweet combination of creamy ice cream and bright, bold mango, I'm struck that Hugh doesn't for a moment question whether I'm qualified, and it's so glorious—to be with a man who simply assumes I'm competent and capable.

When we've finished—a damn near perfect dessert, I decide—I follow Hugh into the small kitchen area. He pulls out two storage containers and hands them to me, and I spoon the meager leftovers into them, while he fills the sink with soapy water and begins to hand wash dishes.

I open the refrigerator, set the containers beside neatly ordered jars of yogurt, a pint of berries, and orange juice that looks to be freshly squeezed—thinking, for a moment, what it would be like to wake up in this apartment with Hugh and share a simple breakfast.

"So where will you be making your comfort foods next?" I ask, my chest tightening at the thought of him leaving. I know I don't have the right to feel this way, since we've only just met, so I struggle to brighten my tone, and ask, "What grand city will you be moving to, once the Emory gig is up?"

"Copenhagen is next on the itinerary," he says, taking a clean dishrag from the drawer and beginning to dry his hands. "But I'm so enjoying these warm Georgia nights"—he gestures toward the screened window beside us, where moonlight shines through a magnolia—"I may just have to stay awhile longer."

The promise of his words hangs in the humid air between us.

I don't want to ruin the moment with questions of logistics, of whether that might even be possible. What do I know about professors and their work? About how long a person can be officially "visiting" a university and not wear out his welcome? I can't imagine someone like Hugh Pridmore ever wearing out his welcome, at least not with me.

Before I can second-guess my decision, before I can think about how fleeting this all might be, I take a step to stand behind him at the sink, place a hand on his waist, and tug, so that he turns to face me. He lets out a soft sigh, and as Coltrane's "Lush Life" pours through the room, I put a hand on his chest and push him gently against the counter. He lets the towel drop to the floor, wraps his arms around my waist, and pulls me in, then leans down to press a kiss against my throat.

"I've wanted to do this since the first moment I saw you," he whispers into my ear, "knocking frantically against the window of my lab, with your hair up in that loose bun."

I wrap my free hand around the back of his neck, feeling the rough stubble, just as I had imagined it. I lean away, look into his eyes. "You mean, when I interrupted your very important research with my silly little lies?"

"There's nothing silly about you, Holly," he says, then kisses me softly on the mouth. "And you can interrupt me anytime. But let's be honest with each other from this point forward." He kisses me again, so lightly that it's almost teasing. "No more lies."

"No more lies," I repeat, running my hand down his chest, loving the feel of linen, rough and cool beneath my fingers.

He pulls me in closer, grazing my hips with his hands, and I kiss him hard, as the intensity rises between us. He tastes of vanilla and cumin and humid summer nights, and I suddenly know that it will be impossible to get enough of this man.

He turns us both around, lifts me onto the counter. Then his firm hands find their way beneath my silk shirt, and I feel them hot and searching against my back. I let my thighs part, and he steps between them. He rises against me, and I pull him in closer, grabbing his hair into my fist. He slips the silk strap from my shoulder, leans down to run his lips along my collarbone. My free hand finds the top button of his jeans and I tug, which produces a hum deep in his throat.

But then he releases me and steps away, fast. I watch, baffled, as he begins to pace back and forth in the small space between us.

"Since we've decided to be honest," he says, his voice a low groan, "I want nothing more right now than to carry you over to that bed and have my way with you."

Jesus, God. I want that, too.

He runs a hand through his hair, frustrated. I suck in a long breath, try to calm my raging hormones. Because I have a sneaking suspicion I know what's coming next.

"But, for better or worse, I endeavor to be a gentleman." He continues to pace in front of me. "And it's our first date, and I already feel a bit lechy, having brought you here, which wasn't my intention, and—"

I slide down from the counter, touch him on the forearm, which stills his pacing. "I get it," I say, trying to sound nonchalant, trying not to worry about whether his hesitation is really about me, trying to remind myself that this man will be in Copenhagen soon, and that the last thing I have room in my life for is complication.

Oh, but Hugh Pridmore is a complication I so very much want to make room for.

CHAPTER 29

Luisa

Eli's room is masculine, neat, simple. The floor is covered in a shag rug, so I kick off my wedges and abandon them by the door before stepping inside.

A cozy, three-person couch is set against a bare wall—not one throw pillow or cuddle blanket in sight. It's wide enough to fit two bodies, I observe, as a current of lust takes over my imagination.

"No throw pillows here, huh?" I ask, running one index finger over the velvety green fabric, fighting the urge to sink into its plump cushions.

"Not a fan of clutter," he says, leaning against the doorframe, casually watching me explore his space. He's also taken off his shoes, stacked them next to mine.

Across the room sits a mahogany desk and chair, with a chest of drawers to one side. A two-month calendar hangs on the wall above it. Pearl's school deadlines, handwritten appointments, and sticky notes with bill reminders take up most of the space. Beside the desk, tucked into the corner of the room, is an indoor woodstove that has me wishing it were the dead of winter. A set of large double windows provides a view of the backyard and illuminates the room with the faint glow of the patio lights.

The queen-size bed is covered with an Oxford Blue comforter and white pillowcases that match the sheets. My fingertips stroke one of the snug feather pillows, my mind already conjuring the cool sensation of the sheets against my skin.

There's a lamp on the side table, next to three small potted plants and a stack of books. I set my clutch on the table, then pick up the books one by one, reading the titles on each cover—*Tuesdays with Morrie*, *The Book of Five Rings*, *Zen and the Art of Motorcycle Maintenance*, *Vagabond Volume 1*.

"What are you thinking right now?" he asks, eyeing me with amusement as I pick up one of the books.

"That you surprise me," I respond truthfully. "And not many people do."

I don't tell him that while he's been playing at being Tripp, I've been cataloging every expression, every posture, every gaze that is only Eli's. I don't tell him that I think of him at random times during the day, and that the thought of him invariably makes me smile. I don't tell him that his scent—a heady mix of musk, spice, and woods—lingering on every textile in the room is making me lightheaded and woozy, like I'm somehow drunk on him.

Eli meets me on the side of the bed and sits on the mattress, drawing me between his legs, hands resting over my hips.

"I can't remember the last time I was so wrong about someone." I run my fingers through his hairline, then caress his eyebrows, following the contour of his nose, the curve of his lips. Eli tilts up his head, closes his eyes. "I'm never wrong," I add quietly.

He takes the palm of my hand in his, kisses it. "That's one of the things I love most about you," he says, pulling me onto his lap. He brushes the tips of his fingers over the delicate skin of my upper chest, up my neck, sinking them into my hair, then angling my head down toward his.

"My charming stubbornness," I whisper, grazing his lips.

"'Endearing' is the word you're looking for," he murmurs, plunging our mouths into a kiss to rival every kiss that came before it. It's achingly unhurried and tender, but also knowing and full of yearning. I want to commit his taste to memory—the minty tingle of his breath on my lips, the hungry lap of his tongue on mine, the fiery intensity rippling through my whole body.

"Can I undress you?" he asks in a breathy voice.

"Please." My heart beats desperately, compensating for the sudden lack of oxygen and the delicious throbbing climbing up my thighs and into my lower belly. One half of me wants to take this slow, stretch out the longing, savor every second as if this night was nothing short of an eternity. The other half—a starving, ravenous wild creature—craves a naked Eli, wants to meld his steely body with mine, until the whole universe shatters behind my closed eyelids.

We stand, facing each other. Eli's hands fall to my waist, and he turns me in place. He sweeps aside my long hair, planting kisses along my shoulder blades as he slowly lowers the zipper of my dress. I close my eyes, dazed with the sensation of his lips skimming across my back. My dress collects in a puddle of gauzy fabric at our bare feet.

Unexpectedly, Eli takes a step back. I turn to find the famished eyes of a wolf, dark and liquid, devoted and also ardently protective. His gaze progresses from my exposed breasts to the swell of my hips, the black lace of my underwear, the pair of legs I know he's admired in the past, my tanned skin glowing with desire.

"Jesus Christ," he mutters to himself. "Luisa . . ." He trails off with a heavy sigh.

Hearing my name on his lips sends a shiver down my almost naked body. I meet his gaze, and in what feels like an act of unadulterated desire, I deliberately slip out of my underwear. I stand tall, offering Eli an unguarded picture of my body, relishing in the greedy expression that takes over his face.

"God, you're fucking beautiful." His voice comes out a strangled groan.

"Will you take off your clothes?" I say, tension coiling inside me.

Eli obliges, and I can't help but bite my lower lip as I watch him tug at the edges of his T-shirt and pull it over his head, revealing the beautiful landscape tattoo over his torso and the sibling birds inked over his heart. My heart expands with the new understanding of the two birds in flight. This man is beautiful inside and out.

And as he zips down his jeans and wriggles himself free of his pants and trunks, I'm left breathless at the naked sight of his glorious body. A pair of defined obliques slope into an inviting V-cut. A trail descends in a straight line from his belly button to his groin, where the most beautiful, fully erect cock stands between a pair of well-toned upper thighs.

We stare at each other for a silent beat, unmoving, as if in a sweet stupor. I'm rapt by every single line and ridge of muscle running across his body. I want to name every color in his tattoo. I want to count the freckles scattered over his upper chest. I want to kiss every square centimeter of his pale skin.

Eli closes the space between us. He reaches for my chin with his fingers, catching my lips with his, then curving his palm around my neck. His free hand languidly follows the outline of my spine, reaching for the curve of my ass. He grabs me from behind and tugs me into him, my swollen nipples pressed against the taut muscles of his torso. My own hands traverse to his cock, stroking him until a raspy moan bursts from his throat and his grip tightens around me.

"I want to taste you," Eli murmurs into my ear. "Would you like that?"

I can barely breathe out a "yes." Because, oh God yes, I want nothing more right now than to have his mouth between my legs.

He lowers me to the bed, kissing me until my head is resting over a pillow. He deftly spreads my legs, as my body welcomes his form hovering over me. My back melts into the pillow-top mattress, relaxing under the weight of him. My arms bend at the elbows, reaching for the support of his shoulders as the head of his cock brushes against the wetness between my legs, teasingly. I instinctively arch against him, consumed with the need to have him inside me.

"Not yet," he whispers, sensing my restlessness. He clutches both my wrists, carefully raising my hands over my head as he kisses his way down my neck, over my breastbone. He cradles my breasts in his hands, gliding his tongue over my taut nipples, sucking and grazing his teeth across the sensitive skin. My fingers grip the comforter, balling the fabric into closed fists. "Do you like that?" he asks.

"Yes," I whimper, licking my lips, pressing my head back into the pillow. Eli's mouth charts a path of kisses over my belly, down to my lower abdomen and the folds between my legs. His hands pull my thighs apart with one torturous, mind-bending motion. And then, his tongue is on me, delighting in my most sensitive flesh. I'm skirting the boundaries of consciousness as intense pulses of pleasure ricochet inside me, searing every single one of my nerve endings.

"You taste so sweet." His lids are heavy and his mouth glistens with my wetness. When he licks his lips, drinking me in, I die a thousand little deaths. "I just want to stay here."

His tongue swirls over my clit and I writhe in ecstasy. It takes every ounce of willpower I have left to say, "I don't want to come yet." I want to stretch my known threshold of pleasure, hoard this exquisite tension until my body simply can't physically contain it anymore.

"Come here," I say, propping myself up on my elbows and beckoning him to me.

He smiles, that pure Eli smile that sends my stomach into a free fall and my heart hurtling. Then he pushes himself up to kiss me on the lips, his arms extended over my sides, elevating his body. "I have to grab a condom from the nightstand," he says.

"Hold that thought—" I extend one index finger between us, gesturing to the bedside table where my things are. Eli falls to his back beside me. I open my clutch, remove a condom, then pass it to Eli.

"Latex allergy," I volunteer.

"Duly noted," he says, tearing open the black-and-gold wrapper with his fingers. He removes the prophylactic, then rolls it down the shaft of his cock, pulling at the end until it's securely in place, and in the process giving me an exhilarating preview of the coming attractions. When he's done, he turns to face me, one hand propped under his head.

"Tell me what you like," he says, softly running small circles around my nipples with his fingertips. "Do you prefer to be on top?"

I turn to face him, getting lost in his gray irises, which are focused intently on me.

"I want to feel you beside me," I say quietly. "Side by side." He nods in understanding. "Is that okay?"

"I just want you, Luisa," he says, staring into my eyes with a gaze so penetrating, it sends a surge of emotion rising inside my chest. "I don't care where or how." He kisses me, and suddenly my heart feels too small for the enormity of everything I feel in this moment.

I press my back against Eli's chest, folding myself into him, attuned to his own heart pulsing rapidly against the back of my shoulder blade. My right hand finds his palm above my head and interlaces our fingers. My left hand rests over his hip, indenting my fingers into the hard muscles of his buttocks, as he eases into me from behind. I curve my back against his torso and his lips brush my ear, sending a warm tingle down my neck. "Slow. Deep," I mutter, turning my face to him.

He pulses deeper into me. I bring down our interlaced hands, wrap them over my torso. His right hand rests on my lower abdomen, drawing my hips to him, rocking me into him with fluid, mind-blowing motions. His hips undulate behind me, and I bear down, feeling him go further inside me. Eli moans with pleasure, exhaling a warm breath into my upturned mouth, kissing me feverishly. We're linked from head to toe, and still, it's not enough.

I take his right hand, resting over my abdomen, and guide it between my legs, gliding over my clit. Eli's fingers move under mine, adding exquisite, agonizing pressure. His right arm tightens over my torso, containing the friction building between us as our bodies harmonize into a steady rhythm. I close my eyes, losing myself to the sensation, only existing within the context of Eli's body, indivisible from mine.

The intensity builds and Eli seems on the verge of release, but then adjusts his pace to match mine, slowing down, stretching the mounting pleasure between us. "I'm so close," I say. My hips press harder into him, his cock sinking inside me so deep that breathing seems impossible. His fingers manipulate my clit until an earth-shattering spasm rips through me as we arrive at a single, blissful crescendo of blinding orgasm.

My body and mind are lost to me, and yet I am everything and everyone, everywhere, all at once. Only the force of Eli's body wrapped tightly around mine keeps my limbs from falling apart.

Eli pants beside me, lips tenderly falling onto my shoulder. Our skin shimmers with sweat, hot and tingling. I am so overwhelmed by this man—wrapped tightly around my very being—that tears sting at the corners of my eyes.

"Stay forever," he whispers in my ear, his voice so vulnerable and sweet, so full of longing that, reason be damned, I believe him.

"Okay," I say back.

CHAPTER 30

Holly

These weeks have been a complete blur—between planning for the Midnight Society's Costume Ball and squeezing in enough official dates with Hugh to merit luring him home to my bed. We've ambled through the High Museum of Art, sipped cocktails on the roof of Ponce City Market, biked the Beltline to my favorite Glenwood Estates taqueria, and even visited the tasting room at the World of Coca-Cola. I figured that if Hugh is really on his way to Copenhagen, it's my duty to show him a selection of Atlanta's best and worst tourist attractions before he goes.

I saved the best for last night: an evening concert and picnic on the lawn of the Atlanta Botanical Garden. I packed the picnic, a simple spread from Alon's Bakery, but he provided a wonderful Spanish cava and a single granadilla—the Bolivian fruit we never had a chance to try on our first date. It was delicious, but I'm not sure whether it was the strange pungent flavor of the seeds or the way he fed them to me under the moonlight, making me hungry for more.

Was it coincidence that the Botanical Garden is a short, four-block walk from my apartment? That I had him park his car at my place? Not exactly.

Through my bedroom door, Hugh lies drenched in morning sunlight, his bare leg tossed casually over my comforter, his dark hair wild against my mattress. He stirs, tucks his arm around my pillow, and then burrows into it. I wish I could go back to bed. I wish I could bring him fruit, and he could feed it to me, breaking it apart with his hands and pressing the sweet-sour seeds into my waiting mouth. But the clock is ticking on the Midnight Society

Costume Ball. I need coffee, a shower, and a quick breakfast before the day's packed agenda gets underway.

I open the fridge and peer inside. It dawns on me that I probably have nothing to feed that beautiful man still sleeping in my bed. I haven't exactly had time to grocery shop. Thank God I picked up a pound of good coffee yesterday morning before meeting with my florist, when I rushed into Dancing Goats for a shot-in-the-dark and a doughnut.

How is it that my refrigerator is twice the size of Hugh's, but contains about a quarter of the food? No yogurt in orderly glass jars, no bright seasonal berries or freshly squeezed orange juice. Just a few stalks of limp celery, a bag of carrots, and a haphazard array of condiments.

At least I have milk. Well, chocolate milk. Does that count as a breakfast food?

I pull the carton of chocolate milk from the shelf, unscrew the cap, and sniff. It still smells like high fructose corn syrup, so I think it must be okay. I head over to the pantry, open the door, and rummage around, until I excavate a few items that might qualify as breakfast foods.

"Good morning, gorgeous," Hugh says, his voice still gravelly with sleep.

Peering out from behind the pantry door, I see him standing in my doorway, in nothing but the crisp white boxers I slid from his narrow hips nine hours ago. I can't resist crossing the kitchen to wrap my arms around his waist. I kiss him softly.

"Thank you for last night," he mumbles into my ear.

"It was my absolute pleasure," I reply, thinking how hilarious it is that he is thanking me. I'm not terribly experienced in this area, but Hugh Pridmore is without a doubt the most generous lover I've ever had. And what do I have to offer in return? Chocolate milk, a quarter loaf of Nature's Own bread, and month-old sugar cereal.

At least I have decent coffee.

Hugh heads across the room toward my bathroom.

"You can use my toothbrush," I tell him, "unless you're fussy about that sort of thing."

He turns to look at me. His eyebrows raise and a knowing grin spreads across his now-stubbly face. Hugh doesn't have to say anything. His teasing expression reminds me of everything I learned about him last night. A flush rises to my chest. This man is anything but fussy.

By the time he comes out of the bathroom, I've set a pot of French-press coffee, two mugs, bowls and spoons, a box of cereal, and chocolate milk on my kitchen table.

"Might I offer you some Frosted Mini-Wheats?" I ask, feigning a formal accent.

"I've long hoped to sample them," he replies, taking a seat at the table.

"With chocolate milk?" I ask, dumping the cereal into his bowl and hoping it's not stale.

"My favorite kind," he says. "How on earth did you know?"

We sit together at my breakfast table, sipping coffee and slurping cereal in comfortable silence. It dawns on me that Hugh is the first man I've ever had at my breakfast table—well, excepting Joel, Peter, Byron, and my smarmy landlord (uninvited, of course). Over these last many years, I haven't been keen to bring men to the apartment I shared with my young son.

But now, here I am, having breakfast with my lover. And it feels utterly delicious. He stands up to take his bowl to the sink, pauses to look out of my kitchen window, where, at the right angle, it's just barely possible to catch a glimpse of the Midtown skyline.

"Ask me again," he says.

"Ask you what?" I reply.

"What's the sexiest city—"

"They don't call it HOTlanta for nothing," I finish his thought, feeling confident that I know the answer.

"And all along I thought it was the extreme late-summer temperatures and obscene humidity," he adds, which makes us both laugh. "Maybe I'll need to stay and find out for myself."

We stop laughing, and an awkward silence fills the room. Is he trying to tell me he wants to stay? Is that even possible? I'm struggling to form the right question when a terrible noise breaks through the quiet.

My doorbell. Buzzing furiously and repeatedly.

"That would be Luisa," I sigh. She was meeting an IRS criminal investigator for breakfast nearby and offered to pick me up after, suggesting in her ever-practical way that it would give us extra time to go over our plan on the drive back to Norcross.

She knew I had a date with Hugh last night, but I never got around to telling her I finally managed to bring him home. I happened to be otherwise occupied.

"I'm so sorry," he says, clearly noting my panicked expression. He heads into the bedroom to pull on his jeans. "I've kept you too long. I'll distract her with hot coffee and probing questions about investigative journalism. You go get ready for your big day."

Hugh returns from the bedroom, struggling to pull on his shirt as I open the door.

Luisa takes one long look at the two of us, laughs, and exclaims, "Well, well, well. Who knew Professor Pridmore offered private lessons?"

Since I came up with the Southern Gothic theme for the staff costumes, I can't exactly complain when Luisa's sister, Carola, leans in, tugs the edge of my eyelid, and begins applying the sort of black liquid eyeliner that hasn't touched my face since I was thirteen and experiencing a short-lived emo phase.

Lord, how my mother hated that all-black era of my life. If we had lived in a slightly different climate, I probably would have stayed blissfully emo through all of high school. But, dang, that first summer in black jeans, black leather combat boots, and trench coats was brutal. By the Fourth of July I was back in my summer uniform of ratty cutoffs and ribbed tanks.

"You scream *seductive kindergarten teacher*," she deadpans, clearly pleased with herself. "It's the whole 'heart-shaped face and rosy cheeks' look. Don't open your eyes, the kohl needs to dry."

I nod in submission, which is basically what I've been doing for the last hour, as Luisa's mom and sister trimmed, combed, teased, sprayed, and arranged my hair into a choppy style that's unlike anything I've ever worn. For starters, it's way bigger.

Luisa told them some version of the truth: We got invited to a Y'allywood Ball at a Midtown country club, costumes required. They were enraptured by the idea of giving us a glam makeover for the event.

"Spread your lips," Carola commands, then applies a thick lip liner, pressing it against the top of my mouth to form a wide heart. "Now pucker."

"Wait," Luisa's mom, Dolores, exclaims—as if Carola is leading me to the edge of a cliff and it's her responsibility to rescue me from the abyss. My eyes fly open and I see her rushing toward me with a tube of lipstick. "She's too blanquita for Chanel Independante. You need to use MAC Ruby Woo."

"Mami's right," Luisa says from the salon chair where she's been sitting for the entire time, observing their progress with razor-sharp focus. "That deep red will wash Holly's complexion right out." Her phone rings, and she walks into the other room, grinning like an idiot. Somebody's gotten under that girl's skin, and I know exactly who it is.

"Make her look sickly," Dolores oh-so-helpfully adds, still focused on my choice of lip color.

"Too pale, on top of how flaquita she is," Abuela Fela observes, unhelpfully. She's been trying to feed me empanadas since I walked through the door, but I'm too nervous to eat. They smell amazing though.

Carola accepts the lipstick from her mom and begins to apply it liberally to my lips, not the subtle tap-tap of soft color that I usually do, when I do lipstick at all.

"My work is done," Carola exclaims with a flourish, then spins me toward the full-length mirror.

I stare at my reflection, barely recognizing the matte-skinned, bold-eyed, fierce-lipped badass of a woman staring back. *Is this really me?*

My phone dings, pulling me out of my daze. It's a text from Hugh with a listing for a rental property near Emory.

What do you think of this place? Has real oven and room for actual sofa.

My heart begins to sputter in my chest, and I let out a tiny squeal.

Oh wow does this mean you're staying?

I typc the response quickly, proud to have avoided the word "really."

Wanted to tell you this morning. Emory's offered a three-year visiting gig. Thinking about it.

And then, before I can chicken out, I reply, straight from the heart:

I want you to stay.

"You look tough," Luisa calls out as she returns to the room, her voice filled with awe.

"I *feel* tough," I say, grateful for the distraction from my phone. I want to be bold, an emotional risk-taker. But I also don't want to be the woman who stares at a string of texts, waiting for a reply.

So instead, I stand to take in the full effect of my ensemble: full-length leather jacket, tight white blouse, black boots, and bright red scarf taut around my neck. My hair falls spiky around my cheeks, which somehow manage to look not round and cute, as they typically do, but chiseled and tough, under the bold liquid rouge Carola applied.

I wanted for the staff to be in costume, but also to wear something that could feel like a sort-of armor against the roving eyes, the subtly and not-so-subtly offensive comments, and the exhaustion that typically come with the Midnight Society Costume Ball. I think I've succeeded.

Carola, Dolores, and Abuela Fela applaud as I spin, and then they drift away to the reception area, where real clients are beginning to gather, since their salon opens for business in five minutes.

"How can we *not* take those assholes down tonight," I say, "looking like this."

"I can't believe it's finally happening," Luisa adds, her voice wistful.

I walk over to her, loving the feel of heavy leather swishing around my ankles. "So what's your next step?" I ask her. "Once you get the scoop of the century in Atlanta's business-news world and take down the bad guys."

"I'm gonna get my fucking job back," Luisa says, her tone defiant.

"And that's what you want?" I ask, unsure of how to articulate my real question, which I think is whether all that we've been through together has changed her. Because, glancing back at my fiery self in the salon's full-length mirror, I know it's changed me.

"It's what I've always wanted," Luisa responds without hesitation.

"What about the lonely apartment? The long work hours? The dying plants, and all the late-night takeout?" I dare to ask. "Is that the life you want to go back to?"

Luisa sighs, her shoulders falling with a long exhale. "I know that I struggle with the whole work-life balance or whatever," she begins, surprisingly self-aware. "But I also love the work. And I'm really good at it. So I'm not ready to give it up." She stands up, slips on her own leather coat. "Why can't I have it all? There has to be some way to make it all work. Right?"

I think of my own path, motherhood and work, and trying to juggle those responsibilities with—well, life. Sure, I've made sacrifices, and I've set more than a few dreams aside. But I've also built a stable, loving community for Aidan, surrounding him with care. I've learned how to rely on people when I need them and also to let people rely on me. I hope I've shown Aidan, through my example, that—when it comes down to it—this is what makes life beautiful.

Letting her question linger in the air between us, I reach for Luisa's red scarf and offer to tie it around her. She stands facing me and I slip the silk fabric around the back of her neck. It dawns on me, suddenly, that Luisa has become one of those people—someone I trust, someone I know I can rely on to get through hard times. I think she trusts me, too.

"If anyone can find a way to make it work," I say, pulling the ends of her scarf together, "you can." Luisa is more determined than anyone I know, and if she sets a goal for herself, she'll find a way to achieve it, come hell or high water.

She inches her chin up so I can knot the fabric over her throat. I finish the double knot, and then she turns to stand beside me. We stare at our reflections in the mirror.

"All right, Jade Jackal," I say, playfully bumping into her shoulder. "Let's do this."

"Yessssss," she replies, bumping me back. "Let's go kick some ass, Honey Badger."

CHAPTER 31

Luisa

The Dogwood Hills ballroom doors open to the all-male members of the Midnight Society, along with their wives and girlfriends, decked out in a blitz of over-the-top, Y'allywood-inspired costumes.

My eyes scavenge the crowd, hunting for Eli and his Wonder Bread racing fire suit. *Is he here yet?* Griggs invited him to his Tuxedo Park mansion for a pregame drink, where Tripp would confide that he's getting pressured from his dad to put his trust fund to work, then ask Griggs for investment advice, guidance on tax shelters and offshore accounts.

As I scan the room, I spot multiple versions of Elvis and also Dolly Parton, Forrest Gump, Ray Charles, Truman Capote, Loretta Lynn, at least a half dozen women dressed in cutoffs with their ass cheeks hanging out—I'm thinking probably Daisy Duke from *The Dukes of Hazzard*—and that one guy from *Smokey and the Bandit*. I also detect a couple in an elaborate Scarlett O'Hara and Rhett Butler period belle gown and suit. Guess they didn't get the whole slavery whitewashing memo.

Everyone seems genuinely awed by the way Holly has transformed this musty club into a fabulous event space—from the massive overhead *Y'ALLYWOOD* sign to the life-size cardboard cuttings of paparazzi; from the flashing camera lights to the red carpet lined with gold posts.

"They may be stuffy high-society muckety-mucks," Holly mutters beside me, "but this is when they get to let their hair down and play dress-up."

"So it's like a debauchery party," I reply, dropping the brim of my hat to cover more of my face. Chip, my former publisher, is on the guest list, and I'm relying on the uniform Holly designed to keep him from recognizing me. I devised a whole plan for slipping some extra-strength laxative into his drink, but Holly put the kibosh on it, arguing that we shouldn't add any unnecessary crimes to our rap sheet. I begrudgingly agreed.

"More like debauchery adjacent," Holly mumbles back through a wide smile. "The women ensure their men keep some semblance of restraint. I've heard their other parties—the ones without wives and dates—are truly obscene."

"As in—"

"I'm gonna spare you the details," she interrupts. "It's the sort of thing you can't un-know, and I really wish I could."

I nod, strangely grateful for her discretion.

Holly repeats a practiced "Welcome," as I usher guests toward the colossal champagne tower and the impressive circular bar at the center of the ballroom, where a small battalion of bartenders is delivering from an extensive menu of signature cocktails, beer, wine, and more champagne.

The buffet is just as opulent, with carving stations for prime rib, tenderloin, and country ham, beside a massive shrimp topiary. The catering staff went all in on the Southern food theme, with a shrimp 'n' grits bar, a biscuits 'n' white gravy bar, a mac 'n' cheese bar, heaps of fried chicken, and an iced raw bar that features dainty oyster shooters—pulled off the shell and served with cocktail sauce inside shot glasses, and paired (of course!) with those delicious buttery saltines.

Beyond the buffet, a Big Band is playing a high-energy, brass-heavy rendition of Earth, Wind & Fire's "September" on a stage overlooking the dance floor. Holly has instructed the staff that, *exactly* as the prop clock on the stage strikes midnight, they will break into Kool & The Gang's "Celebration." Confetti cannons will explode over the dancing crowd, and servers will carry out silver trays of Chick-fil-A mini sliders and glazed Krispy Kreme doughnuts dotted with vanilla ice cream—because this is what rich people like to snack on when they are "cutting loose."

"Excuse me," a honeyed voice in a Mississippi accent says

behind me, "I was told you could get me some Domino's pizza, KFC, and the always delicious Taco Bell."

I snort with laughter, then turn to find a grinning Tripp Reynolds Bedford III—ever the Bubba in his Ricky Bobby fire suit, complete with Wonder Bread racing helmet, which he's cradling in one arm.

"Would you like some Powerade Mystic Mountain Blueberry with that, sir?" I deadpan, making him smile wider.

"Dear sweet baby Jesus," he mutters in a low whistle, running his hungry eyes down my costume and over my waistcoat, pausing at the name tag pinned on my chest. It reads *María*. Common. Forgettable. Invisible. His gaze drifts to the red silk scarf tied around my neck, then to my lips, painted the same color. We look into each other's eyes, willing the senseless spectacle around us to disappear, willing Tripp and María to fade until it's just us: Eli and Luisa.

"Hi," Eli says simply, dropping the Ricky Bobby act.

"Hi." I lean into this new unspoken language between us. It's become our own form of code-switching, a language born over morning pancakes at the kitchen table with Pearl, random *I miss you* texts, spontaneous *I just wanted to hear your voice* calls, whispered secrets spoken in the dark, after sex, and so many plans for the future—our future.

"There you are," Virginia cries out, materializing by his side and snaking her arm around his. "You just disappeared on me."

I almost don't recognize her. Surprisingly, she's gone all out on a matching Cal Naughton Jr. fire suit, dressed as Ricky's best friend and racing partner. She's even wearing Naughton's thick mustache.

Two fratty guys dressed as the Dixon Brothers from *The Walking Dead* wander by with zombie dates. They give Tripp and Virginia a once-over and then call out, in unison, "Shake and Bake, baby." Without missing a beat, Virginia and Tripp fist-bump. "Shake and Bake!" they call back.

Once again, I'm so conflicted about this woman. She seems goofy and kinda cool. It would have been easy to dismiss her if she'd chosen to dress as Ricky's smokin' hot wife. But no, she had to be the wacky, fun teammate. Which begs the question: *What message is she trying to send?*

"What are you supposed to be?" she asks me, grabbing a mini crab cake from a passing waiter with her free hand, while inspecting my costume. "I like it."

I'm rocking the Southern Gothic look, if I do say so myself—mid-calf boots, leather leggings, tight waistcoat over a lace shirt, stand-up collar coat, and wide-brim hat.

"Oh, wait," she adds, eyes suddenly bright and wide. "I've got it! You're Goth—"

"*Southern* Gothic," I correct, brimming with fake politeness. "It's a subtle commentary on the grotesque. Alienation and aberration."

Tripp coughs out a laugh.

"Exposes the dark underbelly of the haut monde," she adds, with perfect French enunciation. "Great for this setting." Unable to produce a response, I stare, agog. Is she not-so-subtly critiquing her own world? "I took a class in college." She shrugs. "Comp-lit major."

As much as I loathe being the jealous type, I can't help but feel a little defensive and territorial around her. She's got beauty *and* brains, as it turns out. How annoying is that?

I don't realize that I'm staring until she asks, "Don't we know each other?" She's tilting her head to the side as if something about me doesn't add up.

"It's Luisa, right?" she exclaims in recognition. "Why are you dressed like the staff?"

"She works here," Tripp says, gesturing to my name tag dismissively. "She just *looks* like Luisa."

"I guess we all look the same to you," I mutter derisively, trying hard to throw her off my scent.

"That's not . . . no . . . what I meant—" Virginia stammers, flustered. "Sorry, I thought—"

I tug at my silk scarf, rattled.

"Should we go find the judge?" Tripp jerks at her jacket, cutting her off. "I think he wanted to introduce me to some folks from out of town." His eyes cut to the ballroom, inconspicuously backing away from her touch. "I'm thirsty," he blurts out. "Let's go get a drink, Magic Man," he tells her, not waiting for an answer.

Tripp drags her to the bar before she can protest, ask any more questions, or offer commentary. But he does manage to turn back and give me a quick wink.

Reassured, I go in search of Holly. Justine directs me to a side room—nicknamed the nightclub—where a second, louder and more rowdy band plays for the younger crowd. It's packed with people, but I find Holly talking to the sound and light tech about an issue with the midnight confetti cannon explosion and something about a guy planning to ride in on a motorcycle.

To her credit, Holly has carved every minuscule detail of tonight's schedule with surgical precision, all while putting out concurrent fires, juggling an unending stream of ludicrous requests, and directing a staff of several dozen. Tablet in hand, she's in her element, and I'm enormously impressed.

I grab two flutes of champagne from behind the bar and gesture for her to follow me down a deserted hallway, furnished with soft lighting and antiques that look like they predate the Civil War. Maybe Scarlett and Rhett brought them as props.

"I swear to God," she grunts, taking a gulp of champagne. "If one more drunken asshole tries to jump onstage to"—she makes air quotes with her free hand—"lip-sync with the band, I will wring his scrawny little neck." She sets the glass on a sideboard and jabs an angry finger at her tablet. "This isn't a frat house, boys! And don't even get me started on the banker who insists on making his grand ballroom entrance—on a freaking motorcycle."

"You're really good at this event planning thing, Holly," I say with feeling.

"I've just been doing it for a long time," she remarks, shaking her head as she marks off another to-do item.

"I mean it," I insist. "Not everyone can keep all these details straight. Execute under all this pressure for perfection." My hand falls over her tablet, forcing her to meet my gaze. "And look smoking hot while barking out orders." I force her to admire her reflection in the gold-rimmed mirror hanging over the sideboard.

"See?" This makes her smile, and the tension in her shoulders eases a little.

"Dolores is a master of her craft," she says, passing one hand over her spiky layers. "My hair has never looked this good." She sets the tablet down, then picks up the champagne glass, taking a sip, relaxing for what seems like the first time in weeks. Well, with the possible exception of the postcoital moment I stumbled into this morning.

"Do you really want this general manager job?" I ask, closely watching her expression.

Holly bites at her lower lip, her entire body sagging against the cabinet. "Honestly, and in spite of all the nonsense unfolding around us, I think I do," she admits. "I filled out the application but I haven't submitted it," she says, dejected. "What's the point? Griggs will block me. Or worse, get me fired." She returns her gaze to the tablet, absently running one index finger over the screen. I abruptly press the sleep button and the screen goes dark.

"Griggs won't be in the picture much longer," I remind her. "If this is what you want, you shouldn't let him stop you."

"What if . . . ?" Her voice trails off. I don't say anything, giving her space to speak her mind. "What if I'm not good enough?"

"Look at me," I say, resting my hands on her shoulders. "You are fucking amazing." I give her a squeeze. "And by now, you should know that I don't go around doling out unearned compliments." She smiles at this, knowing it's the truth. "If they don't want you, then fuck them. Quit. Start your own damn business. They don't fucking deserve you." I drop my hands, resting them on the sides of her arms. "But at least give them the chance to decide."

Before I can react, Holly pulls me into a hug. "Thanks," she whispers. "I really needed the pep talk."

I hug her back, realizing that—despite our many differences—Holly and I seem to have become real friends.

"Let's hit send on that application," I say, leaning back so I can look her in the eyes. "Before you have time to change your mind."

Holly releases her hold on me, then reaches for a file folder inside her bag. She retrieves an old-school, honest-to-God, paper job application she's filled out in blue ink.

"Are you fucking kidding me right now?" I ask, dumbfounded.

"They were very specific about the ink color," she tells me, her tone suddenly solemn. "Legible handwriting in blue ink only."

"What are you supposed to do with it?" I examine the form with curiosity. Remarkably, Holly has very neat handwriting.

"Drop it in the board's mailbox." She gestures down the dimly lit hallway. "Like, an actual mailbox."

"Come on, then," I say. "Bring your champagne."

"Wait," she cries out. "Now?"

"Now." I take the form and my champagne glass, then stride down the hallway, Holly tottering to keep up with me.

"I can't believe we're doing this," she tells me, her voice giddy.

"I can't believe anyone actually still uses paper applications," I scoff, waving the archaic document in one hand. "Is this thing in triplicate?"

"Oh yes," she replies, laughing. "Carbon copies. I had to press really hard."

When we arrive at the mail slot affixed to the wall, I pass her the application. She stares at it for a beat, takes it with her free hand, and then drops it in.

"Ohmygod, ohmygod, ohmygod," she says, suddenly breathing so hard that I think she might hyperventilate. "I did it. I applied."

I take my champagne glass and lift it to her. "To the next general manager of this club," I say, "whose first vital task will be teaching the old-ass men on the board how to use an actual computer."

"To the next department head of investigative journalism at *The Georgia Times*," she says. *Department head?* I like the sound of that. "Whose first task will be to move out of her mother's house so she can finally have hot sex with her boyfriend at her own place." She lifts her glass higher.

"To our bright, sexy futures," I exclaim.

"To our bright, beautiful futures." She clinks my glass, her eyes glinting with hope. We shoot back what's left of our drinks.

"Oh, crap," she says when she's finished her champagne. "I gotta go warn the valets to clear the way for Easy Rider."

CHAPTER 32

Holly

It's not the most absurd request I've fielded, in my almost nineteen years working at this club, but it may be among the more complicated—right up there with the three hundred real wax taper candles Ella-Rose Richmond and her mother insisted we suspend from the ballroom ceiling in delicate glass vases. She was an especially *attentive* bride, micromanaging everything from the shade of natural twine used to hang all those dangling open flames to the type of lemon in guests' water glasses (Meyer, of course). Unfortunately, Ella-Rose seemed less concerned with the details of the special permit I had to procure from the Atlanta fire marshal, leaving that fun task entirely to me.

At least I have this to be grateful for: Linwood Hayes's *Easy Rider* stunt doesn't require any variances from the city. Maybe I also should feel grateful that focusing on the complicated logistics of what's about to happen, keeps my mind off what I've just done. I'm not sure I was ready to submit that application. Honestly, I'm not even sure I want the position. But that Luisa—she can be quite persuasive.

"Mr. Hayes is incoming," I alert Lionel at the gatehouse. Then I head out to the main entrance to ensure the extra handicap ramp has been properly placed and effectively secured. Wouldn't want to repeat the film's tragic ending. I rush back inside to clear loiterers from the foyer, but I'm stopped in my tracks by Loula, who—in a flowing emerald-green dress—has managed to make herself into the spitting image of Anna, the younger sister in *Frozen*. I'm not sure what an animated film set in the Arctic Circle has to do with iconic movies filmed in or about the South, but here we are.

"Oh, Holly," Loula exclaims, her cheeks rosy with pleasure (or maybe wine), "isn't this all just the most fun ever?"

I paste on a huge smile and nod enthusiastically while she gives me a once-over. "You look *hot*," she says, her eyes roving my costume appreciatively.

I'm still a little shocked that I decided to go with this look. After all, it clearly defies my "blend in" approach to dressing for work at the club. But it feels right for tonight—bold, confident, maybe even fierce. Somehow, these past weeks with Hugh, and the radical vulnerability they've brought, are letting me settle into a sense of myself that I guess has always been here, but that I've been reluctant to expose. I think that's what I most love about our time together. Being with him makes me feel more at ease and relaxed. His presence somehow reminds me that I'm enough, just as I am.

In the adjacent ballroom, the band strikes up Rick James's "Superfreak," inducing Loula to quite literally jump up and down, while squealing, "Sexy Holly! You have to come dance with me! Pleeease?"

I'm not even remotely surprised when Marg arrives at her side, in a shimmering blue gown and an ice-queen crown, then gently balances a now teetering Loula with her right arm.

"Oh gosh," I say, trying to sound sincerely disappointed, "I really wish I could. I mean, I do love this song, but, you know—"

"She's working," Marg says matter-of-factly.

"Always working," Loula slurs. "Soooo boring."

I've got to hand it to these two—they've nailed the costumes, and the Anna/Elsa dynamic is pretty on the nose, too. Maybe one day sweet Loula will break through to thaw Marg's cold, cold heart.

I'm glancing around, really hoping to glimpse one of their husbands dressed as Olaf, the heat-seeking snowman, but instead I see Captain America and Black Widow heading directly toward us. The costumes are so realistic that I'm struggling to pinpoint who's inside them, until I notice that Black Widow has bright red fringe earrings dangling beneath her red wig.

Damn, there must be a whole lot of spandex and silicone in that bodysuit. Rail-thin Anna-Byrd is sporting some serious curves.

Griggs arrives at my side, sending a chill up my spine. He's leaning in to say something to me, when the roar of a motorcycle drowns out even the raucous chorus of "Superfreak."

Linwood Hayes, investment banker masquerading as a leather-clad coke dealer, is making his grand *Easy Rider* entrance, and I couldn't be more thrilled with the timing. The crowd parts as he rolls in, revving the vintage Harley lowrider he rented for the night. A young woman I've never seen before, with a fabulous brunette bouffant and perhaps the thickest eyelashes I've ever witnessed, rides behind him in an American Flag bikini top and electric-blue spandex mini shorts, her arms wrapped around his waist.

Their arrival incites so many whoops and hollers that Mr. Hayes, clearly an amateur, gets a little too confident with the bike. He actually attempts a wheelie, which sends his motorcycle out of control. The gathered crowd watches in shock and awe as Dennis, the club's soon-to-retire general manager, appears out of nowhere to try and steady the bike. But it's too late. Both Linwood Hayes and the mystery woman are thrown off the bike, which then careens into a heavy oak sideboard, sending three Ming vases and a sweet little arrangement of miniature spray roses crashing to the ground. The motorcycle lands squarely on Dennis's left leg, but he hops up and brushes himself right off, eliciting relieved cheers as he hobbles away, wincing.

Dear sweet Jesus. I hope Dennis is okay. And I should have thought to move the vases. How could I have overlooked this detail? Someone could have been seriously lacerated. I grasp my headset and send out the call. "Cleanup needed in grand entry foyer. Calling all available staff."

I'm berating myself when Luisa arrives at my side, laughing. She crouches down and begins to gather broken shards of pottery. "You didn't tell me the biker-banker was bringing an escort," she whispers, glancing up at the bikini-clad woman.

Wait, is she a prostitute? I hadn't thought about it, but I guess that would make the *Easy Rider* setup even more authentic. Needless to say, Linwood Hayes didn't fill me in on this detail any of the six times he called me at work to offer step-by-step instructions.

"I actually feel sorry for her," Luisa continues, as *Gone with the Wind*'s Rhett Butler crouches to help the bewildered woman to her feet. "She's not getting paid enough for this shit."

Besides being down three Ming vases, the foyer has been returned to pristine condition, thanks to our excellent cleaning staff, and just in time. I rush through the service corridor to supervise the delivery of hot-glazed Krispy Kremes, fresh off the conveyor belt. They're being transported from a doughnut factory on North Avenue, and I need to be sure the kitchen is prepared to receive them at the service entrance. Heaven forbid they not be pipin' hot from the oven. I'm approaching the staff hallway that also services the men's locker room, when Captain America himself materializes. I glance around quickly, noting that only he and I are present in this long corridor, and that familiar chill returns to my spine.

I am loath to admit it, but I'm becoming physically afraid of this pathetic excuse for a man. I squeeze my eyes shut and try to muster the fierce energy I carried only moments ago, but it has all dissolved in the presence of Griggs Johnson.

"Holly," he calls across the hall, his voice gregarious and chummy. "Just the woman I wanted to see." It strikes me as odd, suddenly, that Griggs is slinking through the service hallway, away from the other revelers. Could he be hiding from someone? Probably just his overbearing wife. "I was upstairs earlier and I saw your application for the GM job," he says. "Good for you. Way to step out of your comfort zone and go for it."

Demeaning, patronizing prick.

"I'm rooting for you to get the job," he adds, scanning my body with an unrestrained hunger in his eyes. "Would give us the chance to work even more closely."

A part of me wants to punch him in the chest, aim directly for that big white star. Another part wants to turn and run like hell away from him. And, also, why is he lurking about in so many hallways tonight?

"What can I do for you, Mr. Johnson?" I ask, my voice tremoring slightly.

"Well," he says, "as you'll recall, the dean over at UGA is joining our threesome for golf in a week."

I stop in my tracks and involuntarily lean against the cold concrete wall.

"And I thought we might reserve the Ivy Room for brunch after the round," he says, his tone still light and jovial. "You know, make it a special, private event, since it looks like I might have some sensitive information to share with him."

By "sensitive information," he means the legal investigation he's planning to open on my son, and the criminal felony conviction that will no doubt ensue. I suddenly feel nauseous. Exactly what kind of man asks a woman to plan the celebration of her own demise? The kind of man who's striding confidently toward me, coming too close.

"Unless," he says, so near to me that his voice is a whisper. Letting the word linger in the still air between us, he uses one arm to trap me against the wall, then lifts a hand slowly to my upper lip. I'm frozen in place, my heart hammering in my chest, my brain willing my knee to find his ball sack. But I can't seem to move. Instead, I'm forced to feel his fingertip drag along my lip, my chin, my neck. "Unless I cancel with the dean and take you out instead." His hand has somehow made its way to my chest, and his finger skirts along the open edge of my shirt. "For a business lunch, of course."

"Stop," I croak. "Stop now."

"Just relax, Holly. All you have to do is quit playing this 'hard to get' game." His finger grazes my left breast, and I feel it, cold and menacing, piercing through the fabric of my bra and button-down shirt.

Suddenly, as if I've woken from some terrible nightmare, I find the will to move. I place my hand firmly on his chest and push him away so that he stumbles backward into the wall opposite us. Seeing him falter brings me just enough confidence to do what I know must be done—consequences be damned.

"I'm going to say this nice and loud, to be sure you hear me," I tell him, planting my feet in a wide stance. "And I'm only going to say it once, so pay attention."

He stands upright, too, his stupid fucking Captain America costume sagging around his narrow hips, and then he pastes a bored look across his face.

"I'm not *playing* hard to get," I tell him. "I am—for you—permanently and forever *impossible* to get." I prop both hands on my hips, hoping that the stance will elicit courage. I need to finish this—to end the sick game I never agreed to play—once and for all. "You might get me fired from my job, you might get my son kicked out of school, but let me assure you—you will never, ever touch my body again."

"Whatever you say, boss," he sneers, giving me a sick little salute. "But just so you know, this is when the game really starts to get fun."

He walks away and I watch, using sheer force of will to stay on my feet, not to collapse into a pile. I stare at his back, hoping he feels my stern gaze through the red, white, and blue of his stupid spandex bodysuit. I hope he feels weak, emasculated, and rejected. I hope he feels like the small, idiotic man that he is. But I also know, with absolute clarity, that Griggs Caldecott Johnson III won't stop until he wins—or gets sent directly to jail, without passing Go.

He opens a service door and exits to the courtyard, where I see Judge Thacker and Jim Wade standing expectantly, as if they've been waiting for him. As the door slams shut behind him, I feel a wave of relief.

This is almost over, I tell myself. *We are so close to ending this nightmare forever.* It's Eli's turn to roll the dice, and my bet's on him.

CHAPTER 33

Luisa

"Jade Jackal on the move," I whisper into our radio's private channel. "Eyes on the target." Tripp, Griggs, and his cronies step onto the club's vast lawn, where cocktail tables and plush patio furniture have been arranged for private conversations. Metal floor lanterns line the steps down from the ballroom and strings of light run the length of the garden, casting a warm glow over the guests.

"Roger that," Holly responds, as I pretend to clear out glassware and plates. "We're getting really good at this," she adds, more animated. "Maybe we should start a PI agency after this is all over."

"Over and out, Honey Badger," I deadpan, unable to stop myself from smiling at her shenanigans.

The men move down a second set of stone steps toward a secluded courtyard, away from the other guests. I watch from the terrace above, as musty-scented cigar smoke bellows into a clear summer sky. They make for a bizarre menagerie of characters: Captain America, Ol' Mags the banker as Jumaji's murderous big-game hunter, Judge Thacker as an exact double of Colonel Sanders, and Jim Wade in a . . . *Is that a Godzilla cosplay suit?*

The deal is about to go down and Tripp is perfectly situated to record the whole thing, ask the right questions, make sure Griggs and the others incriminate themselves. A thrill of excitement coils through my body in anticipation of our big payoff.

"Back at the house, you asked me if I knew of any solid investment opportunities," Griggs says, gently tapping his cigar.

Tripp nods but doesn't say anything. He knows better than to look eager.

Everything is unfolding exactly as we planned. Griggs has taken the bait. Holly was right, this man would never be able to resist a gullible young angel investor with a trust fund to burn.

"I'm working on this development down in Westlake," Griggs continues. "High-end luxury homes, restaurants, golf course"—he motions forward with the hand holding a cigar—"that kinda thing."

"It's gonna be one helluva course," Ol' Mags remarks, puffing on his cigar.

"More than one course," the judge says. "Three. Heck, maybe we'll play a round on all of 'em, and I just might have a chance at winnin' back my money." He nudges Tripp, and they all laugh.

"You set up the tee times, and I'll be there," Tripp replies cheekily. "Hard to resist a winning streak." They chuckle at his brashness, and once again I'm awed by Eli's sagacity when it comes to telling these people what they want to hear.

"We're closed to outside investors," Griggs offers, gesturing to the other men, in a confidential tone. "But we agreed that you're just the sort of man we want to be in business with." He drops one hand on Tripp's shoulder, and I lean closer to the railing, careful not to be seen. "You in?"

"Sounds intriguing," Tripp says blithely—interested, but not *too* interested. "I'm listening."

"The situation over there in Westlake is a bit delicate," Griggs says, a conspiratorial grin spreading over his villainous face. "So here's what you need to understand—"

Yes. Yes. Yes. Fuck yes. I want to pump my fists in the air, victorious.

"I think we got 'em," I can't help but call out to Holly over the headset. "Deal's going down, and Griggs is about to spill."

Holly starts to reply, but her words are drowned out by none other than Virginia, striding across the lawn, crying out, "There you are!" I'm too dumbstruck to react, much less stop her as she steps down to the courtyard below, where the men are assembled. "We've been looking *everywhere* for you." A young man trails after her in a black football jersey, the phrase *MEAN MACHINE* stitched in red over a white number 18.

Tripp reaches out a hand to the newcomer, his voice dropping to a deep baritone as he recites what must be a line from a movie, "We may not have the most talented team, but we'll definitely have the meanest."

"Who we gonna crush?" the guy calls back.

"The guards!" Tripp exclaims in response, as both burst into laughter. "I loved that damn movie, *The Longest Yard.*"

"I knew you'd hit it off." Virginia claps in delight. "This is Little Shuggy. Remember? I told you about him at the derby party?"

I clutch the railing with sweaty hands, trying to steady myself. How can this be happening? Why is Shuggs here?

"Your cousin, right?" Tripp's eyes go wide, but he still manages to paste on a welcoming smile. "I thought you were off on a European adventure."

"Had to cut it short," Shuggs says. "Turns out they don't love Americans who carve Greek letters into walls in Pompeii."

"You didn't," Virginia exclaims, aghast.

"Hell no," he replies. "I've got better sense than that. But my buddy Tabs, not so much."

The whole crowd laughs in a shared understanding that boys will be boys, and on occasion, they're entitled to a little bail money. Meanwhile, I'm sweating buckets and my mind is racing to catch up. Little Shuggy was decidedly *not* part of our surgically stitched plan for this evening. I force my nerves to remain calm and think clearly: How can I remove Virginia and her cousin from the picture before they inadvertently blow up our scheme?

"Sorry to hear," Tripp says, laughing as he grasps hands with Tripp, then pumps twice. "I'm Tripp Bedford."

Shuggs's head tilts sideways. "Tripp Bedford?" he asks, his laughter dying off as he grasps hands with Trip. "From Ole Miss?" He releases Tripp's hand.

"The very one," Virginia adds, stepping beside Tripp, resting one hand on his bicep.

"Theodore Reynolds Bedford the Third," Tripp says, his voice faltering slightly.

Shuggs stares at him, confused.

I blink repeatedly, a sense of foreboding rising from deep in my gut. My pulse quickens as I take in Shuggs's mystified expression. He cuts his gaze to his grandfather, the judge, then back to Tripp. "I don't know who you are, man," he says, more certain this time. "But you're not the Tripp Bedford whose family is from Greenwood—the guy whose grandfather everyone calls 'The Colonel.'"

I watch, panic-stricken, as if having an out-of-body experience.

"What do you mean?" Virginia asks, her tone still light, half laughing at her cousin's confusion. "Of course he is."

"I've met Tripp Bedford," Shuggs tells his cousin. "Last fall, at an Ole Miss alumni event for premed students." Then to the judge, he says, "He's one of those Doctors Without Borders types—was on his way back to some jungle in Cambodia. But he gave me his contact info, said he'd write me a letter if I decide on Bama for med school." Shuggs pulls out his phone, begins to scroll.

My stomach bottoms out. Suddenly, I can't breathe. Even from a distance, I can sense the tension building below. The friendly banter has vanished, replaced by a shroud of suspicion and hostility.

"Oh, I know that guy," our Tripp says dismissively, an attempt at regaining control. "People always confuse the two of us." He removes his phone from his suit, too, pretending to scroll, surely buying himself some time. "I'm pretty sure I have a picture of us together. At a frat party, way back when."

There's no such photo. I know because I would've been the one to create it. Why the hell didn't I think of it before?

"So, you're a Phi Delt, too?" Shuggs asks, still befuddled.

"Sure am," our Tripp says, trying his best to project confidence. I recall all that Holly has taught him about the fraternity and start to feel the tiniest flicker of hope that this will get back on track.

"Well, then, we can clear this up right now—" Jim Wade says, gesturing to Ol' Mags.

"Absolutely," the banker says. "You're looking at a proud Phi Delt from the great class of '78 at Washington and Lee University." His right hand protrudes from under the safari cape draped over his shoulder. His creepy Van Pelt grin, muttonchops, and handlebar mustache make me shudder.

Tripp pauses, staring at the extended hand for a beat. Is this some insider frat bro joke? It doesn't sound like a joke. And why is Tripp not shaking the man's hand?

"Come on, don't leave the man hanging," a belligerent Griggs demands. "What's the Phi Delt handshake?"

There's a *literal* secret handshake—of course there is. Because frat guys are perpetually stuck in a childish game of "who gets to play in my super-secret tree house."

Tripp hesitates, and I can practically read the thoughts that must be swirling inside Eli's head. He could attempt to fake the handshake, or just try to play it off.

"You don't fucking know, do you?" Griggs's nostrils flare, eyes going wild behind his Captain America mask.

An ominous, damp chill crawls over my skin. I reach for the call button on my walkie-talkie, my tone clipped and frantic as I urge Holly to come meet me in the courtyard.

"You're gonna regret you ever set foot in this place," Griggs barks, quickly taking a combative stand.

Eli's lead foot is angled forward, back foot angled out, knees bent slightly, body weight shifted back, readying himself for a fight.

To her credit, Virginia remains by his side. I don't know if I should be pissed or grateful. She may be the only thing preventing Griggs from physically going after Eli.

"Hotty Toddy, my ass," Griggs says, baring his teeth like an animal, spittle flying, his polished Atlanta accent gone. "You're a fucking fake." Eli flinches at the accusation, balling his hands into fists beside him. "And you've fucked with the wrong people."

Holly appears beside me, breathing hard from exertion and nerves. "What's going on?" she asks, but I don't have to respond.

"Surely," Virginia ventures, her tone honeyed sweet, "this is all one big misunderstanding." She places one hand on Griggs's chest, right above the star, trying to build some space between them. "Tripp is a common name. Maybe we shouldn't jump to conclusions."

"Fine, you got me," Eli says with a dismissive shrug, trying to regain his cocky Tripp persona. "I don't remember the fucking handshake. Sue me."

Judge Thacker steps forward, somehow even more menacing in his white suit and black Western bow tie. "We're gonna do a little more than that, son." He leans forward, hands resting over the round handle of his costume's cane. "If my grandson is correct, it seems that you've stolen this young man's identity." He takes Virginia by the arm, moving her away from Tripp and toward himself. "Georgia carries a maximum ten-year prison sentence for first offenders." He stabs his cane in Eli's direction. "More for subsequent offenses."

My vision blurs. *Eli can't go to prison*, I think erratically. *Who will help me save the Castillos' home? Who will take Pearl to Savannah in the fall? How will he get Mabel to Wyoming?* All at once I'm dizzy, my thoughts careening into a tailspin.

"We have to do something," I hear myself cry out in a whisper. I move toward the steps, but Holly catches the sleeve of my jacket, pulling me back.

"Where are you going?" she whisper-yells.

"We can't let him get arrested." My mouth goes dry. My body is on the verge of a panic attack, but it will have to wait. We need to intervene before the judge puts in a call to his buddy the sheriff. "Follow me," I say, clutching my drinks tray, doing my best to calm my wobbly legs as I take the steps, one at a time, Holly moving beside me.

"Can I get you gentlemen some drinks?" I ask, forcing my face to rearrange itself into a servile smile.

"Holly," Griggs snarls, ignoring me. "Get security."

"Is there something the matter, Mr. Johnson?" Holly asks, her voice remarkably measured and steady. She makes a point to glance up the steps, conveying with one look that there are other guests in the courtyard who might be listening, appealing to their need for discretion.

Seeming to read the room, Virginia nudges her cousin. "We should get out of here." They head back up the steps to the lawn, but not before Virginia tosses one last look in my direction, her expression shaded by something like remorse.

"A fraudster has infiltrated the club," Judge Thacker concludes, stabbing the ground with his cane.

"Just can't trust anyone these days," Griggs interjects, folding his arms across his chest.

"Holly," Judge Thacker says, reaching for her shoulder. "Please call the police."

The glasses on my tray rattle, turning everyone's attention to me. Everyone except Holly looks genuinely surprised to see me standing there.

"María, is it?" Jim Wade says, rolling the *r* unnecessarily. His pale face pokes out from the toothy mouth of the giant lizard. "Why don't you run inside and grab us a round of bourbons?" He smiles as if nothing's the matter. As if he's not about to wreck our lives, obliterate our futures.

"Happy to," I manage, avoiding Eli's hard gaze as I turn back toward the ballroom, uncertain of what to do next. I stride across the courtyard, berating myself. *How could I dismiss Virginia's comment about her cousin when we first met her at the derby party? Why didn't we cross-reference the guest list? Why didn't I follow up, do a deep dive? Why did I agree to this godforsaken plan in the first place?*

I abandon the drinks tray at the bar, where I catch sight of Chip, the publisher of *The Georgia Times*, enjoying a cocktail and flirting with a younger woman, decidedly not his wife.

You won, asshole. And I should've fucking given him explosive diarrhea when I had the chance. Too late now.

Half an hour later, Holly and I idle in the parking lot behind the club, watching as Eli's wrists are encased in handcuffs and he's loaded into the back of a patrol car.

Holly asked the officer to turn off the patrol's lights so as not to disturb the party's guests. I get that she's also doing her job, but who cares about a bunch of rich hedonists when we're now responsible for getting Eli arrested? A crushing sense of desperation has settled at my center, wringing my chest with pain.

"What happens now?" Holly asks quietly beside me.

I know she's not expecting an answer. I know this is one of those rhetorical questions we ask ourselves when there is nothing left to say. But the fact that we didn't anticipate this as a possible outcome; the fact that we are not fucking prepared for this turn of events; the fact that I was stupid enough to trust Holly when she said she knew all the rules, and we would be "in and out, with the proof we need," makes me want to break something. Because I know better than this. I know to always have an exit plan. And I know never to rely on others when I should be relying on myself.

"This was such a stupid idea," I snarl in frustration. "Why did I let you drag me into this?"

"I'm sorry?" Holly turns to face me, eyes narrowed, cheeks glowing red. "Who dragged who? You're not putting the blame on me."

"I trusted you with my whole fucking life," I shriek, shaking my head in disbelief. "How could I have been so naive, so reckless?" I bark. "God, this was such a dumbass plan. And the worst part about it is I knew not to get involved—I *know* better."

Holly tenses, exhaling hard beside me. "We were supposed to be in and out—"

"Stop saying that!" I cut her off angrily. "You found Tripp's identity—" I tick off each charge with my fingers. "You called the house mother at Phi Delt. You dug up the details from Ole Miss." I throw both hands in the air, exasperated. "Why did I trust an amateur sleuth and a pool hustler, when I'm the one with the college degree?"

Holly shrinks at the accusation. "Stop," she tells me, "before you go too far."

"Too far?" I gesture to the patrol car with my open palm. "It's the end of the line, Holly. I followed your lead and look where you got us—a fucking dead end."

Eli's vacant stare is fixed on the windshield, his expression inscrutable.

"I'm not gonna go down this road with you, Luisa." She yanks off the earpiece on her headset. "You're trying to hurt me—pushing me away because you're scared." Her shoulders sag as she entreats, "Don't you see?"

"Oh, I see perfectly," I say, jaw clenched, arms folded over my chest. "I brought you in. You came up with this harebrained scheme. And now, we've gone from bad to dumpster fire," I huff. "I should've gone at it alone."

"This is what you do." She splays her hands in my direction. "You push everyone away when things get too real." Blotches of red take over her neck, blending into her silk scarf. "News flash: just because your father left you half a lifetime ago, doesn't mean the whole world will let you down."

"Are you kidding me right now," I hiss back, glaring. "You want to talk about people who've let their family define them?" There's a vein pulsing in the back of my neck, bringing on a blinding headache. I push past it, too enraged to stop. "You've let your parents' judgment define your whole life. You're stuck in a rut at this stupid, vacuous country club, afraid to take any risks because you still believe what your mother said about you all those years ago." I pause, letting my words land. "Maybe you should stop seeing yourself as a teen mom, Holly."

Holly stares back like I've just slapped her across the face. She opens her mouth to respond, but a voice comes through the earpiece, cutting her off. She slips the earpiece back on with trembling hands.

"Holly here," she speaks into the microphone, steadying her voice. She listens, her thumb and index finger squeezing at the sides of her head. "I'll be right there." To me, she says, "I have to go."

"What?" I spit as she's walking away. "Problem with the confetti cannons?" She turns, and I tap at my temple with my index finger, tilting my head as if I'm remembering something. "Or maybe it's the midnight doughnut run?" I'm being a jerk. This is low even for me. But I want her to stay and fight me. I don't want to face this alone. Why can't she see that?

"I'm not doing this," she says, quietly. More chatter comes over her walkie-talkie.

"Go back to your party, Holly," I say, despondent. "Because let's face it, it's not like you ever escaped the country club scene, did you? You're still living in your parents' shadow, hoping that someday you'll be accepted by these people."

She turns to leave, takes a few steps, then stops, whirling around. "You're wrong about us, Luisa," she says slowly. "Eli may not be an award-winning investigative journalist, but he is just as smart as you, and a hell of a lot more emotionally intuitive." She lifts her chin, looking me in the eyes as she says, "And I don't have a college degree because I had the audacity to put my son's needs before my own."

As soon as the words leave her mouth, I know I've gone too far. I've aimed for the jugular and managed to wound with surgical precision.

Holly turns to leave for good. I should chase her down, apologize. I should say that I didn't mean it, that I'm frustrated, angry, stressed, heartbroken—all the things! But my feet don't move and the words don't form in my mouth. There's only one thought drowning out everything else: *What chaos have we unleashed with our sloppy, half-baked plans?*

I'm standing alone in the parking lot as the patrol car hauls Eli to the Fulton County Jail, when Virginia appears beside me, her costume's wig and mustache discarded.

"Oh God, I'm so sorry about this mess," she says, genuine concern in her voice. "Is he gonna be okay?"

I can't muster the breath to respond, because I have no idea.

Inside, the clock strikes midnight, confetti cannons go off, and the band breaks into Kool & The Gang's "Celebration." That's when I do something I haven't done in more than a decade: I pray.

CHAPTER 34

Holly

It's Monday morning, technically my day off, and—once again—I'm scrambling to get ready, then heading into work to put out fires. At least, I think that's why I'm going to the club. It's also entirely possible that I'm going to *get* fired.

The club president, James "Buck" Dorsey, called my cell phone a half hour ago, sternly instructing me to come in for an impromptu meeting. Frankly, I have no idea how he got my cell number. Probably from Jancy. All I know is that I need to be there in a half hour, and I can't seem to track down any clean underwear.

Aidan arrives at the doorway of my bedroom, his unruly auburn hair flopping over his eyes. He's wearing torn-up jeans, a dingy Goodwill T-shirt that reads *Starlight Motel*, and a look of significant concern.

"You okay, Ma?" he asks. "Lots of banging around in here."

"Absolutely," I say. "Just rushing to get to a meeting."

Honestly, I'm not okay at all, but he doesn't need to know that. I'm freaking out because after Saturday night's motorcycle debacle, I worry that Buck Dorsey is bringing me in to demote me. Or maybe Luisa—in her fury—marched up to him after the Midnight Society Costume Ball and tried to blow the whistle on Griggs and the others, somehow implicating me in the process.

"Anything I can do to help?" Aidan asks, his brow etched deep with worry.

He returned from Athens last night, and—looking at him—my heart almost bursts with pride. The kid may look like a street urchin, but he finished his first year of college with a 3.95 GPA. Pretty damn impressive.

I guess he inherited his father's brains, as well as his musical talent.

A huge pit opens in my stomach, knowing that all of Aidan's hard work was for nothing. In six days, Griggs Johnson will play a round of golf with the Undergraduate Dean at UGA, then take him to the Ivy Room and tell him, while nibbling on eggs benedict and sipping stiff Bloody Marys, that my sweet boy is a felon. And there's not a damn thing I can do about it. Well, except plan the meal, which I've already taken care of.

I've been carrying my phone around, watching obsessively for any communication from Luisa, hoping that she's found some way to get Eli out of jail, praying that this isn't all as completely awful as it seems. I tried to go see Eli first thing yesterday morning, but the Fulton County Jail requires at least twenty-four hours' notice for any visitors. I left my contact details in case he needs to make bail. I sure wish Luisa would call to give me an update. And I wish we both could take back the awful things we said to each other Saturday night.

"Sure I can't get you anything?" Aidan asks, still standing in the doorway. I hate to make him worry—parents aren't supposed to do this to their kids.

"How about a coffee," I say, pasting on a reassuring smile. "That's exactly what I need."

"Great," he replies, clearly relieved that I've identified something for him to do, besides stand around awkwardly and worry about his mother. "I'll go make you a double latte for the road," he says. "Then I'm heading out to play some music with Jay."

"Perfect," I say. "And don't forget family game night tonight, next door."

Joel and Peter established the tradition way back when Aidan was starting kindergarten. They'd have us over for dinner on Monday nights—my night off—and after a good hearty meal, with enough leftovers to last me and Aidan at least through Wednesday, we'd dive into Aunt Edna's game night.

"How could I forget game night?" he teases. "Especially since we've got a guest player."

I feel a blush rise to my cheeks, thinking about what it will be like to introduce Hugh to my adopted family. I think he'll jump in and enjoy the games, but it's hard to know. He is, after all, a British professor. And, while I'm not exactly feeling in the mood for fun and games, I know that canceling would be a terrible mistake. Family game night is an almost sacred tradition, and if I miss it, especially on Aidan's first Monday home, Joel, Peter, and Aunt Edna will gang up on me, demanding that I tell them what's wrong.

First, I have to muster the courage to tell Aidan.

I watch him turn to go, my beautiful, sweet, shaggy-haired boy. My heart clenches with love and dread and a deep, haunting melancholy. I know that the time has come for me to explain the entire situation with Griggs, and to face the effect it will have on his future.

I meant to do it this morning. Really, I did. But then the call came in, and I found out Buck Dorsey is waiting for me in the boardroom. I'll tell Aidan tonight, for sure.

I take my last swig of Aidan's strong coffee, toss it in a hallway waste bin, paste on a smile, and stride into the Dogwood Hills boardroom, feigning a confidence I don't have.

The first big surprise awaiting me there is Dennis, the current general manager, leaning back in a club chair with his leg propped on the conference table—in a full cast. The second, to my enormous dismay, is Griggs, standing beside Buck Dorsey, arms crossed over his chest, and an evil grin on his smug little pretty-boy face.

"Ohmygod, Dennis," I exclaim, rushing to his side. "Are you okay?"

"Honestly," he says, looking up at me pathetically, "no. I spent thirty-six hours in the Grady ER. Multiple fractures. Hurts like hell."

"Terribly unfortunate accident," Buck says. "And of course we intend to cover all of Dennis's medical expenses, but in these circumstances, discretion is key."

Ah, discretion. The highest value of the Southern Country Club set.

"With the board's full support," Buck continues, "and a generous severance package, Dennis has drafted an announcement explaining that he's decided to retire, effective immediately."

So they're sending poor Dennis out to pasture early, to avoid any untoward gossip about Linwood Hayes's botched motorcycle stunt. No surprise there. I bet they've paid the escort off nicely, too, but only after having her sign a nondisclosure agreement. I just hope she wasn't permanently injured in the fall.

I've been around the club for long enough to know exactly what's coming: Dennis will submit an open letter, sharing his heartfelt appreciation for his years here, and expressing his desire to spend more time with his wife and grandbabies. No one will wonder why he's disappeared (family values!), and no one will see his serious injury, thereby protecting Linwood Hayes from liability and the Midnight Society from scandal.

But what the hell does all this have to do with me, and why in the world is Griggs hovering over the whole situation while looking positively triumphant?

Griggs makes his way around the table to stand beside me. For a moment, it appears that he's intending to place a hand casually on my shoulder, and so I shoot daggers of fire through my eyes, then hazard a quick glance from my knee to his balls. He seems to get the message, and instead he pulls out a chair and gestures for me to sit.

"I'm fine standing," I say.

"Suit yourself," he tells me.

"Only one problem with Dennis's big plan to retire early," Buck asserts jovially, leaning forward and placing both hands on the table. "Somebody's gotta run this place."

Well, yes, that's true.

"Griggs, buddy," Buck says, patting him heartily on the shoulder, "as the newly minted chair of the Staffing Committee, why don't you take the reins?"

"Absolutely." Griggs nods, turning to face me. "We've called you in here today because we want you to be the interim general manager, Holly," Griggs says, with that overly amiable Southern drawl he loves to put on. "Starting right now."

My head spins, and I lean on the heavy oak conference table for balance. What the hell kind of game is this man playing? And how am I ever going to make it stop?

"I'm honored," I reply, one hand grasping the edge of the table. "Though I do have some questions—"

"You're the only person who can do it," Dennis interrupts, "the only member of this staff who knows the place well enough to step in right away." Of course, this is true, but still. "With you," he says, gesturing toward me, "the transition will be seamless."

Again, he's right. No one will really miss Dennis, though he's a perfectly nice man. He just doesn't actually do much around here. In fact, I've wondered more than a few times why he showed up at all. Probably to get face time with the members of the Midnight Society—the biggest of the club's bigwigs. And look where that got him. Poor guy.

"We'll offer a thirty-percent raise, effective immediately," Buck tells me. "And, since you've submitted your GM application," he continues, "we feel confident that you'll slide right into the job permanently, once the dust has settled."

Permanently. The word reverberates in my mind, and I recall what Luisa said—well, yelled—to me on Saturday night as we were watching Eli get handcuffed and taken to jail. Am I stuck here forever? Will I always be trying to prove to myself that my mother was wrong? I never, ever have wanted to fit in with the members of this country club, and I certainly have no intention of becoming one of them. But why haven't I found the courage to try something new? Is it because of my co-workers and how much I adore them, or is it because I'm afraid?

I set aside my worry for a moment to focus on the practical: I need a raise. My mind frantically races to crunch numbers, determine how long I'd need to hold on to the job to potentially cover Aidan's tuition and Eli's legal bills—but even with the significant salary increase they're offering, it's not enough.

"Make it forty-five percent and I'm in," I tell them, my voice strong and unwavering. "I should earn as much as Dennis."

I'm thanking my lucky stars that Janey also gossips about salaries, and that I've become pretty good, over all these years of negotiating with vendors, at doing quick math in my head.

"She drives a hard bargain." Griggs laughs, then looks directly at me. "But let's not get ahead of ourselves."

Motherfucker.

"She's highly qualified," Dennis interjects, "with much more experience than I had when I took the job. I think the salary increase is merited." And for the first time in our relationship, I find myself wanting to hug that dull, sweet man.

"It's settled, then," Buck says. "I'll have our lawyer draw up a contract."

"One more thing," I tell them, looking directly at Griggs. "If I take the job, I'm bringing Reginald Lewis back as chief of security. He's excellent, the best there is."

Griggs's jaw clenches, but he stays silent.

"I always liked the guy." Buck shrugs. "Sure, let's give him another chance."

I let out a sigh of relief. Janey can help me track down Reginald. Who knows if he'll want the job, but at least I can offer. And my raise will help Eli pay for an excellent lawyer. I'll need to figure out how to talk to Joel about it tonight at dinner. I'm sure he knows a good criminal defense attorney.

Even with so much uncertainty—with so many unanswered questions rushing through my mind—I still feel triumphant. I'm about to be the first woman to run this place in its hundred-and-forty-year history. And, sure, I'll only be interim at first, but I've successfully negotiated an excellent salary, my work will be worth every penny of it, and in light of Saturday night's turn of events, I definitely need the money.

Maybe, if I really pinch pennies, I can chip in and help the Castillos find a new place to live. I've never met them, but it just about does me in when I think about that family being evicted, all because of Griggs. Plus, I've relied on the generosity of others a time or two in my life, and I'm not ashamed to admit it. That's how life works, or at least how it should work.

Dennis struggles in his chair to extend his right hand toward me, and I reach out to shake it. "Congrats, Holly," he says, his voice feeble. "You'll do great."

"I'm sure she will," Buck says, and then he turns to face Griggs. "Why don't you go on and give her the keys to the kingdom, buddy," he says, patting Griggs on the shoulder—again. "No need for Dennis here to exert himself any more than necessary"—he tosses a pitying look in Dennis's direction—"in his condition."

"It would be my pleasure," Griggs drawls, then steps to the other side of the table to retrieve a full set of master keys, which he then dangles in the air, and I listen as their subtle metal clink cuts through the thick silence that has suddenly descended on the room. "I'm really looking forward to our close working relationship, Holly," he says.

To my profound shock, I feel a sudden rush of pity for this sad man. He looks so perfectly put together; he acts so smooth and debonair. He seems always to be entirely in control. He smiles and laughs, he plays all the parts so well. But, wow. He is broken. It dawns on me that Griggs Johnson has not the slightest idea what makes a life worth living. He knows nothing of love, of joy, of friendship, of community. All he knows, all he cares to know, is power.

For the briefest of moments, I wonder what happened to break him so entirely, to make him such an empty shell of a human being. But I don't have time to muse about this man's childhood, to worry about his daddy issues or household trauma. I have my own beautiful life to save, and that of the person I love even more than life itself. I'm going to find a way through this because I have to. And no matter what suffering Aidan or I endure because of Griggs Johnson, I'll forever be grateful that the life I've built with my son is—and always will be—infinitely better than his pathetic existence.

It seems to dawn on Griggs that I have no intention of responding. I've taken a pass on my turn in his insidious game. So he tries a new tactic: He extends his hand as if to pass me the keys, but releases them before I have time to catch them. They land on the floor in front of me. We both crouch down at the same time to pick them up.

"Welcome to the next phase of our game," he hisses against my ear, like the snake he is. I recoil at the words, aware that we are partly hidden under the conference table and the others can't see or hear the exchange. "When I get the pleasure of watching you enjoy, for the briefest of moments"—he pauses, smiles so wide that I can see his gums—"the fabulous job that you can't permanently land without my help." He smiles even wider. "Not here. Not anywhere. Not while I'm the boss. I could get you fired tomorrow and then make damn sure no other club in this city hires you." He cocks his head to the side, studies my expression closely. "But I'm feeling generous, so I'll give you another chance to play by my rules."

All the familiar anxieties threaten to rush back in, but after I pick up the keys from the floor, I find myself standing tall, and I'm surprised to feel a sudden release of tension from my body—a tension I've been holding for so long that it's served as my constant companion over these many months. Now, it's gone.

I don't have to worry about whose turn it is, or about who wins, because this isn't my game. These aren't my rules, and they never will be.

Tucking the keys into my suit pocket, I thank the gathered gentlemen for the opportunity, then turn to leave.

I've got a family game night to attend.

CHAPTER 35

Luisa

After my red haze of anger subsided, I called Augusto and filled him in on every detail of the last three months. He listened, asked probing questions, went over crucial details, and promised to help, before reprimanding me for being "so dumb and reckless."

My saint of a brother-in-law worked around the clock, calling in multiple favors and expediting the investigation into Eli's possible impersonation charges. He met with Judge Thacker, Griggs, and the other witnesses. Aided by Virginia's unexpected assistance with the judge, Augusto somehow managed to convince them—or to be more precise, create the illusion that it was their idea—that it was best for the club's reputation if they dropped the charges and buried the paperwork, or risk ending up as a headline in a major news outlet. *What journalist worth their salt would resist outing the fraudster who infiltrated one of the most prestigious country clubs in the country?* The subtext being that by outing Eli, they out themselves.

Augusto swatted away every one of my attempts to help. *You've done enough, Luisa*, he'd said in a tone that reeked of disappointment. His rejection was one more item on a growing list of my self-inflicted losses: Augusto's respect, Holly's friendship, Eli's freedom, Pearl's and Aidan's college prospects, the Castillos' home, my career, my life, my future.

Eli spent all of Sunday held at the Fulton County Jail, awaiting a Monday morning hearing. Meanwhile, I sat on my hands, spiraling. Alone in my room, I pulled up Gloria's phone number a dozen times but couldn't bring myself to dial. It was over. Her prayers had gone unanswered, just as mine had all those years ago. All I had left to do was question the trail of bad decisions I'd left behind since the morning my editor, Nina, fired me.

I've never been a sloppy investigator. I lean on facts, research, analysis. I excel at identifying patterns and inconsistencies. I'm guided by evidence and logic. And above all, I know to remain objective. Emotions are a nuisance in the news world.

Which is how, by the time the sun has set on Sunday, I have reached a self-evident conclusion: I trusted two people with my life, and yet again, everything has fallen apart. Adult Luisa is not much different than teenage Luisa, it seems. Again I put my life in the hands of a naive woman and a con man. And a plan, as it turns out, Chip could've rightly compared to a hunk of Swiss cheese.

Looking back to my meeting with Holly at Ginny's bar, I should've paid closer attention to the red flags, starting with the stupid karaoke bet. Who bets their life on a song?

Apparently, I do.

And then there's Eli. A self-avowed professional trickster. Did the man mean a single word he said to me? Were his feelings truthful? And even if they were, what's preventing him from duping me in the future? Is this the man I want to gamble my happiness on?

I think of my mother and how much direct evidence she dismissed or outright ignored over the years. She crafted excuses for my dad when he was away for longer than could be justified. She blamed our friends when our landline rang, only to have the caller hang up. She took his lipstick-stained dress shirts to the laundress, not once confronting him about it.

She actively chose to believe the lie.

I, by contrast, transact in facts.

And the fact of the matter is that I will be better on my own.

I'll give Mami credit for this, though: she taught me how to pack up my life and start over again somewhere new.

So, yesterday, I reached out to every one of my professional contacts and applied to jobs in news markets as far as Honolulu. I began to make plans for a future 4,490 miles away from here.

I just need a fresh start, I told myself over and over. I could take up surfing, rent a little condo by the beach, enroll in some law courses at the University of Hawaii, and be an island girl again.

Now it's noon on Monday—thirty-six hours since Eli's arrest at the club. I'm loitering in the waiting area of the Fulton County Jail, sleep-deprived, physically spent, and emotionally drained, but eager to get this over with. The quicker I blow up the bridge between me and Eli, the sooner I can move on with my life away from here.

A guard buzzes the doors to the holding section of the building. Eli steps out in the black T-shirt and gray sweats I gave Augusto to deliver yesterday. His clothes are rumpled, his hair is sticking up in a mess. He's got dark circles under his eyes and a beard shadow. I force my body not to respond to his physical presence, tamp down every feeling of affection, longing, and want in my heart, because now is not the time for sentimentality. Now is the time to take care of myself, do what needs to be done, be practical, pragmatic, and get myself back on track.

"Christ, Luisa, it's so fucking good to see you," he says warmly, extending both arms as if to embrace. I step back, out of reach. "Did something else happen? Is Holly okay?" His expression shifts to concern.

"Let's go," I respond, briskly moving out the main doors into the blistering midday sun.

Eli jogs to catch up with me.

"Luisa, we'll figure something out," he says, falling into step beside me on the sidewalk. "I'll help you. We'll regroup. I had time to think, and I have some ideas—"

I stop abruptly. "I don't need your help," I snap, cutting him off. "I don't need anyone's help." I'm breathing hard, internally gasping through the rush of rage, dejection, and grief surging inside me.

Eli examines my face, the lines between his eyebrows and forehead deepening. "You haven't slept," he observes, reaching for a loose strand of my hair, which is haphazardly up in a bun. "You're not okay, Luisa. You're a live wire."

"I'm fine," I insist, avoiding his touch. I can't let him touch me. If I do, I may come undone. And I'm barely hanging on by a thread.

We stand on the blazing sidewalk in silence. Families go in and out of the building, patrol cars cruise through the parking lot, the U.S. flag ripples at the end of a post, rows of barbed wire crown the high-security wall behind it. I think back to all the hours I've spent in this very spot, reporting on the atrocious conditions inside the jail, holding officials accountable. But my Atlanta journalism career is over now, gone forever.

I need to move on, do what I came here to do, before he has an opening to change my mind or stop me.

As if reading my thoughts, he says, "Don't do this." He reaches for my hands, but I tuck them away. "We can fix this together. We're a team."

I scoff at the idea. "We're not a team, Eli. Holly and I hired you to do a job. And it was a mistake."

"I'm calling bullshit," he says. "You wouldn't be here if you didn't care."

"You don't know me like you think you do." I pull an envelope out of my bag, shove it into his open palm. "Here's the rest of your payment."

He stares at the cash, then back at me. The wounded expression in his eyes makes me want to vomit, but guess what? I've got nothing left inside me.

"Augusto is handling the charges," I explain, my voice so detached it barely feels like my own. "They'll be dropped." I add in a more biting tone, "Virginia—of all people—came through for you in the end." I avert my eyes from his pained expression. "So we're good."

He releases a heavy sigh, shaking his head at the envelope in his hand.

"You got some new clothes out of the deal. A new haircut," I remind him bitterly. "What more do you want from me?"

"To get your head out of your ass," Eli shoots back in that backwoods accent I used to loathe, and which, strangely, I've missed. "I'm not just some disposable thing," he exclaims. "If I wanted to be used and thrown away, I would've called my dad."

The accusation lands like a closed fist to my sternum. My

lungs constrict to a breaking point, but I don't let it show. I need to get out of here, put distance between us. I remind myself again and again that if I don't get this man out of my life now, I'll pay for it later. Love like this doesn't last. And the more I let him in, the more he'll be able to hurt me.

"You're not a piece of garbage, Eli. You're just a silly bet," I spit, pushing past the knot in the back of my throat. "Holly thought we could turn you into a country club gentleman. I bet her otherwise. I guess I won."

I expect him to storm off, walk away and not look back. But he just stares down at me with those wolfish gray eyes, something like pity behind his gaze.

"Yeah, you won," he says, his expression vacant. "I never mattered to you one bit. I reckon you should've just left me back at the Happy Hooker."

Eli forces the money back into my hands. Within seconds, he's disappeared out of the parking lot, and out of my life.

I guess I won. What a stupid thing to say.

Later that evening, someone knocks on my bedroom door, and I lift my head from my pillow, bleary-eyed and confused. I have no idea what time it is or how long I've been drifting between asleep and awake. I stood on that hot sidewalk for God knows how long before getting into my SUV and driving straight home. Then I climbed into bed fully dressed, sneakers still on, and passed out from exhaustion.

"Luisa?" Carola peers into my room, backlit against the hallway's bright light. I squint, then cover my face with my forearm, sinking deeper into my pillow.

"What?" I reply groggily.

"I brought you some of Abuela's asopao," she says, letting herself in. "Mami says you haven't eaten anything." She turns on the lamp on my nightstand, then sets down a tray carrying a bowl of chicken-and-rice soup. My stomach growls at the enticing smell of sofrito, tomato, and cilantro, but it's hard to make myself sit up. I'm so tired.

"Is this about your job?" she asks quietly. I turn my head to meet her gaze, telepathically willing my thoughts into her mind. "Or is it about the actor and what happened at the country club on Saturday night?"

She takes off my shoes, drops them by the bottom of the bed. I slide over and make room for her beside me. Carola sits in the empty space, resting her back against the upholstered headboard.

"Eli," I mutter, my voice croaky, my throat dry. "His name is Eli." I curl up beside her, laying my head on her lap. "Did Augusto tell you everything?"

"Um-hum." She runs her fingers through my curls, caressing my hairline.

"Did you tell Mami and Abuela?" I ask, resigned to have every detail of my life up for family consumption. I'm too tired to argue.

"No," she says, surprising me. "Let's just keep this one between us. There's too many others involved."

"You must think I'm an idiot," I say, holding on to her legs the way I've seen my nieces do so many times.

"I just wish you would've trusted us to help you from the start," she says, gently stroking the curvature of my ear. "I wish you would've let us in."

I turn my head to face her. Immediately, I'm hit with a pang of grief. Carola inherited Papi's high cheekbones, his thick eyelashes, and the amber highlights in his irises. As is always the case when I think of him, I'm torn inside. I hate what he did to us, and yet I miss him so much. Mostly, I hate that I never got to be angry with him—or forgive him.

Holly's rebuke comes back to me, cutting me to the core: *Just because your father left you half a lifetime ago, doesn't mean the whole world will let you down.*

Is she right? Am I stuck? Pushing away everything good in my life as a result?

My thoughts turn to those fateful days, more than fourteen years ago. Carola and I came home from school like we had every other Friday, heavy backpacks hanging from our shoulders, eager to shed our hideous polyester tartan uniforms. Papi and I had big plans for the weekend. I had just gotten my learner's permit, and he'd promised to take me out for driving lessons.

Carola and I headed straight for the kitchen in search of an after-school snack. We had yet to put away all the decorations left over from my quinceañera, and there were storage bins stacked beside the kitchen table. Carola was telling me about this guy she had a crush on. He'd caught her leering at him, and she was so embarrassed that she'd tripped, missed three steps, then face-planted on the concrete. He came to her aid, but she was so mortified that she couldn't even thank him. We were laughing over grilled cheese sandwiches when Abuela came into the kitchen to break the news. Our papi was dead.

"Do you remember the night before Papi's funeral?" I ask quietly.

Carola nods. "Mami was obsessed with cleaning the floors in the kitchen."

"I was so worn out, I just wanted to go to bed," I say. "But she made me carry those bins with all my quinceañera decorations to the storage shed."

"I remember." She takes a strand of my hair, curling it between her fingers. "Mami and I almost got into a fight. She kept yelling, holding up the mop in one hand, shoving the bucket with her foot in my direction." Carola drops my hair. She gestures with her hands, mocking Mami's shrill voice as she says, "I want to be able to eat off these floors!"

We burst into a full belly laugh, booming and uncontrolled. It feels so good to laugh with my sister.

"She was kinda unhinged, to be honest," Carola says, catching her breath.

"I stayed up and helped you clean," I remind her.

"You were so brave," she says, her voice dropping above a whisper. "You didn't get angry. You didn't cry once. I kept expecting you to fall apart, but you never did."

"I wanted to," I admit for the first time.

"Why didn't you, Luisa?"

I shrug on her lap, tears stinging my eyes. "Mami said . . ." The rest of the sentence gets caught in the back of my throat, too tight to utter another syllable.

My mother's words echo in my mind: *Don't you dare cry,*

Luisa. I was fifteen, my father was inexplicably gone from our lives, and his second family would soon make themselves known. There were funeral arrangements to make, a coffin to buy, friends and family to notify, flowers and catering to order, a message to write for those little *En Memoria* cards the funeral home insisted on. We had to be strong for Mami.

"We couldn't cry," I whisper. "Not in front of Mami, anyway."

"I'm sorry, Luisa," Carola whispers back. She slides down on the bed until her head is resting on my pillow and we are facing each other under the low light of my bedside lamp. "I love Mami and Papi so much, but they really fucked things up for us." She takes my hands, holds them in hers.

"Can I ask you something, and will you tell me the truth?" I ask, squeezing her hand in mine.

"Always."

"Do you think I push people away?"

Carola sighs. "Amor, you've designed your life to keep everyone at bay." I open my mouth to protest, but she doesn't let me speak. "Luisa," she says in that mommy tone she usually reserves for her girls, "you moved out the day after you graduated high school. You chose a career where you succeed by being distant and uninvolved. You're always working. You have zero friends. And you find fault with every guy you date."

I roll my eyes at this. "Not everyone is Augusto, Carola. You got lucky."

"Augusto is a good man, the best dad. And the love of my life," she says, her voice growing thick with emotion. "But he's not perfect. Not by a long shot. Love is an act of faith, Luisa." She holds my chin in her hands, forces me to look her in the eyes as she says, "It's okay to be vulnerable. Life is gonna suck at times, regardless of whether you're ready, shielded, protected, or whatever it is that you are trying to do. So why not try to be happy along the way? Love with all you've got," she says. "And let us love you back."

Carola's words, the kindness in her gaze, peel back the scab of a deep injury. I'm too tired to fight it. Suddenly, every part of me feels exposed and raw, as if she's pouring antiseptic on a long-festering wound. It hurts like hell.

A deep sob, fifteen years in the making, rips through my chest and bursts out of me. I'm crying and shaking, releasing my grief into my sister's chest. She pulls me into her, kissing the top of my head, telling me everything is going to be all right.

We stay like this for a while, and in that time, I venture a hard look at my choices. Carola is right. And so is Holly, for that matter. I've built a life devised to keep people away, so that I never again have to feel the kind of loss, or pain, that turns your world upside down.

The problem with that life plan is that you end up all alone.

I don't want that anymore.

"I really messed everything up," I say through the tears that won't stop. "I ruined my friendship with Holly. Pushed away Eli."

Carola holds the sides of my face, wiping away the tears with her thumbs.

"Do you love him?" she asks knowingly.

I nod, relieved to be telling someone how I feel.

"And you miss them both?"

"You have no idea," I acknowledge.

"Then go tell them," she urges. "Admit you were wrong and get them back."

CHAPTER 36

Holly

It's Aunt Edna's week to choose the game, and Twister has long been her favorite, so I should have seen this coming. Still, though, it's hard to anticipate straddling one's new boyfriend (can I call him that?) while my own son snakes his hand past my armpit.

Aunt Edna—always the referee these days, since she claims to be too old for such elaborate maneuvers—spins.

"Right foot, red!" she calls out with sadistic glee.

Why couldn't it have been Peter's turn to choose the game? We'd all be gathered around the breakfast table, sipping on good bourbon, and crafting esoteric Scrabble words. Sure, I'd almost definitely lose. But a loss at Scrabble is infinitely less humiliating than these acrobatics.

Joel and Hugh, partners competing against Aidan and me, easily shift into place, which elicits an exuberant cheer from Aunt Edna and Peter, this round's observers.

Aidan and I, in something of a pickle, crane our necks to look at each other, dismayed. Sure, Aidan's a long, bendy nineteen-year-old, but still, the only red dot available to him seems an impossible reach.

"Let's just go for it," I sigh, signaling for him to make his move.

Peter and Aunt Edna watch, with matching evil grins, as we simultaneously lift our right feet. I lose my balance, causing all four players to tumble into a tangle of arms and legs.

"Sweet victory!" Joel exclaims, while Hugh laughs warmly, then gently extracts his elbow from my cleavage.

That's when the doorbell rings insistently, not once, but six times. My first reaction is profound relief that attention has been drawn away from my cheeks, bright red with embarrassment. My second is a slightly irrational fear that the gig is finally up, and the cops are coming to arrest me for pawning a stolen sapphire bracelet.

Joel throws open the door to reveal Byron, Justine, and Irma bearing a couple dozen balloons and what appears to be a cake box.

"Whose birthday is it?" Hugh asks, bewildered, just as my three co-workers call out a simultaneous "Congratulations!"

They tumble inside and, just as I get to my feet, crush me into a group hug.

"She got the GM job," Justine exclaims, squeezing me tight.

I wonder for the briefest of moments how they found out so quickly. I haven't even had the chance to tell Aidan about Griggs's pending meeting with the dean. He came straight here from an all-day jam session with his friends Jay and Nikki, and I couldn't figure out a way for the two of us to talk alone. It felt somehow wrong to burst into game night with exciting news when I know that—despite the promotion—there's little to celebrate. So, this afternoon, I made a plan: Try to enjoy game night, then talk with Aidan, and tomorrow somehow figure out a way to let everyone know about the promotion. Okay, yes, a loose plan, but still. I thought it would work.

I wish I could talk to Luisa and Eli—they're the only people who would understand the untenable situation I find myself in. But Luisa's still ignoring me, and Eli—thank God!—got released from jail this morning. He texted to let me know the charges are being dropped, and he's on his way back to Westlake, where he plans to spend a quiet evening with his sister. Not a word about Luisa, which makes me very nervous. I hope she didn't torpedo the whole thing with Eli, but I have a sneaking suspicion that she did. I'll get the story from Eli tomorrow. I don't want to interrupt his time with Pearl.

"I knew good fortune was coming your way," Irma pulls back from the group hug to tell me. "Jupiter just entered your eleventh house."

How can I possibly begin to explain that none of this feels exactly like good fortune—though, admittedly, the raise will help, for as long as I'm able to stay in the job. I'll just have to figure out how to keep avoiding Griggs. Or, who knows? Maybe once the truth about Aidan's crime is revealed, I'll find the courage to go ahead and sue Griggs's ass for harassment. In which case, I'll definitely lose my job. Strangely, the prospect is both terrifying and exhilarating. Could I be ready for something new? Maybe start my own business, as Luisa suggested?

Byron brushes Irma off with a wave. "Don't you dare go giving credit to some distant planet," he chastises. "Holly earned this one all on her own." Dear Byron always seems to know the right thing to say. I did earn it—this much is true.

"Why the hell didn't you tell us?" Joel says, trying to act stern, but instead sounding utterly delighted. "We should have been the very first to know!"

"No one knows," I say, brushing him off. "I haven't even signed the contract."

But who am I kidding? Obviously, Janey found out, and then she told, well, everyone. Everyone but Joel, it seems. He's probably got a string of texts from Janey awaiting him on the phone he judiciously set aside for Twister.

The entire room begins to barrage me with simultaneous praise and questions, while Hugh stands aside and looks on, smiling warmly. It strikes me that all the most important people in my world are right here, in Peter and Joel's living room, together. Well, almost all of them.

How did it happen so fast? How did Luisa and Eli become my friends, my confidants, my real-life partners in crime, and then disappear, just like that? I wonder where Eli will go now that he's been released and absolved. I wonder what Luisa plans to do, now that her big story will never break. Will I ever know? Or are we completely over?

I push aside the ache, and instead watch the glorious chaos unfolding around me. Justine tugs an elaborately iced cake from the box, while Irma traps Hugh in a corner, deep in conversation (no doubt asking the exact time, date, and location of his birth so that she can determine whether our stars align). Byron is wrestling too many helium balloons around the grand piano, trying to stabilize them with Peter's prized bust of Shakespeare. Aidan does his best to assist, hugging pink, yellow, and purple balloons to his chest as he shimmies past a piano bench. Joel comes rushing in with a sterling silver cake knife, and Peter follows along with a stack of crystal plates.

"Hold on, people," I call out. "No reason to work yourselves into a tizzy. I'm just the interim."

"Hogwash," Aunt Edna exclaims, waving her bejeweled cane energetically. "You know they'll keep you. How could they not?"

And watching my beloved aunt Edna make that pronouncement, I decide not to protest, not to resist this moment, even though I know it's utterly fleeting. I'm not going to think about Griggs right now, because when life brings us joy, even for a few moments, and especially when surrounded by the people we love, we have no choice but to lean into it.

"I'll go down to the cellar and get a few bottles of chilled Dom Perignon," Peter announces. "We've got some serious celebrating to do!"

Two hours and two bottles of Dom Perignon later, Aidan and I finally find ourselves alone in Peter and Joel's kitchen. They wandered up to bed, and Aunt Edna followed close behind them, as soon as Byron, Irma, and Justine took their leave. Hugh had to sneak out early, since he's catching a red-eye to Los Angeles tonight to give a keynote at a linguistics conference. I managed to slip away with him, for at least a few moments. We made out under the moonlight, champagne lingering on our breaths, pressed against his Honda. It felt delicious and a little silly—two full-on adults sucking face against a parked car, especially since—soon enough—at least a half dozen spectators were observing not-at-all discreetly through the living room window.

Joel even had the audacity to applaud when I came back inside.

Now I'm elbow-deep in foamy water, washing champagne flutes. Aidan, standing beside me, carefully dries them as he listens to the explanation I've been spooling out for several minutes:

Dennis's surprise departure, Griggs's terrible advances, my reaction and the threats that ensued. By the time I get to Griggs's upcoming meeting with the dean, I'm starting to worry that he's gone catatonic.

"You okay, Aidan?" I pause to ask him, wiping my hands with a dish towel. "I know this is a whole lot to process all at once."

"Why didn't you tell me sooner?" he asks, his voice filled with hurt.

"I thought I could handle it," I say, putting down the tea towel and turning to face him.

"It just kills me that—"

"That I kept a secret from you?" I interject. "I'm so sorry—"

"No, Ma. That you've had to go through all of this alone. I would have been there for you if I'd known."

It dawns on me that I wasn't alone at all. In fact, I felt deeply supported and sustained through those many ups and downs by two people who were strangers to me before this all began.

"So, about that," I begin, and then I muster the courage to tell him about Luisa and Eli, and the completely nutty plan that we tried to execute. Remarkably, he doesn't berate or scold me. Instead, he just throws his head back and laughs, so hard that his Adam's apple bobs wildly.

"That's amazing," he says, once he's caught his breath. "I can't wait to meet those guys."

"I'm not sure you will," I say, feeling the sadness well up in my chest. "It didn't end so great between us."

"Maybe just give it time," he says. "Sounds like y'all went through a lot together. That kind of thing has a way of bonding people. You know?"

Yes, I do know, because I miss them both like hell, but I'm pretty sure Luisa and Eli don't see it this way. We took advantage of Eli, never truly valuing his talent and commitment. I never gave him the respect he deserved. I wouldn't hold it against him if he wants nothing more to do with me. And Luisa? It's pretty clear that she's falling back into Lone Ranger mode, pushing away anyone who cares about her. I'm guessing she'll strike out on her own, find some intense job that sucks up all her time and energy in another city, throw herself into it, and never look back. I really hope she hasn't irreparably damaged things with Eli. Those two are so good for each other. As for me, I'll respect her wishes if she thinks we can't be friends.

I just want a chance to tell them both I'm sorry.

"Sucks that it didn't work," Aidan continues. "It was a fucking awesome plan."

"Watch your language, young man," I snap.

This is a thing I still do with Aidan, and I'm not sure why. I, of course, curse occasionally, but it feels somehow wrong to let my own kid drop F-bombs in my presence. I mean, doesn't that make me a bad parent, or worse, a "cool" parent? I've spent much of my adult life trying to avoid the trap of becoming a "cool" parent. Wouldn't want to ruin it all now when I'm out here on the home stretch.

"Anyway," I say, "it's quite possible that after Saturday your scholarship will disappear. But I don't want you to worry."

"I'm not worried," he says, but his scared eyes tell a different story.

"I'm making an excellent salary now," I say. "I can save for your tuition."

"But I thought you said that dickwad Griggs was harassing you—"

"Language!" I call out again.

He rolls his eyes, then puts the last of the champagne flutes into Joel and Peter's glass-front cabinet.

"You can't stay in that job if you're being disrespected, Ma," he says.

I lead him to sit beside me at the kitchen table, place a hand, palm-down, on the smooth oak, trying to steady myself for what's coming next. Once we've settled, I continue, "I've taken some time to think about this, and I have a plan," I tell him, my voice as even as I can manage. "If I have to leave my job after this all goes down, we'll ask your dad for money to pay your tuition. I'm sure he'll be willing to help."

I'm not sure of anything when it comes to Aidan's father, but he doesn't need to know. Well, I am sure he became a doctor, just as I anticipated he would. He married shortly after college, a lovely woman from Fort Worth. As far as I know, he still lives with her and their three beautiful daughters in a stately brick Colonial in Jackson's old-money neighborhood, and he still attends the church where he once led the praise and worship band. I've cyberstalked him a handful of times, just out of curiosity. I feel certain that Aidan has, too.

"I don't have a dad." He looks directly at me, his gaze unwavering. "I have a biological father."

"Okay," I say, since I can't deny this fact. "We'll ask your biological father for help."

Aidan leans toward me, wraps my hand in his. I watch as his long, slim fingers weave through mine. "We don't need his help, Mom. We never have needed it, and we never will."

My mind races back through all the times we were on the edge of poverty, all the times I desperately needed money, support, someone else to rely on. But I never resorted to asking Aidan's father for it, on principle. He didn't want a son, and so he doesn't get the privilege of supporting one. He knows that Aidan exists. I've made sure of that. But he chooses to ignore this fact, which is fine by me. The man has no idea what he's missing.

"Here's the thing, Ma," Aidan says, squeezing my hand. "You are all the parent I've ever needed. You've been everything for me."

I look away, through the kitchen window, as my eyes well with tears.

"Ma," he says gently. "Look at me, please."

I turn to look at him, my heart full to bursting. "I've never lacked for anything, especially your love. You are a good mom. No, you are a fucking great mom, and a fucking great dad, too."

I ought to say *Watch your language* again, but I know that if I open my mouth, all that will come out is a sob. So I nod and smile, holding back the tears.

"You are the most responsible and hardest-working person I know, and the best role model I could ever have," he continues, his voice rising with intensity. "You always have been there when I needed you, and you've also managed to always do your job well. You're fucking amazing and competent and a total boss, and everyone knows it but you, Ma." He places another hand over mine, and I feel them both, warm and strong. "And I'm not gonna 'watch my language,' because I want you to understand how much I fucking mean all of this."

I laugh then, and somehow manage to squeak out a "Thank you."

He stands up and pulls me into a hug—not just any hug, but that perfect Aidan hug, the one that swallows me whole and fills me all the way up. We stay like that for a while. I decided years ago that when my kid hugs me, I'll never be the one to pull away first. I want him to know I'm here, for as long as he wants or needs me. And on this particular night, in this particular hug, I feel like I could stay forever.

When Aidan does finally release me, he leans back and a sly grin creeps across his face. "Oh, and also, you've raised a fantastic son—kind, loving, responsible, handsome. Potty mouth notwithstanding. Pretty much everyone agrees on this point." He shrugs, nonchalant.

Cocky bastard. But how can I protest? He's absolutely right. This boy is my pride and my joy.

"I made a mistake last spring, a big stupid one," he continues, his voice resolute. "It doesn't matter why I did it, I'm not going to make excuses. I should be ready to accept whatever consequences come my way." Aidan places both hands squarely on my shoulders. "You don't have to protect me, Ma. I can go to community college, get a part-time job. We can figure this out." He squeezes my shoulders gently. "Whatever happens, the two of us will find a way through it together." Aidan smiles a crooked smile, then says, "Without the help of my sperm donor."

And just like that, my sweet boy has become a good man.

CHAPTER 37

Luisa

I pull up to the Dogwood Hills Country Club's iron gate, then flash my deactivated *Georgia Times* badge at the guard. "I have a meeting with Holly Simmons," I say, my voice so self-assured that he doesn't question me. I don't have a meeting, in fact. I thought about calling, but groveling over the phone didn't feel like the right thing to do. Not after how things ended between us. So I got in my SUV and drove to Midtown, praying she wouldn't have me escorted off the grounds.

I check in at the front desk, where Janey does a double take, asking if we've met before. I'm certain she's picturing the nonexistent *María* in her head. I did my best to stay clear of the club's staff during the gala, but Janey has the optical dexterity of a scallop, with two hundred tiny eyes gathering information from all directions.

"The annual Philanthropy Banquet—" I say, trying to divert her recollection. "I covered the event." Satisfied, she leads me down a corridor to Holly's new office.

Janey is a journalist's dream. She runs her mouth unprompted, telling me about the old GM's ill-fated accident and Holly's interim appointment. The woman could start her own Chismosa Social Club. But what she doesn't know—and I don't say—is that, unless Griggs is dead and buried, Holly won't be able to retain the position. Not now, when there's no hope of outing his evil machinations.

We find Holly sitting behind a monstrous cherry desk, like something borrowed from the Oval Office.

"A reporter is here to see you," Janey says eagerly. "She said you're expecting her?"

I stiffen, hovering by the doorway, studying Holly's reaction.

"Huh?" Holly glances up from her computer screen in confusion. She looks at Janey, then to me. I offer a tentative smile and a pleading gaze. To my surprise, Holly responds with her most genuine, rosy-cheeked, thousand-kilowatt smile. Relief floods my entire body. I've missed her so much.

"Oh yes," she exclaims in Janey's direction. "Luisa is working on a piece about . . ." Her voice trails off, eyes cutting to mine.

"Buttered saltines," I interject helpfully. "I'm doing a comparative taste test at all the clubs in Atlanta."

"Well, I'll be. Are you really?" Janey's eyes widen before dropping her voice into a conspiratorial whisper. "Did you know our recipe was stolen from the Altamaha Country Club?" She nods vigorously as if sharing a state secret. "Back in the early seventies. The sous chef at Altamaha had run out of oyster crackers and came up with the buttered saltines. Word got around."

"I'm going to need a copy of that recipe," I say, matching her conspiratorial tone.

"Of course! We can arrange that." Janey is quick to oblige, but seeming to remember Holly is now the boss, she adds cautiously, "If that's okay with Holly."

"Thank you, Janey," Holly says, standing. "I can take it from here." She steps around her desk to usher her out, then closes the door to the office and turns to take me in.

"Are you okay?" she asks, closing the space between us. "I've been worried sick."

I have a whole apology speech prepared, but before I can get one word out, Holly has her arms around me, pulling me into a hug.

"It's been almost a week." She exhales over my shoulder. "I was starting to think I'd never see you again. Why didn't you call me back?"

I lean back, staring at her stupefied. "Because I was horrible to you," I cry out, tears pricking at the corners of my eyes. "I was cruel and a shitty friend."

"I was a shitty friend, too," Holly cuts in, in a tone that implies our blowout, for her, is water under the bridge. "I'm just so happy you're here." She beams back at me, holding on to my arms.

"Seriously, Holly," I urge, a little annoyed that she's not more upset. "I was a fucking nightmare. Just let me apologize!"

"Okay. Fine," she says, releasing her grip on me. "Let's apologize." She waves one hand in the air. "But for the record, I think we were both freaking out, worried sick about Eli, and we took it out on each other." She holds on to herself, the memory of that night darkening her expression. "All I'm saying is, we can't judge others by their worst day, and judge ourselves by our best intentions."

I tilt my head sideways, flummoxed by her words. "Are you really quoting President George W. Bush right now?" I bark out a laugh.

"Maybe?" she says sheepishly, then gestures to the wall behind us, where one of those derivative office quote posters hangs. "It was the old GM's," she explains. "Ol' Dennis loved W." The former president smiles down placidly at us. "It's true, though—we can't just throw away our friendship over one argument on one disastrous day."

Holly leads me to a tufted dark leather couch, and we sit. Everything about this office, from the oversize furniture to the collection of muskets displayed in a glass cabinet to the tweed wallpaper screams hypermasculine.

"Luisa," Holly says warmly, reaching for my hand, "we may be about to lose everything we've worked for"—her eyes travel around the room—"but I don't want to lose you, too." She squeezes my hand, and with it my heart. And before I have time to retreat into myself, put up any walls, or send for emotional reinforcements, I'm ugly crying. Again.

"What in the world is happening right now?" Holly's gone slack-jawed, seemingly stumped by a mix of concern, disbelief, and surprise. "Is the tough-as-nails investigative journalist Luisa Martín Moreno crying?"

"This is what I do now." I motion to my face, pulling in a long calming breath, trying to regain control. "I cry in front of people." I fan my eyes in an almost comical attempt at drying my tears. "I hate this so much."

Holly reaches for a box of tissues on a side table, then pulls out a handful and passes them to me.

"You have to let me apologize," I demand, dabbing at my eyes with a tissue.

"Okay," she acquiesces. "You go, then me."

"You were right," I admit thoughtfully. "Something changed inside me when my dad died." I tap at my chest with my fingers. "I keep expecting the worst, for things to go wrong or for people to disappoint me."

"It was a traumatic event, Luisa," Holly says in understanding. "So to cope, you learned to always be prepared, react first, be hypervigilant." I nod, wringing the tissue with my hands. "All the traits that also make you a great journalist."

"But it's also the reason I try to anticipate rejection and sometimes bulldoze the people I love." Shame at the things I said and the pain I've caused spreads hot over my cheeks. I stare at the balled-up tissues. "I pushed you and Eli away in a preemptive strike." Fresh tears well in my eyes. I let them fall, feeling every bit vulnerable and raw, but also open and tender. "I don't want to be that person anymore. I want to be a good friend. To expect good things instead."

"You deserve good things, Luisa," Holly says quietly. She covers my hand with hers, and I allow myself to be soothed by her touch, to let my friend care for me.

"We both do," I say. "You are an incredible mom, and excellent at your job." I look her straight in the eyes so there's no doubt I mean every word. "You should be the fucking boss lady. For real. Not just this interim bullshit."

"Thanks," Holly says, two circles glowing red over her cheeks. "Is it my turn now?"

"I'm pretty sure I have no more tears left," I joke. "But sure, go ahead."

"I'm sorry I hurt you." She gazes at our hands, now clasped together. "I don't think it's a secret that I've been insecure about myself and my abilities for as long as I can remember." She releases a deep sigh, her shoulders relaxing a little. "But you were right. I'm not a teen mom anymore. I'm a grown-ass woman. I can more than take care of myself, and my son is an adult now. It's time for me to start really thinking about what I want and need, about what's next for me, and to find the courage to go after it."

"Damn straight," I assure her.

We smile at each other, and it feels so good to have Holly back in my life.

"I missed you," she whispers, pulling me in for a side hug.

"I missed you, too," I whisper back, my heart full of gratitude for my friend and for this moment.

My face is a mess, so Holly passes me a few more tissues, along with one of those toiletry boxes they keep in the women's powder room. I hold up a small mirror to my face, then freshen myself the best I can.

"What about Eli?" Holly asks, passing me the makeup remover. "Have you talked to him?"

I shake my head in response, then cover my eyes with both hands, probably smudging wet mascara all over my face. "We had a big fight outside the jail." I fall sideways on the couch, hiding behind Holly. "I doubt he ever wants to see me again."

Holly jumps to her feet. "Luisa Martín Moreno," she exclaims. "Get your ass off that couch."

"What?" I whine. "Can I sulk for like a minute?"

"You're not a sulker, Luisa," she goads. "Clean your face. I'm driving you to Westlake."

"Aren't you supposed to be working or something?" I survey the papers on her desk. "Maybe you can get them to change out these musty carpets."

"It's not like I have to clock in and out," she says, already reaching for her phone and purse. "Remember, I'm the boss now." She holds up a bulky metal ring with dozens of keys, including a few ancient skeleton ones. "I've even got the keys to the kingdom," she calls out in a town crier voice, jiggling the ring in midair and grinning.

"Please don't do that anymore," I say derisively.

"So glad you're back." She links her arm with mine, leading me out of the office.

"I hope you know," I tease, my tone a warning, "I'm not leaving this club without the recipe for those buttery saltines."

My stomach does a gravity-defying triple somersault the second Holly pulls off the Westlake Highway into the parking lot of the Happy Hooker, Inc.

"I can't do it," I groan from the passenger seat. "I was awful to that man."

Holly shifts the car to park, then turns to face me. "Just tell him how you feel."

I gaze at the red shack and the multicolor strands of Christmas lights twinkling over the porch, even in the summer.

"From the heart, Luisa," she adds gently. "Don't get stuck in that head of yours."

I sigh, leaning the side of my head into the windowpane. "When did I become such a coward?"

"You're not a coward." She clasps my arm encouragingly. "You're just in love."

I gaze back at the building, knowing Eli is inside. My chest expands, then just as quickly contracts with ache and yearning.

"What do you have to lose?" she asks.

"My dignity," I offer reluctantly.

"Oh, honey," Holly scoffs. "We left our dignity back in that pawnshop on Cheshire Bridge Road." This makes her laugh. "We're just a pair of lowlife criminals."

"Remind me not to drive off a cliff with you," I deadpan, opening the passenger door, then stepping out into the sweltering afternoon.

Holly lowers the passenger window. "Don't take no for an answer," she calls out. "And if he offers to take your jewels to the back room, just let him." She bursts into a fit of adolescent laughter, but I'm too nervous to join her.

I push my way through the front door. Above me a bell tinkles, causing Eli to gaze up from the register. A deep frown takes over his face at the sight of me, his fingers frozen over a laptop, mid-keystroke. Neither of us speaks. Eventually, he sighs, takes off his trucker hat, and scratches the back of his head.

Suddenly, I've lost all my words. Why does it feel like I have absolutely everything to lose right now?

"Luisa . . ." He trails off, fitting the hat back on his head. "If you're here about the charges, Augusto took care of it," he says, matter-of-fact. "And I already told you, I don't want your money." He folds his arms over his chest protectively, shielding himself from me.

The realization sends a stab of pain through my heart. Holly is right, I need to be honest. But where to begin? Should I tell him that all I think about is meeting his gray eyes the second I wake up in the morning, kissing those soft lips just because I can, running my fingertips through his messy hair, smelling the scent of soap and laundry on his skin, telling him every insignificant detail of my day, and then climbing into his bed at the start of every night, staying there forever?

I stare down at my feet, unsure of where to start.

"That's not why I came," I say after a long pause. He raises a questioning eyebrow in response, so I step closer to the counter, across from him. "I made a huge mistake, Eli." He opens his mouth, but I put up a hand to stop him. "Please, before you say anything, hear me out. I know I probably don't deserve it, considering how I acted, but if I don't say what I came here to say, I also know I'm going to regret it for the rest of my life."

His expression softens at this. His shoulders drop slightly as he gestures for me to continue. I take a deep breath, fill my lungs with resolve, and launch in.

"If I'm being honest, I can be pushy, maybe a little difficult, and—"

"A total pain in the ass," he cuts in pointedly, but there's no real bite to his words.

"But if I'm also being honest," I press on, ignoring his jab, "I care about you. And I love how much you care about Pearl. I want to be a part of her life, too." He listens, some of the apprehension draining from his face. "Eli, I don't let many people in," I acknowledge, pushing past the thick knot of emotion in the back of my throat. "Letting people get too close gives me all sorts of anxiety."

"You're not the only one," he says quietly.

"I know," I respond. "But as Holly rightly pointed out, you have more emotional intelligence than me." I shrug, self-aware. "I'm a work in progress." I offer a half smile, hoping to disarm him, but his expression remains impassive. "Anyway . . ." I continue, undeterred, "what I came here to say is . . ." I swallow hard, my blood pumping so hard that I can barely hear myself. I'm about to put everything I have left—my heart, my trust, and my future—in Eli's hands. Carola's words echo in my mind, *Love is an act of faith, Luisa.* And so I close my eyes and leap. "What I came here to say is that you and Pearl are already inside my heart." I bring my open palm over my chest, meeting his gaze as fresh tears run down the sides of my face. I don't wipe them away. "And more than anything"—I swallow hard—"I'm scared of losing you."

He exhales, staring down to the floor. It hurts to look at him. So I close my eyes and just stand there, reminding myself to breathe. I said what I came here to say, now it's time to leave.

I don't hear him step off the chair or walk around the desk. Instead, I feel his arms reach around me, his fingers digging up my neck into my hairline, cradling my head against his chest.

"Come 'ere," he whispers, pressing a kiss to the top of my head.

I breathe him in, melting into his body without reserve. His heart is beating just as hard as mine.

"I'm not going anywhere, Luisa."

I let out a long, easy breath. This time, I believe him.

The bell dings behind us, and we turn to find Holly peering in.

"Y'all decent?" she bursts in impishly. I shake my head, too happy to be annoyed. "Can we go to Ginny's now and day drink?" She pulls out those ridiculous keys. "I would like to celebrate my kinda-sorta promotion."

"You a janitor now?" Eli observes wryly.

"She's the interim general manager," I fill him in. "But there's still the matter of King Griggs, ruling the world."

"But for now, I've got the keys to the castle," she bellows, rattling the keys. She probably thinks this is funny. "I can open every door at the club." Her eyes go wide, as if she's just been struck with an idea. "Maybe we can find a secret closet to lock Griggs in?"

"Pretty sure that constitutes kidnapping," I offer, holding on to Eli with one arm. I may never let go of this man.

"Wait," Eli breaks in, snapping his fingers. "Does Griggs keep an office at the club?"

"No," Holly says. "Why?"

"That night that I went to his place, to pregame before the costume party," Eli explains, "we had drinks in his home office." He rubs thoughtfully at the stubble over his jaw. "I made a joke, something like, 'Oh, is this the place where you keep all the classified information,' and Griggs laughed." Eli looks from me to Holly, then back again. "He said Anna-Byrd was too nosy, so he kept everything locked safely away at the club."

"Sonofabitch," Holly booms, so loud that Eli and I jump. "It's the second locker." She takes in our puzzled expressions. "He leased a second locker last year," she explains. "I had to fill out one of those carbon copy forms with him. In triplicate!"

"You have to press really hard," Eli sympathizes.

"Exactly," Holly says, as if he's just vindicated years of pointless paper bureaucracy.

"Remind me again why I decided to keep you two clowns?" I ask, trying really hard not to laugh.

"Because you love us," Holly chirps.

I roll my eyes, unable to contain a smile.

"Can we get into the club tonight?" Eli asks.

"Guess who can get in anytime she damn well pleases?" Holly says, jingling the keys triumphantly.

A few hours later, we're striding into the men's locker room on the ground level of the Dogwood Hills Country Club, wondering why in God's name there's an adjacent bar and grill (in a locker room!).

"Let it be said," Holly says, "that I will only cross this threshold for you." We pause, taking in the enormity of the space. "I've never been here before."

To our right, there's an actual restaurant and a full bar stocked with top-shelf drinks. To our left, polished dark mahogany lockers rise from floor to ceiling. Wood benches and sitting lounge areas are interspersed throughout. There's a shower room, a sauna room, a steam room, and a marble vanity countertop with multiple sinks and a lit wall-length mirror. There are also plenty of amenities—Q-tips, razors, shaving cream, combs . . .

"Are these Goldfish crackers?" Eli asks, helping himself to the orange contents of a glass jar tucked inside a nook.

"Wait—" I say, my tone indignant. "Are those regular Goldfish, or do you also have some special, super-cheesy Goldfish recipe y'all are hoarding away?"

"I will neither confirm nor deny the source of the Goldfish," Holly deadpans.

Eli drops a handful of crackers into my hand. I shove them in my mouth and chew, disappointed that they are, in fact, regular Goldfish.

We go in search of Griggs's two lockers. When we open the first one, our spirits fall. We find a couple of golf shirts and pants, silk briefs, a pair of spiked shoes, and a bottle of Tom Ford Oud Wood cologne.

"Nothing," I say after a thorough search. Could we be wrong?

That all-too-familiar hopelessness starts to expand in my chest as we approach the second locker.

"Here goes nothing," Holly says, inserting her master key into the lock. She opens the door, and I almost fall to my knees.

Before us, there's a hard drive and massive cache of documents. I rifle through, pulling out folders one by one, laying them out over one of the benches. We find copies of checks from Griggs's family foundation to the various nonexistent nonprofits, and a trail of cash that funnels into the offshore bank in Panama, only to be laundered back into shell companies like Peachtree Holdings, LLC. The Lake Chiaha development sits at the center of a massive fraud scheme.

But there's more—enough financial data to build a case on tax evasion, and a ledger containing a list of fake investors, records on bribes and political donations. Before I know it, I'm so overwhelmed that I'm wiping away tears of relief.

"The Castillos' fake deed," I say, holding up the certificate for Eli and Holly to take in.

Eli sighs and then releases a long, drawn-out "Hot diggity damn."

CHAPTER 38

Holly

Luisa's perched on a barstool, sipping from a bottle of beer, when I walk into the Road Queen Grill. She's looking drop-dead gorgeous, and she knows it—all curves and shining wavy hair and thick red lips. Luisa doesn't belong in this place any more than I do. But, of course, she's a total chameleon, and she has managed to blend right in, wearing silver-studded Italian leather boots, light-wash jeans, and a snug T-shirt.

Then she pulls out her laptop.

I pause by the doorway and watch, amused by the reaction of the biker sitting on the stool beside her. He's in a denim vest straight out of the 1980s, covered in an enormous red-and-black patch that reads *Hog Mountain, GA*. The biker's got a nice build and a tight salt-and-pepper beard, and I wondered briefly whether he's been trying to pick her up—until she slid that computer out of her bag and propped it onto the bar. Now he's looking a little bewildered—probably wondering why she's not over at the cute little coffeehouse on the Westlake town square.

"Luisa," I call out, crossing the room.

I'm a little late to meet her, since I've been juggling a lot these days. My job as interim GM of the Dogwood Hills Country Club is going great—I've been working hard to spruce up the common areas and digitize the records, basically to bring us into the twenty-first century, while also maintaining the Old South feel of the place. This morning, I had the great pleasure of posting on the central bulletin board three terse but oh-so-civilized letters of resignation from Griggs Johnson, Jim Wade, and the judge. Not only is a greatly coveted Sunday morning tee time now up for grabs, but the members get to avoid the indignity of rubbing elbows with high-profile criminals.

As has been the case for almost nineteen years, I'm grateful for the club, for my fellow staff members, and for all the kind members who have made a place for me there. But also, I know it's time for a change. I've already told Buck Dorsey that I'll serve as interim for a year, and then—with the nice little nest egg my forty-five-percent raise and frugal lifestyle provide—I'll branch out on my own as an event planner.

Luisa and Eli will be heading out on a road trip to Jackson Hole, Wyoming, next week, to deliver an old truck Eli fixed up and sold to some billionaire. Eli promised that, with the profits, he wants to invest a little something in my business, which means the world to me. Who knows? Maybe, under the shadow of the magnificent Teton Mountains, they'll get swept up in the romance of the landscape and decide to tie the knot. I'm kinda hoping a Luisa and Eli wedding will be my first gig. But I'm not going to push it and risk spooking Luisa. She needs to do things in her own time, in her own way.

Luisa looks up from her laptop and waves, then gives me a not-so-subtle once-over. I've learned a thing or two since my last visit to the Road Queen, and I ditched the flowery sundress—choosing instead fitted jeans, a pair of cowboy boots I scored a decade ago at the Goodwill on Northside Drive, and a black ribbed tank. Her eyebrows arch, and she nods in a way that suggests I've won her approval.

Not an easy task, but I'm getting better at it with each passing day.

I weave through several tables crammed full of bikers engaged in boisterous conversation over copious pitchers of beer. I pass a small stage where a woman is setting up equipment. She looks to be about my age. And, in a torn-up KISS T-shirt, with about a dozen tattoos snaking across her chest and arms, she also looks like a real badass.

When I arrive at the bar, the Hog Mountain man sitting beside Luisa stands to offer his stool. So chivalrous! I thank him and start to sit, but Luisa gestures toward the corner of the room, where a four-top remains remarkably empty.

"I got Ginny to save us a table," she says, snapping her laptop shut and leading me across the room.

Rhonda looks up from the grill, where she's expertly smashing about a dozen burgers. "Well, hey there, Southern Belle," she says. "Welcome back."

Oh well. So much for trying to blend in.

Ginny passes me a cold PBR without even asking, and then Luisa and I head over to the table, just as the badass in the KISS T-shirt takes the microphone, introduces herself as Crystal, tonight's emcee, and launches into "Wagon Wheel."

It takes approximately fifteen seconds for the beer-swilling biker ladies at the long tables in the center of the room to jump to their feet and sing along. When I saw her setting up, I was sure that woman's voice would be all raspy and breathy—she strikes me as a smoker—but her voice is clear and low, and her song choices are turning out to be both surprising and epic. Crystal really knows how to get this crowd going.

I can barely hear Luisa over the raucous cries of "rock me, mama," when she resolutely sets her laptop on our table, opens it, and then asks: "Are you ready for this?"

I nod.

She refreshes the home screen of *The Georgia Times*, and the headline appears: *Atlanta Developer at Center of Multimillion-Dollar Embezzlement, Fraud, and Bribe Scheme*. Luisa scrolls down, and I skim the summary line of her long-form piece. "'Griggs Caldecott Johnson III, real estate developer and son of renowned Atlanta architect, indicted for years of criminal activity involving a prominent local judge, a chair of the State Board of Natural Resources, and a Southern banker working in Panama. Former publisher of *The Georgia Times* conspired to cover up the scheme,'" I read, rapt, as Luisa's article unspools the entire complicated scenario. Of course, Griggs was able to post bond, but the evidence is stacking up against him and his cronies. There's no doubt that after their embezzlement, tax evasion, money laundering, and racketeering trial plays out, the whole bunch of them will be spending quality time together in federal prison. Maybe they'll find a new Sunday morning hobby, in the absence of a swanky golf course.

Luisa finishes the article with a heart-wrenching account of the travails those selfish, power-hungry men put the Castillo family through. The final quote is from Gloria, framed with a beautiful photo of the entire family standing proudly in front of their Westlake home.

"Our prayers have been answered," Gloria said. "And even though these men and their greed caused our family so much suffering, we have renewed faith that there are good people in this world. People with the courage to fight for the truth at their own personal risk."

"This is absolutely incredible," I tell her, looking up. "You're a master of your craft!"

"And that's not all." Luisa grins, clicking on the paper's Cooking section, then gesturing to a headline that reads *Country Club Buttery Saltines, For the People.*

"A real coup!" I laugh, delighted.

Luisa leans back in her chair, props both hands on the back of her head, and grins from ear to ear. "Nina called the Griggs piece top-notch—a masterpiece of investigative journalism," she tells me. I know Nina is her new boss, now the publisher of *The Georgia Times*, after the paper's board fired Chip Marshall. "And then she gave me a promotion," Luisa tells me, still trying to seem nonchalant, but I can see the absolute thrill in her eyes. "You're looking at the new head of the paper's investigative unit."

Feeling anything but nonchalant, I jump to my feet and squeal with delight, then attack her with a bear hug, just as Crystal eases into "Wonderwall." I release Luisa and return to my seat, while Crystal croons those overplayed lyrics of winding roads and blinding lights, then launches into a chorus about the surprising people who just might save us. And, to my own enormous surprise, both Luisa and I are gazing at each other, across our half-empty PBRs at a biker bar, tears in both of our eyes.

"Thanks," she says. "For doing all this with me."

"Yeah, thanks," I say back. "I couldn't have done it with anyone else."

And that feels like enough. There's really not more to say, because we both know what an incredible gift it was that we stumbled into each other's lives at just the right time—well, technically, I stumbled; Luisa marched confidently. We took risks together, some of them wild and scary and not exactly legal. We trusted that we'd somehow get through it all. And now, here we are, together, and we've each saved the other from our worst nightmares. In the process, we've managed to take down the bad guys, which feels pretty damn incredible, since it's not like that happens every day.

We exposed the sort of powerful criminals who think they're untouchable, while giving a helping hand to a few people who really needed it . . . one of whom happens to be walking through the door, with my (now official) boyfriend following a few steps behind him.

I stand up and wave them over, trying to peer around Eli to catch a glimpse of Hugh, but I'm frankly unable to avoid the way Eli looks at Luisa, as if he wants to devour her right here and now. Who can blame him? As I mentioned, she looks hot. Eli steps aside and I'm finally able to get a full view of my favorite professor. In his signature crisp white button-down and leather loafers, Hugh looks both out of place and perfectly at ease. I can already see his mind working as he takes in the array of Georgia accents that fill this crowded room.

For Hugh, every new place offers an opportunity to listen carefully and attentively, to learn. It's become one of the many things I love about that man. I can't wait to one day travel the world with Professor Hugh Pridmore.

"Hello, gorgeous," Hugh says, which—even though he says it all the time—still makes me blush. He kisses me gently on the lips, then sits down and slides his hand into mine, while Luisa excitedly shows Eli The *Georgia Times* article, and he beams with pride for her.

Rhonda, wearing a mildly offensive T-shirt that reads *Merry Christmas, You Filthy Animal*, a callback to one of the *Home Alone* films, arrives with a tray stacked with smashburgers, fries, and enough crispy onion rings to float a boat.

"On the house," she says.

"No way—" Eli begins to protest.

"Aw, shut your fuckin' mouth, pretty boy," Rhonda interrupts. "It's not every day we get an award-winning newspaper writer, a Southern belle, *and* a college professor in this dump."

She sets the tray down with a thud. "Just let Ginny treat you, for Chrissake."

"Hey," I scold, feigning offense. "Don't you dare call the Road Queen Grill a dump. This place is absolutely perfect."

I take in the room as we dive hungrily into our feast, and I mean it. There's nowhere I'd rather be right now than in this dive bar with these beautiful people.

Crystal, closing out a truly earth-shattering version of "You Shook Me All Night Long," leans in, and announces, "Mic's open. Who's up?"

"Y'all ready for this?" Eli asks in his deepest Georgia twang, as a mischievous grin spreads across his face.

Luisa and I have discussed that silly bet we made so many months ago. And we finally decided that, technically, neither of us won. Sure, Eli was revealed as a fraud in the end, but it was a fluke, a coincidence. And the truth is, he worked his ass off to become a Southern gentleman, and he succeeded. So we decided Eli's the real winner, and he gets to pick the song.

"Go easy on us," I plead.

"I'm thinkin' we'll go with my favorite lady rocker, Pat Benatar," he announces, quirking an eyebrow.

"You have a twisted sense of humor," Luisa says, amused.

"I'm not joking," he tells her. "I'm serious as a heart attack." Which seems like an appropriate metaphor, given the large amount of fried food we're devouring. I wash down a catsup-drenched onion ring with a deep swig of beer, stand up, and announce to Luisa, "Let's do this thing."

And then the two of us take the stage together. Luisa grabs the mic from Crystal, and we throw our arms around each other's shoulders, while the classic opening guitar riff brings the crowd to their feet.

Luisa and I lean in together and belt it like we mean it—because Lord knows we've earned the right.

Hit me with your best shot. Fire away.

Country Club Buttery Saltines, For the People

A Note from the Authors:

Just like Luisa, Mayra fell in love with the country club's buttery saltines while conducting research for this book. At one of the (several) Atlanta clubs we visited, she peered into the kitchen and asked for the secret ingredient—clarified butter!

"Buttery crackers for the people!" she cried out in triumph, fist up in the air, as she walked away beside Marie, passing one of the club's many bright green lawns. Everyone deserves to have the bliss of warm, buttery crackers, specially made.

To make these at home, you will need half a pound of unsalted European-style butter and forty-eight square Nabisco saltine crackers. They *have* to be Nabisco—or so says the club's chef.

For the clarified butter, add the butter to a small saucepan and melt on low, undisturbed. Clarified butter is just butter with the milk solids and water removed. It requires a lot of patience, so if you're like Luisa, find something else to occupy your mind, for about 20–30 minutes.

While you wait, preheat the oven to 400 degrees and lay the flat crackers on a baking sheet, side by side.

When the butter has melted, skim the foam off the top. Keep skimming until the butter is clear and golden. Once the clarified butter is done, use it to coat the crackers, then bake for three minutes or until golden brown.

For maximum buttery bliss, serve warm and enjoy with friends over a tall glass of iced Southern sweet tea.

ACKNOWLEDGMENTS

This novel was a craft of love, friendship, and faith. It required taking creative risks to learn a new way of storytelling. Like Luisa and Holly, we wouldn't have chosen to go on this journey with anyone else but each other.

We are deeply grateful to the many extraordinary people who supported us during this process, including our literary agents, Saritza Hernández at Andrea Brown Literary Agency and Erin Harris at Folio Literary Management, and also our development team at Alloy Entertainment, Joelle Hobeika, Josh Bank, and Jessica Harrinton. Y'all cheered for us all the way to the finish line (and taught us the power of a pithy, short chapter). Thank you for sharing your many talents, editorial skills, golf tips, and publishing insights.

Our team at Primero Sueño/Atria, Simon & Schuster, includes the most badass crew: our publisher Michelle Herrera Mulligan; editor Yezanira Venecia; associate editor Norma Perez-Hernandez; publicist Maria Mann; copyeditor Stacey Sakal; cover artist Vi-An Nguyen; production editor Emma Navarro; and interior designer Davina Mock-Maniscalco. You make us feel seen, validated, and ever so grateful to be working with you—it still feels like a dream.

To all the kind friends who invited us to visit their Atlanta country clubs, shared their juiciest stories, and trusted us to use our best social graces and table manners, we hope we didn't let you down.

This book required a ton of research and we are thankful to all the professionals who generously lent their time and expertise. Reis White schooled us on linguistics, morphology, and phonology.

Criminal defense attorney Joey Burby; real estate attorney Josh Rand; former City of Norcross mayor Bucky Johnson; and bank comptroller Beth Roseberry all helped us sort through the complicated details of Griggs's many crimes. Hair designer Felistas V. Mhute gave us a crash course in hair salon essentials, and Radhika Behl helped us craft a mouthwatering Punjabi feast that could be prepared on the fly. The wonderful staff at Chip's Bar and Grill and The Happy Hooker Inc. in Winder, GA, kindly answered our most absurd questions about everything from smashburgers to cricket cages.

We are deeply grateful for all the family, neighbors, and friends who shared their expertise and beautiful spaces with us. Madeleine Zacks and Harrison Lawrence endured a barrage of detailed questions and taught us all things Ole Miss. *Hotty Toddy!* Alex Perry generously shared his auto-mechanic and car repair knowledge. Laura Rogers and Greg Heim's Victorian home and annual Derby party provided much inspiration. Bill and Mary Long kindly lent us their lake house so we could get through the last stretch of the first draft.

For constant support and encouragement, we thank our local writing community; our neighbors in Atlanta, Decatur, and Norcross, and Puerto Rico; our familia at the Latinx Kidlit Book Festival and the Latinx Storytellers Conference; and the spiritual communities of Kadampa Meditation Center Georgia, St. Thomas More, and El Refugio. A special shout-out to the Not Your Mama's Rosary "ladies" for always reminding us to lean into joy.

Without the unshakable foundation of our families, we'd never find the courage to take these creative risks. To our husbands, The Chrises; our children Alex, Caleb, Mary Elizabeth, Nate, Pixley, and Annie; our mothers Zulma and Elizabeth; and our sisters Lourdes, Lee, and Carroll Ann: Thank you for loving us beyond words, and for giving us the joy of loving you.

ABOUT THE AUTHORS

Mayra Cuevas is the award-winning author of picture books and novels for readers of all ages. Her young adult novel *Does My Body Offend You?* (co-written with Marie Marquardt) was long-listed for the PEN/Faulkner Award. Born and raised in Puerto Rico, Mayra is a former award-winning CNN producer, and currently, a creative writing professor. She co-founded the Latinx Kidlit Book Festival and its Latinx Storytellers Conference. Mayra keeps her sanity by practicing Modern Buddhism and meditation. She splits her time between Atlanta and Puerto Rico. You can find Mayra on Instagram @Mayra.Cuevas and her website, MayraCuevas.com.

Marie Marquardt is the award-winning author of four YA novels, including *The Radius of Us* and *Does My Body Offend You?* (with Mayra Cuevas). Marie has also published two nonfiction books and several articles about Latin American immigration. She lives in Decatur, Georgia, with her spouse and four kids. You can connect with her on Substack @mariemarquardt and through her website, MarieMarquardt.com.